HE WAS IN A PLACE HE COULDN'T IMAGINE, WITH A WOMAN HE COULDN'T FORGET. . . .

Dylan slowly opened his eyes. His head felt like he'd just survived ten rounds with Mike Tyson—in jail. After his eyes adjusted to the dimness, he examined his surroundings and frowned.

The cellar.

Memories of his terrifying fall flooded back as he struggled to a sitting position. Closing his eyes, he tried to convince himself he had to be dreaming—it seemed of late that he'd done more than his share of that.

But when he opened his eyes, Dylan knew this was no dream. On the floor, not more than a few feet away, was a girl—a woman.

Impossible.

It was her—the woman who had haunted his dreams for as long as he could remember.

Her hair was black and shiny, spilling in a cascade of wild curls about her face and shoulders. Her breathing, the doctor in him noted, was deep and regular. From a non-medical perspective, he couldn't help noticing how beautifully she filled out the tightly stretched fabric of her old-fashioned dress.

She was real. Her flesh was warm to the touch. Her breath was soft and moist, not ghostly by any means.

This was definitely not a ghost.

She moaned again and her eyes fluttered open, wide and frightened, the shade of cornflowers.

In his dreams, he'd known this woman in the most intimate sense of the word. He helped her to her feet. She was small, barely reaching his shoulder. Her hair still smelled of roses. She didn't seem in need of medical attention, nor was the thought of giving it uppermost in his mind at the moment.

"So, dream lady, we meet again," he whispered, and his lips descended to claim hers.

TURN THE PAGE FOR RAVES FOR DEB STOVER AND *SHADES OF ROSE*. . . .

DEB STOVER
SHADES OF ROSE

PINNACLE BOOKS
KENSINGTON PUBLISHING CORP.

PINNACLE BOOKS are published by

Kensington Publishing Corp.
850 Third Avenue
New York, NY 10022

First Printing: June, 1995

Printed in the United States of America

This rose would never have bloomed without the super-human patience of my family, the magical assistance of The Wyrd Sisters—Laura Hayden, Pam McCutcheon, Karen Fox, and Paula Gill—and Denise Little's belief in me. This book's for all of you.

Prologue

The Ozark Mountains, 1894.

"Mule, this be the answer to all my prayers." Tom Marshall tugged on the reins until the weary pack mule reluctantly trudged through the thicket surrounding the spring.

"Lord, if only I could've found it sooner." He spat on the ground, then shook his head. "It's gold. Gold! Right here on my farm all along."

Under cover of darkness, he turned toward the cabin he'd constructed many years earlier. "I know'd this old cabin'd come in handy for somethin' someday." He chuckled to himself as he paused before the abandoned structure.

"I gotta be careful, mule. There's thieves around every holler in these hills." He looked anxiously around the spring, half expecting someone to leap out from behind a tree to steal his treasure. "Can't even trust my own family, I reckon. The durned fools'd tell me to give it to the sheriff."

After assuring himself he was alone, Tom went inside the cabin and opened the heavy cellar door. "Nobody'll find it here, mule," he said to the animal as he stepped outside to retrieve a bag of gold. "Nobody but me."

Carrying the bags of gold into the cabin and down into the cellar exhausted his strength. Again, he lamented the fact that he hadn't discovered the fortune in his youth. What he could've done with it then . . .

After several trips, he'd stashed all but one small pouch safely in the corner of the musty cellar. "Mine," he whispered to himself as he stood in the cellar admiring his cache.

Ascending the ladder, he shook the heavy pouch and chuckled. His family need never learn of his stroke of luck. He'd spend the gold as needed, never revealing the source of his wealth.

At the top of the ladder, Tom half-turned to peer down at his prize. His eyes watered at the glorious sight—his lifelong dream fulfilled at last. With a satisfied grunt, he pivoted again toward the opening in the floor.

"Hello." A young woman peered down at him with large blue eyes. Then she made a mistake—she looked beyond him to the pile of bags, visible in the lantern's luminous glow.

"What's that, Mr. Marshall?"

Recognizing the intruder, Tom cleared his throat as his heart collided with his ribs like a logjam on the White River. He stepped out onto the cabin floor. "Whatcha doin' out at night, Rose?"

She continued to stare beyond him . . . into the cellar. "My stepbrothers and their father went hunting. I decided to go for a walk . . . then I saw your light down here by the spring. I couldn't imagine who might be out here."

"Well now." He studied her, wondering how much she'd seen. Could she know the contents of the cloth bags? Several of them gaped open, revealing the glittering gold coins.

My gold.

Tom felt that familiar fever possess him. When he'd traveled to California in '49 to seek his fortune, frustration had been his hard-earned reward. Now this young woman on the threshold of spinsterhood stood between him and his dream.

His destiny.

"Is that . . . money, Mr. Marshall?" She pointed toward the corner of the cellar, her eyes still wide and curious.

Tom cringed—sweat moistened his brow. "You wanna see it?" With awkward movements, he stepped aside to permit the girl access to the ladder. A few moments later she was down in the cellar, peeking inside one of his precious bags—touching *his* gold.

"My goodness." Rose ran her fingers through the gold coins. "Send that lantern down here. It sure is shiny."

Tom retrieved an old lamp from the mantel and touched its wick to his lantern's flame. Enough oil remained in the lamp to burn for a while. He carried it a few steps down the ladder and handed it to Rose, watching as she placed it on the floor. He glanced once more at the girl as she ogled the fruits of his labor.

The sight of *his* gold passing between another's fingers was his undoing. Tom leapt up to the cabin floor with an agility his body hadn't seen in many years and dropped the trap door.

The thick floor planks muffled Rose's scream. He hurried to the corner of the room and found a heavy table, constructed from the stump of a huge oak tree.

Before he returned with his heavy burden, Rose managed to partially open the heavy door. Her terrified expression tore at him, but gold fever willed Tom to struggle against her efforts. Silencing the nagging voice of his conscience, he shoved her back into the dark hole and secured the door.

With desperation enhancing his strength, Tom pushed until the heavy table covered the opening, sealing the girl inside once and for all.

Protecting his gold—his dream.

The strain of moving what had once been a giant oak tree took a toll on his dwindling strength. Fatigue obscured Tom's vision as he led the mule up the hill. Still clutching a single pouch of gold, he paused on the twisting path to catch his breath. He was hot and tired—perspiration trickled down his face, into his eyes and mouth.

An ominous sensation swept through him as he looked around at the strangely silent night. He wasn't alone. Had someone seen him in the cabin?

With Rose?

Frantic, he hurried up the hill, erratically looking over his shoulder. Tom's heart battered his chest like a bird flapping its wings in a feeble attempt to escape the claws of a hungry bobcat. But each time he looked behind him he saw nothing but darkness.

The excitement of the night's events had sapped most of his strength—fear seized the remainder. The long sloping hill which led to his home seemed endless. He stumbled several times before cresting the knoll.

Panting as he paused in front of the house, Tom glanced over his shoulder again and smiled. He held the gold up in front of his face . . . then froze as realization struck.

I buried my gold with Rose.

He felt cold, then hot. His heart accelerated as a pain was born in the center of his chest and spread throughout his midsection and down his arm. He clutched at the crushing sensation and gasped for air. The sweet Ozark Mountain air . . .

Stumbling, Tom's gaze landed on a pair of piercing black eyes, mere inches from his own. The eyes belonged to a man in full ceremonial regalia of a Cherokee medicine man. Legend claimed the old Indian was a ghost—Keeper of the Ozarks since the passage of his tribe through the region back in '38.

"I saw," the spirit said in a voice which surely did not belong in this world. "The woman's life must be restored by the blood of your blood."

Closing his eyes as the apparition vanished, Tom imprisoned the pouch of precious gold in his grasp. He took one last shuddering breath as the image of Rose's terrified face flashed through his mind.

A word commenced in his soul, never to see fruition.

Serenity.

One

Her lips were soft and sweet, like superb wine. His hand crept up her spine to stroke the nape of her neck where fine, dark hairs blended with the ebony tresses trailing across his face and chest.

Kisses caressed his cheek, neck, shoulder and crept down his torso toward the part of him that screamed for release. Raven curls tickled his abdomen as her tongue made its way downward, like a torch gathering fuel as it went.

Dylan moaned when her teeth nipped at the base of his shaft. He was crazy with desire. She'd been teasing him for weeks now. It was far past time for their relationship to progress.

Her breath was hot against his turgid flesh. A quiver unfolded in the pit of his belly and shot through his body. If she didn't take him soon he'd explode.

Her velvety lips found the tip of his erection and toyed with it—arousing him beyond anything humanly endurable. With her tongue, she traced teasing circles around him before she enveloped his entire shaft.

Moaning when she seemed hungry for all of him,

he winced. He was certainly more than willing to accommodate her.

She left his engorged manhood, slithered up his body and kissed him on the lips again. Her tongue playfully explored the recesses of his mouth as if seeking some hidden treasure. Dylan returned her kiss, savored the sweet-hot fires of passion which flailed his soul . . . his very core.

He gasped when her mouth left his and she rose above him, permitting him to see her entire body in all its naked splendor. Flesh as soft and white as the petals of a flower, dusky nipples and the crisp, dark hair at the juncture of her thighs beckoned to him. He was beyond any semblance of comfort, so engorged with passion he could scarcely breathe.

"Why do you torment me so?" Not waiting for, or expecting an answer, he reached out, guiding a passion-swollen nipple to his mouth. He relished her sweetness as his hands roamed over her body. She moaned as he released one breast to bestow equal treatment to the other.

Glancing up, he found an expression of confusion and perhaps desperation cross her features as she sank against his arousal without taking his agonized body within her silken loins.

Dylan gasped in surprise. Though his dream woman had visited him nightly for three weeks, she'd never consummated their relationship. Always she'd left him gasping for more, perspiring with unfulfilled lust. But this time she was pressing her soft woman's flesh against his urgent erection. At last, he had reason to hope his tortured body would soon find release within her receptive folds.

She ground her hips against his, making Dylan pray for her to receive his manhood with the voraciousness he knew from the fervor of her movements that she possessed. Perhaps she wasn't real—but if this was a dream, he wanted never again to wake.

She leaned forward to tease his lips again with her swollen nipples. Dylan grasped the magnificent globes in his hands, glorying in her perfection. Whoever she was, she was all his, from the crown of ebony hair to her slender, white ankles. His, at least for now.

"God." Dylan arched his back in a futile attempt to infiltrate the secret she kept just beyond his reach. It seemed as if hours passed while he stayed at the mercy of her teasing and tantalizing, urging him on, torturing him with flagrant intensity.

He climbed, soared, reached for that pinnacle of pleasure he knew was just within the scope of his arousal—but the gratification he sought so desperately was not to be.

Suddenly, he was alone in his bed. The sweat-soaked sheets were on the floor and his body was exposed to the cool night air. Frustration born of raw, sexual hunger raged within him. He was tense, on the verge of . . .

Where the hell is she?

"Damn." Dylan sat up on the edge of his bed, fully awake, but hadn't he been awake all along? Throughout her delicious lovemaking? It had seemed so real. He looked at the bed, crumpled and smelling like . . . a bed. Surely she'd really been here—in this bed. There was no other explanation for the state of his body.

He ran his fingers through his sweat-dampened hair

and reached for the water glass on the nightstand. The glowing red numbers on the digital clock read *12:00.* Midnight. Every time she came to him, she left at exactly the same time. He was starting to feel like some wildly skewed, adults-only version of Prince Charming.

Was this insanity?

Looking around, Dylan remembered that he was at his grandfather's farm. The memory of the old man's funeral assailed him anew. Dylan was really alone now. Completely.

He padded barefoot into the bathroom and flipped on the light. He winced at the bright intrusion and filled his water glass, popped two aspirin into his mouth, and swallowed until the glass was empty. The dry taste in his mouth, the aftermath of shock and frustration, remained. He refilled the glass and drained it again.

Great. Now I'll be up all night pissing.

"Your grandfather didn't leave much, Dylan," Jeff Bentsen said quietly as he peered over his glasses. "The house, lands, whatever livestock was left . . ."

Dylan balanced his ankle across his knee, fidgeting with—the frayed hems of his jeans where they'd worn along the backs from dragging the ground. He had no family left anywhere that he knew of.

"There are no liens on the property." Jeff hesitated, knitting his brows together. "However, there is a stipulation concerning the inheritance."

"Stipulation?" Dylan leaned forward to listen to the man. He hadn't paid much attention up to this point, since he planned to sell the property as soon as the estate was through probate. "What?"

"It's rather . . . strange." Jeff drummed his fingers on the desk. "I didn't understand it, even when he asked me to draw up his will."

Dylan sighed. "Jeff, we've known each other a long time. What is it?" An alarm went off in the back of Dylan's mind. Any stipulation, whatever it was, could prolong the entire process. That meant trouble when it came to closing a real estate deal.

Jeff laughed, but it was strained. "Remember the old cabin down by Serenity Spring?"

Dylan nodded and a chill passed through his body. "Sure. How could I forget?"

"Yeah." Jeff rubbed the back of his neck and looked at the papers in front of him. "Well, it's mentioned in the will."

Dylan was conscious of his pulse accelerating and his blood pressure rising. "I didn't even know Grandpa owned it. I thought that property simply adjoined his."

"So did I." Jeff laid the document down and stared at Dylan. "We're both educated. I'm an attorney, you're a doctor, for Christ's sake. I'm sure neither one of us believes in—"

"Ghosts?" Dylan supplied, chuckling nervously in recollection. "God, when I think about how scared we were . . ."

"Yeah. How old were we? Twelve? Thirteen?"

Studying his friend's expression, Dylan shrugged. "Yeah. Something like that. I can't believe the old man owned that cabin all this time."

"According to the records it's always been in your family. Hell, it was part of the original homestead."

Jeff cast him a sheepish expression. "I really didn't know until I drew up his will."

"Why didn't you tell me?" Dylan crossed his leg over his other knee and glared at Jeff. "You must have realized I'd want to know."

"Client confidentiality." Jeff gave him a grin reminiscent of his twelve-year-old self. "I was surprised, but not totally convinced you didn't know. The old man spelled out his conditions. It seemed very important to him."

"I'm sure it did." Dylan stood and paced the room, pausing only to gaze out the window at the cars tooling down the main street. "I've planned to sell the rest of the farm all along, though." He turned to study Jeff's expression. His gut twisted into a knot at the disappointment he saw in his best friend's face. "All right. Let's have it."

"Okay." Jeff hesitated and frowned.

"C'mon, Jeff." Dylan laughed derisively. "This is the Las Vegas of the Ozarks, complete with tourist traps and neon lights." He waved his arms to emphasize his disgust concerning the changes which had taken place in his home town. "Country music extravaganzas on every corner. You didn't really expect me to come back to Branson?"

"I know, but—"

"You did, didn't you?"

"Well . . . why not? After all, I came back after law school."

"You have a wife and kids." Dylan clenched his teeth as memories of what he'd almost had flooded his mind.

"And you're divorced. I know." Jeff nudged the papers aside and turned to face him. "Hell, Dylan. It's past time you got on with your life."

Dylan walked back to the desk and leaned on it with the palms of both hands. "Like Cindy? She sure as hell got on with hers in a hurry."

"Put it behind you. Why don't you settle here? Lord knows we could use another doctor."

Dylan laughed. "I'm a pediatrician, Jeff." He slammed his hand down on the table. "Not a small town family practitioner."

"There are children in Branson." Jeff's face reddened, his voice strained and low. "Maybe we should just get back to business."

Dylan threw his hands up in defeat. "By all means, do get on with it."

Jeff sighed. "I'm sorry, Dylan. What you do is your business. But . . . it'd be nice to have my best friend move back home."

"Well, sometimes it doesn't sound like such a bad idea," Dylan said, dropping back into his chair. "The pace in the city . . . well, you remember how it was when we were at the university."

"I remember."

Dylan shook his head. "And with eight years of marriage down the drain . . ." He put his feet on the corner of Jeff's oak desk. Could he actually settle down in Branson again? Sometimes it didn't seem like such a bad idea. He surprised himself with his next admission. "Tell you what—I'll think it over."

"Good. Now, I'll thank you to remove your feet from this expensive desk. Let's get back to the conditions for your inheritance of Serenity Spring."

"Do people still call it the ghost cabin?" Dylan

laughed, but the memory of what he and his friend had seen so many years ago was as fresh as the day it had happened.

Jeff nodded. It was obvious from his expression that his thoughts mirrored Dylan's. "There are still occasional sightings, too. The Indian and the . . . the woman."

Dylan felt his muscles tighten. "Let's get on with the will." But a more recent memory took root and grew, becoming even more disturbing. The beautiful woman in his bed—why hadn't he realized before where he'd seen her? Tugging at his collar, he knew now why the room had grown so warm.

Jeff looked at the document in silence for a few moments. "There's a condition pertaining only to the property down by the spring . . . with the cabin."

Dylan sensed something coming he didn't want to hear. "You're stalling. Cough it up or I'll tell everyone in town you wear a toupee."

"You wouldn't dare." Jeff made a face and patted his head. "Anyway, the stipulation is that you must live in the cabin for at least thirty consecutive days." Jeff's gaze met Dylan's. "This is to prove yourself worthy of—"

"Hold on—you've got to be kidding? Live with—"

"The ghost?" Jeff shuddered visibly. "I'm sorry, Dylan. I know if it were me—"

"You'd just give up the property."

"Maybe not."

"Why? Is there more to this?" Dylan used what he hoped was his most sarcastic voice. "Please, enlighten me."

"All right." Jeff flipped the page over. "Old man Sawyer wants the property to build a resort."

"Undoubtedly. Mineral springs are big business." He shrugged. "When you mentioned it was part of the property, the thought crossed my mind, too."

"Right." Jeff smiled. "This all boils down to money, Dylan. *Dinero. Pesos. Lira.* The terms of this will must be met by the end of the year or Sawyer can exercise his option."

Dylan slapped his leg in frustration. "Sawyer? Why? It's *my* family's heritage."

"Nevertheless, for some reason your grandfather felt if you couldn't move into the cabin for at least thirty days, then you really don't want the property bad enough. Who knows why?"

Dylan's face grew warm. "So, you're telling me that the only way out of this mess is for me to actually move into the cabin."

"For thirty days." Jeff glanced up from the papers. "Remember, Sawyer had an option on the property. It was quite specific. Your grandfather was seriously considering selling. That option's almost up, so if you can't meet the terms of the will . . ."

"This is weird. Would you do it?"

"Not on your life." Jeff paled significantly. "I remember that day too well."

Dylan swallowed hard. "Me, too." *God. That's not all I remember.*

Jeff avoided Dylan's gaze as he doodled on a piece of scrap paper. "Tell me, have you heard the stories about a . . . treasure?"

Dylan stood and walked over to the window again. "Sure, but what does that have to do with anything?"

Jeff leaned back in his chair and turned slightly to face Dylan where he leaned against the window sill. "Well, suppose the rumors are true."

"That's ridiculous. Treasure? Jeff, you've been in the sun too long."

Jeff tapped the pencil he held against his knuckles. "C'mon. We've both heard of tourists coming to the Ozarks looking for lost silver and gold."

"Sure. What of it?" Dylan shrugged.

Jeff tilted his head slightly and his eyes glittered. "There have always been rumors about the cabin and spring. With its reputation, no one ever looked there, to my knowledge. You could have quite a treasure hidden there after all these years."

Dylan glanced speculatively at his friend. For some insane reason he wanted to hold onto the property. "I'll have to sleep on it. Maybe you should approach Sawyer with an offer. Find out how much he'll take to tear up his option."

Jeff grunted. "Don't hold your breath. That greedy old man was in here the day after your grandpa died, before you even got here."

"Maybe he believes in the treasure." Dylan considered this last bit of information. "Might bear a little investigation at that. It could set me up in practice anywhere I wanted."

"What are you going to do?"

"Think about it." Dylan surprised even himself with his words. He swallowed hard, but realized he'd spoken his gut feelings. There was some sort of mystery at Serenity Spring. For some reason, he felt certain it dated back long before his birth and his encounters with the ghost.

Jeff leaned forward. "A treasure—just think of it."

"And a spell . . . with a ghost." Dylan shook his head in disbelief. "What the hell am I getting myself into?"

"A chance to discover the truth, maybe?"

Dylan stood with a long sigh. "I don't really have much of a choice."

"Yeah, I understand that, but if there's a real treasure . . ." Jeff stood and extended his hand. His eyes twinkled. "Good luck."

"Does your diploma from law school say anything about avarice, Jeff?" Chuckling, Dylan moved toward the door, but hesitated and swallowed as he turned to face his friend again. His stomach churned. "Do you remember what . . . *she* looked like?"

"The ghost?" Jeff smiled, but his face paled. "She was the most beautiful creature I've ever seen."

"Yeah. That's what I remembered, too." Dylan chuckled nervously. How could he, a grown man, confess to such a dream? He swallowed hard. "It's kind of funny . . . this happening right now."

"Why?"

Dylan knew he'd sound like a fool, but he needed to share this enigma with someone. His best friend seemed the logical choice. "Since I came back to stay in Grandpa's house, I've been having a dream."

Jeff's brow furrowed. "You mean a recurring dream?"

"Exactly. I've been here for almost three weeks and had the same dream nearly every night." Dylan couldn't shake the notion that his dream was associated with the unfurling mystery.

Jeff sat back down in his chair. "Tell me about it."

Dylan followed his friend's example, rubbing the stubble on his chin with his thumb. It made a rasping sound in his ears.

"I think it's the wom—ghost from the cabin."

Jeff whistled. "You mean *that* kind of dream?" He stopped to shake his head in apparent disbelief. "Man, I haven't had one of those in—"

"I know. I'm too old for wet dreams." Dylan scowled, silently daring his friend to laugh. "But it's much more than that."

Jeff folded his arms across his chest. "This sounds interesting."

"She seems . . . *real,* Jeff." It was clear his friend was no longer making fun of him. He was deadly serious. The fright they'd suffered—shared—so many years ago created a unique bond between them. "I know this sounds crazy, but it's just so . . . damned wonderful."

"Wonderful?" Jeff chuckled. "I wish you could bottle that dream. I could use a little of it myself. We'd make a fortune."

Dylan leaned forward and rubbed his temples with his thumbs. "This is getting to me."

"I think so, too." Jeff's words hung in the air between them. "Is the money worth it? I mean . . . if it really is her—the ghost—visiting you up at the big house, just imagine . . ."

Dylan stared in silence. His body could well imagine, or at least hope, what might happen. The dream woman had tortured him. Maybe, if he moved into the cabin for a month . . .

"Shit!" He leapt to his feet and paced. "What am I going to do?" He stopped to peer out the window again. "Why have I been dreaming about her now, Jeff? After all these years?"

"Beats the hell out of me. I know when I was a teenager I dreamed about her all the time. So did you."

"Man, I sure did." Dylan returned to his chair. "It must be the old house. The memories."

"Sure." Jeff seemed unconvinced. "I wish I could come with you, but—"

"But you've got a wife and kids to worry about." Dylan knew his tone was mocking and cruel. Jealousy did that to a person, at least it sure as hell did it to him. "I'll just have to do it alone. That's all."

Jeff stood and walked toward the door with him. "Just think—once you've done this the land will be yours."

"Then I can sell it and do what I want?"

"Or stay here and keep it. Maybe your dream will end." Jeff lifted one eyebrow. "Or come true."

"If it is a dream." Dylan recalled the vivid image of the woman. Lord, he couldn't remember ever experiencing such intense sexual arousal in any other context. Even in adolescence, when he'd walked around, hormones running amuck, trying to seduce every girl he met, nothing had ever matched his dreams.

"Let me know when to start counting the thirty days."

"Gee, thanks."

"No problem." Jeff laughed and rolled his eyes. "Maybe you should have a phone put in out there, or at least a generator."

"No, I don't want to take the time or spend the money right now. Besides, I'll have my cellular phone.

Let's just get this over with, *if* I decide to do it at all."
Dylan hesitated at the door. "Who says you can't
come visit during the daytime?"

"Well . . ."

"Jeff," he warned.

"All right. I'll bring my fishing pole."

Dylan raised his eyebrows and punched his friend
on the shoulder. "Good—*if* I go through with this."

Dylan turned and left the office, muttering under
his breath. His heart pounded hard as he trotted down
the stairs and out into the brisk March air. The near
cloudless sky seemed to taunt him.

Haunted cabin, my ass.

As he settled down for the night, his grandfather's
house seemed determined to remind Dylan of how
many different sounds a house over a century old
could produce with no help from man or machine.
Settling into this house after the funeral had seemed
logical, since he needed to remain nearby until the
terms of the will were met.

*And spend thirty days and nights in a haunted
cabin.*

His mystery woman failed to appear that night, even
though he'd stayed awake waiting for her. The least
she could do was return to finish what she'd started.

Perhaps she didn't come because he was awake.
Was that the problem? Had she been nothing more
than a dream? A catalyst for his starved senses?

After shoveling down a breakfast of dry cereal, Dylan packed a few provisions and headed down the hill
toward the spring. As he neared the familiar area, his

throat constricted and memories waged a full-scale attack on his waning resolve.

As if in answer to the unspoken questions ricocheting around in his mind, a deer leapt out in front of him on the trail. Startled, Dylan stopped and shook his head.

This is asinine.

He gathered his courage together and turned toward the cabin and the spring at the bottom of the hill. All his life he'd wanted to explore the ghost cabin. Unfortunately, that term still seemed appropriate.

The sun was barely above the horizon when he caught sight of the cabin. The early morning light cast long shadows around the picturesque structure as Dylan approached. Willow trees, wisteria and various other vines had nearly choked the small building with their exuberant growth.

But it was still the most compelling place he'd ever seen.

He paused directly in front of the modest shelter, studying the expert workmanship which had gone into its construction. The foundation was of native stone, as was the chimney. A trellis at each end of the small porch supported heavy vines of climbing roses.

His ancestors had built this cabin with their bare hands. A sense of pride filled him, overshadowing some of his fears.

He drew in a deep breath of the cool morning air and took a tentative step onto the porch. A rotted board gave way beneath his foot, pitching him sideways. He hadn't considered that the logs and lumber could be rotted and hazardous. But he was still going inside, after he collected water for cleaning.

Turning, Dylan started to make his way down to
the spring to fill his bucket when a sound drifted from
the cabin. A chill passed through him.

He froze.

"Help me," came a muffled cry.

He was afraid to turn—afraid to continue. But he
couldn't ignore that voice. A voice calling for help . . .

"I don't believe in ghosts," Dylan whispered—
lied—to himself as he turned very slowly toward the
cabin. Surely it was just his imagination. What else
could it be, after all?

But if he didn't believe in ghosts, then what had he
and Jeff seen at this very cabin nearly twenty years
earlier?

"Help me."

His body tensed. He forced his gaze to sweep the
front of the structure for any sign of . . . life.

"Help me."

"Damn." Dylan squinted as he searched the front
of the cabin again. He sighed. Relief flooded him.
"Nothing."

Abandoning his plans to clean the cabin, he moved
away from the spring, but something compelled him
to turn back before he left the overgrown area. His
breath caught in his throat as he stared directly at the
decrepit front door.

A face seemed to float in the portal. A woman's
face. A beautiful face.

Her face.

"No," he whispered, but no amount of logic
changed the obvious.

After rubbing his eyes, he shook his head and
looked again. The image was gone.

He turned away and started toward the larger house up the hill, but as he glanced up, he stopped in mid-step. Across the spring was the unmistakable and unforgettable figure of a Native American in ceremonial dress. Dylan's gaze never wavered from the formidable figure.

These paranormal beings—or whatever—were ganging up on him.

The man—the image—the *ghost* lifted a hand in greeting, nodding to Dylan.

God, I must be crazy. You're a legend.

It had to be the Keeper of the Ozarks.

If he's real, he'll still be there when I reach him. If not . . .

He hesitated.

Dylan's courage vanished along with the Indian. Striding over to where the figure had been only a moment ago, he grasped a tree and felt its roughness.

This tree was real. He leaned against the bark with his forehead, wondering if he was losing it, if this was what insanity felt like. He grasped—reached—for anything tangible to anchor him in reality.

How could he actually *live* in the cabin for thirty minutes, let alone thirty days? He'd been a fool to ever consider it. He'd call Jeff the minute he got back to the house.

Sawyer can have the damned place.

Dylan walked away from the cabin fast, looking back over his shoulder every few steps as if expecting to find someone following.

Someone or some*thing*.

An unshakable sense of dread elevated his blood pressure as he rushed up the hill. Near the front porch, he paused to stare at his grandfather's house. He swallowed hard, sat down on the front step and waited for his breathing to return to normal.

Dylan leaned against the porch railing and remembered the face in the door. He felt cold—colder than he had since that long ago day when he and Jeff had first seen the woman—ghost—at the cabin.

Recalling her beauty, Dylan knew beyond a hint of uncertainty that she was a ghost. What else could she be?

He shook his head. The flesh of his dream woman had been more perfect than any he could imagine. But of course she was a ghost. Or was she a dream *about* a ghost?

Though the air was cool, perspiration dripped from Dylan's face. Indecision returned. How could he sell the cabin without first learning the answers to the mystery? And what if there was a treasure? Didn't he owe his ancestors something?

And why was he dreaming about a ghost?

His grandmother's prize tulips were beginning to open their red and yellow petals to the sun. He could almost see Grandma—smell her raw apple cake baking in the oven, the aroma wafting through the open windows of this house.

This very house.

His heritage.

The only thing still connecting him to a family he'd once cherished. They were all gone now.

"Damn." Dylan stood and looked across the field and forest that separated the house from Serenity

Spring. Doubts flooded him. Angry, he stormed inside, letting the screen door slam behind him.

He clenched his fingers behind his back and paced.

A car stopped in front of the house. Cursing, he stepped back onto the porch and spotted Jeff's red Volvo. He waited as his friend came up the steps and paused in front of him.

"I laid awake thinking about this all night, Dylan." Jeff knitted his brow in obvious concern. "You have to do it."

"What do you mean I have to do it?" Dylan shook his head in disbelief. "I just decided to let Sawyer have it all."

"Don't. Hear me out first." Jeff stepped closer. "I went down to the newspaper and did some research. The Sawyer family has been trying to buy the property for years. You and I both know there's never been good feelings between your family and theirs."

"Dammit, Jeff. You're not telling everything. Give." Instinctively, Dylan looked toward the spring—again.

"Zeke Sawyer killed Jim Marshall. Your great-great-grandfather, I think. Did you know about this?"

Dylan shook his head and stared in disbelief. "When?"

Jeff handed Dylan a photocopy of an old newspaper clipping. "See for yourself."

"May 11, 1894?" He scratched his head and read the article. "Says here Sawyer shot my great-great-grandfather over a pouch of gold Tom Marshall—I guess my great-great-great-grandfather—had at the time of his death. Gold? Interesting."

"That's for sure."

Dylan paused to watch a scissor-tailed flycatcher

sail by, then perch on the porch railing to sing for a moment. It didn't have answers either. "Then why would Grandpa consider selling out to Sawyer?"

"It doesn't make much sense." Jeff put one foot on the step and rested his palms on his thigh. "My gut just tells me you shouldn't let him have it. I can't exactly explain it. Instinct, I guess."

God, I don't believe this. "Mine, too."

"I—I know you have reservations about—"

"Reservations, hell." Dylan paced the length of the porch as Jeff stared at him. "I went down there today."

"Alone?"

"Yeah." Dylan stopped to stare at his friend. "Guess who was waiting for me?"

Jeff's eyes grew round. "Her?"

"And the old Indian." Dylan shook his head and sighed. "But I didn't dream last night."

Jeff's expression was solemn. "Well, that's something. What are you going to do?"

"Sleep on it and decide by morning." He reread the newspaper clipping still clutched in his hand. "Then, by God, I'm not going to change my mind again. Understand?"

"I'm sorry. I'll stay out of your decision."

"No. Irritating as you may be, you're the only person who understands what I know is down at that damned cabin."

"Gee, thanks for the vote of confidence." Jeff chuckled. "All this makes me feel like a thirteen-year-old boy again. I'm too old for this."

"Huh. That makes two of us." Dylan forced the memories from his mind. He needed to think rationally and at the moment that simply wasn't possible. "Dinner?"

Screwing up his face and doing his Festus imitation, Jeff said, "Thanks, Marshal Dylan, but Miss Shari's holdin' dinner."

"Sure." Dylan watched as his friend got in his car and drove away.

Hot meal, warm woman . . . or the reverse.

Lucky bastard.

"Only my imagination . . ." Dylan forced his eyes closed in order to blot out the image of the shadows on the wall. His body was tense, tied up in knots. He knew sleep would be a long time coming, if at all.

He put the pillow over his head. "Only my imagination." She hadn't been—couldn't be—real. Dylan trembled, but despite his anxiety, his body warmed and relaxed. The long day of deliberation combined with the fresh air and sunshine had made him sleepy.

Dreams possessed him. A moan escaped from his lips as her hands roamed over his body. He responded immediately to her touch. Her efforts became fevered, intense as she pressed against him, then moved away.

He opened his eyes and saw her hovering over his bed. Her eyes seemed sad as she gazed down at him. The expression on her face blended regret with desire.

She moved closer until Dylan recognized the details of her luscious form. A blue dress slipped from her shoulders and fell in a wrinkled heap to the floor beside the bed.

He didn't move.

He didn't dare.

Her silken flesh beckoned to him, begged for his touch, as she descended to cover him. Dylan felt an almost electrical charge between them the moment she reached him.

Her dark hair smelled wonderful—like roses. Strange, he couldn't recall experiencing a sensation of smell before in a dream. Her raven tresses formed a veil, cascading over his face and chest as she came more fully against him.

Her contact ignited a quaking in his loins which would not be quelled. She pressed her full breasts against his chest, rubbing her dusky nipples against him until he groaned.

"God, what are you doing to me, woman?"

As if in answer, her lips claimed his in a kiss so intense it took his breath away. A charge like liquid fire leapt between them. Never in his life had he wanted a woman as much as he wanted this spirit who'd plagued him for so many weeks. His body burned to possess her fully.

Feeling as if he would explode, Dylan suddenly took command. He rose on one elbow to gently press her to the mattress. He paused to study her features.

Was she real? His starved senses found it nearly impossible to doubt her authenticity. It seemed impossible for her not to be real. Her body was passionate and vibrant, entirely alive. He pressed himself against her, displaying how successful her seduction had been.

"You'll not elude me this night. I don't know who you are, but you'll not leave here before I've had my fill of you. You've tormented me long enough."

She nodded almost imperceptibly. Her lips curved in a bewitching smile.

"God." Dylan buried his face in her silken hair, savoring its fragrance. He explored the side of her throat with his lips, relishing the sweetness. No ghost could feel or taste so remarkable. Could it?

She moaned beneath him, urging him to further explorations. He trailed kisses across her shoulder to the valley between her glorious breasts. Lifting himself slightly, he admired the twin globes beneath the moonlight streaming through the window. Their tawny peaks beckoned to him.

Perfection.

He sampled one puckered peak, drawing it deeply into his mouth until she pressed herself against him to offer more of the bounty nature had provided. His hand found her other breast and caressed it until she writhed enticingly beneath him.

Dylan toyed with one, then the other of her delectable breasts as his hands roamed over her, feeling, exploring, seeking to bring them both to the pinnacle of pleasure which had eluded them so often in the past. His fingers found her hot woman's flesh and probed her depths until her hips rose from the bed.

Enough was enough. Three full weeks of foreplay should satisfy any woman. Poised between her thighs, he pressed his engorged manhood against her soft folds until she opened unto him. Like the petals of a rose seeking the sun's warmth, she unveiled her essence to his manhood. A sigh of satisfaction escaped his lips as she sheathed him. He paused, gritting his teeth to prevent his climactic explosion from commencing prematurely.

Gaining control, he plunged into her again and again, climbing, soaring and feeling her accompany him to that perfect peak of pleasure they each sought.

She ground her hips against his, angling to meet his powerful thrusts. This was a passion born from weeks of frustration and seduction, culminating in a glorious obsession. He took her like a fire ravishing a forest too long denied quenching rain. His body soared until he thought he would surely die before the release he so desperately needed finally came to pass.

A liquid fire suffused him. His body felt as if it had separated from his mind. Swells of grandeur washed over him. Tidal waves of rapture swept him away in a pinnacle of pure ecstacy. Everything he possessed seemed to converge for this singular purpose— his strength, his body, his spirit.

She moved beneath him; her body contorted around his shaft, swallowed the molten lava of his seed with a voraciousness which left him breathless. She seemed to draw from him all he could give, siphoning every ounce of strength and substance she could. This woman was a greedy lover, but as eager to give as she was to take.

Dylan rose up slightly to see her face as she found the same joy he had. Pleased with his performance, he strained against her, felt her quiver and buck beneath him, cry out her pleasure and cling in the way a woman did only during savage, sexual bliss.

Their movements stilled and he continued to stare at her. His breath came in short, rapid bursts as he waited for it to return to normal.

He was reluctant to leave her softness. His body was still buried deep within her. The moon-maiden, ghost, or whatever she was, certainly had a way about her. He reached down to kiss her parted lips, closing his eyes in the process . . .

Dylan awoke with the first violet streaks of dawn. Uncertain, he looked around the room in confusion, wondering where he was.

Then memory made him bolt from the bed.

He paced the room, looked out the window and returned again to the bed. But there was no sign of her—no evidence that she'd ever even existed.

The best sex I've ever had—or hope to experience in my life—was nothing but a dream?

Running his fingers through sleep-mussed hair, Dylan threw back the sheets in search of something—*anything*—which might offer a clue.

But the truth hit him in a crescendo of introspection he wished fervently to deny, but he couldn't. He sat down on the edge of the bed.

Only a dream. Nothing but a dream.

Two

Dylan decided to look upon his decision as kismet. He'd been . . . invited by something or someone to that cabin.

Along with food and cooking utensils, he loaded a backpack with two flashlights, spare batteries, and various tools. He stuck his cellular phone in his hip pocket. As an afterthought he collected a few items from his medical bag and stuffed them into a fanny pack, which he buckled around his waist.

Whistling, he made his way down the hill. He slowed as he neared the spring. It was midmorning, so he had a full day of sunlight to guide him. Nightfall was many hours away. But that didn't really matter since he was going to stay for at least thirty days.

And nights.

For a few moments he considered the possibility that the treasure legend might be true. What if a fortune in silver or gold awaited the lucky individual who happened across its hiding place?

Such a prize could set him up for the rest of his life. He could practice medicine in style, free from the stresses and savagery of group practice infighting, for the remainder of his days.

He could do all that without selling the farm.

Dylan paused for a moment. His mercenary instincts superseded his emotions for a change and took command. He glanced back toward the house. If a treasure existed—and he found it—he could keep the farm. Surprised at his pleasure in this bit of internal revelation, he nodded in satisfaction, then continued his journey.

He hadn't realized how much the farm meant to him. His father had died ten years ago, his mother seven. Cindy'd left him eighteen months ago. Maybe all the hours of loneliness were making him mushy.

His mother had been a hippie back when the word was a noun rather than an adjective. Dylan chuckled as he recalled her long straight hair and the beads she wore even after they'd gone out of style. His father never seemed to notice . . . or care. He didn't even object when his wife insisted on naming their only child after her favorite poet. It was only coincidence that he also happened to bear the name of her favorite folk singer a few years later.

A dogwood tree had burst into bloom overnight in front of the cabin. He paused to admire the delicate white blossoms, reminded of the story of Christ's cross. Even though there were those who believed ghosts were somehow "unholy," his instincts told him the spirit of Serenity Spring wasn't evil.

After all, he knew that spirit in the biblical sense of the word. His body tightened with longing when he thought of his nocturnal visitor. Never in his life could he recall such explosive sexual release. It was the kind of lovemaking men dreamed of.

Literally.

He paused in the same spot he had the day before

and waited. Dylan refused to consider exactly what he was waiting for. He didn't have to.

After several moments, no voices had called out to him. *That figures.*

Now that he was determined to discover the truth about the mysteries of the cabin, they weren't around to study. Dylan wasn't certain if he was relieved or disappointed, but the day was young. Somehow he knew that eventually the ghost would confront him.

The memory of his mystery lady's lovemaking invaded his thoughts again as he climbed the steps, avoiding the rotted board he'd stepped on the day before. Would he find her inside? His body responded to the memory and he cursed his weakness.

The narrow door hung crookedly from leather hinges. He pushed at it, and the portal swung open.

He hesitated, drew a deep breath. Ducking beneath a portion of the door which had remained stuck to the frame, Dylan hummed the theme to *"The Twilight Zone"* as he flipped on his flashlight.

He paused while his eyes adjusted to the light. He'd done it—crossed the threshold of the infamous ghost cabin.

Where was the applause?

No drum roll?

No fanfare?

He shook his head in disbelief.

Taking a deep breath, he looked around. Tattered remnants of curtains hung by the lone window. Dust coated everything, including the cobwebs which clung to every nook and cranny. He sneezed, then froze as if expecting someone or some*thing* to rush forward.

Nothing happened.

After a few heart-stopping moments, he sighed. Sweeping the room with the flashlight, Dylan realized that at this particular time of day, sunlight spilled through the window. He turned off the instrument, deciding it best to save his batteries for later—when it was very dark and he was alone—or not alone?

"Stop it, Dylan," he whispered as he looked around, forcibly quelling his rising unease. Adventure awaited, and possibly a fortune as well.

The ceiling was a network of enormous bare beams which had obviously taken more than one man to construct. Logs, as big around as Dylan, crisscrossed in a precise pattern to support the sturdy building. He stepped near the center of the room and stared upward in awe.

Thinking it a waste that no one but a few termites had inhabited the cabin for over a century, Dylan became enthralled with the history about him. Some old cooking utensils remained near the hearth in the end of the room. A bed constructed of bent willows tied with leather thongs was pushed against the far wall. It seemed improbable that no one had set foot inside a cabin which had so much intrigue in its history, but the appearance of the place suggested that it was untouched since the day his ancestor had last shut the cabin's door.

Of course, the thought also crossed his mind that perhaps people had tried to enter and been deterred by the occupant. Would he be considered an intruder? But then—he *had* been invited in a rather unorthodox manner.

Hadn't he?

Dylan's sturdy work boots made far too much noise

to suit him as he made his way across the small room. Many birds had obviously built their nests in the eaves, both inside and out. Their droppings covered the oak floor.

Then he noticed the huge table made from the trunk of a mighty old oak in the center of the room. Avoiding the bird droppings, Dylan leaned against the table, marveling at its immense proportions. He couldn't help wondering how many men it had taken to haul the tree stump into the cabin. It would have been easier simply to construct the cabin around the tree.

He was avoiding the real issue. "Ghost, are you here?" He chuckled at what he'd said, then repeated his question. His medical training insisted he double-check everything. "Hello."

Still no ghost.

He shook his head. He was being absurd. Dylan told himself to get on with cleaning the filth from the room. If he was going to live here for thirty days the place needed a thorough disinfecting.

And an exorcism.

Rolling up his sleeves, be grabbed the bucket and stepped outside to fill it at the spring.

Serenity.

It was easy to see why the place had received such a name. Graceful willow trees surrounded the large spring. Wild violets, his grandmother's favorite flower, grew along the bank on the far side where he'd seen the Keeper yesterday.

Where I saw the Keeper yesterday . . .

It couldn't have been his imagination. He moistened his lips and raked his fingers through his hair as the image flashed through his mind, as clear and undeniable as the day before.

So what if the Keeper was real? The old Indian hadn't seemed threatening. Neither had the woman in his dreams. The Keeper wanted him here. Dylan knew it—felt it. This was right.

"So stop procrastinating and get on with this."

He took a deep breath, feeling his unease begin to dissipate, though he wasn't totally ready to abandon his internal arguments yet. Dylan wanted to convince himself that last night had been a dream.

And without a doubt, one of the best dreams he'd ever experienced. In fact, he looked forward to another. What man wouldn't?

Not that he was thoroughly convinced it was a dream, of course. "Damn." Pushing himself away from the table, he decided some good old-fashioned work would take his mind off ghosts and things that go bump in the night. Time for some serious scrubbing.

A few hours later the cabin had returned to a bit of its former glory. Tired and weary, Dylan stood back to admire his success. A century of dust and bird droppings had hidden the true beauty of the oak flooring. Even the window was clean. He knew the glass panes, now uneven and warped with age, must've been quite a luxury when the cabin was originally built. Beams of sunlight danced in the newly clean room.

Something was wrong with the look of the place. He examined the huge tree stump which had obviously served as a dining table. It didn't belong in the middle of the room. In fact, he was certain the original occupants wouldn't have wanted it there either. It was really in the way, not that he was planning to entertain during his stay.

Walking around the ancient tree stump, Dylan doubted he could move it alone. He gripped its edge and pushed. Nothing. It didn't even budge.

Where's Superman when you need him?

Dylan walked away from the tree-table and retrieved his pack from the floor in the corner. His stomach rumbled, reminding him he'd missed lunch.

"Dylan." A man's voice carried across the spring and through the open door.

Dylan jumped. His heart leapt into his throat until he recognized the visitor. *Next I'll be afraid of my own shadow.*

"Jeff."

Slinging the pack over one shoulder, Dylan stepped outside onto the porch and grinned when he saw his reluctant visitor. His best friend from childhood had made one hell of a sacrifice in coming down to the dreaded ghost cabin.

"Well, you did it, then." Jeff folded his arms across his chest and looked around.

"What are you looking for, Jeff? Lawyers aren't afraid of anything."

"Nothing we can confront in a courtroom." Jeff laughed as he walked around the spring, but never stopped his visual sweep of the area.

"So, what brings you out here?" Dylan asked. "Must be damned important to get you all the way out to the haunted house. Come in and set a spell. Take your shoes off."

"Very funny. You can cut the Jed Clampett routine

anytime now." Jeff scowled and stopped at the base of the steps. "So you've really been inside?"

Dylan grinned. "Come on in. I've been inside all day and nothing's happened. No strange noises or ominous sightings." He shrugged. "In fact, I was just thinking about lunch."

"Nothin' strange about that. All right." Jeff mumbled to himself as he and Dylan knelt beside the spring to wash their hands. Then they entered the dreaded room. "I can't believe I'm doing this."

"Anything for a friend. Right?" Dylan placed a reassuring hand on Jeff's shoulder. "Go on. Be brave. If I can do it—so can you. You're Super Lawyer, remember? Faster than a speeding ambulance—you can leap tall briefs in a single—"

"Right." Jeff stepped through the door and paused. "So far, so good."

"Explore new frontiers, man. Go where no one has gone before. Except me, that is." Dylan felt almost high with his newfound courage, disregarding the memory of how frightened he'd been earlier. The cabin was beginning to grow on him already. "You know, I really kind of like the place."

Jeff looked around the room. "I see what you mean." He glanced upward at the impressive ceiling and let out a low whistle of appreciation. "This is quite a piece of Americana."

Dylan remembered the table. "Hey, as long as you're here, give me a hand shoving this table out of the way."

Jeff chuckled and removed his double-breasted jacket and placed it over Dylan's pack near the door. "Jeez—put me to work the minute I get here."

Dylan smiled, remembering their childhood. They'd spent many pleasant hours fishing in the creek behind the cabin until the day they saw the ghost for the first time.

As they inched the table toward the wall, Jeff grunted. "So, you haven't seen any . . . ghosts today?" His gaze scanned the room as he spoke, betraying the seriousness of his inquiry.

Dylan gave the table one more good shove and stood back to admire their conquest. "That's better." He brushed off his palms and looked at Jeff and shook his head. "Nothing yet."

"That's good. *Real* good."

Feeling a growing need to change the subject, Dylan went to his pack and removed the sandwiches he'd thrown together that morning. "Now, how about some lunch? And speaking of food, is there anything in Grandpa's will that says I can't go up to the big house or to town for supplies on a regular basis?"

"No, I don't think that would be a problem." Jeff smiled, accepting one of the sandwiches his friend offered. "It'd be hard not to have a refrigerator."

"Right." Dylan took a big bite of his sandwich and stepped back onto the porch to enjoy the view. "It really is nice down here."

"Makes you think about moving home, eh?" Jeff nudged him as he joined Dylan on the porch. "You know, I still can't help but wonder about your grandfather's motivation for all this."

"What about it?"

"Well, do you suppose it could've been his way of encouraging you to move home?" Jeff arched a brow and took a bite of his sandwich.

Dylan smiled, but didn't speak. They ate in silence for several moments. His thoughts had been heading in that definite direction all morning. He'd forgotten about the peace, so prevalent here it was often taken for granted. Quiet was another one of those things he didn't realize he'd missed until he found it again. There was nothing quite so healing as silence.

"I just might give it a try." Dylan faced Jeff when he finished his sandwich. "I didn't tell you, but I resigned my position at the hospital before I left St. Louis."

Jeff lifted a curious brow. "Oh? Interesting."

"It was hard being around Cindy all the time." Dylan shrugged. "Besides, you were right about one thing."

"What's that?"

"I do need a change."

Jeff looked across the spring and sighed. "I'd forgotten how wonderful this spot is."

"You've been reading my mind." He chuckled. "Yeah, me too. My thirty days starts today. Right?"

"Right."

"And you'll come down to . . . check on me regularly?" Dylan winked, fighting the uncertainty threatening his resolve at every opportunity.

"Sure. I'll check on you." He sighed in obvious resignation. "If I have to."

"Yeah, you have to. And thanks." Dylan took a sip of water from his canteen and offered it to Jeff.

"Had any good, uh, dreams lately?"

"How did you . . ." Dylan nodded and his voice roughened. "Yeah."

Jeff grinned mischievously. "You don't seem as tense today."

"Smart-ass." He avoided Jeff's gaze. He wasn't ready to share the intimate details of his dream. For some reason he couldn't bring himself to kiss and tell.

Even if it was just a dream.

"Sorry, Dylan. I remember what it's like to want a woman and not be able to have her." Jeff ignored Dylan's scowl by glancing at his watch. "I have a late afternoon appointment so—"

"Coward."

"You got it." Jeff walked tentatively back into the cabin to retrieve his jacket. "Did you know there's a trap door in the floor where the table was?"

"I hadn't noticed before." Dylan shrugged. "You're right. Must be the cellar."

"Hmm." Jeff slipped on his jacket and offered Dylan his hand. "Reminds me of a story I read once."

"Let me guess." Dylan smirked at his friend. "The Telltale Heart."

"Good luck, Dylan."

"Gee, thanks. But I hope I don't need it."

"Yeah. Me, too." Jeff whistled "We're Off To See The Wizard" as he walked away from the cabin. He paused near the spring and glanced back over his shoulder. "I'll come back on Friday."

"You have my cellular number."

Dylan watched Jeff until he was nothing but a tiny speck on the horizon ascending the hill toward the road, then he turned toward the cabin again.

He saw the trap door the moment he entered the cabin. For some reason it disturbed him. Maybe he should have left the table where it was.

Curiosity gnawed at him. What was down there? It could be very interesting to explore. Old jugs of moonshine?

Treasure!

What better hiding place? Dylan broke into a cold sweat. His stomach lurched. Could that be why the table had covered the opening?

His raw nerves twitched. He wanted to find the treasure, but entering a cellar that hadn't seen fresh air in over a century wasn't on his agenda.

Get a grip, Dr. Marshall.

Dylan stepped onto the porch and took a deep breath. He'd just open the trap door, then let the cellar breathe for a while before he ventured down into it. Convinced he'd found his nerve, he went back inside the cabin and retrieved the flashlight from his pack. Checking the batteries to assure himself they worked, he knelt beside the opening.

He grasped the leather handle on one edge of the trap door and gave it a tug. *Snap.* The rotting leather disintegrated in his hand. Dylan removed the crowbar from his pack. It was lucky he'd brought it.

He went to work on the trap door again, discovering strength in determination. If there was a treasure in the cellar, he'd damned well find it.

The door was stubborn. Over a century of dirt had filtered in around the edges of the opening, forming a seal. The weight of the heavy table sitting on it hadn't helped the situation, either.

Dylan scraped some of the caked dirt from the crack and tried again. It moved a fraction of an inch. He smelled the dank, musty odor which wafted through the tiny crevice.

Smells like something crawled in there and died.

Another sniff. *Though it did it a long time ago.*

Flinching in disgust, he grew more determined to open the trap door and let the cellar air out before night fell. Stupid as it seemed, he'd prefer to climb into the pitch black cellar during the day rather than the night. At least the thought that it was daytime offered some psychological comfort.

Dylan took a deep breath and pushed with all his strength on the crowbar. Little by little the door began to rise.

Give me a lever and I can move the world.

Sweat drenched his brow by the time he forced the trap door open enough to wedge his foot beneath it and kick it completely open. He sat down beside the opening and mopped his brow. Tossing the crowbar to the floor with a crash, he reached across his lap and grabbed the flashlight.

A premonition gripped him. He peered down into the dark hole. He felt a sudden chill across his sweat-dampened shirt. Positioning the flashlight, Dylan leaned forward and flipped it on. When he did, he gasped, dropping the light into the cellar. Surely, he hadn't seen a . . .

A skeleton?

A human skeleton.

His imagination must be on a psychedelic high of some sort. But he was a scientist. He knew what human bones looked like. It wasn't some animal. His medical training wouldn't permit such an error. A skull returned his stare when he leaned over again and gaped at the spot where his flashlight had landed. The device macabrely lit the human remains. It looked like something Indiana Jones might have discovered.

"Shit." Dylan backed away from the opening and ran his fingers through his hair, which had worked itself loose from its short ponytail. Glancing in the hole again, he confirmed what he'd seen. Common sense told him it wouldn't matter how many times he looked into the opening.

The skeleton wasn't going anywhere.

He looked beyond the remains to the corner of the cellar where the flashlight cast a glow on several tattered cloth bags stacked against the earthen wall. Somehow, he was sure of their contents.

"The treasure."

He found his courage. There was something about the prospect of actually discovering a fortune in silver or gold that gave him the strength to face any foe.

Dead or alive.

His future looked sweet indeed. Dylan stood and put one foot into the hole until he found the ladder. Common sense warned him the ladder would be old and frail as he eased his other foot into the opening beside the first.

As he began his descent into the cellar, a strange feeling riveted him. It was almost like an electrical current of some sort. His head swam and a low humming sound enveloped him.

"What the hell . . ."

The humming grew more insistent and his head felt light. It was as if he'd passed through a force field. Dizziness claimed him as he swayed and gripped the ladder, bracing his head against it.

The room began to spin. Blackness surrounded him

as he struggled for control, only to find it eluding his every effort.

He was in a vacuum, a vortex of sorts, rushing toward bright light. The ladder gave way beneath him and he was sucked into the cellar, drawn in against his will.

For a fleeting moment he recalled the stories of patients who'd experienced death and been brought back to life. They'd all reported a bright light and a tunnel.

But before he could sort through his jumbled thoughts, unconsciousness took him in its soothing hand.

An image—a face—flashed through his mind before he lost consciousness completely.

Would she be in heaven waiting?

The Keeper grunted in satisfaction, then moved across the spring and floated into the cabin. The time had finally arrived.

With a wave of his hand, he willed the heavy tree stump to move. Slowly, he slid the table across the planked floor until the cellar door was exposed.

With a sigh, he pressed his open palm upward in a gesture which simultaneously lifted the door, allowing the light from within to escape into the cabin.

Now all will be as it should.

Three

Dylan slowly opened his eyes. His head felt like he'd just survived ten rounds with Mike Tyson—in jail. After his eyes adjusted to the dimness, he examined his surroundings and frowned.

The cellar.

Memories flooded back as he struggled to a sitting position. His flashlight was nowhere in sight, yet light bathed the dank cellar in a golden glow. He scanned the floor for its source.

"What the hell . . ." He winced at the sound of his own voice. Closing his eyes, he tried to convince himself he must be dreaming—again. Seemed of late he'd done more than his share of that.

But when he opened his eyes, Dylan knew this was no dream. On the floor, not more than a few feet away, was a girl—a woman. In fact, she was in the same position as the skeleton he'd seen earlier.

Impossible.

She moved and moaned. Dylan's medical instincts surged through him as he crawled over to her. He checked her carotid artery for a pulse. It was strong and regular. She pushed at his hand, then curled away from him. He was convinced by the way she moved that there were no spinal injuries. He rolled his patient from her side onto her back. He gasped.

It was her.

Dark lashes rested against her cheeks which were, at this moment, very pale. Her hair was black and shiny, spilling in a cascade of wild curls about her face and shoulders.

Her breathing, he noted, was deep and regular. However, from his nonmedical perspective he couldn't help noticing how beautifully she filled out the tightly stretched fabric of her old-fashioned dress.

Despite his concern for her health, he couldn't help recalling how she'd looked, felt and tasted during their lovemaking. She was real. Her flesh was warm to the touch. Her breath was soft and moist, not ghostly by any means.

He noticed a lantern not far from her grasp and, wondering briefly about its origin, he moved it nearer. Dylan lifted the lid of one of her eyes to assure himself her pupils were equal and reactive. And he'd been right—they were blue.

This was definitely not a ghost.

She moaned again and her eyes fluttered open. Her bewildered expression soon gave way to panic, however, and Dylan found himself on the receiving end of several surprisingly vicious blows.

"Help!"

"Settle down." Dylan gripped her shoulders and gently restrained her. "I'm not going to hurt you. I'm trying to help."

She looked at him with wide, frightened eyes the shade of cornflowers. Her trembling became more pronounced as she flinched away from him.

As if remembering something, she jerked her head toward the corner of the cellar.

The gold.

She tried to get up, but Dylan tempered her efforts. "Don't try to stand yet. You were unconscious." He noticed the color returning to her face. "Are you feeling better?" When she nodded, he helped her up. She swayed and fell against him.

Dylan was consumed with the memory of her luscious body bared before him. For a moment he forgot his dilemma. Passion flooded him as her breasts pressed enticingly against his chest. Suddenly, she became a woman rather than a patient.

A woman he'd known in the most intimate sense of the word . . .

She was small, barely reaching his shoulder. Her hair still smelled of roses. The memory made his body nearly burst with carnal urges. He turned her toward him and cupped her chin in his hand. She didn't seem in need of medical attention, nor was the thought of giving it uppermost in his mind at the moment.

"So, dream lady, we meet again," he whispered, and his lips descended to claim hers.

She gasped when his mouth covered hers. But the gasp was extinguished when his kiss achieved its intended effect. Dylan sensed her response when her lips parted, permitting him to explore her more thoroughly.

Though he knew this was the same woman, he was somewhat baffled by the difference in the way she returned his kiss. The wild abandon he recalled was curiously absent. In fact, she seemed naive as hell.

But of course, he knew better than anyone how erroneous that assumption was.

Dylan lifted his head to study her. Her eyes were glazed with passion as she stared up at him. Her body leaned full against his, reminding him of his urgent physical need. The raw sexual hunger she'd awakened in him during her nocturnal visits emerged with a lusty fury.

He reached out to test the weight of her breast, but his efforts were not rewarded with the intense passion he recalled. Instead of welcoming his touch, she returned his caress with a smart slap across his face.

"Why the hell'd you do that?"

He stared at her in shock as his hand covered a stinging cheek. "You didn't mind when I did that *and* a whole lot more last night."

"Why you filthy swine." She came at him with a fury that made *Mommie Dearest* seem more like *Pollyanna.* "I've never seen you before in my life, and I'll thank you to unhand me."

"Unhand *you?*" Dylan tilted his head, still rubbing his injury. "Make up your mind, love. You're the one who's been coming to *my* bed ev—"

"Well, boys." A voice filtered down from the oak flooring above. "I done heard enough."

Dylan looked up and swallowed hard. Staring down into the hole was the ugliest man he'd ever seen, with thin silver hair and a tobacco-stained beard. A pair of young men flanked him. They were obviously twins, and easily the largest, gawkiest teenagers he'd ever seen.

"Who are you?" Dylan asked, forgetting about the

gold, the girl and his location for the moment. These were intruders on his property.

"Zeke Sawyer, but I reckon I'm the one what oughta be askin' questions, stranger," the ugly man said with a toothless grin. He patted the shotgun resting across his knees. "Unless you wants to meet up with the other end a Old Bess here."

"This is my property," Dylan said with more bravado than he felt.

"Well, I'm sure the Marshall clan'll be right surprised to hear that." The three men laughed again, then Zeke's face grew dark with anger. "I never would come in here if'n I hadn't seen the light. S'pose I got the good Lord ter thank for it." His expression softened as he glanced at the girl. "He hurt you, Rose?"

Marshall Clan? Rose?

Dylan looked with astonishment at his mystery woman. Rose. That shouldn't come as a great surprise, considering the wonderful fragrance which seemed to radiate from her when he held her in his arms.

She shook her head. "No, Stepfather." She sniffled loudly. "He just . . . just kissed me." Rose blushed and avoided Dylan's gaze.

"How many times I gotta tell you, Rose—don't call me Stepfather?" He glanced at Dylan again. "Kissed you, eh? Well, we can't have none of that." The ugly man seemed quite pleased with the turn of events. "I reckon we're gonna need the preacher, boys."

"Preacher?" Rose scurried up the ladder, which Dylan suddenly realized was no longer decrepit.

With a frown, he took a quick glance around the cellar floor. It seemed so different. Even the cloth bags—the treasure—looked cleaner and untorn. The intruders obviously hadn't noticed the bags, and there was still no sign of his flashlight.

Or the skeleton.

He turned his gaze toward Rose again. The skeleton—Rose. Dylan jerked his head around to look at the place where he'd found her. It couldn't be.

"Stepfather, I don't intend to marry . . . *him.*" Her glance toward Dylan was scathing, to say the least.

Marry? She certainly had his attention now. He scowled, continuing to watch the exchange between the strange family.

"Rose, don't call me Stepfather." The man seemed disgusted with the title. It did seem rather formal. "This might be your last chance. You're gettin' on in years." He scratched his head. "Since you been so highhanded with the beaus who come courtin'—"

Rose snorted derisively. "Beaus, indeed."

Dylan couldn't help noticing the flagrant difference between Rose's manner of speech and her family's.

"Stepfa—Pappy Zeke—I'm not a spinster. I'm one of the New Women. We don't have to marry." She clung to the ladder with both hands, unaware that Dylan could see right up her skirt from the floor below.

My God, the woman's wearing bloomers.

"Besides, I don't want to marry . . . him."

She looked over her shoulder at Dylan and stuck out her pink tongue. Dylan shuddered. Seeing slender, shapely legs beneath her skirt and that tongue . . . well, he couldn't help but recall with a jolt how talented that tongue was.

Marry? Old Maid? Spinster?

Reluctantly abandoning his entertaining view, Dylan stepped to the side where he could see up the ladder beyond Rose. "Excuse me?" He called up and was rewarded with Zeke's ominous scowl. "Could I have a word with you, sir? Upstairs?" *Away from my gold.*

The man seemed to contemplate the matter with a great deal of effort. "I reckon. But don't try nuttin'."

As the threesome cleared the way for them to vacate the musty cellar, Dylan wondered what he could possibly "try." They had the gun.

Besides, he must be dreaming. That was it. He'd fallen and hit his head. This was nothing but a hallucination.

One helluva realistic hallucination, Dr. Marshall.

Rose peered at him as she rushed to her stepfather's side and grasped his arm. "Pappy Zeke, he didn't . . . do anything like what you mean." She glared at Dylan. "Besides, he has red hair. I don't care for men with red hair."

"Auburn." Dylan could have kicked himself for that.

"Huh?" the twins asked in unison.

Dylan sighed. "As . . . Rose explained, sir, nothing *happened.*" He shrugged and shook his head in disbelief. "We simply found ourselves in this cellar together for a time. That's all."

Some dream. At least in my other dreams Rose was—

"Trapped in this here cellar . . . *together?*" Sawyer asked, lifting his shotgun until it was leveled at Dylan's midsection. "I heard enough." He nodded as if issuing a command.

"I'll fetch the preacher, Paw." One of the twins moved toward the door.

Dylan couldn't help noticing the boy's clothing. Wearing overalls and red flannel underwear in lieu of a shirt, the youth was barefoot despite the cool evening.

"Naw." Sawyer grinned. "We'll take the happy couple to the preacher fer the hitchin'."

Hitching?

"I told you." Dylan was beginning to sweat. If this was a dream, then shouldn't he be waking up soon? Surely this cruel and unusual punishment was a violation of the Eighth Amendment. "Nothing happened."

"Maybe not." The man tilted his head sideways and spit on the floor. "But I reckon it will after the weddin'. Lord knows it's high time somebody took the uppitiness outta Miss High-n-Mighty Rose Jameson."

"High-and-mighty indeed." Rose glared at her stepfather and Dylan, then back again.

Amazing. He could almost forget his predicament while comparing the difference between Rose's refined speech and her stepfather's hillbilly *patois*. She certainly didn't seem like the same woman from his dream. But as his gaze traveled downward and came to rest on the swell of her breast where the shape of a nipple was boldly outlined by her thin dress, he was certain of her identity.

When he looked up again, Dylan found the old man's gaze on him. There was a knowing smile on his lips. "Yup," he said again. "I reckon it will after the weddin'. The Sawyer clan is gonna have us a weddin'."

Sawyer?

"Oh, this is rich." Dylan laughed aloud and slapped his thigh, amazed he hadn't made the connection sooner. "Old man Sawyer thought he could pull a fast one on me, but he's sadly mistaken. How much did he pay you? You guys are really good." His gaze rested on Rose's confused expression. "Especially you."

"That's all she wrote." Sawyer swung his shotgun around level with Dylan's nose. "March, stranger."

Dylan shook his head and chuckled, but complied with the man's wishes. When they reached Branson, he'd set things straight. But Sawyer wasn't getting his hands on the treasure or the property. Dylan was more determined than ever. At least the three men hadn't discovered the gold. Of course, Rose knew about it. He glanced back at her.

What an enigma.

But then, she was a paid participant in this carnival, wasn't she? Had she actually slipped into his bed at the other house? How else could he have dreamed her so . . . accurately? He recalled the devastating sweetness of her surrender when she'd finally allowed him to consummate their relationship.

God.

Once this indignity ended, he was determined to ask her out. Actress or not, no woman could feign the passion she'd displayed. Yet he must have been drugged to be so foggy on whether her visits had been dreams or reality. How had they managed it? Drugs? Hypnotism?

All the way to town—on foot, no less—Dylan listened to the exchange between the family who held him prisoner. They certainly were accomplished actors. It was all he could do to keep from laughing aloud. Their dialect, vocabulary, mannerisms all screamed "hillbilly." Except for Rose—she was different.

Still, if this was a dream, then why were they heading away from town, rather than toward it? They were going toward the lake.

He'd fallen down the ladder, bumped his head . . .

But the hallucination theory no longer held much plausibility. These were actors hired by Sawyer to perpetrate a scheme to try and force him to abandon Serenity Spring.

Convincing himself of this, Dylan turned his attention to his dark surroundings. They were definitely heading in the wrong direction.

And where were the city lights? In recent years, Branson had turned into a tourist trap that glowed neon bright at night, nearly blotting out the stars in the Ozark sky. As they walked down the dirt road, which he felt certain should have been a paved highway, his resolve began to dissipate.

"Excuse me, but we're not heading toward Branson."

Zeke spat on the ground before answering. "Nope. Dogwood."

"Dogwood?" Dylan had never heard of such a place. "Where's that?" *Maybe what's that would've been a better question.*

His gaze strayed to Rose who continued to plead with her stepfather. Moonlight bathed her in a halo that danced in her dark tresses. He sighed. He was obsessed with the recollection of her lush form pressed wantonly against him nearly every night for the past three weeks.

He wished they were alone in his bed right now, recreating the ecstasy he'd found in the arms of Rose—the temptress from hell. Her face was so innocent and angelic in the moonlight.

How could he think her guilty of such treachery? To steal her way into his bed because she was on old

man Sawyer's payroll? And yet, the vivid memory of
her naked form in his bed couldn't be denied.

"Here we be." Sawyer's voice interrupted his pondering as Dylan glanced up at a log structure not much
larger than the cabin at Serenity Spring.

"And where might that be?" Dylan's voice dripped
with sarcasm.

"Church." Sawyer spat tobacco juice on the ground
near Dylan's booted feet. "Them's mighty fine-lookin'
boots you got there."

Dylan ignored the man's interest in his choice of
footwear. He was cold, tired and his head ached from
the fall.

And what about that fall?

Dylan knew there was no point in trying to explain
the spinning vortex which seemed to have drawn him
into the root cellar. The experience defied any plausible attempt at justification.

"This has gone on long enough. I'm going home."
He chuckled and shook his head. "Go on back to
whichever amusement park you're from. You can tell
old man Sawyer to go to hell for me."

"You just did." Sawyer leveled the shotgun at Dylan's
midsection again. "An' I don't much like it neither."

Dylan swallowed hard. "This really has gone on
long enough." He tried to laugh, but it sounded more
like a snort. "C'mon—cut the crap."

"Don't appear to me you're in a position to do much
bossin'." Sawyer grinned and prodded Dylan in the
ribs with the barrel of the shotgun. "What's your
name, boy?"

"You know very well what my name is." Dylan
placed a tentative finger on the barrel of the gun and

gently steered it away from his ribs. "Dr. Dylan Marshall."

"Marshall? I know every one of them Marshalls and you ain't one." His scowl soon turned to a smile as he burst out laughing. "Imagine that, boys—a Marshall a doctor?"

While the three men laughed, Dylan ventured another glance at Rose. She was silent now, her blue eyes wide with what looked like genuine fear. For some reason, despite his predicament, Dylan felt sorry for her. But he quickly reprimanded himself for such foolishness and turned away.

Feeling sorry for Rose is sort of like feeling sorry for Leona Helmsley.

Sawyer pounded on the heavy door with the butt of his shotgun until a light appeared inside. Within a few moments, a man of indeterminable age, dressed in a long nightshirt, swung open the door. Lamplight spilled out onto the ragtag assortment of people on his threshold.

"Sawyer." He acknowledged the eldest of the group. "What brings you to town at this unholy hour?"

Dylan felt the man's gaze on him. His flesh began to crawl. A nagging suspicion sparked in the very confused recesses of his mind. Could he be mistaken? Were these people actors, or were they for real? It couldn't be, yet doubts nagged him.

The man held his lantern higher until the light fell across Dylan's face. A smile spread across the gnarled features.

"Why, this must be Joe Marshall's boy." His smile broadened. "He's the spittin' image of him."

Joe Marshall?

Sawyer turned to look speculatively at Dylan's shocked expression. "Says he's a Marshall, but I don't recollect ever seein' him before." He squinted. "They be a resemblance all right, though."

"Well, now Zeke . . ." The man with the lantern scratched his head. "Joe's widow had a youngun after she left Dogwood."

"Yup, that's right." Sawyer looked at Dylan again and nodded. "Anyway, he's marryin' Rose tonight."

"Ah, it's like that. Caught one, eh?" The man in the doorway shook his head. "Compromisin' a lady's virtue's an abomination, boy. What, if anything, do you have to say for yourself?"

This was insane. "I didn't *do* anything," Dylan said in a voice he felt certain betrayed his anxiety. Of course, he understood deep down inside that he had slept with Rose. Or with someone—some*thing*—that looked a hell of a lot like her.

At least he thought he had. Jeez, he was confused. He looked at her again. A ghost? A dream? An actress? Which one had visited his bed?

Zeke spat on the ground to the left of the open door. "You ready to do some marryin', Preacher?"

"Preacher?" Dylan swallowed, wishing he'd stayed in his cramped apartment back in St. Louis. At least there he'd be warm—and alone.

"If you insist, Zeke," the man said with a long suffering sigh. "Bring in the betrothed."

"Betrothed?" Dylan balked, but one of the twins grasped his arm and steered him into the log church. Pews of split oak sat in neat rows from front to back. A rough cross hung from the rafters behind the pulpit. "I told you, I'm not marrying anyone."

Rose began to cry. "Oh, don't you see? He doesn't want me any more than I want him." Her tears fell in droplets to the floor near Dylan's feet.

Dylan looked at her uncertainly, wondering why he should care about her feelings. "This is wrong. I don't know why you came to me last night, but—"

"Heard enough, Preacher?" Zeke grinned maliciously. "Now, hitch 'em."

"I never saw this man before in my life." Rose tugged at her stepfather's sleeve. Her eyes were wide and pleading. "Please, don't make me marry him." A huge tear rolled down her cheek.

Dylan shifted his weight from one foot to the other and applauded. "Bravo. He tilted his head sideways to survey the gathering. "I'll vouch for your performance to the Academy."

"Ac—ademy?" Zeke knitted his dirty brow in obvious confusion.

"Right." Dylan sighed in exasperation. "I don't care how much Sawyer paid you. I'm not going to let him have the property."

"Boy, is you tetched?"

"'Tetched?'" Dylan repeated, casting the man what he hoped was his most derisive glance. "You can cut the 'Lil' Abner' routine now. I'm onto your scheme."

"Preacher, marry 'em fast before I shoot him." Zeke poked Dylan in the ribs again with the shotgun, maneuvering the reluctant groom farther up the church aisle, toward the pulpit.

"Is there a phone in this place?" Dylan looked over his shoulder at the preacher, who either didn't hear or chose not to respond. "I want a telephone so we can clear up this mess, once and for all."

"Tely—fone?" Zeke looked at the minister again and laughed. "Huh. Only city folks got them new-fangled talkin' things."

"Nary a clue." Shaking his head, the preacher stepped behind the pulpit and withdrew a well-worn bible. "Dearly beloved—"

"I'm not marrying anyone!" Dylan's shout was completely ignored. He looked down at his feet and shook his head in disgust. Well, at least it wouldn't be legal. Jeff would have it annulled—no problem. He doubted whether even that would be required since there was no marriage license, no blood tests . . .

Suddenly, he recalled the cellular phone in his hip pocket. Reaching back with a tentative hand, he sighed in relief and withdrew the coveted object. After flipping it on, he punched in Jeff's home number.

Nothing but static.

"What's that?" the twins asked in unison, stepping forward to admire the instrument in Dylan's hand. He punched the numbers in again, glancing warily at the two huge predatory animals.

"Put that gol-durned thing away an' pay attention, boy." Zeke didn't seem the least bit impressed with the cellular phone and at the moment neither was Dylan. A whole hell of a lot of good it did him if it didn't work.

"Do you . . ." The preacher glanced at Zeke, who still had his gun wedged between two of Dylan's tender ribs. "What did you say this fellow's name is?"

"Dylan, so's he claims." Zeke gouged the barrel deeper into Dylan's side. "He best be tellin' us right, too, if he wants to see the sun rise agin. Hold her hand, boy."

"Dylan Marshall, M.D." Dylan winced. He'd be damned if he'd hold the hand of the seething woman at his side. She was doing a fine job of imitating his outrage. "This isn't legal." After a third futile attempt to call Jeff, he returned the worthless phone to his hip pocket.

"You already married?" The very convincing actor portraying the minister frowned.

"No," Dylan said impatiently, immediately regretting his hasty answer. That could have been a means of halting the ridiculous proceedings, but he'd let it slip right by him. Of course, these people already knew very well who he was and that he most definitely was not married—anymore.

"Well, then . . . I reckon it's legal enough." Zeke nodded to the preacher, who cleared his throat and looked down at his Bible.

"Do you, Dylan, take Rose to be your lawful wedded . . ."

Dylan tried to tune out the preacher's nasal voice. It was very late and he was exhausted. He'd be damned if he'd return to the cabin tonight—not after this. He was going to make a straight path to the farmhouse and a nice, soft bed. Right after he called Jeff and woke him up.

"Say 'I do,' boy." Zeke prodded Dylan's bruised flesh and bone again.

"Easy with that thing, old man." Dylan glared at his captor. Zeke gouged even deeper in response. "All right. I do, but I really *don't.*"

The minister sighed. "I reckon that's good enough."

At Zeke's nod, the man smiled. "I now pronounce you man and wife. You can kiss her now, boy."

"Kiss her . . . *Son,*" Zeke said ominously, though he was grinning like some kind of maniac. "Now I reckon we got us a real doctor in the family. How about that? Jim ain't gonna like this one bit."

Dylan stood frozen. Jeff's voice returned to haunt him.

Zeke Sawyer shot Jim Marshall.

Old man Sawyer had certainly done his research. History made a strong ally when properly utilized. Someone sure as hell had the facts down pat and knew exactly which buttons to push.

He felt Rose's gaze on him, but refused to meet hers. Somehow he knew she was crying, and for some inexplicable reason, he felt responsible. She was an actress—a very talented one—both here and in his bed. He glanced askance at her again. Wasn't she?

Of course she is. Get a grip.

With a sigh, he turned to face his captor again. He could play their little game if it would get him out of here. "Are you happy, now?" Dylan finally asked Zeke, pushing the barrel of the gun away. "You've managed to keep everyone up all night and make Rose cry."

"Miss High-n-Mighty's your problem now." Zeke scowled. No humor remained on his grizzled features. "Now . . . I said *kiss her.*"

Dylan saw murder in those rheumy eyes. Something deep in his gut hinted that this was no game, and the man who held the gun so expertly was no actor.

Logic demanded it wasn't so.

Instinct screamed otherwise.

He nodded, then looked into Rose's eyes. His breath caught in his throat at the pain, anguish and fury he saw so plainly. Academy Award material if he'd ever seen it. Such expressive, traitorous eyes—tears glistened in their depths and trickled down her cheeks. Very effective. Her face was so lovely he ached to touch it, though her gaze sparkled with anger and rage behind the tears.

"Damn." He cupped her chin in his hand. Another tear escaped and rolled down her cheek. He caught it with his fingertip and brushed it away.

Her angry gaze wavered. "I'm sorry," she said so softly he thought at first he was mistaken.

Dylan frowned. Why would she be sorry? If indeed she was only performing a role, why should she regret success? None of this made sense.

"Kiss her!" Zeke's voice was fierce.

Dylan lowered his mouth to hers, intending to deliver only a brief peck, but he'd forgotten how sweet she tasted. Once his mouth made contact with hers, instinct took over. He kissed her as if staking a claim.

Claim—like husbandly rights?

He tried to fight his natural urges, but it was a futile campaign. The influence of her soft, warm frame pressed so enticingly against his, combined with the memory of the "ghostly spirit" who'd made unrestrained love to him.

The amalgamation was the fatal blow to his self-restraint. He kissed her with the raw yearning her repeated visits had created and now commanded. His body responded as if it was at a hormone smorgasbord.

Take what you want and leave what you don't.

Unfortunately, he had no concept of moderation where this woman was concerned.

"There, now." Zeke's voice intruded on Dylan's foggy mind. "I told you this'd happen after the hitchin'."

Dylan jerked himself away from Rose and exhaled with a loud whoosh. Obviously startled by his abrupt release, she wavered and nearly collapsed at his feet. An entire lifetime of practicing good manners demanded he offer a steadying hand. She looked up at him with eyes so clear and bright he felt certain she wore tinted contact lenses—a tool to lure her victims into her lair. Yet she seemed as confused by her reaction as he.

"Damn."

"I'll thank you to mind your tongue in here, boy," the preacher scolded, though his eyes reflected a glint of humor.

"Sorry." *Why the hell am I apologizing to* him? Dylan looked steadily at Zeke Sawyer, or whatever his real name was. "I'm getting out of here. I'll have this thing annulled by tomorrow. It isn't legal to marry without a blood test and license."

Zeke guffawed with his sons. Rose's lower lip trembled slightly, forcing Dylan to look away. The minister seemed nonplused.

"Oh, it's legal, son." He shook his head and offered Dylan a parchment. "I don't know about a license and . . . blood test? But here's your certificate—all legal and binding as can be."

Dylan grabbed the document and clutched it in his hand, taking every ounce of self-restraint he could muster to prevent him from ripping it to shreds. He'd just give this to Jeff . . .

Considering the various ways he could get out of the ridiculous liaison, Dylan scanned the forgery. His confidence was unwavering . . . until he read the date just beneath the actor-minister's ostentatious signature.

March 30, 1894.

He did a double-take.

Four

"Hey, where you think you're goin'?" Zeke's voice followed Dylan as he walked stonily from the church.

He was vaguely aware of Rose running in the opposite direction with her entire family in hot pursuit. Better her than him.

1894?

Dylan struggled to grasp the meaning of this latest blow. This was baffling, to say the least. But was it possible? Had he actually traveled back in time a hundred years?

No, of course not.

Dylan looked around, half-expecting to discover he'd been abducted by aliens and transported to another planet. Unfortunately, no such obvious explanation presented itself.

The night was still dark, though he sensed the sun would be peeking above the horizon at any moment. With leaden feet, he trudged along the dirt road in the general direction of his grandfather's property.

His property.

Or was it? If, in fact, he'd traveled back in time— though the mere notion was ludicrous—who owned the farm? His great-great . . .

No.

Yet he had to at least consider the possibility. After all, how much more outlandish was the concept of time travel than haunted cabins, buried treasure . . . and beautiful, insatiable ghosts?

Dylan shook his head and paused on the road to watch the first violet smudges of dawn streak the eastern sky. A faint mist rose from the valley which stretched out before him. The view was breathtaking and strangely unfamiliar.

He threw his hands up in the air in frustration when he realized what was wrong with the visual images his eyes were sending to his brain. Something very large was curiously—impossibly—absent from the scene. "Where the hell is the damned lake?"

This was ridiculous.

Impossible.

Undeniable.

A few cabins dotted the valley floor, with smoke curling from their chimneys. He rubbed his eyes and looked again, half-expecting the smoke to have been replaced by the hum of microwave ovens nuking instant oatmeal.

No power lines.

No highways or automobiles.

No lake.

He rubbed his eyes and looked again. The sun reached above the horizon now, blotting out most of the spectacular bloom of first light. Much to his amazement, the daylight revealed many familiar sights.

To the south, the winding creek splashed along as if nothing had changed. He was almost positive the road he now stood on would one day be paved and known as U.S. 160.

His eyes stung. He hadn't cried since he was eleven years old. Except once—privately—after Cindy'd first announced she was leaving him.

He wasn't about to start now.

Dylan swiped angrily at his eyes until he felt some control return. A twig snapped and his head shot around to check his surroundings. Had the Sawyers followed him after all?

A squirrel chattered, voicing obvious displeasure with a human's presence. Shaking his head, Dylan emitted a sigh of reluctant surrender. "I sure as hell don't want to believe this."

He turned and continued toward the farm. If his calculations were correct, he'd soon come face to face with his great-great-grandparents.

And just how would he explain his identity?

"Hello, I'm Dylan, your great-great-grandson." A laugh that sounded more like a howl of anguish rose from his chest at the absurdity of such a scenario.

He recalled the preacher's reference to Joe Marshall's son. Apparently no one had seen him, and Dylan knew he possessed the family characteristics—the genes. The auburn hair and hazel eyes were Marshall trademarks regardless of the century. Could he assume the identity of Joe Marshall's son until he sorted through this mess?

What choice do I have?

Running his fingers through his hair, Dylan wished he could take a hot shower and grab a shave. He rubbed his chin, where he knew reddish brown stubble covered his usual clean-shaven mug.

He paused again. A flock of birds settled down to search the ground for their breakfast directly in front of him. He watched intently while one very small bird devoured a juicy worm nearly as large as itself.

Taking a deep breath, Dylan remembered how long it had been since he'd eaten anything. Of course, he'd have to be starving to death before he'd join the bird in its juicy repast . . . and even that was questionable.

He'd need money. The currency and credit cards in his wallet were worthless. And a whole hell of a lot of good his driver's license would do him in 1894. Then another, more disturbing thought crossed his mind.

The treasure.

Rose must have seen the gold. That was probably why she'd been in the cellar in the first place. Dylan took a few steps and stopped again. A chill passed over him as realization thrust itself forefront in his mind.

Someone sealed Rose in the cellar.

There seemed no other explanation, since she'd been inside the cellar and the only exit was blocked with the heavy oak tree stump.

But how? Who? Why?

The fury in her blue eyes had been undeniable . . . and directed at him. Because she wanted the treasure for herself?

Dylan's heart raced. Jeff's words echoed through his mind.

Zeke Sawyer shot and killed Jim Marshall over a pouch of gold.

Had he stumbled across the cause of his great-great-grandfather's murder? And more importantly—could he prevent it?

Dylan had no choice. He must move the gold to a place where no one would ever find it. If he succeeded in hiding it well and could find a way to return to the future, he'd be able to walk straight to it in his own time.

He ran the remainder of the way to Serenity Spring, relieved when he found the cabin unoccupied. Rose hadn't returned for the gold.

Yet.

The cellar door was still propped open. Dylan hesitated before descending the ladder, wondering if he'd be whisked back to the future.

If so, then it stood to reason the gold would be where he'd first seen it. He hesitated, recalling the human skeleton.

Rose.

Dylan bit his lower lip in contemplation. If he returned to his own time, would she die? Or had he already changed history with his little adventure?

"Damn."

Nausea churned in his stomach as he considered all that had transpired during the past twenty-four hours. Rose must have been murdered, obviously because of the gold. He came back in time to . . . save her life.

To marry her?

Completely baffled, Dylan shook his head. He'd never considered himself capable of doing anything notable. He wasn't exactly the kind of guy people erected statues to honor. Yet it was becoming obvious that he'd inadvertently traveled back through time and saved a young woman from a horrible death.

And married her.
Inadvertently?

"Damn," Dylan repeated, as he climbed down the ladder, not knowing which century he'd find at the bottom. With any luck, he'd swirl his way back through the vortex. The time tunnel? Time portal?

Whatever.

Nothing happened. Assuming traveling forward in time would involve at least as much spinning and special effects as going back had, Dylan could only conclude that he was still stranded. His feet were firmly planted on the dirt floor, still very much in the nineteenth century.

"Beam me up, Scotty?"

Nothing.

"Hell." He opened a bag and stared. His pulse took off like a thoroughbred darting from the starting gate at Churchill Downs. Yes, this was gold all right. Glittering circles of yellow coins—hundreds of them. He picked up two of the heavy bags and climbed the ladder again. He knew exactly where to hide it. With any luck, it would never be discovered.

Except by him if—no, *when*—he returned to his own time.

He remembered a cave where he and Jeff had played as boys. Located about a hundred yards behind the cabin, it was the perfect place to store his cache. Dylan made several trips to transfer all the gold to its new, secret, resting place.

Old Zeke Sawyer had missed the prize in the cellar when he found Dylan with Rose. Amazing. The old hillbilly'd missed his golden opportunity. Fortunately, so had his stepdaughter.

Dylan retrieved a few coins for his pocket, realizing he'd have to go to town for supplies. These weren't ancient Spanish coins by any stretch of the imagination. From a nineteenth-century perspective, they were recent issue.

Grimacing, he removed his wallet, the now less-than-impressive cellular phone, and all his futuristic currency, placing them inside the cave as well. But he kept the fanny pack, recalling the medical supplies he'd brought along.

Grunting with the effort, Dylan rolled a boulder over the cave opening. There was sufficient space for him to squeeze through to retrieve the gold as needed, but the mouth of the cave was obscure enough to deter any curiosity seekers, at least for a while.

Satisfied with his morning's work, Dylan staggered to the spring and splashed his face with cool water. Reminded unpleasantly of the cold showers he'd been forced to endure at the hospital during his residency, he removed his shirt and bathed as best he could with the frigid water. He was a little less dirty, but a whole lot hungrier by the time he'd finished his ablutions, such as they were. All he really wanted was a hot shower and a rare steak.

To hell with my cholesterol.

He went back inside the cabin to close the cellar door and determine what supplies he'd need to make his auspiciously brief stay in the nineteenth century a bit more bearable. Chuckling, he shook his head at the irony of his situation.

What a stink he'd made about moving into the cabin when Jeff had first read the will. Imagining his best friend's reaction when he learned about this latest episode, made Dylan laugh even harder.

Another thought stole his laughter. What if he never found the way back to his own time?

"My God." Dylan stood frozen in the center of the one room cabin that had so altered his life. "What the hell am I going to do?"

He had to make the best of things until he could sort through this predicament. At least he was alive.

"Jeez—am I?" Dylan patted his abdomen and pinched his forearms. "I feel alive. Hungry and dirty, but alive."

Shaking his head and laughing at his foolishness, he jingled the heavy coins in his pocket and stepped outside, closing the cabin door as if it really belonged to him. For the time being at least, this was home.

The time being?

Resigning himself—at least temporarily—Dylan whistled as he walked slowly up the familiar hill toward the farmhouse. His heart began to hammer as he crested the rise which would permit him a full view of his ancestral home.

Dylan froze.

The house looked very much the same, with its broad front porch and gabled roof. The lawn was not well manicured as it would one day be, and the house didn't gleam with white paint accented with green shutters. But it was achingly familiar and comforting.

He walked slowly up the slight embankment which led to the front porch. What would he say to his ancestors? Would they recognize him as a member of the family?

That was a laugh.

Before he reached the porch, Dylan knew something was wrong. A black wreath hung ominously on the front door. Its meaning was obvious to anyone who'd been reared in the Ozarks in any century. His throat constricted as he rushed up the steps to pound on the door, suddenly frightened for relatives he'd never met—never should've met.

Dylan held his breath in anticipation, wondering whose face would greet him. He licked his cracked lips and prepared himself to meet with a slice of history. The door swung open slowly.

"Lan' sakes." The woman gasped and covered her mouth with the corner of her apron. She was in the advanced stages of pregnancy and stared at him with open curiosity. "Are you . . . Joe's boy? You're sure enough the spittin' image of him."

Dylan held his breath, but managed a weak smile. If he resembled Joe so much, then far be it for him to argue the point. "I wasn't sure I'd be welcome." *That's no lie.*

"Pshaw!" The woman reached out and literally dragged him into the painfully familiar, but different, house. White cloth hung over the antique looking glass that had been his grandmother's prized possession.

Ozark superstitions were fierce even in his time. The clock on the mantel was stopped. These signs, along with the wreath at the door, confirmed a recent death in the household. It was too early in the year for it to have been Jim Marshall's shooting.

Offering no explanation for the obvious signs of death, the woman led Dylan to the kitchen, devoid of the cabinets and modern conveniences he knew. An old cook-stove in the corner provided unnecessary warmth; a pot of beans already simmered on its top.

"I'll bet you're hungry. Set yourself down here an' wait for your cousin."

Cousin? "Are you . . . ?" Dylan smiled tentatively at the woman who boasted hair as red as any he'd ever seen and eyes the color of a mountain spring. She was pleasant and cheerful, which seemed rather odd, considering the wreath he'd seen on the door.

"Cousin Martha, by marriage."

Martha Marshall.

She gave him a smile that made him feel like a child again. He guessed her age as very near his own. His great-great-grandmother . . . so young? How peculiar.

"None of your folks ever learnt your name. All they know'd was that Mary had a boy after she left here. She was . . . in a family way when your paw died." She shook her head for a moment and studied him as if she thought he wasn't real. "We always hoped to meet you. Is you really Joe's boy?"

Dylan swallowed hard. The lump which had formed in his throat would gag him before this deception was finished. *Damn.* What choice did he have?

Dylan nodded, hating himself for the lie. He wanted to change the subject—he *needed* to. "The wreath on the door . . . ?"

"Your grandpa. Lordy, he woulda loved meetin' you." Failing to notice Dylan's guilty wince, she placed a plate of ham and eggs in front of him and filled a cup with steaming coffee. "He come home last night from his crazy wanderin'. Dropped dead before he got in the door." Her face reddened as she related the story while avoiding his gaze, almost as if she wasn't telling the entire tale and feared he might read something in her expression.

Dylan's thoughts went crazy with possibilities. Tom Marshall—his great-great-great-grandfather. His gaze dropped to Martha's swollen abdomen, wondering if his great-grandfather was the child she carried. Considering the month and year, it had to be.

Martha blushed. "Oh, I reckon you noticed the babe."

"I'm sorry . . . Cousin Martha." Dylan reminded himself that women in the nineteenth century weren't as open about pregnancy as they were in his time. "I didn't mean to embarrass you, but see—I'm a doctor."

"Doctor? Well, I'll be. What's your given name?" She waited while he gathered his thoughts. The tension he'd noticed when they'd spoken of Tom had passed. "You do know it, don't you?"

Dylan nodded and his face flashed hot. "I'm sorry. Dylan."

"Dylan." She seemed to test the name on her tongue. "That's a queer name, but I kinda like it."

"I believe it's Irish." Dylan grinned. He liked his "Cousin" Martha.

"My, you sure talks real fine." She sat down opposite him at the large oak table. "Where'd your mamma raise you? Last we heard from her, she was still in Springfield."

Dylan shuddered. He didn't like to deceive her, but there seemed no other alternative. "St. Louis."

"Oh, I ain't never seen a city that size." She seemed duly impressed, then took a sip of coffee. "You be wantin' some more?"

"No, thanks." Dylan finished the ham and eggs just as a very tall man entered the room. His gaze went directly to Dylan, then a frown knitted his brow as he studied the uninvited guest with open inquiry.

After a moment, a tentative smile tugged at the corners of the man's lips. "Well, I know you're a Marshall. There ain't no denyin' that."

"Plain as day right there on his face," Martha said in agreement, then shook her head and stood to fill another cup and plate for her husband. "He's the spittin' image of his paw."

"Joe. Sure as ticks on a dawg." Jim Marshall sat down at the table, accepting Dylan's identity without question. "There ain't no other relatives I knows of. You gotta be Joe's boy."

Dylan nodded again. The lying tore at his gut, making him feel as if he'd been found guilty on "The People's Court" of running over his neighbor's dog.

Jim ate his breakfast in relative silence, though his gaze rarely strayed from Dylan. "I was just a pup when my Uncle Joe—your paw—died an' your maw left here. But I'm glad to finally meet you."

"I'm pleased to meet you, too." Dylan had expected grandparents—older people—not peers. "My . . . my mother told me about the family and after she died I wanted to meet you." That seemed plausible.

Jim nodded and rubbed his bearded jaw. "What'd you say your given name was?"

"Dylan."

"Dylan. Hmm." Jim's smile revealed straight white teeth in the midst of a dark brown beard. His hazel eyes crinkled at the corners when he smiled. "Dylan Marshall. That's a right fine name."

"Thanks." Dylan sighed. As long as Joe's real boy didn't show up, he might pull this off yet.

"I can tell you've had schoolin'."

Dylan smiled, but before he could respond Martha supplied the additional information.

"He's a doctor."

Jim smiled. "Oh, that's fine. Yes, indeed. Dogwood needs a doctor in the worst way."

"Dogwood?" That was the second time since his journey through the Twilight Zone that he'd heard the name of this mystery town. It was almost as if he'd stumbled across the "Brigadoon" of the Ozarks. "Where's Dogwood?"

"Down by the river."

Dylan's mind raced, then he recalled the lake. The town of Dogwood must have been covered by the huge reservoir he knew so well. Now that he considered it, where the Sawyer clan had escorted him last night would definitely be under water in his time.

"Of course—the river." He smiled, wondering if he should tell his "cousins" he had no intention of staying around long enough to establish a medical practice. Yet what else was he supposed to do with himself while he waited for another miracle to thrust him back to his own time?

None too soon.

Jim Marshall set his coffee cup down and stared at Dylan in silence, obviously waiting for him to speak.

"I was wondering about the cabin." Dylan took another sip of coffee, discovering a mouthful of grounds for his trouble. Reminded he wasn't consuming a beverage brewed by Mr. Coffee, he managed a semigraceful rescue with the cloth napkin Martha had provided.

Only a minuscule portion of the gagging grounds made their way down his gullet. "Down by the spring. Do you suppose I could . . . stay in it for a while? I guess while I'm here I could see some patients."

Jim glanced at his wife. His expression was filled with concern and love. Dylan's heart skipped a beat as another memory tore at him. The newspaper article.

Zeke Sawyer killed Jim Marshall.

As Dylan considered the enormity of leaving Martha widowed with a small child, Jim reached across the table to cover his wife's hand with his large, tanned one.

Dylan searched his memory for information about his family tree. As he recalled, his great-grandfather had been Jim and Martha's only child.

"I kinda hoped after hearin' you was a doctor . . ."

Dylan rubbed his forehead, trying to follow Jim's thoughts. Then he realized the man was worried about his wife and the baby. Though fairly young by Dylan's standards, Martha was considerably older than most nineteenth-century first-time mothers.

"Leave him be, Jim." Martha hurried to the stove and refilled her husband's coffee cup. Her face flushed and she avoided Dylan's gaze when she returned to the table.

"I don't see why you can't stay in the cabin for as long as you like." Jim shrugged and exchanged glances with his wife. "Martha tell you about Grandpa?"

"Yes, she told me." Dylan hesitated. "I was sorry to hear about his death."

"Crazy old fool." Jim shook his head in apparent disgust. "He was always chasin' rainbows. He built that cabin down by the spring, you know."

"So I've heard." Dylan smiled and swallowed. *The ghost cabin.* His memories created a knot in his gut he was powerless to unravel.

"He built this house, too." Martha sighed and cast her spouse a wistful glance. " 'Course he had three big sons to help him by then."

"So he did." Jim smiled meditatively. "They're all dead now. My paw was the oldest. He was kilt in the war when I was still wet behind the ears."

Dylan hung on their every word. He had heard the tales of his ancestors' arrival in the Ozark region prior to Missouri statehood. The homestead was quite large and had considerable improvements.

Compared to what he'd seen from the bluff earlier— when he'd had to admit the truth to himself—the Marshall family seemed quite prosperous. The large frame house was an austere contrast to the rough cabins he'd already observed.

"The funeral's tomorrow," Jim said finally, pushing away from the table. "That'll be your chance to meet the townfolk. Most of 'em'll be glad to hear we got us a doctor."

"Most of them?" Dylan grimaced and his heart sank. He had to return to the twentieth century.

"Some folks is superstitious about real doctors." Martha chuckled. "They visit old Maggie Mae when they needs healin'. We all do mostly. She's been the closest thing Dogwood's had to a doctor for years. She was a slave before the war. Owned by a real doctor, she was. That's how she learnt everything about healin'."

Jim chuckled and nodded along with his wife. Sighing, he walked toward the door, and removed a battered hat from a peg near the wall. "You up to some chores, Dylan?"

Dylan smiled and immediately rose to his feet. Though he hadn't slept since night before last—plus a century—he was eager to spend some time with his ancestor while he had the opportunity. "Thank you for the best breakfast I've had in many years, Cousin Martha." Bending, Dylan delivered a kiss to her soft cheek.

The woman blushed and slapped at his arm. "Git on with you."

Just before he stepped out into the midmorning sun with Jim, Dylan couldn't help noticing that Martha was still smiling. It felt good to have family again, despite the extreme lengths required to find them. Many years had passed since he'd felt this kind of kinship with anyone. He paused for a moment, then hurried to catch Jim.

If he could keep Zeke from killing Jim, would there be more children? Would Dylan return to the future to find an extended family?

That thought boggled his mind.

Here was the perfect opportunity to rejuvenate the Marshall clan. Jim Marshall had been killed in the prime of life. If he were to live, then there was a good chance of cousins, aunts and uncles.

A real family.

"I don't usually lay about of a mornin', Dylan," Jim said almost apologetically, as they walked toward the barn. "Was because of Grandpa. An' Martha weren't feelin' too pert earlier."

"Of course." Dylan slowed his pace when Jim did. "Do you know the cause of death?"

Jim shrugged. "Old age, I reckon. Martha's done washed him. I put twenty-five cent pieces on his eyes and she put the soda rag over his face to keep it . . . well, you know. He's laid out in the parlor if'n you've a mind to pay your respects." He swung open the gate and stepped into the barnyard. "He was almost eighty. Way too old to be trompin' 'round like he did, always lookin' for a treasure or somethin'."

So Tom was the one. Dylan hid his wince from Jim. He knew all too well the treasure Tom Marshall'd been searching for. He patted his pocket as if to reassure himself it still existed.

"I couldn't help noticing, Jim . . ." The doctor in him would not be deterred. "You and Martha don't have other children?"

Jim reddened beneath the brown beard and shook his head. "In the buryin' ground. Three of 'em."

"I'm sorry." Dylan searched his mind for clues to this enigma. When was his direct ancestor born? It had to be *this* baby. "If there's anything I can do, as a doctor, to help when Martha's time comes . . ."

Jim sighed in open relief. "I'm glad to hear that. Thank you. Martha ain't had no real doctor through none of the births. Reckon somethin' ain't right inside her."

"Could be." Dylan prayed when Martha's time came he'd be able to help. He had very few medical supplies, and definitely wasn't an obstetrician, though he'd learned to deliver babies during his internship, of course. He could even perform a cesarean section under dire circumstances. He shuddered at the thought of performing surgery without modern technology.

But should he meddle with history? Was it his right

to do so? He shook his head in consternation. He knew what his answer would be. There was no way he'd let a baby die if it was within his ability to save it.

No matter the consequences.

Dylan nodded. "Do you know a family by the name of Sawyer?" He had to determine what might be expected of him once word leaked out about his marriage to Rose, as he was confident it would. Zeke didn't seem the type to let it pass. He'd been more than eager to see his stepdaughter wed. And there was still the mystery about Jim's death at Zeke's hands.

"Yep." Jim scowled. "White trash, except maybe for the stepmamma who died, an' her girl."

"Oh." Dylan followed his cousin into the barn where they collected an ax, a wedge and two saws. He should tell Jim about Rose. "Are we going to cut firewood?"

"Fenceposts." Jim swung the heavy ax over his shoulder and turned toward his cousin. "Why'd you ask about the Sawyers?"

Dylan sighed. "It's a complicated story, but it would seem I'm ma—"

"Marshall."

Jim and Dylan turned toward the visitor. Zeke Sawyer, with his twins and stepdaughter, approached on foot. Dylan wasn't surprised to note that the clan—excluding Rose—appeared no less dirty in the brilliant light of day.

His gaze went to Rose, who returned his look with an open glare. That hardly seemed appropriate. He'd half-expected diffidence. But she stared at him with a fury blazing in her blue eyes that took his breath away.

God, she's gorgeous.

Zeke stopped in front of the pair near the barnyard gate. "Jim, I got biz'ness with your kin."

Dylan sighed, but his cousin squared his shoulders and stood his ground. "Whatever biz'ness you got with Dylan here, concerns me, too."

Zeke shrugged and spat on the ground. "Suits me." He reached behind him and grabbed Rose by the arm, pulling her forward. "Found him havin' his way with Rose last night."

Dylan noticed the anger continuing to flash in Rose's eyes. The only thing subdued about her at the moment was her mouth—for a change.

Jim glanced sideways at Dylan, who shrugged in confession to his reluctant role in the wedding. There was, after all, no point in denying the truth at this point, even though he'd hidden the marriage certificate with the gold.

"Marched 'em right down to Preacher Ross, I did." Zeke shoved Rose toward Dylan. "I s'pects the boy to do right by the girl, Jim."

Jim nodded. "He's a Marshall."

Zeke seemed quite pleased with himself and offered Jim his right hand. Dylan couldn't help noticing the strained expression on his cousin's face when he accepted Zeke's handshake. There was obviously no love lost between the two families.

When had the killing taken place?

Or, when will it occur?

For some reason he couldn't recall the exact date from the newspaper article. The article. The memory flash made him momentarily forget those around him. Reaching into his pocket, he retrieved the crumpled photocopy Jeff had given him.

May 11, 1894. Six weeks.

Heat suffused Dylan's face when he looked up from his reading to find everyone staring, as if waiting for him to explain his actions. Guiltily, he stuffed the article back into his pocket and grinned.

Zeke lingered. "Rose ain't talkin' about last night," he said quietly, then shrugged.

"Don't really matter now." Jim seemed impervious to the situation. "Deed's done and penance paid."

Zeke nodded. "Heard in town about Tom."

Again Jim's only response was a cursory nod. Before Dylan could take into consideration the full significance of the young woman standing before him, her father and brothers turned and walked away.

" 'Pears you got yourself a family, Dylan," Jim said, and looked at his cousin in a manner that spoke of tolerance and judgment all rolled into one pithy glance.

Dylan had been watching Rose for several minutes and hadn't missed her flinch at the mention of Tom's name. He was the one, then—the murderer.

Or almost murderer.

She looked up at him with a blazing expression that still astounded Dylan. The woman was downright fiery. She was drop dead gorgeous—a ten—and Lord knew he wanted her physically. But after Cindy . . .

"Well, Rose, I reckon we'd best git you inside to Martha." Jim took Rose by the elbow and escorted her inside, ignoring the baffled bridegroom.

Dylan merely stood and stared in silence. What was he going to do with a bride? His face grew warm when he considered what he would be expected to do with his new wife.

I've already done it—sort of.

He grew suddenly cold as a new fear leapt to mind. Genetics. How could he ensure that by living in and procreating in 1894, he wouldn't jeopardize his entire lineage in the future?

Not that he was even considering the possibility. Yet, as he recalled her fiery lovemaking in his dreams . . .

Had it been just a dream?

Or was it her ghost?

Or . . . maybe a dream about her ghost?

Whatever she'd been in his bed, he couldn't say he'd regret a repeat performance. The thought certainly had possibilities.

And problems.

Dylan chuckled, but before he could turn toward the house, Jim returned alone. He considered offering an explanation, but before he could, Jim put a brotherly arm across his shoulders.

"Dylan, I coulda picked a better family for you to hitch up to, but Rose is one fine piece of womanflesh." He grinned. "She ain't Zeke's blood kin, you know. Her maw married 'im when Rose was near grown."

"I see." Dylan kicked at a rock near his feet. "That explains some differences about her."

Jim chuckled. "Lordy, she's different all right. Carryin' signs about women's sufferin', er somethin' like that, all the time." He shook his head. "But unless I miss my guess, if you can keep 'er in line, she'll warm you at night."

Dylan stared at his cousin in amazement. "If she were willing." *Keep her in line?*

Jim guffawed and slapped Dylan between the shoulder blades. "C'mon, Doc. We got fenceposts to cut."

Five

Tired and hungry, Dylan trudged back up the hill from the stand of hickory he'd helped Jim clear. They'd split the hard wood into fenceposts, placed them in deep holes and surrounded each one with rocks gathered from the field and creek bed. They hadn't returned to the house for a noon meal, as Jim informed him he customarily would, because of the late start they'd gotten on the day's chores.

Bread-and-butter sandwiches and cool spring water stored in a burlap-wrapped ceramic jug had been their only sustenance during the day. Dylan's stomach growled in anticipation when the farmhouse came into view and Jim prodded him to go inside while he put away their tools.

Dylan had forced himself all day to think of Jim and Martha as his cousins. He had to. The possibility of slipping and revealing the truth was too great.

And too bizarre.

Dylan hesitated. He wasn't really prepared to see Rose again. Some primitive part of him wanted nothing more than to take her to his bed, make love to her and live with her as man and wife.

In the nineteenth century?

Dr. Dylan Marshall, pride of his graduating class,

remain in the nineteenth century? Just to be with a woman?

But his educated, reasoning persona was determined to avoid what his body wanted more than anything else. To bury himself deep inside Rose, to relive that last erotic, wondrous dream he'd experienced before being whisked back in time . . .

A cold sweat popped out on his forehead and he swallowed hard. It would take all the self-restraint he could muster to avoid seeking what he'd encountered so vividly in his dreams.

"Go on," Jim urged, nudging him. "That pretty wife's waitin' for you."

Dylan sighed and rolled his eyes as his cousin guffawed good-naturedly. "Thanks, Jim. But I'd better wash up first."

"Well's out back."

Yeah, I know. "Thanks."

Dylan splashed his face with cool well water until he felt in control. He took a moment to look around him. So many things were the same. The garden was in the same spot. Even though there was still a slight danger of frost, it was obvious the potatoes had been planted already. Tiny green shoots he recognized as wild onions sprouted up on the far side.

His gaze swept the hill behind the house. Downhill, appropriately so, there was an outhouse. That was certainly different. Farther out was a spring house at the mouth of a cave. He knew that cave well. There was an icy spring gushing from the bowels of the earth inside. Sort of a primitive refrigerator.

"All right, Dylan," he muttered, mentally kicking himself for procrastinating.

What the hell was he going to do with a bride in another century? Again, his body knew exactly what to do with her, but his mind was waging a full-scale battle.

Perhaps that was it. He was crazy and none of this was really happening.

Or dead.

But that would have been too easy. No, he'd been through too much hell already to be dead. This was definitely real.

Replacing the bucket in the well, he went in the back door, wiping his feet on the mat out of habit. His grandma had never tolerated having dirt tracked in the house by "folks who was old enough to know better." Dylan wasn't about to put his great-great-grandmother to the test just yet.

He paused just inside the door, half expecting and half fearing he'd find Rose. But he found Martha grinning.

She clicked her tongue in answer to his unspoken question. "She ain't here, Dylan."

Dylan sighed. Perhaps Rose had seen the wisdom in returning to her stepfamily. Good. Now he could get the annulment. He knew, even in 1894 there was a court system. Lord knew he had grounds for seeking the dissolution of the ridiculous marriage.

"I suppose she went home to her family, then." Dylan felt a pang of something he refused to identify. The part of him that wanted so desperately to know Rose in the flesh as intimately as he'd known her . . . ghost, screamed foul with a vengeance.

"Well, I reckon you could say that." Martha grinned and handed him a covered basket. Fragrant steam rose from beneath the edges of a bright cloth, making Dylan's mouth water. "She's down at the cabin waitin' for her new husband."

Dylan's breath came out in a loud rush. He silently reprimanded himself for feeling relieved that Rose was still his. "I see."

"Git on with you." Martha crossed her arms over her ample bosom. "We took some things down to the cabin for you both. Should be a might more . . . cozy now."

Dylan forced a smile and thanked Martha for the food before stepping out into the evening air. The door squeaked and slammed behind him, making him jump. He was as nervous as a . . .

Bridegroom?

"Damn."

Anxiety mingled with anticipation and flooded his senses as he walked down the hill toward the spring, noticing, but not pausing to admire the sunset.

The ghost cabin.

What had prompted Tom Marshall to lock Rose in the cellar? She should've—would have—died last night, but Dylan's appearance had already modified history. He shook his head in total bewilderment.

The legend of Serenity Spring always referred to a spell of some sort, allegedly cast on the premises. Was that his explanation? Had a one-hundred-year-old curse drawn him back in time for this purpose—to change history?

The learned physician in Dylan couldn't fathom such a bizarre concept. Yet the kid who'd grown up in Branson and spent endless hours on his grandfa-

ther's farm—*this* farm—knew otherwise. Yes, Serenity
Spring was enchanted. There had been a ghost.

Rose.

"Damn." No amount of contemplation could change
his predicament, so why bother. Forcibly, he squelched
thoughts of subjects beyond his control, which included
almost everything.

Blackness gradually swallowed the last streaks of
twilight as he reached the spring. The typical evening
mist romped in the treetops. He grinned as a childhood
memory returned. His grandfather had insisted the
misty creatures were "hants."

The region abounded with legend.

And now Dylan was living one.

When he reached the cabin porch, the sounds coming from inside were anything but welcoming. This
wasn't the warm homecoming a new groom might expect. But then, this was no ordinary marriage.

Opening the door, he saw Rose. Her hair clung in
damp tendrils at the nape of her neck and along her
hairline. Her cheeks glowed with perspiration. His
gaze traveled down to where her breasts strained enticingly against her modest dress.

As she moved about tearing up the room, obviously
unaware of his presence, her hips swayed slightly, making the full skirt swish and swirl around her ankles.

Dylan closed his eyes for a fleeting moment, recalling with wrenching accuracy the way she looked
completely naked. Dusky nipples contrasted sharply
against white, silken skin. Her long dark hair, always
smelling of roses, tickled and tantalized his body as
she . . . .

"God." He wasn't aware he'd spoken aloud until

Rose turned to stare at him. Her blue eyes immediately glazed over with nothing less than pure rage.

"Where is it, Dr. Marshall?" Her voice was soft and cultured, dripping with anger tinged with sarcasm.

Dylan's gaze swept the small cabin, taking in the disarray. Martha and Rose must have spent the better part of the day cleaning and preparing the cabin for occupancy, only to have Rose tear everything apart in search of the gold. "Where's what?"

"You know very well what I'm looking for." Her words were clipped. "It's mine. *Mine.*"

Choosing to ignore her tirade, Dylan stepped completely inside and shut the door. "We should talk about our situation."

Despite all the uncertainties, having her stand before him as a flesh and blood woman instead of an apparition that would vanish in the night, made him happy. Rose was real, alive and . . . his.

"Your cousin seems to think we'll be living here like happy newlyweds." Rose cast a derisive glance around the unpretentious cabin.

"That's right." Dylan nodded, noting the flash of disbelief in her gaze. "Does that disturb you?"

A strange expression flamed in her blue eyes only to vanish just as quickly. "Of course it does." She lowered her lashes for a moment, then opened her eyes wide to glare. "Yes, Dr. Marshall—indeed it does."

"What do you want me to do about it?" Dylan asked quietly, though his own ire was being severely tested. "You're the one who came to my bed." He could have kicked himself for that—and did mentally—knowing his brain was probably black and blue by now.

Rose gasped. "That's the most ridiculous thing I've ever heard." With arms crossed over her middle, she turned away, but not before Dylan saw tears glistening in her eyes. "We never met before last night and you know it."

"Damn." Dylan glowered down at his feet while anger and confusion battled his libido. There was no way Rose could know about his dreams, let alone have been a willing participant. Yet the memory of her beauty made it difficult to believe the experience hadn't been real . . . at least, for him.

"I want the gold." Rose wiped her eyes angrily and looked at him again. "It belongs to me."

Dylan felt pinpricks of guilt sting his conscience as her expression blatantly accused him. "Gold?"

"Come now. You must have seen it." Rose moved toward the hearth. She pressed on several stones as if searching for a loose one.

"Can't say that I did." Dylan shuffled his feet, wondering how he would manage to pull this off. "Did your stepfather see it?"

Rose muttered angrily to herself. "My stepfamily is rather stupid, Dr. Marshall. I'm surprised you didn't notice."

Her muttering continued, with only a recognizable word here and there, and some of them definitely not what he would have expected from a well bred, nineteenth-century lady.

Dylan stepped toward her and waited while she turned to stare at him. "Rose, this wasn't my idea."

"No, that's true." She pursed her lips. "Nor was it mine, Dr. Marshall—*if* you really are a doctor."

"Oh, I most certainly am." Dylan clenched his teeth

and shifted his weight. How had he gotten into this mess in the first place? And how the hell could he prove he was a doctor, if it became necessary?

He had to change the subject, get her mind off the damned gold. "I know what's bugging you. You're mad because you harbored a romantic desire for me to carry you across the threshold, such as it is."

Rose stomped her foot, then turned away again to gaze at the cold hearth. Dylan's heart swelled in his throat at the anguish he sensed she must be feeling. Why was the gold so important to her? He needed some answers.

And the first question was easy.

"Did Tom Marshall lock you in the cellar, Rose?"

In profile, he saw her blanch, then lean her forehead against the mantel. Her lower lip trembled. "How did you know it was him? I was so frightened. He was a crazy man. He forced the door shut and put something heavy over it. I tried and tried, but I couldn't open it. I guess I must've fainted."

Dylan nodded and indicated the huge tree stump. "This table. I had a heck of a time moving it." *I had help, actually.*

"And for that I'm eternally grateful. I could have— would have—died." Rose's expression softened as she lifted her face to look directly at him. The shift in her expression and intent was overt. "I have to get out of the Ozarks, Dr. Marshall. I don't belong here. Surely, you must realize that."

You're not the only one, lady.

Nodding, he took a step toward her and reached out to touch her face with the back of his hand. Why did she have to be so damned beautiful?

"My mother made a grave error in marrying Zeke Sawyer. She didn't think she had a choice, though," Rose said in a voice that trembled, as she shied away from his caress. "I was fifteen when we came here. I've vowed to find a way to return to my grandmother in Georgia one day. That gold would have enabled me to do that."

"But Tom . . . entombed you." His hand fell to his side and he sighed. "I don't know exactly what happened here last night, but do you realize how lucky you are that I . . . happened along?"

"How was it that you just happened along, Dr. Marshall?" Rose's expression became accusing again. "You're not from around here, and to my knowledge you've never visited your family before."

"True." Dylan leaned against the table—the murder weapon. "My . . . mother died. I always wanted to meet my father's family." He shrugged, praying he could live out his lie. The old saying that truth was stranger than fiction seemed more than appropriate in this situation.

Rose sighed and strayed toward the cellar door. "Well, whatever brought you to the cabin instead of the farmhouse, I'm grateful." She glanced at him with that indicting expression again. "You hid it, didn't you?"

She sure as hell is determined. Indecision flashed through him. Dylan straightened and took a step toward her. The gold had cost Tom Marshall his life. All Rose wanted was enough of it to return to her home in Georgia. But for some insane reason, he couldn't bring himself to give it to her and let her just walk out of his life. Not yet.

"Hid what?" He smiled through his guilt. "I haven't been here since your stepfather dragged me out last night." The lie fell with difficulty from his lips, but it was necessary until he figured out what was going on.

Rose reddened. She bent over and grasped the leather handle and lifted the heavy door.

Shrugging, Dylan walked over to help her, fighting his contrition with the physical exertion. She would investigate thoroughly—he was certain of that. But until he sorted through this quandary, she wouldn't learn the gold's whereabouts. There was something volatile about Rose Jameson . . . Marshall.

Carrying a lantern, Rose descended the ladder and walked directly to the corner where the gold had been stacked. She covered her face with her hands.

Dylan felt certain she'd been in the cellar to investigate already as he followed her down the ladder. Perhaps she thought the gold would reappear as magically as it had vanished.

Remorse built a wall in his gut, but his resolve remained. "What are you looking for?"

She whirled on him like an alley cat. "You know very well what I'm looking for." Her words snapped and sliced through the cellar. "I'm quite certain a more thorough search would be wasted effort."

Swirling, she ascended the ladder. The lantern swung precariously from her fingertips. When they reached the cabin floor again, she turned and stood before him, trembling with rage. "All I want is out of this place." After situating the lantern on the table, she held her outstretched hands in a pleading gesture. "But you refuse to see that. Don't you?"

Oh, if you only knew.

"God, this is like something out of a B movie." Dylan threw up his hands in frustration and walked over to the basket to lift a corner of the cloth to peer inside. "I'm starving and not in the mood to talk about chasing rainbows right now. Unless, of course, I've been reincarnated as Darby O'Gill."

Rose stiffened and sighed, apparently uninterested in exactly what a "B movie" or Darby O'Gill were. "I suppose you expect me to play the role of a dutiful bride and prepare your dinner."

Dylan cursed softly and removed a neatly wrapped platter of fried chicken. A cold jar of milk, and bread and butter pickles soon followed.

"I've been seeing to my own needs for some time." Dylan offered her a piece of chicken, but she simply shook her head, making those wild curls fall in even more disarray around her lovely face. He took a sharp intake of breath to steady the desire that surged front and center . . . in his jeans. "Suit yourself."

Sitting on the floor near the door, he devoured the food, washed it down with milk and reached for more, again extending a piece of chicken to his bride. "Sure you don't want some?"

Rose reached for the proffered piece of poultry with dainty fingers. Dylan watched as she took tiny bites. He poured some milk into one of the tin cups Martha had provided, and he passed it to her.

"Thank you." She lowered her lashes to nibble, following the effort with a sip of milk. "I'm sorry about what happened with Pappy Zeke last night, Dr. Marshall." She took a deep breath. "Since my mother died last year, I've been searching for the means to return to my grandmother in Georgia, if she's still alive."

"I see." Listening intently, he finished the milk and discovered raw apple cake in the bottom of the basket. If he was correct, this would be from the same family recipe his own grandmother had used. Taking a bite of the delicious sweet, Dylan closed his eyes for a moment to savor the familiar flavor of his favorite dessert.

"Some things are always changing, but others stay the same—thank God," he said in appreciation, finishing the cake and licking his fingers.

Rose sniffled and wiped at her eyes with the back of her hand. "Mother hated it here even more than I."

"Seems odd that someone of your . . . background should end up here." Dylan smiled in a way he hoped was encouraging. The truth needed to be told—at least her part of it. His would have to remain a secret.

Rose returned his smile with a shaky one of her own. "To say the least." She took another sip of milk. "I discovered Mr. Marshall last night quite by accident. I was trying to run away again, and Pappy Zeke followed, as usual. He always said he owes it to my mother to take care of me. I guess, in his own way, that's what he was doing."

She sighed and took another sip of milk from the tin cup. "When I saw a light in this cabin, my curiosity demanded I investigate." She laughed nervously—too nervously. "My mother often said my curiosity would be the death of me." She covered her eyes for a moment with a trembling hand. "It almost was."

If only you knew, Rose.

Dylan's guilt escalated as he listened to her story. "All this is real interesting," he said steadily, hoping his emotions didn't betray him. "But that doesn't change the fact that you and I—whether we like it or not—are husband and wife." He arched an inquisitive brow. "What do you propose we do about that?"

"Have it annulled, of course." Rose scrambled to her feet and walked to the door, opening it to peer outside. "It's late. We should decide what we're to do for the night, Dr. Marshall." She crossed the room to the table and reached across the basket for another lantern.

Dylan swallowed, watching intently as the woman removed the chimney and turned up the wick. The cabin brightened immediately. Her movements were delicate and refined, so very different from the strong Ozark women, like Martha. She didn't belong here any more than he did. But at the moment he was powerless to change that.

The glow from the second lamp bathed Rose in golden light. Dylan gasped when she turned to face him. The illumination created an aura around her, reminding him of her ghostly rendition from his dream. How could a mere dream be so damned accurate? *Had* she been a ghost rather than just a dream? He'd known Rose in the most intimate way a man can know a woman. Yet he hadn't.

"So, will you give me enough gold to leave here, Dr. Marshall?" Rose put one hand on her hip, breaking the spell she'd inadvertently cast upon him. "I don't have to take it all."

"No." Dylan struggled to his feet and rubbed the small of his back. Cutting fenceposts was harder labor than he'd performed in his entire life. He stretched and groaned. "I can't give you what I don't have."

"Damn you." Rose gritted her teeth and clenched

her fists at her sides. "You're just as bad as the rest of them, holding me here against my will."

Dylan shrugged. "You can always return to your stepfather's house." It was idiotic to goad her, because the last thing in the world he really wanted was for her to leave.

Rose shuddered and her eyes were round and sincere. "Much as I hate to admit it, Dr. Marshall . . . I'd rather be here with you than with the Sawyers."

Dylan held his breath, wondering at her true meaning. "Here . . . *with* me, Rose?"

Rose blushed and lowered her gaze for a moment. When she looked up at him again the expression in her eyes made Dylan moan. Exquisite innocence mingled with open desire in her gaze to create an invitation, though he felt certain she didn't realize it.

"Yes." Rose smiled timidly as he stepped toward her. "If the alternative is returning to the Sawyer cabin, then even here with you."

Desire raged through his veins as he gazed into her eyes. He cupped her face in his hands, recalling her enthusiasm during their kiss following the wedding ceremony. She was such an enigma. Did she want to become his bride in *every* sense of the word? Or did she only wish to leave the Ozarks—and him—forever?

"Rose," he whispered her name, lowering his head to taste her lips. The first contact was explosive. She threw her arms around his neck and whimpered as his kiss deepened. Dylan was unprepared for her response. Raw need erupted deep within him. This woman who had tormented him in sleep for weeks was now his wife.

Rose leaned full against him. Her breasts pressed

and flattened against his chest. Dylan moaned as his hands roamed over her back and shoulders, caressing and kneading her flesh through her threadbare dress.

He explored her mouth with his tongue, savoring the intoxicating sweetness. She was like a drug he was addicted to and couldn't get out of his system. He deepened the kiss again as she began to counter his movements with her tongue. She seemed intent to torment him and Dylan felt obligated to return the favor.

Heat suffused him. He recalled the willow bed in the corner. There was a small feather mattress on it now which Martha had obviously sent down to the cabin during the day. It was covered with a bright—inviting—patchwork quilt. His lips never left hers as he lifted and carried Rose the short distance to the bed.

She moaned as he laid her down. When his lips left hers for a brief moment, her gaze locked with his. The expression in the blue eyes tore at him. It was identical to the combination of desire and despair he'd noticed in his ghost lover's gaze.

The memory of her ghost—of her near-murder—thrust reality into Dylan's thoughts. He couldn't do this. He had no right. "What am I doing?" Dylan straightened and ran his fingers through his hair. "What the hell do I think I'm doing?"

Rose winced beneath his verbal agony. Her expression changed from desire, to confusion, then anger again.

"Exercising your husbandly rights, no doubt." She sat up and patted her hair, obviously avoiding meeting his gaze as she swung her legs around to place her small feet on the floor. "In these hills, I'm quite powerless to stop you. You have every legal right to take me to your bed, Dr. Marshall."

"Dylan." He glared at her. "Your stepfather was right to call you 'Miss High-and-Mighty.' " The agony of desire waned in light of the fury surging through him. "I liked you better as a ghost."

"What?"

Dylan turned and stormed to the door, then paused. Without looking at her, he braced himself in the door frame with both hands. His knuckles turned white from the force of his grip. Lowering his head, he clenched his teeth in frustration. "You won't get what you want from me through deceit, Rose."

"Deceit? What *I* want?" Rose took a step toward him, but hesitated. "You're the one who insists I've been to your bed before."

"Oh, trust me, Rose . . ." Dylan laughed in self-derision. He didn't look at her, but continued to stand braced in the doorway. "I know your delectable body *intimately.*"

"How *dare* you?" Rose stomped her foot in open aggravation.

"It was kind of Martha to provide the bedding." He paused as he stepped off the porch. "But I believe we'll be needing firewood for the night. It's getting chilly and it's quite apparent you won't be keeping me warm."

"You are very astute, Dr. Marshall."

When the door slammed behind him, Rose wandered over to the lamp on the table and lifted it. The cellar door was still open, so she carefully descended the ladder with the light to search again for the gold. She'd seen it with her own eyes—touched it with her hands.

Perhaps if she looked often enough it would return. But no. She knew very well that Dylan Marshall had returned to hide the precious treasure from her.

Deliberately.

She trembled as she surveyed the dusty cellar—empty of the gold—then scaled the ladder to the cabin floor. Sighing, she lowered the trap door and returned the lamp to the table.

The table that held me prisoner . . .

She shuddered as fear gripped her again, consuming her with the pure terror of being buried alive! Her dream of finding the treasure had finally become reality, until she'd turned to meet the maniacal gaze of Tom Marshall just before he entombed her in the cellar. Involuntarily, she brought her knuckle to her mouth and bit down hard, trying to bring her trembling under control.

"Told you so." Dylan leaned against the door frame and stared at her.

Rose bit her lip as she turned to look at this man. *Really* look at him. He was her husband, a doctor, inordinately handsome. His auburn hair was pulled back and secured at his nape with a thin strip of leather. Dark, spiked lashes framed hazel eyes which observed her with mind-boggling intensity just now. He was quite intriguing.

Tall and slim, with broad shoulders and corded muscles in his exposed forearms and neck—all in all, Dylan Marshall was one fine specimen. Back in Georgia she would have been proud to have him court her.

He awakened in her something she hadn't known she could feel—until last night when he'd kissed her in the cellar. Her body had exploded with unleashed passion so powerful it frightened her. At twenty-five, she was a spinster by the code of the hills. Even back East she would be considered one.

She sighed and met his gaze, recalling against her will the power of his touch. "For now, my gold appears to be gone. But I'll find it."

Dylan shook his head as a smug expression crossed his handsome features. "Yeah, I definitely liked you better as a ghost."

"What is all this about a ghost?" Her heart raced and her face flashed with the heat of anger. "We never met before last night, and you know it."

Something resembling regret flashed in those hazel eyes, making Rose wonder about its cause.

"Rose, I . . ." Dylan slapped his thigh and bent down to retrieve an armload of firewood at his feet, then he carried it to the hearth. "I hope the chimney's clean."

Good. He was changing the subject. She could deal with that. "Birds, probably."

"Yeah, when I first came in here yesterday there were bird droppings all over the place."

Rose frowned. "There were? I don't recall seeing—"

"Oh, I cleaned it up." Dylan reddened as he straightened to light a piece of paper from the lamp's flame. In a few moments he had a cheery blaze started. "We need to make a decision about our . . . marriage." He simply stared at her without moving.

"You mean fish or cut bait, Dr. Marshall?"

Dylan grinned and continued to study the fire for a few moments. "Something like that. Like it or not, we *are* married."

"Yes, we are." Rose nodded and walked slowly toward him. "So, you want me to become your domestic slave in this . . . palace?" She shuddered at the prospect of living in the Ozark Mountains for the rest of her life. Her parents paid with their lives for the time they'd spent here. The past ten years had seemed an eternity to her. "I should rather die."

"Which you almost did last night." Dylan glanced at the fire, then cast her a crooked grin that made her knees go weak. "I'm glad you didn't, though."

"You are?"

"Yeah." He reached out and lifted a strand of her dark hair between his fingers. "Then you really would be a ghost to haunt me." His voice grew husky, his expression so intense it took her breath away. "You're beautiful, you know."

Rose stomped her foot. *"What is all this about a ghost?* I am not a ghost, as you surely know. And I most certainly have never visited your . . . your bed." Her voice dropped to a faint whisper with the last word, but she refused to lower her gaze.

Dylan smiled. It was the most ingratiating smile Rose had ever seen, displaying even white teeth amid his auburn whisker stubble.

She couldn't believe he was actually smiling. What nerve. "I haven't." Why didn't he believe her?

"Yes, pretty lady. You have . . . in my dreams." Dylan laughed aloud when she gasped in shock.

"Well, I never . . ." She averted his gaze, trying to hide her grin from him, but his laughter was infectious. "In your . . . dreams?"

"Oh, yes." Dylan stepped toward her. He wasn't laughing now. His breath became a warm caress against her cheek. Dropping the strand of hair which he'd wound around his index finger, he reached up to rub her shoulder. "The most exquisite, exotic, erotic . . . *stimulating* dream I've had in my entire life."

Rose swallowed with difficulty. He was much too close. Her clothing felt tight and uncomfortable. A strange but wonderful warmth spread throughout her body. Her breathing became labored as he slid his hand down her arm to her elbow. He caressed the side of her rib-cage with his thumb.

"A dream?" she whispered as his mouth covered hers.

Six

Rose leaned into his kiss. Though her mind screamed frantically that she should resist the potency of his embrace, she couldn't. Her body yearned for this intimacy. She was a grown woman and alone. Her mother was dead and now this man—her *husband*—wanted her.

Wanted—really wanted. It felt so strange, yet so wonderful. Not since her mother's death had she experienced the simple but crucial feeling of being wanted by someone—anyone.

At least, he certainly kissed her as if he wanted her.

Dylan brought his hand around to the bodice of her gown. His physician's fingers deftly released the tiny buttons which lined the front of her modest frock. She moaned when he pushed aside the garment to boldly caress her flesh. With his free hand, he cupped the back of her neck and tilted her head to deepen their kiss as his thumb rhythmically stroked her throbbing nipple.

How strange to feel such longing from the touch of a man's hand to a part of her body she'd always thought had a single purpose in life—to nurture an infant. But the barest brush of his calloused fingers against her tender flesh made her lose all sense of reason.

Her blood seemed to surge to the surface, making her flesh quake and swell with longing. The core of her turned hot, moist, hungry for something. She felt all quivery inside—like preserves left sitting in a sunny window too long. What was this obscure yearning that Dylan Marshall created within her formerly cooperative body?

He left her lips to gaze into her eyes. Rose allowed his arm to support her weight, fearing her own legs could not. She was in some sort of daze, unable to stop his intentions—nor was she even certain she wanted to.

She trembled with desire. He'd awakened a sleeping giant within her, one whose existence she'd been blissfully ignorant of only a few short hours ago. Despite her ignorance of such matters, Rose realized the significance of this awakening. Passion was a potent drug—once tasted, it would be nearly impossible to resist.

When he lifted her to carry her to the bed a second time, she didn't protest. Something inside her wanted to know Dylan in the same wondrous way he claimed to know her from his dream.

He propped himself beside her on the narrow bunk to stare intently into her eyes. His hazel gaze possessed her, evoking a shudder of longing from deep within. Instinctively, she reached out to caress the side of his face. His beard stubble raked and stimulated her palm. Was no part of her body immune to his power?

His expression was solemn as his questioning gaze probed hers. She gasped when he slid her dress from her shoulders and raised her chemise to completely expose her breasts to both the cool evening air and his heated desires. A protest commenced and died on her lips when he sat up to remove his own shirt, exposing an expanse of male flesh that made her breath catch in her throat. His rippling muscles glistened in the golden light which filled the room.

Rose was grateful for the light. She'd always imagined lovemaking would occur in total darkness. This was much more pleasant than anything she could have imagined. Her body transformed into liquid fire as she memorized each rib, every muscle of his tawny flesh.

She should make him cease this insanity. Her mind tried again to do battle with her senses, but longing quelled such rebellion when he touched her.

His lips caressed the hollow at the base of her throat, teasing, tickling until she moaned aloud. No part of her was exempt from his torment—her starved senses reveled in his touch until she thought she'd go mad. She didn't demur when he lifted his head to gaze at the swell of her breasts as they rose and fell with her rapid breathing.

"You're exquisite, dream lady," he whispered, just before his lips found the lobe of her ear and teased the presumably innocent flesh until she writhed and moaned beneath him.

A quivering mass of sensation, oblivious to the cause or consequences of her predicament, Rose knew this man possessed more power than any she'd ever known.

Making him far more threatening.

The thought of danger reminded her of her mission—her purpose in life. *Daddy's legacy.*

"No." She knew her weak protest was inadequate at best. She shoved against his chest with both palms, but he seemed unaware of her efforts. After another moment, the mettle to halt this madness succeeded in eluding her.

Dylan's lips traveled down the side of her neck to tease and tantalize. He found and caressed her surprised nipple with his warm tongue, laving it, then drawing it into his mouth.

It was like an Ozark thunderstorm within the confines of her flesh. So startled by the intimacy of his mouth on her breast and the red-hot longing shooting through her body, Rose whimpered . . . stupefied.

She arched her back—her hips thrust against his as the onslaught continued. She prayed he'd never stop, then groaned when he released her eager nipple to find the other and impart equal attention. Defenseless against herself, she savored the hot, liquid inferno which engulfed her.

She noticed—how could she not?—the long, hard shaft at the front of his trousers pressing intimately against her hip. Becoming aware of it created a peculiar ache deep in her loins. Like a spring wound too tight, waiting, begging for release, her body responded to his in primitive tribute.

With trembling fingers, she sought the back of his neck where his hair was soft and curling. No longer capable of reasoning, she held his head against her as he alternated from one nipple to the other, holding her breasts in his two large hands. Rose watched him through a cloud of desire as his mouth claimed her. For some inexplicable reason, this seemed so right.

Yet somewhere in the recesses of her subconscious,

she knew how very wrong it was. This wasn't a marriage of love or even mutual consent. She wasn't so naive that she didn't realize the paramount consequences of consummating the marriage.

"Rose, Rose . . ." His breath was hot against her breast. She watched in awe as his tongue flickered to taste and tease—making her feel like screaming and dying all in one glorious moment of bewilderment.

Why didn't you tell me, Mamma?

The image of her mother's face when she'd agreed to marry Zeke Sawyer assailed Rose. It was like a bucket of spring water thrown in her face, dousing the flames of desire in an instant as cold reason returned.

"No."

When Dylan lifted his flushed face to gaze at her, his eyes darkened several shades. Something passed between them so profound, so significant, that for a moment she regretted stopping his seduction.

Fighting her body's betrayal, Rose took a deep breath and tried to look away from the intensity of his gaze. It was disturbing, almost as if he could read her thoughts, knew her emotions, was aware of her reluctance to end their lovemaking.

"This is wrong." She slid away from him and into a sitting position, clutching her arms across her bosom, which continued to beg for more of his magical touch even while her words demanded it wasn't so. She felt swollen and empty—painfully abandoned.

He nodded almost imperceptibly, seeming to weigh his options. There weren't any as far as Rose was concerned. If they made love . . .

"If we . . . do what we almost did, our marriage would—"

"Be permanent?" His laugh was harsh and belittling. "There's no such thing, sweetheart. That 'til death do us part' crap is about as durable as a disposable diaper."

Rose winced. How quickly he'd changed from tender lover to angry cynic. Surely he must see the wisdom in maintaining a chaste marriage. There was far too much at stake. At least for her . . .

"I don't want to remain in the Ozarks." Rose inched farther from him, managing to swing her legs half-off the bed before Dylan's steel grip pressed her flat against its surface again.

"Women are all the same," he said fiercely. His expression was ruthless as he scrutinized her with his glittering gaze. "You only want what a man can give or buy for you. You don't give a damn about human emotions."

"No, that's not true." Rose looked at him in confusion, wondering how he could think such a thing after what had almost transpired between them. The emotions she'd felt—still felt—made her shudder in anticipation of a second dose of his powerful elixir. "No, that's not true."

"Then how can you be so—never mind." Dylan stood and pulled on his shirt, moving quickly to the closed door. "I'm going for a walk."

Rose stood to follow him to the door. "Wait. You don't understand. I—"

"I have to, Rose." Dylan's voice was raspy. His anger was obvious. "I can't deal with this right now. I shouldn't have tried . . ."

Rose blinked back her tears. When his gaze dipped to where her flesh pressed out around her folded arms as if to tempt him again, she was reminded painfully of her partial nudity. The candid desire in his gaze made her lower hers until she noticed how sensitive and swollen the tips of her breasts were as they pressed against her forearms. She looked up at him in stunned horror, wondering if she'd ever stop wanting him now that he'd touched her.

Dylan winced as if mortally wounded. He stepped outside, leaving her to wonder about the enormity of what had just ensued.

"God, I didn't know it would be like this," she whispered to the empty room.

Dylan walked to the far edge of the spring and sat on a fallen log. He picked up a few pebbles and tossed them into the moonlit pool.

A cacophony of sounds filled the night. An owl hooted from a tree behind him—frogs croaked their nocturnal songs. No wind stirred the trees and the stars seemed closer than Dylan had ever seen them.

Just yesterday his life had seemed fairly normal. Divorced and between positions was nothing he couldn't deal with.

This was.

He'd been lonely, but relatively complacent, until those damned dreams. Of all the people in the world, why had this happened to him?

He chuckled to himself. What would Jeff think when he went to the cabin to check on Dylan? He'd probably have the sheriff out to investigate Dr. Marshall's mysterious disappearance.

Will they find a skeleton in the cellar?

He knew the answer. Dylan Marshall, M.D. had managed to alter history at least that much. Rose didn't die in that root cellar in 1894.

She got married instead.

He shook his head and laughed again. It was more of a frustrated cackle than anything.

Frustrated.

Rose Jameson had managed to drive him crazy in two centuries. How much power could one woman have? He'd known she was special from his dreams. But he'd had no idea just how special until now. No woman had ever aroused him to such a fevered pitch before—not even Cindy.

Oh, how Cindy would hate that bit of trivia. The lovely, long-legged, doe-eyed physical therapist had been outdone by a proper lady from the nineteenth century.

Dylan threw back his head and laughed aloud. It wasn't what he'd call a sane sort of laugh by any stretch of the imagination.

But why me?

In an entire century, it seemed logical there could have been another more likely candidate to travel through time and rescue Rose. What logic could be found in selecting him?

None.

Even Mr. Spock would have difficulty with this one.

Of course, he was assuming some force had brought him back for just this purpose. No other explanation seemed plausible.

As long as he was performing miracles, there was another bit of history he'd like to change during his exile, before he returned to the twentieth century, which he was determined to do. Jim Marshall would live to a ripe old age if Dylan Marshall, certified—or certifiable—time traveler had anything to say about it.

"You have done well, my son."

A chill swept through Dylan as he turned his head to determine the source of the voice. It carried through the trees like the echoing utterances in a Halloween haunted house attraction. It seemed to emanate from everywhere at once.

"You have broken the spell generated by your blood."

"My blood?" Dylan leapt to his feet and whirled around. Instinct told him who was speaking. It was a waste of breath to even ask the voice to identify itself. There was no doubt. He squinted as an image took shape near the edge of the trees.

Swallowing the lump of fear in his throat, Dylan faced the ghost. "What do you want with me?"

"I am Keeper of the Ozarks." The figure didn't move. It was the same Native American Dylan had seen before . . . a hundred years in the future. "It is I who brought you here to undo the deed of your ancestor."

"Tom." Dylan clenched his fists at his side. Why the hell was he being held responsible for a crime he didn't commit? Anger, determination and desperation gained control of his fear.

He took a step toward the shimmering figure. "This isn't fair, buster. I'm not the one who pushed that table over the cellar door. Why the hell should I have to suffer because of what my great-great—whatever did?"

The figure loomed in silence for several moments.

Dylan was cold . . . and petrified. Most of his bravado beat a hasty retreat as the reality of his words penetrated his thick skull. His big mouth had managed to get him in trouble before, but this was unprecedented, to say the least.

In a more controlled voice, he decided to try a different—safer—approach. "I want to go home. Why'd you bring me here? For God's sake *why?* You had no right. I had a life, you know."

"The spell had to be broken by the blood of Tom Marshall." The figure began to fade.

"Wait! How do I get home?"

The figure almost vanished, then reappeared. "This is your home," the spirit insisted.

"Home—in—my—own—time?"

"You must seek and find the right path. It will lead you."

The spirit vanished entirely. Dylan rushed forward to where it had been. He walked in circles for several moments trying to convince himself that this was real—all of it.

"Damn." Dylan looked up at the sky. He groped about for the trunk of a tree, anchoring him in reality like before. The rough bark was comforting. Still, he needed more proof.

The right path. What did that mean? Dylan racked his brain in a feeble attempt to understand the complexity of things which defied explanation.

He ran his hands through his hair in turmoil, then turned toward the cabin. Indecision gripped him. "This is worse than Philosophy class," he whispered into the darkness. " 'If a tree falls in the forest . . .' "

Lamp and firelight flickered from within the cabin.

The single window was a golden square in the night. A beacon for his starved senses.

Rose.

She moved around inside, passing by the window several times. Dylan sighed. All she cared about was the gold, despite the delicious passion she'd displayed. She was, in all probability, a virgin. But innocent?

How could a woman accomplished enough to tease a man with her tempting body be innocent? She'd nearly been his, but something had stopped her. What was it? Was she merely keeping him dangling a bit longer until she drove him so crazy he'd give her the gold?

Had her passion been feigned for the purpose of monetary gain? The thought revolted him. It was too devious. Surely Rose was incapable of such subterfuge.

Something—his heart?—in his chest swelled until he thought it would burst. He swallowed hard to quell the quivering deep in his gut. Only two women had ever gotten to him so completely in his life.

And he'd be damned if one ever would again. Rose and Cindy were enough for any man to deal with in a lifetime, let alone in two different centuries.

Dylan took a tentative step toward the cabin, but froze again. He was weary. He hadn't slept in thirty-six hours. That in itself seemed almost enough explanation for the Indian.

Sleep deprivation psychosis?

But that hardly explained the other time the spirit had appeared before him.

In broad daylight.

It was too easy. But perhaps exhaustion might rationalize his behavior with Rose. He'd nearly succumbed to his primitive instincts. Having her in his arms had been like a testosterone heaven—or something dangerously close. Between the dreams and reality—

"You ain't gonna find yer answers in the night sky, boy."

A woman's voice intruded on his thoughts. Whirling around, Dylan saw the dark form of a stooped old woman moving toward him. She had a basket slung over her arm and a shawl draped over her shoulders.

"Who are you?" Dylan asked without fear as the woman stopped in front of him. Her black face split into a wide, toothless grin. Her hair was as white as the dogwood blossoms which dotted the countryside.

"Maggie Mae." She stared at him steadily. "And who might you be?"

"Dylan Marshall."

"The doctor," she stated, rather than asked. "I thought so."

Chuckling, Dylan shook his head in amazement. He was from the age of communication, where electronic mail could be sent anywhere in the world within a matter of seconds. This nineteenth-century community had a considerable jump on technology, judging by the speedy spread of the news of his arrival

"And you're the healer." Dylan smiled despite his state of mind. He recalled what Jim and Martha had said about Maggie Mae. "I'd planned to visit you. I'll be needing all the information you're willing to share about the herbs and such in the area."

She nodded. "I'd be right pleased to share my healers with you. You'll be surprised, I reckon."

"Why's that?" Dylan crossed his arms, sensing a challenge and welcoming the diversion.

"You'll find out what grows in the forest works jes as good as the finest remedies of modern medicine." She chuckled again.

Modern . . . medicine? "Such as?"

"Wintergreen tea stim'lates the heart, but too much'll cause vomiting."

"All right." Dylan smiled to himself. "What else?"

"Wild plum bark eases the breathin'. You ain't jes makin' fun of me. Is you?"

"No, ma'am. I most certainly am not." He surprised even himself with the truth of his statement.

"Well . . ." She seemed uncertain, but continued anyway. "Bull nettle root is for the skin ailments. Slippery elm helps with the stomach complaint, but it also works on boils."

"Slippery elm?" Dylan shook his head. "Okay."

"O—K?" She stopped to stare at him again. "What's that mean?"

"All right. Go ahead. I'm sorry." Dylan rolled his eyes in self-chastisement. It was only a matter of time before he made a big slip.

"Garglin' tea brewed from white oak bark'll ease the throat." She coughed a bit and spat on the ground away from him. "Feel like I could use a bit of that myself 'bout now."

"The night air?"

"I guess you might be a doctor at that." She nodded. "Yep. The night air always torments me some."

"Then you should stay in at night," Dylan said in his most serious "doctoring" voice.

She laughed again with a peculiar wheezing sound.

"May apple and dandelion helps with the liver. There's lotsa healin' in these hills. I reckon in time you'll git the hang of it."

"You're pretty smart for a hillbilly." His voice was deliberately light and teasing. He hoped she'd take his jest as intended.

Maggie Mae laughed. "I ain't no hillbilly." She put her hand on her hip. "I was owned by a doctor down to Washington County, Arkansaw before the war. I was homeless after Mr. Lincoln's 'Mancipation—drifted some, 'til I come here."

"The Emancipation Proclamation?" Dylan held his breath in awe and shame. This woman had been a slave. The disgrace of his entire race was his to bear. With a shudder, he changed the subject. "So, tell me . . . what are you doing out at night?"

"Workin'." She nodded and pointed toward the forest. "I was gatherin' roots that is best dug by the light of a new moon."

"It's kind of hard to see. Isn't it?" This woman was a delight. A curious delight. "Mind if I tag along?"

"You plannin' ter stay on a while?"

"If I say no?" Dylan sensed he was being tested. What the penalties were for failing, he wasn't certain. But he realized Maggie Mae was someone worth taking the trouble to impress.

"Well?"

"For a while." That was no lie, for he had no idea how long he would be stuck in this ridiculous situation.

Her gaze was the most intense scrutiny he'd ever been subjected to. Now he knew what bacteria and cells felt like beneath the examining eye of a microscope.

When she spoke, her voice sounded suspicious. "I thought you was tired."

"How did you—"

"I just knows things. Like I knows you is from here, but you ain't." She tilted her head to the side. The whites of her eyes were visible in the darkness. "They's somethin' queer, but I ain't figgered it out yet. I will, though. Gimme time."

Time.

Dylan winced and was thankful the cover of darkness hid his expression from her probing gaze. "I'm sure you will." He took the basket from her arm and followed her into the woods.

"Seems kinda strange, leavin' a bride on her weddin' night, though."

"Hush, old woman." Dylan knew somehow that the old face was smiling. He sighed, relaxing in her presence. "The bride is happier without me around. Trust me."

"I think you's the one what needs ter be a trustin' folks." Maggie Mae sang softly to herself as she walked deeper into the woods. Suddenly, she stopped and turned to stare at him.

The flesh on the back of Dylan's neck crawled. Her penetrating gaze pierced straight through him. It was almost as if she probed deep into his mind for answers to her questions.

He swallowed hard. Could she possibly know? His heart raced. Instinct told him this old woman had vision into another dimension.

Maggie Mae studied him for several moments. Even

though it was very dark, he had no doubt that she could see him . . . and beyond.

"You didn't wanna come here," she finally said in a knowing way.

Dylan laughed and shook his head. "I wasn't consulted about my . . . journey, or about the wedding either."

"Well . . ." She chuckled. "Happens that way often 'round these parts. At least you got ter skip the shivaree by doin' it this way."

"So it seems." Even Dylan was familiar with that Ozark custom. Being kidnapped by well-wishers on his wedding night might have been more pleasant than the sexual frustration he was experiencing now.

"Zeke Sawyer's slippery." Maggie Mae began to slowly walk again. "He wanted a husband for Rose and you got in the way."

Dylan nodded, feeling some of his burden lift. For a moment he'd feared his secret was lost. Her attention was diverted again, though. Maybe his imagination had secured the better of him. After all—with ghosts, time portals and spells, what could possibly surprise him now?

"Yeah, I got in the way all right." He cleared his throat, which seemed extremely full for some reason. "I need to make the best of my situation while I'm here. It's my intention to practice medicine until . . . until I find the right path."

"Dogwood had a real doctor for a while. He had a real office in town. Some of his stuff might still be there. Worth havin' a look." A breeze filtered through the trees, carrying with it the scent of rain in the distance.

He was actually looking forward to seeing the mystery town. "I'll have a look."

"Reckon it's gonna rain. Guess we best be headin' back." She stared at him in silence again, as if choosing her words with great care. "Doc, sometimes things happens for the best, even when it seems like they's really the worst."

"Worst?" Dylan stared toward a flash of lightning in the distance. "I'm not sure even this is the worst thing that's ever happened to me."

"That's prob'ly so, boy." Storm clouds blotted out what little light the crescent moon and stars had offered. "Your bride's a waitin' for you."

"I guess so."

Silently, he wondered if he would return to find the cabin empty.

Seven

Rose awoke when the sun streamed through the lone window to bathe the tiny cabin in pink light. She turned to her side, stretched in cat-like fashion and yawned widely.

"Sleep well?"

His voice was a startling reminder of her near-indiscretion. She sat up and rubbed her eyes. Dylan was stretched out on the floor beside the bunk wrapped in the tablecloth which had covered the basket of victuals. He looked cold and miserable.

"I'm sorry you had to sleep on the floor," she said, swinging her legs around to stand. She yawned again despite her best efforts to the contrary. "The bed is rather small, though."

Dylan smiled. For a moment it was in that same soul-searing way she recalled from the night past. But it soon faded to a smile of obvious self-reprimand.

"It was big enough . . . for a while."

Rose blushed as his hazel gaze scrutinized her unkempt appearance. She was painfully aware of how messy her hair was and her blue calico frock was wrinkled from having been worn to bed. Zeke Sawyer hadn't even allowed her to pack her few measly belongings before thrusting her into the reluctant arms of her new husband. She didn't even have a brush for her hair.

Her lower lip began to tremble despite her silent vow to remain strong and unemotional in this obscene situation. Hot tears stung her eyes and trickled down her cheeks. Ashamed, she covered her face with both hands and ran out the door into the early morning air.

She went directly to the spring and knelt to splash her face with cold water. It startled her senses and cleared her mind. She would face this day, confront her . . . husband, and get the gold.

Determination filled her as she straightened. She sought the outhouse behind the cabin, then returned to the spring to wash again. The cold water was cleansing not only for her flesh, but for her soul as well.

Satisfied she now had control of her wayward emotions, Rose turned toward the cabin. She paused for a moment to ponder the exquisite beauty of the structure. The sun bathed the little valley in light. It was quite majestic for something so small.

My honeymoon cottage.

Or my tomb?

Rose bit her lower lip to halt the telltale tremor. She drew a deep, steadying breath and walked to the cabin, then stepped inside.

Dylan turned from the basket which still sat on the table from last night. In his hand he held a brush, a hand mirror and a neatly folded dress.

"Martha must've put these in the bottom of the basket," he said in a voice so gentle it seemed to caress her. His expression grew solemn. "Rose, you brought nothing of your own with you?"

She shook her head, uncertain of her ability to speak without crying. "I have nothing." Stepping forward, she took the brush from his hands and returned to the porch where she sat to brush her tangled hair. Dylan's steps sounded behind her. She stopped brushing for a few moments, sensing his nearness.

He reached down to touch the inside of her wrist. His touch created a fluttering sensation throughout her body. She closed her eyes as he caressed the soft flesh of her inner arm with the tips of his fingers. Then, quite tenderly, he took the brush from her hand and began to untangle her hair himself.

Rose didn't move. The delicious feeling of Dylan brushing her hair made her warm and languid. She watched the reflection of the cabin on the water as the sun rose higher in the sky behind them. The sky was cloudless—last night's rain had cleansed the air. She couldn't recall a more perfect morning.

"It's a lovely day," Dylan said, as if reading her thoughts. He dropped to one knee behind her as he continued to brush her now tangle-free hair. "We're expected at my gra . . . cousins' for the funeral this morning."

"Yes, of course. Imagine attending a funeral for your own would-be murderer." The memory threatened her resolve, making Rose wish he hadn't spoken—that he'd continued to brush her hair in silence for an eternity. But that was quite foolish. "I'll change my dress."

"There's bread and cheese for breakfast." Dylan smiled at her, causing Rose to freeze as she turned toward the cabin. "Rose, I—"

"Don't." She pushed past him and went inside to

change into the clean dress. It was dark green sprigged muslin with long sleeves and a high neckline. Perceiving herself in the hand mirror, she realized it must be one of Martha's finest dresses. But of course she wouldn't be able to wear it right now because—

Stunned by her thoughts, Rose's hand flew to her mouth. If she and Dylan had followed through with what they'd started last night, she could have found herself in the same condition as Martha. What would she do with a baby?

Alone?

She dropped the mirror. Terror gripped her as her hands continued to tremble. Last night when she had . . . followed her more base instincts into the bed with Dylan, the possibility that she could conceive a child hadn't occurred to her. But now—in the light of day—it was an entirely different matter.

Dylan didn't want a permanent marriage any more than she did. It stood to reason he wouldn't want a child either. How fortunate she'd found the wherewithal to halt the consummation. In the future, she must be far more circumspect with her behavior.

Dylan stepped inside and paused. His face was freshly shaven. "Jim sent a razor." He rubbed his chin thoughtfully. "It's not a Norelco, but it'll do."

"Norelco?" Rose looked at him curiously.

"Oh, nothing, just a bit of slang from home." Dylan pointed to the broken mirror at her feet. "Seven years of bad luck, Rose."

"I've already had that," she said, kneeling to retrieve the larger pieces. "I don't suppose there's a broom in that basket."

"No." Dylan shook his head and took a step toward

her as she straightened. "Rose, we need to talk about what happened last night."

"Nothing . . . happened." She skirted his gaze and carried the broken pieces of mirror to the ash can near the hearth. "We should both try to forget about it, Dylan."

"Forget it?" Dylan exhaled loudly as he came up to grasp her arms from behind. "Rose, look at me."

She turned slowly. His hands loosened just enough to permit her to shift in his grasp and face him.

"Rose." He touched her face with his right hand. "Why do you have to be so damned beautiful?"

Rose knew she was blushing from the intense heat suffusing her face. Lowering her lashes, she captured a deep breath and forced herself to meet his gaze. "Dylan, surely you realize there could have been a . . . a child. I was so foolish to—"

"Not you, Rose. It was my fault." Dylan smiled indulgently. "I'm a doctor."

"Yes, so you've said, but—"

"Rose, I *am* a doctor." He sighed exaggeratedly. "I was a pediatrician back in St. Louis."

"I see." She blinked to hold back the tears which had threatened to emerge since the moment he touched her face. "A pediatrician?"

"A doctor who takes care of children."

"Oh. I guess you probably thought of . . . that already then."

"Well . . ." Dylan had the decency to blush himself. "I didn't think about it until this morning, actually."

Rose giggled. She couldn't help herself. Their almost lovemaking had been so spontaneous there hadn't been any possibility of rational thought by either of them. Soon, Dylan's deep chuckle had joined her mirth.

"It really—isn't funny, Dylan," she said brokenly, grasping her side as their laughter intensified.

"No, it isn't." His chuckle became a guffaw. He put his arms around her and drew her against him.

The laughter ceased.

"Rose, I don't know what's happening between us, but—"

"Don't." Rose reached up to press her fingertip to his lips. "I don't understand it either, but it's kind of . . . wonderful."

"Wonderful." Dylan released a sigh. "That's precisely the word I used when I told Jeff about my dre . . ."

"There you go again about that dream." Pulling away, she jerked on the sunbonnet she'd worn with the blue dress yesterday. It didn't match the green muslin, but it was better than getting freckled in the sun. "We'd better go up to your cousins' house for the funeral."

Dylan nodded and tugged at his belt. The movement made Rose's gaze drop low enough to notice his reaction to her this morning. Male anatomy was somewhat of an enigma to her, but the memory of the long, hard ridge hidden within the confines of his trousers last night brought a flash of heat to her face . . . and other parts of her body.

A blaze of raw yearning brandished through her anew. A tremor dawned in the depths of her belly and spread throughout her. Her face warmed and she looked quickly away, but not before she was certain he'd noticed the direction of her gaze.

"Rose, I still want you," he said soberly. "Refusing to talk about it won't make it go away. We're married, living in this cabin together, and I want you in the worst way. No, the *best* way. Even though I have no right, I can't help wanting you."

Rose turned away and took a step toward the door. She stopped near it and looked down at the floor. "I . . . guess I want you too, Dylan," she said softly, wondering if he'd even heard her when he didn't respond. "But we can't always have everything we want."

When she felt his hot breath against the back of her neck she knew he'd heard her confession. He slipped his arms around her waist and pressed himself against her from behind. Rose gasped in shock when his right hand boldly and gently stroked the side of her breast.

"God, woman," he said in a husky voice which seemed to vibrate through her bones and fluster her brain. "You make me crazy with wanting you."

Rose leaned her head back against him for support. Her body felt as if it would burst from the ache of desire. With his long, lean frame pressed enticingly against her backside, she couldn't help but feel his hard, pulsing erection through her skirt and petticoat.

Maybe she'd been wrong to resist him. It seemed so natural for them to succumb to their carnal urges. They were man and wife. Making love was a normal and expected part of their relationship.

But they didn't have a relationship. They'd never even met until night before last, when Pappy Zeke escorted them to the church against their combined wills.

This was so wrong.

Yet so right.

All she had to do was turn in his arms, lift her face and his lips would find hers. She knew it like she knew the sun would set in the west at the end of the day. He could be hers with very little effort.

Her body began to follow her thoughts, inching very slowly around until she was at an angle to his muscled torso. He continued his exploration of the sensitive underside of her breast. The fabric of her chemise and the green dress created a distressing barrier between them.

"Dylan." Jim Marshall's voice carried across the spring and into the cabin.

"He's got rotten timing." Dylan pulled her even closer, gave her a chaste kiss on the cheek and a hug before releasing her. "Later."

Later?

Rose wasn't sure if she was relieved or angry about the interruption. But she knew how she *should* feel, and forced a deep breath into her lungs to fortify her steadfastness.

She followed Dylan from the cabin to find Jim Marshall waving as he stepped onto the porch.

"I'm sorry to interrupt you so early," he said with a blush and a grin. "But Martha reckoned you might prefer a hot breakfast down at the house before the buryin' commences."

Dylan's stomach rumbled audibly as if in answer to the question, permitting some of the tension to dissipate on the morning air. "Thanks, Jim," he said on behalf of them both. "I think that would be fine."

"Yes, thank you for asking." Rose forced a smile and pulled the door closed behind her. She tied her bonnet strings beneath her chin and stepped off the porch, where Dylan tucked her hand in the crook of his elbow.

Jim talked incessantly as they walked up the hill. Rose heard very little of the conversation. Her mind was in a frenzy, wondering what would happen when she and Dylan returned to the cabin later in the day. Should she permit it? Common sense demanded she deny herself the indulgence of succumbing to her unruly appetites.

Yet she feared that when alone with Dylan again there would be no forbearance. A few moments longer this morning and she might have surrendered to the raw, hungry ache deep in her loins. Oh, how she'd wanted to. It would have been so much simpler than fighting her natural instincts.

As if reading her mind, Dylan gave her hand a squeeze and smiled in the way she'd already grown fond of.

Fond of?

She trembled as that consideration surged through her mind. This wasn't for her. When her mother'd died, her determination to find the treasure and return to her grandmother in Georgia had been all that had mattered.

That was still true. It had to be.

"Folks'll be arrivin' soon for the funeral," Jim said matter-of-factly when the house came into view. "Martha was up at dawn cookin'."

"I'll have a talk with her about taking it easy until after the baby comes." Dylan's brow furrowed in open concern. "With her history, she really should."

"I already told 'er that, Dylan." Jim didn't seem offended by the offer of help. "She won't hear of it. Maybe comin' from a real, bona fide doctor, though . . ."

Dylan smiled. "It's worth a try."

"I'll go help Martha." Rose turned toward the kitchen when they entered the house through the front door, surprised when Dylan kissed her on the cheek in front of Jim.

Rose found the woman on the kitchen floor clutching her swollen abdomen. "Martha!" She rushed to Martha's side and dropped to her knees. "The baby?"

Martha managed a nod. Her brow was covered in perspiration—the veins on her neck bulged. Her eyes were wide with obvious fright. Leaving her for a moment, Rose ran back to the front of the house.

"Dylan." She ignored the body laid out on boards stretched between a pair of sawhorses. "Martha—the baby!"

Without a word, Dylan rushed to the kitchen, followed closely by Jim. The physician knelt beside his patient and placed his hand on her abdomen, nodding as if his suspicions had been confirmed.

"I'll need Maggie Mae's help, Jim," he said over his shoulder as he continued to check Martha's pulse. "I haven't had time to purchase medical supplies. All I have is what's in my fanny pack."

"Fanny pack?" Rose shook her head.

"I'm sorry." Dylan lowered his gaze for a moment and she was aware of him gritting his teeth. "One of you go for Maggie Mae, and the other go after my fanny pack at the cabin. It's a pouch with a strap that wraps around my waist. It's dark blue. I remember putting it on the mantel."

"I'll get both," Jim said hurriedly, already heading

toward the door. "Maggie Mae's cabin's just above the spring."

Rose recognized Jim's need to keep busy. Besides, he could move much faster. Dylan nodded.

"Rose, I don't know if people were going to come here for the funeral or meet in town. You'll have to explain what's going on until Jim returns." Rose followed when Dylan lifted Martha's distended body in his arms and carried her up the stairs.

He paused in the hallway upstairs. "Do you know—"

"This one." Rose opened a paneled door, admitting Dylan and his patient into the bedroom she'd learned yesterday belonged to Martha and Jim. She rushed over to the iron bed frame and pulled back the colorful quilt.

Dylan laid Martha down gently. "I'll need hot— boiled—water, soap, clean towels, rags, whatever you can find."

Martha moaned and pointed to the bureau by the window. On it sat a pitcher and bowl. Rose opened the drawers and withdrew a stack of clean, white linen towels. She placed them on the nightstand beside the bed.

"Will you help me undress her, Rose?" Dylan smiled apologetically to Martha. "I'm a doctor, Cousin Martha. I've seen women undressed before. It's my job."

She nodded and bit her lower lip, then doubled into a ball as another pain obviously tore at her. She didn't scream. Rose was certain if it were her lying there, she'd not only scream, but probably swear as well. For her, personal comfort definitely took precedence over being ladylike in this situation.

"Dylan," Martha whispered, her blue eyes wide and pleading. "Don't let my baby die. Jim needs a son. Promise you'll save our baby."

Dylan winced. Rose saw his pain—felt it. She reached over to squeeze his hand just before they eased Martha's dress from her shoulders and slipped a clean nightgown over her head.

Rose's gaze locked with his after Martha was settled beneath the blankets. For some reason, she could almost sense his thoughts. She knew, just as she was certain Dylan did, that Martha meant for him to save the baby instead of her if it came to that.

"I need to examine you, Martha." Dylan laid his hand across her abdomen again. "Rose will be here while I do it. All right?"

Dylan washed his hands meticulously with strong lye soap, then dried them with one of the clean towels. His hazel eyes were solemn when he returned to the bed, but the expression he allowed Martha to see was confident and encouraging.

Martha nodded and grasped Rose's hand. Sweat beaded Dylan's brow as he pushed Martha's knees up until they fell naturally apart. He felt her abdomen with one hand and probed her with the other.

"I'm sorry I have to do this, Martha," he said when she closed her eyes in understandable embarrassment. His voice was soothing and apologetic. "But it's the only way I can check on you and the baby."

Rose squeezed Martha's hand reassuringly during the examination. She saw the frown knit Dylan's brow as he completed his analysis and washed his hands again. But when he turned toward his patient, the frown was replaced by a promising smile.

"You are definitely going to have this baby today," Dylan announced in a carefully controlled voice. Even though Rose had only known her husband for a short time, she already recognized many characteristics of his deep voice.

"He must be in a hurry to meet his mamma," Rose said, smiling at Dylan. His inner strength was inspiring. She'd known he was a special man, but seeing him work as a doctor provided insight into his character she knew she'd not seen before. He was a good, strong man.

Martha managed a weak smile before another pain tore at her. Dylan drew Rose away from the bed and led her to the door.

"Rose, listen carefully," he whispered. His expression was very serious. "The baby's in the wrong position. I'm going to need the sharpest knife you can find in the kitchen, a large embroidery needle with heavy thread or cat gut if there is any, plenty of boiled water, scissors, more rags . . ." He hesitated. "Liquor. Whiskey. Moonshine, or whatever they've got."

"Do you think you should be—"

"For Martha, not me, silly." Dylan managed a smile. "Now, hurry."

Rose left the room to search for the items Dylan would need. The knife worried her. What was he planning to do? She gathered the necessary items while waiting for the water to boil. Once the water started to bubble, she removed the kettle from the stove with a crocheted potholder, tucked another one under her arm and retrieved the items Dylan had requested from the table.

When Rose walked back into Martha's room, she

froze. Dylan was on his knees near the window, obviously praying. Martha's eyes were closed as she murmured her own words to her Maker.

She swallowed as the significance of this simple act overwhelmed her. She placed the items on the nightstand, trying to be as quiet as possible. Dylan got to his feet with grace and strength, turning to meet her gaze.

He did not blush or appear to regret being seen on his knees in prayer. His hazel eyes were frightened when he looked at Rose, but as his glance returned to Martha there was no sign of concern.

"Well, we need to have another look at this situation." Dylan nodded to Rose, who assumed her position at the head of the bed again. Martha's grip was fierce as Dylan examined her.

Dylan looked up from his position at the foot of the bed. "You're having a contraction right now," he said knowingly. "That's not uncommon during the examination, Martha."

As the pain ebbed, Martha nodded. Rose waited until Dylan completed his exam, then released the woman's hand to cross the room.

Dylan washed his hands again. Rose had never seen anyone wash as often as her . . . husband. She felt warm when she thought of him as hers. It was thrilling—yet terrifying.

"I can't wait much longer," he said quietly as he dried his hands. "The baby will be in the birth canal. His best chance is with a cesarean."

Rose frowned. "A what?"

Dylan sighed. "I'm going to have to . . . to cut the

baby out." His expression was one of determination. "That's the baby's best chance."

"And Martha?" Rose touched his arm with her hand. She swallowed hard, waiting breathlessly for his answer.

"If only I had some supplies." There was anguish in his voice.

The door opened and Jim rushed over to the bed, handing Dylan the strange fanny pack in passing. Dylan met Maggie Mae at the door and stepped into the hall as he pulled the door shut behind them. Rose wondered what was being said in the hall, but thought perhaps she was better off not knowing.

Jim and Martha spoke in quiet tones. The sadness in their voices made Rose want to reach out to them. She ached for these people, though she hardly knew them except from occasional meetings in town and church. Right now, their vulnerability was oppressive.

After a moment, Dylan returned with Maggie Mae. He walked over to the bed and waited until Jim looked up at him. "Jim."

Jim straightened. The pair of men stood on opposite sides of the bed. "How's it look, Dylan?"

"I'll speak the truth." Dylan took a deep breath and clasped his hands in front of him. "The baby's very large and turned the wrong way. If he's born the . . . usual way, he might not make it."

"Oh, Dear God—not again." Martha looked frantically at her husband.

"But . . ." Dylan's gaze swept both of them. "There's another way."

"What's this?" Jim clenched his teeth, obviously waiting for an answer.

"I learned in medical school how to . . . to cut the baby from the mother."

Rose stifled a gasp with her knuckles. She stared in horror at Dylan. Even though he'd partially prepared her a few moments ago, hearing him explain it to Jim and Martha was horrible. How great a sacrifice was this woman expected to make to bring her baby into the world alive?

Did he mean to sacrifice Martha for the child? No—Rose wouldn't let him do it. But before she could intervene, Jim's uncertain words did.

"Cut?" Jim's voice was wretched. "And what about Martha?"

"With the proper supplies, that wouldn't really be in question." Dylan's mouth was set in grim lines. "But all I have here is my first aid kit and Maggie Mae's skill with herbs. There are no guarantees, but my intention is to save them both."

"Yes." Martha's voice was surprisingly strong. Trust and confidence filled her expression. "Do it, Dylan."

A muscle worked in Jim's jaw. He looked down at his wife, then back to Dylan. "Do it."

"You're sure this'll make her sleep, Maggie Mae?" Dylan held the cup for Martha to sip from.

"Pos'tive." Maggie Mae walked around the bed sprinkling something on the floor. When Dylan looked at her curiously, she grinned. "For luck."

"Every little bit helps. That's true." Dylan returned her smile. "How are you feeling, Martha?"

She murmured drowsily. Her head lolled to one side. Dylan lifted her lids to examine her pupils. "I'll be damned." He glanced up at Maggie Mae. "It worked. Why won't you tell me what's in it?"

"Mebbe later." Maggie Mae stood beside Martha, bending over to check her breathing. "She's ready."

Dylan had explained to Maggie Mae exactly what he would be doing. The woman never questioned his ability or motives, though he had considerable reservations about both. He was meddling with history.

"God, I hope I'm doing the right thing." Dylan laid his instruments out on a clean strip of linen on the nightstand. His hands were as clean as possible. He slipped on the only pair of surgical gloves from his first aid kit.

Maggie Mae pointed at the strange gloves. "What's those for?"

"They're sterile—cleaner than my bare hands." Dylan looked at Martha's exposed abdomen which had been wiped down with the alcohol pads from his first-aid equipment. There was a scalpel and kit for emergency stitches as well. Thank God Jim had returned with them in time. The thought of using a kitchen knife in surgery had terrified him. The term "butcher" came to mind. He simply wouldn't have been able to do it.

"I'll do a bikini cut," he said to himself as he began the incision, wishing suddenly he'd served his residency in obstetrics rather than pediatrics. He glanced up at Martha several times to ensure she wasn't feeling any pain. She made no sound, but did flinch slightly in her sleep.

"Bikini." Maggie Mae shook her head, watching in awe at his work. "What magic is they teachin' doctors these days? This be a gift fer sure."

Dylan didn't take time to consider her words. Busy at his work, he exposed the uterus and within a few moments miraculously lifted the baby from his warm environment. Dylan tied and cut the cord, and he used an empty syringe from his bag to suction the infant's nose and mouth. Then he passed the boy to Maggie Mae.

The old woman wrapped him in several towels and blew in his face. Dylan glanced up once or twice to make certain the infant was breathing. Maggie Mae didn't turn him upside down and spank him as he'd expected. She tickled his feet and blew in his face until the baby wailed in protest.

Dylan grinned. Maggie Mae returned to his side, observing his handiwork as he cleaned out the after-birth and began to close.

"The Lord is workin' through your hands, boy. It's the only answer."

"I think He had a lot to do with this, Maggie Mae." Dylan glanced up at his patient's face. At Martha's request, he'd prayed today for the first time in more years than he could remember. Maybe he should try it more often. "She seems to be doing well."

Maggie Mae nodded in agreement while Dylan completed his handiwork. She clicked her tongue in obvious awe. "This young feller ain't gonna believe how he come into this world."

Dylan applied clean strips of linen over several gauze pads from his meager supplies. He bound the incision and Martha's entire circumference with an Ace bandage. With only a moderate amount of bleeding, he felt it had all gone well.

God, I hope I've done the right thing.

"I just delivered my own great-grandfather." Dylan voiced his innermost thoughts in a ragged whisper, then recalled Maggie Mae's presence. Looking up quickly, he met her amazed stare and realized his error.

Maggie Mae looked back down at the child's healthy, pink face. She didn't speak, but simply smiled. Dylan had no way of knowing if she'd overheard his unbelievable words, or if she was simply smiling because of the successful delivery.

"I'd like ter learn some of this fancy doctorin' stuff." She looked directly at him as she spoke. Her expression was fathomless.

Releasing the breath he'd been holding, Dylan told himself Maggie Mae surely would have said something if she'd overheard him. "Sure. As soon as you teach me about the herbs and stuff."

"You come on over ter my cabin real soon." Maggie Mae flashed him a toothless grin, wide and inviting. "I's glad ye're here, boy."

Martha moaned and shifted slightly. Dylan hurried to the head of the bed and looked into her eyes. "She's coming around."

"Great-grandfather . . . ?" Her whispered words were barely audible. Dylan's flesh crawled as he contemplated his dilemma. How much had Martha overheard? He shook his head. Patients coming out of anesthesia rarely remembered details. Glancing up at Maggie Mae, he was relieved to find her busy with the baby.

After replacing the sheets with clean ones, he called out into the hall where Jim leaned against the wall. Dylan couldn't shake the feeling that he'd conducted the surgery for selfish reasons. History proved that this child had lived. But then, history also showed that Rose Jameson had died. How could he take the chance that Jim and Martha's son wouldn't survive?

"I heard the babe." Jim swallowed hard. His Adam's apple bobbed up and down in his long, thin neck. "Is my Martha . . . alive?"

Dylan laughed and cried at the same time. "They're both fine, Jim." Tears trickled unheeded down his face as he nodded for the new father to enter the room. Suddenly, he knew beyond any doubt that he'd done the right thing. This couple had paid dearly to have the little boy. They deserved every chance for success.

"Praise be."

Dylan watched with a trembling chin as his great-great-grandfather knelt beside the bed to peer at the newborn swaddled at his wife's side. Martha managed a weak smile.

"We'll call him Dylan," Jim said reverently, glancing once in the doctor's direction.

"No, don't!" *That was brilliant, Einstein.* "It's just that—since Tom Marshall died almost the same day this Marshall came into the world—I thought . . ."

"That seems fittin'," Jim said, and Martha nodded in agreement. "How can we ever thank you, Dylan?"

"You already have." He closed his eyes for a moment of silent gratitude. "Believe me—you already have."

Eight

Dylan watched Preacher Ross during the graveside service. The man nodded in his direction, obviously acknowledging that Dylan was the only family member present, since Jim had understandably remained behind with his wife and newborn son.

"Ashes to ashes . . ." The man's nasal tone droned on. Realizing something was expected, Dylan stooped to retrieve a handful of soil and tossed it into the grave. The clods struck the coffin with a sickening thud.

My great-great-great-grandfather. Rose's almost-murderer.

He clenched his teeth as that realization struck anew. Rose stood at his side, a silent reminder of Tom Marshall's crime. As far as Dylan knew, he and Rose were the only two people aware of the truth. The rest of the community merely assumed Tom had wandered off, as he was known to do, and overtired himself.

Perhaps Dylan did owe Rose some compensation for Tom's crime. Saving her life wasn't enough? Could giving her the gold be the right answer? Was it rightfully hers?

Of course, he realized the gold had at one time been

the property of the Confederate States of America. But since that government no longer existed . . .

Lifting his gaze, Dylan surveyed the mourners. They were a ragtag bunch. The men all wore the typical overalls or dungarees, clean ones for the funeral, of course. Most of the women wore calico, and one older lady was dressed in black crepe that hung to her heels in the back.

The mourners looked toward him expectantly when the service ended. Clearing his throat, Dylan scanned the faces in the crowd. The Sawyer clan wasn't represented, an oversight on their part for which he was extremely grateful.

Dylan was a stranger in their midst. How was he going to pull this one off? "Well, Tom Marshall's gone to meet his glory." He glanced around at the expressions on their faces as if checking an applause meter. They seemed satisfied.

A few mourners began to move away. He knew how suspicious people in the Ozarks were of strangers. His only redeeming quality was his kinship to a respected family.

Rose tugged on Dylan's sleeve. "It's customary to invite them back to the house." Her voice was a quiet, and very welcome, whisper at his side.

Dylan smiled, relieved. Of course, he should have known. But Martha certainly wasn't able to entertain. "It seems rather fitting that Tom's namesake chose this day to come into the world."

A murmur swept through the crowd. The news of the baby might help alleviate the open curiosity he and Rose would be faced with, regarding their sudden marriage. Dylan recognized an opening and continued. "That's why Jim wasn't able to be here himself."

"Martha's done had her youngun?" A woman with hair the color of corn rushed over to grasp Rose's hand. "Rose, is she all right? Last time—the baby?"

"They're both fine." Rose's voice was steady and confident. "But the doctor who delivered him is right here. Why don't you ask him for yourself?"

A man dressed in a dark suit with a brocaded vest stepped away from the crowd. Dylan was amazed he hadn't noticed him earlier since his clothing certainly distinguished him from the others.

"So, you're a real doctor?" The man had a cigar clenched between his teeth. He was tall and heavy with a balding head.

Dylan extended his hand. "Dr. Dylan Marshall."

"You aimin' to set up practice here in Dogwood?" The man seemed more than a little suspicious.

"I might." Dylan hated to talk about the longevity of his stay in Dogwood, since he had no way of knowing when—or if—he'd be able to return to his own time. A lump of guilt formed in his throat when he felt Rose return to his side after assuring all the ladies present that both Martha and the baby were doing well.

"I'm Jesse Whorton, owner of the Dogwood Mill," the man said, as if that should impress anyone and everyone. Whorton rolled the cigar between his teeth, shifting it to the other side of his mouth. "If you've a mind to practice medicine in Dogwood, the office 'round back of the mill is yours. We used to have a doctor for a while."

Taken aback, Dylan wondered how he should respond to such a generous offer? He felt almost cornered. "I can't commit myself for any period of time," he said tentatively. "But I'm more than willing to make myself available while I'm here."

The man sighed in open disappointment. "Reckon that's your right."

Most of the mourners had abandoned tradition and gone their own way. Tom Marshall's funeral was officially over. It seemed somehow fitting that a man who'd declined to attempted murder should have a funeral lacking the usual fanfare and ceremony.

"If you've got a minute, we can have a look at the office now."

"Sure." Dylan couldn't pass up the opportunity to obtain any medical supplies which might have been left behind. There could be something there for Martha or the baby, though they were doing well despite the primitive conditions. He glanced at Rose, who nodded almost imperceptibly. Dylan's face burned. He was being rude—neglecting her.

"Uh, I take it you've met my wife?" His wife? He couldn't believe he actually said that.

" 'Course. Miss Rose. I didn't recognize you at first . . . without your sign." The man grinned in Dylan's direction. "Zeke got to you, eh?"

Rose blushed and Dylan felt a protective rush sweep through him, choosing to ignore the second reference he'd heard to his wife carrying signs. He couldn't let the public believe he was forced to marry Rose, even though it was the truth. It simply wasn't fair to her. Once he returned to his own time, she'd be forced to face them. Her neighbors might ridicule and chastise her for the circumstances of their marriage.

"Rose is all the wife a man could ever want," Dylan said, and meant it. Side-glancing at his wife, he saw her small intake of breath and the sudden flush to her cheeks. Gorgeous. She truly was all the wife a man could want. It just wasn't the right time or place.

"Uh . . . 'course." The man appeared properly embarrassed as they walked down the main street of the small town of Dogwood, Missouri. "Congratulations, Doc."

Dylan nodded and took in his surroundings, ignoring the strange swell of pride he felt with Rose on his arm. On his wedding night, he hadn't been allowed the opportunity to see the town. He now realized that the log church where he and Rose had been married was right at the edge of the small community.

The modest town would one day be completely obliterated—covered with water. It seemed like such a waste as he looked around. Though the few buildings were constructed mostly from plain clapboard or logs, they were obviously well cared for. Flowers bloomed along the boardwalks as if defying the civil engineers of the twentieth century ahead of time.

One wide thoroughfare ran the length of the town. All in all, Dogwood was only about an eighth of a mile long, and half that in width. Dylan saw a saloon, post office, general mercantile and the church, which doubled as a school. On the far side of town, the White River bubbled past on its journey to the south. The mill was an imposing structure with its huge water wheel spinning ever onward.

Jesse Whorton paused in the center of town and took a deep breath. "We're a progressive little town, Dr. Marshall."

Dylan stifled the comments threatening to erupt from his somewhat devilish sense of humor. Dogwood looked like the amusement parks which had sprung up all over the Ozarks with the need for people to make a living in his time. Every little bend in the road had a sign boasting of a spring or cave, or some other type of tourist trap. Dogwood would fit right in—no doubt about it.

Except this was a real town with people who called it home. What right did the government have to build a dam on the river, to submerge this thriving little community under millions of cubic feet of water?

"Here we be." Whorton escorted them to the side of the mill, where a flight of stairs led to an outside entrance on the second floor. "This is private. There ain't no access from the mill."

"I see." Dylan smiled at Rose. He was increasingly surprised at how simple it might be to forget about the twentieth century, to stay here . . . with his bride.

But that was insane.

Ridiculous.

Unthinkable.

Yet think he did.

His chest tightened as he motioned for Rose to precede him. He followed her up the wooden steps to the landing at the top, where Whorton opened the door and swung it open wide.

Rose's skirts swished enchantingly in front of him as Dylan enjoyed the spectacle her backside presented for his simultaneous pleasure and torture. He couldn't help recalling how warm and soft she'd been—how receptive to his ardent advances—to a point.

He had no right.

It had almost been too late. Had he taken her virginity, he'd be unable to return it.

No right at all.

But if he'd never traveled back in time, Rose would be dead by now. What of his reward?

Tacky, Dylan.

Self-loathing shot through him as he shook his head. He wasn't the kind of guy who expected compensation for gallantry.

Gallantry?

He was definitely suffering from delusions of grandeur. However, telling himself he didn't expect a reward for saving Rose's life offered little in the way of persuasive argument against his physical urges.

What had Maggie Mae said about things being "meant to be?" Were he and Rose one of those circumstances? Could that possibly even begin to explain his absurd predicament?

Forcing images of her bare supple flesh from his mind, Dylan drew a ragged breath, then released it as they entered the dusty office. Later, when he and Rose were alone at the cabin . . .

As Jesse Whorton entrusted Dylan with the key to the small office and left them there alone, Rose stared in awe at the man who was her husband. They were alone for a while until they had to walk back to the farm.

And then what?

Swallowing, she turned her attention to the man who walked around the room, examining its contents as if he were a child in a candy store.

"You did a good day's work, Dr. Marshall," Rose

said softly, battling a riot of conflicting emotions. But her praise was genuine.

Dylan paused from his investigation of the office and its contents to reach out and touch her face. "Thank you, Mrs. Marshall."

He'd called her Mrs. Marshall. Rose felt warm all over.

Mrs. Marshall!

Deep inside, she wished desperately for him to pull her into his arms, and that he would kiss her as he had last night, but he didn't.

"Thank you for what you said to Mr. Whorton about . . . us." She lowered her gaze from the flash of desire she recognized in his eyes.

How could she have any regrets about being married to Dylan? He was everything any woman could ever want in a man, and so much more. Yet she mustn't permit the day's events to cloud her vision.

The strange, haunted expression had returned to his hazel eyes. Was it because of her? Did he resent having been forced to marry her?

Of course he resents me. And he hid the gold—my gold. Why should I trust a man who would do such a thing?

But he was tall, strong, handsome and intelligent. More than that, he was good in the very best way a man could be. He had a warm and caring heart.

Except for hiding her gold.

How could she forget the reason for her Ozark exile? How could she abandon all efforts to escape, now more than ever? Now that she'd seen her daddy's gold with her own eyes? Just that tiny glimpse had been enough to convince her that her mother's death was not in vain. She couldn't give up—not now.

"Tell me, Rose . . ." Dylan looked at her with a quizzical expression. His smile was filled with mischief. "I've heard references to you carrying some kind of sign twice now, and—"

"Dr. Marshall?" A young woman stood outlined in the doorway with a baby in her arms. "I heard you was plannin' to stay around to doctor folks."

Dylan appeared nonplused by the question. He cleared his throat and smiled. "I will be, but just for a while, Mrs. . . ."

"Dylan, this is Ida Whorton." Thankful for the interruption as her husband's hand fell to his side, Rose smiled at the woman who was probably a year or two younger than herself. She'd already given birth to three children and been married since she was fifteen. "Her husband owns the mill."

"Oh, of course." Dylan nodded. "Pleased to make your acquaintance, Mrs. Whorton. I met your husband earlier and he was kind enough to loan me the use of this office."

"He had to get back to the mill." Ida Whorton hesitated. "Dr. Marshall, they's somethin' wrong with my babe. She ain't gainin' even though I gots plenty milk. My husband said if'n he weren't a good Christian, he'd leave her in the woods. He thinks she's . . . queer."

Dylan's expression froze for a moment as if pondering the enormity of the woman's words. Rose also wondered how a father could be so callous. She glanced at the baby's face. The tiny bundle did seem frail. The skin on her face was thin, permitting thin blue veins to show through. Her eyes were . . . different.

"Bring the baby over here and I'll examine her, Mrs. Whorton." Dylan patted Rose's hand where it was cradled on his forearm. "It may be an allergy or something. Babies can have all sorts of allergies that go away as mysteriously as they appear."

"What's an allergy?" She smiled brightly and brought her petite bundle over to the exam table as Dylan had instructed.

"An allergy means someone's sensitive to a certain substance in the air, or food, a pet, even fabric."

Rose watched as Dylan unwrapped the baby and examined her from head to toe. He removed all the child's clothing and checked her eyes, ears and nose. Then he removed the instrument he called a stethoscope from the bag he now wore buckled around his waist.

His expression was solemn, but not grim as he listened to the child's breathing. "Mrs. Whorton," he said after a few moments. "Was the baby early?"

"Yep." Ida leaned forward to stare at the stethoscope. "What's ailin' her, Doc?"

Dylan straightened and allowed Ida to fasten the child's clothing. "I'm not sure ailing is the right term." He cleared his throat and hesitated as if considering some great problem. "Your daughter has something called . . . Down Syndrome. It isn't an illness, though sometimes there can be heart involvement. Her heart seems sound, though. That's good news."

"What's this . . . Down Syndrome?" Ida appeared confused. "You say it ain't a ailment. What is it then?"

"I don't like the term, but some people still call

it . . . Mongolism." Dylan visibly winced. "Mrs. Whorton, children with Down Syndrome are . . . different."

When Ida gasped, Dylan smiled in obvious encouragement. "Your daughter will grow, but more slowly than other children. We may need to have you nurse her more frequently. As often as she's willing. Don't feed her anything else till I tell you to, though. Just all your good milk she can handle. Understand?"

"I been givin' her mash. Is that what made her sick?"

Dylan sighed and gave Mrs. Whorton's hand a squeeze. "No. She really isn't ill. It's just that if you fill a tiny baby up on solid food, there's not enough room for what she really needs. *Your* milk. Understand?"

"Yep. I do about the feedin'."

"But not about the rest of it." Dylan rubbed his chin before continuing.

Rose thought at this moment he was the most wonderful person she'd ever known. His hazel eyes were expressive and sympathetic. His voice remained level and patient despite Mrs. Whorton's obvious difficulty in comprehending his simple instructions.

"Mrs. Whorton, people with Down Syndrome are usually . . . slow learners."

"Oh." Her voice seemed very small. "You mean she'll be an idiot. My husband said maybe she was."

Dylan winced again, then took the child by the hands and pulled one across her chest until she rolled onto her side. "Her muscle tone is very low. I'll show you some exercises to do with her at home. This is very important. If you want to help her learn to walk and talk, you'll need to do these exercises every day.

It's playing, really. Don't treat it like work. And sing to her—talk to her all the time. Every time you're changing her, nursing or whatever."

"Oh, I will." Ida brightened. "You reckon she'll walk an' talk then, Doc?"

"In time." His voice was cautious, but encouraging at the same time. "You'll need to have great patience with this child, Mrs. Whorton. You have other children?"

"Two more. Girl an' a boy." Ida beamed with pride. "They weren't like this, though."

"No, of course not." Dylan patted the woman's shoulder. "Your older children can help. What's your baby's name?"

"Sarah Jane."

"Sarah Jane's brother and sister will be great helpers with what we're going to call therapy. Understand?" Again, she nodded. "I'd like to come to your home to show you and the children the exercises. Do you think your husband would like to help, too?"

Ida lowered her gaze. "Nope. I don't reckon he would."

Dylan sighed as if he understood far more than was being said. "Fine. Maybe he'll come around when he sees Sarah Jane's progress."

Ida looked up and seemed encouraged. "Thank you, Doc." She opened her tapestry purse.

"No charge, Mrs. Whorton." Dylan covered her hand with his. "You're my first patient in Dogwood. It was my pleasure."

Rose stared long and hard at Dylan after Mrs. Whorton left with the child. She'd heard of Mongolism before, but never Down Syndrome. It made sense that medical science was learning more about things as time went by.

Despite her warm feelings toward Dylan, she could not prevent herself from thinking of the gold. With the gold in his possession, it stood to reason he wouldn't need to charge for his medical services. He had all the money he'd ever want or need.

Her money.

"That was very generous of you," she said quietly, wishing she didn't feel this way. "Her husband is the wealthiest man in town."

Dylan shrugged and reddened beneath her curious gaze. "She'll have her hands full with this," he said, as if that more than justified his generosity. "I don't need the money that bad."

"No, I suppose you don't." Rose frowned, lamenting she'd remembered the treasure so soon. The past hour had been wonderful. The depth of her husband's character gave her argument to consider him as more than merely an obstacle between herself and the treasure.

Dylan put his stethoscope back in the strange pouch and closed it. "I need to check on Martha and the baby before we go . . . home."

The moment was gone, lost to whatever fates were in control of their situation. Rose sighed and nodded. They could talk all day and night, but it wouldn't change facts. Dylan had been forced at gunpoint to marry her, despite what he'd told Jesse Whorton.

Not that she wanted to be married to him, of course. On the contrary, what she wanted was out of the Ozarks with her gold. Then she intended to join the National American Woman Suffrage Association. There was no way she would permit herself to be sub-

ordinate to any man. Not even this one. It had been
her intention never to marry. How ridiculous that she
should find herself in such a situation, whether the
man was desirable or not.

"It's time we headed back," he said quietly, seeming
to share her melancholy.

Rose nodded, feeling as if she'd just shot herself in
the foot. As Dylan escorted her down the stairs, she
chastised herself again for nearly succumbing to his
charms the night before. How could she have come
so close to forgiving herself that easily? She was one
of the New Women, determined to fight for women's
suffrage and not be simply a man's plaything.

Oh, but she'd had no idea exactly how wonderful
being a plaything could be.

Though, her attraction to Dylan seemed so much
more than that. As she studied his profile during their
walk to the farm, she saw his intelligence, his caring,
his dedication to his profession. His character was
etched across his handsome face. Dylan Marshall was
a good man—the kind of man her mother, had she
been alive, would have chosen for Rose.

They remained silent during the walk back to the
farmhouse. The mere thought of being alone with him
again at the cabin was almost more than she could
stand. She hoped her face wasn't too terribly flushed
and that her hands didn't tremble to betray her anxiety.

Rose sighed. Dylan Marshall was quite an enigma
indeed.

Rose and Dylan walked back to their cabin at nightfall. Maggie Mae insisted on staying at the Marshall

farm temporarily while Martha recovered from her surgery. It had been quite an exciting day for them all.

Dylan ventured a glance at his wife. His *wife!* The thought still made his stomach tie up in knots each time he allowed himself to dwell on it. A portion of the euphoria remained from the adventure of delivering his great-grandfather. Had the joy he felt today interfered with his true feelings for Rose?

Was it possible to forget about his former life and just enjoy his new present?

Dylan's gaze swept the forest which closed in to form a triangle down by the cabin and spring. Serenity Spring. He'd never known before exactly how the place had received its name, but he was beginning to understand.

Not that he felt particularly serene. Being forced back one hundred years in time hardly inspired feelings of contentment. Nor did wondering if he'd be permitted to return to his own time. Did he really want to?

His presence in 1894 had already modified the past. A glance at the beautiful woman to his right confirmed that—thank God.

A knot formed in his belly again as he pondered whether or not he'd done the right thing by delivering Martha's baby by cesarean section. His great-grandfather had survived the delivery without his assistance— Dylan wouldn't exist otherwise. Had he interfered where he shouldn't have?

Assuming, of course, that he existed at all. Did Dylan Marshall, M.D., exist at all? He shook his head, dismissing such thoughts as a waste of time.

Twilight—his favorite time of day. He sighed, look-ing around him and realizing how unchanged the area was even a hundred years in the future. A huge oak stood in the center of the meadow, which in his time would be nothing but a large stump—not unlike the one which had confined Rose to the cellar.

Don't think about that. She's alive—that's what mat-ters.

"This has always been the most beautiful place in the world." Dylan took her hand in his, determined to push away the disturbing memories of her near death . . . and her first death.

"You talk as if you've seen it a million times be-fore." Rose's gaze was curious. She didn't pull her hand from his grasp as they paused for a moment to look at their surroundings. "I thought you just ar-rived."

Dylan didn't respond to her remark. How could he? Either he could tell her a lie or the truth. But the truth would be impossible for her to believe. Rather than lie, he chose silence.

"It is beautiful," she finally agreed when he didn't answer. A mist rose from the spring and the creek, shrouding the tops of the trees. Light from the setting sun played in the haze, casting surreal shadows and arcs of color for their entertainment. Dylan recalled again his grandfather's tales about that natural occur-rence, which was relatively frequent due to the high humidity in the Ozarks.

He shook his head as an unusual, but relieving thought occurred to him. By changing history, he'd altered part of his own past as well. "No one will ever call it the ghost cabin now."

"What?" Rose tugged on his hand when he didn't answer right away.

"Oh, nothing important." Dylan looked down at his feet, mentally cursing himself. "The mist looks like ghosts dancing in the trees. That's all."

Rose looked beyond him and nodded. "Yes." She giggled. It was a joyous sound to Dylan's ears. "The locals would call them 'hants,' though."

He laughed along with her and proceeded slowly toward the cabin. He didn't talk for several moments even after their laughter subsided. "Martha and the baby should be stable in a few days."

Rose's expression grew tight and drawn. She avoided his gaze and toyed with the pleats on her skirt. "Will you leave then?" Her expression was strained, her tone tight with obvious uncertainty.

Dylan's stomach churned. How could he answer such a question when he had no answers for himself?

If he had to stay in this century, he wanted very much to remain with Rose, right here at Serenity Spring. This realization struck him like an eighteen wheeler, though he was certain he'd entertained the notion at least subconsciously.

Today's incident with the Whorton baby had reminded him how desperately the rural people needed a doctor. How many lives could he save if he remained in the nineteenth century? If he returned to his own time his patients would be far different. Could the monetary reward be replaced by the satisfaction of really helping people in need?

He couldn't give her a definite answer. "I don't belong here exactly either, Rose," he said finally.

She didn't respond as they started walking again.

Rose kept her face averted, but he wished she'd look at him. He wanted—needed—to see her face. The expression of sadness he'd seen in her eyes during his dream returned to haunt him. She was a woman filled with sorrow—stranded far from her home and what remained of her family. He was contributing to her isolation.

But he wanted her. *Damn.* Though his mind and heart constantly battled one another over his predicament, other parts of his anatomy had absolutely no doubts. The firm ridge filled the front of his jeans, making him uncomfortably aware of just how ill-mannered the male libido could be when properly enticed.

And he was definitely enticed.

"I know we didn't ask for each other, but I can't say—after what almost happened last night—that I'm disappointed. Can you?"

Rose looked at him with wide eyes. Her mouth formed a perfect circle as she stared at him in obvious amazement. "Disappointed?" Her tremulous smile caught him off guard. "Dylan, if not for you I'd be dead or dying in that cellar by now. You're a good, honest man, but that doesn't change things. I still don't belong here and you were forced at gunpoint to marry me."

Dylan thought of one woman who was definitely disappointed with him. Cindy'd been dissatisfied enough to divorce him after eight years of marriage. But that was another time and place. This was different—people in the Ozarks married for keeps.

Even if I return to my own time?

How could he continue to behave as Rose's husband,

and even consider taking all the privileges that role entitled him to, when he knew at the first opportunity he would return to the twentieth century? "Rose, I'm so confused by you—by us."

At her look of surprise, he smiled, pulling her hand until she turned to face him as they stopped just beyond the spring. "We hardly know each other, but I'm already very . . . attached to you. Maybe I don't have a right to feel anything, but I can't help it."

"Attached?" Rose repeated as if the word had been something much more specific. She smiled and reached up to caress his face with her hand. Sighing, she trailed her thumb across his lips.

Dylan felt an electrical jolt of desire surge through him. He recalled the last time Rose had come to him as a dream—or ghost—how he'd noticed such a rush between them.

Was this destiny? His body throbbed in response, ignoring propriety and who had a right to what. His anatomy wasn't nearly as confused as his mind.

Though at the moment his mind was conjuring up all sorts of delicious possibilities.

"Maybe more than attachment," he whispered, stepping nearer.

Her breath was sweet and warm against his face as he bent to kiss her perfect lips. Throwing her arms around his neck, she mewed a pleasurable sound as his tongue stroked and probed. Her response was far more earnest than what he expected.

Dylan caressed the back of her neck, bringing his hands down to cup her firm buttocks and press her against him. His blood surged like molten lava, heated to a boiling point and about to erupt. She pressed herself against him and parted her lips, empowering him to sample her particular captivating flavor.

She was so like the ghost who'd tortured him for weeks that Dylan almost forgot where—and when—he was. Again, he lost himself in a dream of exotic seduction with a woman who had lured and baited him until he was nearly insane from wanting her.

"God, woman," Dylan murmured against her lips when he came up for air. "And Madonna thinks she's sexy."

"Who?"

"Never mind."

Groaning, Dylan resumed and deepened their kiss, lifting Rose off her feet to press her against his full length. Her softness fit well against his extremely enthusiastic erection.

Darkness enveloped them as the sun completely vanished behind a mountain. Their hearts seemed to thud in unison as they crushed themselves together almost as one flesh. Almost. Dylan ached to merge his body with hers in the ancient way of man and woman.

The last time he dreamed of Rose, when she'd finally consummated their relationship, was the most fulfilling, wondrous sex of his entire life. How could he resist the temptation pressing so ardently against him now?

He couldn't.

It was nearly impossible to remember that his dream lover had been the ghostly Rose, not Rose herself. His confused body obviously felt they belonged together in these intimate circumstances, though they'd never been together in the literal sense.

Just thinking about burying himself deep within her velvet folds made Dylan shudder. Groaning, he picked her up and carried her around the edge of the spring to the cabin. She murmured no sound of protest as he kicked open the front door and let it slam shut behind them.

Not bothering with the lamp, he laid her down on the quilt and unbuttoned the green dress. Their lips parted and she sighed, reaching boldly for the buttons at the front of his shirt. They worked together to reveal heated, inquiring skin.

Dylan's need became more urgent as he bared her extraordinary breasts to his touch. He was too inspired to practice reserve as he stripped himself completely within a matter of seconds. This wasn't his dream-world, though he grew comparably oblivious to consequences and reality.

Rose slid her hands down his back and squeezed the muscles in his buttocks when he lowered himself over her. He groaned and covered her lips with his, savoring her eager response. Leaning on his elbows, he traced circles around her puckered nipples with his thumbs, playing with them until she arched against him. Her breasts were perfect twin globes, round and firm, beckoning to him and far too delectable to resist.

His heart pumped wildly in his throat when she brought her hand around to grasp his hard shaft. Her intentions were obvious. Any reservations he may have still harbored about consummating their marriage became kindling. Like a fire so concentrated, so calamitous, it could only be thwarted by annihilating itself, their hunger mounted.

Unwilling to adjourn the kiss, Dylan's hands encompassed her satiny midriff as his thumbs proceeded to tease her pebbled nipples. His jabbing erection pulsated against her hip. His hands fixated on her responsive breasts until his mouth displaced them, relishing her response.

Much to his pleasure, Rose lifted her breast more fully against his mouth. More than willing to accommodate her, he grasped her ample breasts in his hands to press them upward for their mutual pleasure. *So sweet . . .*

Driven beyond tolerance, Dylan positioned himself between her silken thighs. He hesitated to gaze down into her eyes, wishing he could see her passion, yet sensing that her expression would reveal desire as extreme as his own. Would there be fear mingled with her desire this time?

"Rose." Her name sounded so good coming from his lips. Dylan sighed, then buried his face in her hair to inhale the sweet fragrance. "God, I think—"

Rose winced beneath him, his words left hanging incomplete in the charged air between them, interrupted by a resolute rapping at the cabin door.

"Open up, Doc."

"Oh, not now—*not now!*" With his despondent erection poised just on the verge of entering her forbidden flesh, Dylan hid his face in her hair while he grappled with a surge of conflicting emotions. Foremost in his thoughts were a variety of torture techniques he might utilize against the intruder, though they paled to insignificance when compared to the blow he'd been dealt. Fighting the memory of that other night—the one before he'd moved into the cabin, when his dream had allowed him to finally, miraculously . . .

Dragging in a deep breath, he held it for a few moments as the pounding at the door continued.

"So it begins," Dylan said flippantly, though his mood was far from glib. Sexual frustration ripped through him. "I thought Marcus Welby was the only doctor who had patients call at his house."

He stood and pulled on his trousers and shirt, gingerly buttoning his fly to conceal his stymied manhood. He'd been so close to realizing pure bliss.

"Curses, foiled again—or saved by the bell," he whispered when the rapping resumed. "Just a minute. I'm coming." After lighting the lamp, he walked over to the door and opened it just a crack. "Sawyer, what the hell do you want?"

Rose cringed and covered herself with the quilt. Dylan flashed her a crooked grin, despite the unwelcome visitor on their doorstep. Sawyer pushed on the door, which Dylan held closed part way with his knee.

"Chill out, man." Dylan waited a moment, then swung open the door and stepped outside, taking the lamp with him. Rose needed a few moments of privacy to cover that gorgeous body. And he needed to distance himself from the sight of her delectable flesh in order to regain his self-control. "What do you want?"

"Enjoyin' that stuff, boy?" The old man swayed. Dylan waved his hand in front of his face when the man belched corn liquor.

"Man, you're pickled. Don't breathe on my lamp unless you want to blow us both clear to Iraq." Dylan shook his head. "I thought you needed a doctor. Since what you really need is a traffic cop with a balloon, I'll—"

"What the hell you . . . talkin' about, boy?" Sawyer's words were slurred and broken.

"What do you want?" Dylan leaned against the porch railing and sighed in exasperation. "It's late, Sawyer, and I'm tired." *And I want to pick up exactly where I left off inside.*

"Heard you cut Martha's babe right outta her belly." Zeke gave a low whistle of admiration. "Guess you really is a doctor."

"That's what my diploma says." Dylan thought again how impossible it would be to prove he'd graduated from medical school at all—especially in 1982.

"Well, maybe you can help me with somethin'."

Dylan hoped silently that Zeke had a raging case of kidney stones, or something equally painful. *Poetic justice.* "What's that?"

"Appears I got plugged with buckshot."

Dylan caught Zeke as he pitched forward. Lifting his hand, he discovered it sticky with blood. "What were you doing? Stealing?"

"Nope." Zeke's words were fading. He was losing consciousness. "Bushwhacked."

Dylan swung open the cabin door, supporting Zeke with one arm as he peered inside. "Rose, you decent?"

"Yes. What does *he* want?" She rushed over and picked up the lamp Dylan had left behind on the porch. "I see he's drunk, as usual."

"Says he's been shot." Dylan dragged his patient over to the tree stump table and laid him on it with far more gentleness than he would have liked. But the doctor in him wouldn't permit him to deny even this patient his best. Somehow, it seemed appropriate that the very table which had once been wielded as a murder weapon was now being used to save a life. Even if it was a miserable life at best.

The life of the man who would kill his great-great-grandfather in less than six weeks—unless Dylan found a way to prevent it. Allowing Sawyer to die at his hands wasn't the answer. Not one Dylan could live with, anyway.

Rose placed the lamp on the mantel and light shined across the table and the patient.

"Someone visited us today, Dylan," Rose said with a wave of her arm around the room. "Must have been an angel of mercy."

Dylan glanced around the room as he peeled Zeke's soaked shirt away from his wound. "Great." The tiny cabin was fully furnished. It was a miracle he and Rose hadn't fallen over the furniture when they'd come in earlier in such a fervor. Glancing at her now fully clothed form, he swallowed hard. "Jim must've done it."

Rose glanced at her stepfather and sighed. "You want me to help?"

Dylan nodded and looked up at her. "If there are clean towels or rags in any of those cabinets against that wall, they'd be much appreciated."

Rose went immediately to her work, gathering several clean strips of muslin and linen. She went to the hearth and laid a fire, which soon flickered cheerfully in the semidark room. Without being asked, she delivered a pail of water from the spring and soon had a kettle hung over the blaze to boil.

"You learn fast," Dylan said in praise of her labors. Of course, there were other things he'd like to teach her besides nursing skills. After her response to his seduction, there was no doubt in his mind she would learn those skills with equal success. "Thanks."

"I just wish it was a different patient." Rose folded her arms across her bosom. A malicious twinkle gleamed in her eyes. "Then again . . ."

"Doctors don't get to choose their patients, Rose." Dylan determined Zeke's wound wasn't fatal. "He'll be all right if an infection doesn't set in."

"Hmm." Rose grinned when Dylan scowled at her in mock fierceness.

"Could you please pass me my fanny pack, Rose?" Dylan grinned as he contemplated what an anomaly his little zippered pouch was in this time and place. He wasn't even certain zippers had been invented yet, but was positive Velcro hadn't been. Thus far, no one seemed to have noticed the unusual fabric or fasteners.

"What do you need from it?"

"Uh, tweezers."

She seemed to understand what he wanted and opened the pack to peer inside. Within seconds she retrieved the instrument and handed it to him.

"Thanks." He smiled when she turned her attention to the Velcro on the adjustable strap.

"This is interesting." She pulled it apart and stuck it together again. "Works, too. Must be something new you can get in the city."

"Something like that." Dylan looked up at her again. "See if Zeke had a jug with him, Rose."

"For . . . medicinal purposes?" She arched a quizzical brow and smiled wickedly.

Surely she was totally unaware of how devastating her innocent banter was to his self-restraint. Dylan sucked in his breath at the suggestive smile she broadcast. He couldn't wait to get rid of his patient. But maybe the interruption should be considered a blessing, rather than a curse.

Looking down at Zeke, Dylan saw clearly that the hillbilly'd be out for the night. At least in his drunken state he wouldn't feel the pain.

Unfortunately.

Rose stepped onto the porch and returned a moment later with the jug.

"Of course—have jug, will travel." Uncorking it, she handed it to Dylan who passed it beneath his nose, then jerked it quickly away.

"This stuff would sell for a fortune on the streets of St. Louis."

"The Sawyers are known in the hills for the quality of their moonshine." Rose's lips were set in grim lines. "You're not a drinking man. Are you, Dylan?"

"On occasion." He grinned at her and sprinkled the corn liquor over Zeke's wound. "What a pity the old man can't feel that. It probably burns like fire."

"I suppose that's permissible." When Dylan looked up in confusion, she added, "Drinking on occasion."

"Better watch out. You're starting to sound like a wife." Dylan plucked the buckshot from his patient's hairy abdomen. "It's just a flesh wound. Nothing serious."

"Am I?" Rose's voice was light and teasing, her expression warm, almost caressing. "Starting to sound like a . . . wife?"

"God, woman." Dylan shifted his weight to the other

foot to accommodate his responsive body. "You're lucky my hands are occupied."

Rose moistened her lips. "I'm not so certain, that's . . . lucky at all." She pursed her mouth into a pout.

Dylan's blood boiled. What kind of game was she playing now? He'd been certain of her innocence. Now he wasn't so sure. Was she using herself to get to the gold? Whatever her motives, at the moment he was unable to prevent his immediate physical response.

"You're a cruel woman." Her gaze held a promise in it, one he wasn't sure he could—or *should*—hold her to. "I'm hungry."

"Me, too. I'll see what we have around here." Rose walked over to the freestanding cupboard their benefactor had delivered. "Oh, it's full of food."

"I didn't mean for food, Rose." Dylan taped two gauze pads over Zeke's wounds, noticing her confusion when she turned to face him again. "There."

"If not food, then—oh!" Rose's silken voice closed the space between them as her face turned crimson.

Dylan cast her a suggestive glance. "It's too cold to swim."

Her voice diminished to a whisper. "You're hungry for a swim?"

"Among other things," he said suggestively and stepped toward her. "I need to wash up."

"A hot bath would be divine." Rose tipped her face up to meet his kiss. He kept his hands out to his sides, as they were still covered with blood and moonshine. When they separated, he sighed.

"My patient will likely sleep the night where he is.

We'll have no privacy for washing . . . or anything else." Dylan tilted his head. "Unless . . ."

"Unless what?"

Dylan's memory provided a possible solution. "I remember—hearing about—a hot spring bubbling up inside a cave around here somewhere."

"Oh, I know where it is." Rose's expression was eager. "My mother went there a lot when she was . . . ill. It seemed to ease her pain for a while."

Dylan gazed into her blue eyes, sorry for her grief, but relieved she hadn't asked how he knew about the hot spring. "I'm sorry she suffered. If I'd been here, I could have tried to make her more comfortable."

Rose nodded and bit her lower lip. "Let's go to the hot spring for a bath."

"I'm right behind you," Dylan promised, wondering if she really understood what she was inviting. "Just let me give old Zeke a blanket."

"If you must."

"I must."

Nine

It's a little different than I remembered. Shaking off his overwhelming desire for a moment, Dylan looked away from the slim back directly in front of him to glance around the cave. He longed to wrap himself in her silken flesh.

Rose seemed oblivious to her appeal. She stood so near him that as he inhaled her sweet fragrance, his remembrance of her warm flesh was pure torture. Having her so close and not touching her was agony.

"Damn." His curse caused her to turn toward him. A deep blush crept to her hairline. The heat in his loins kindled to a flame, threatening his continued temperance. "Rose, I—"

"Shh." She stepped toward him and, standing on tiptoe, wrapped her slim arms around his midsection. The lantern they'd brought along bathed the cave in golden light.

"Are you still . . . hungry?" Her whispered query echoed through the chamber.

Dylan sucked in his breath. His narrowed gaze swept her upturned face. "You're playing a dangerous game, Rose. I told you, not for food. But I'm very definitely still hungry." Was this for real? Did she want him as much as he wanted her?

Or was she merely teasing him? Taking advantage of his primal male nature? Should he put her to the test—discover how far she was willing to go in order to get her precious treasure?

Dylan laid his head against her shoulder, savoring the feel of her arms wrapped tightly around his waist. They were warm, possessive arms. When he cupped her face with his hand and lifted it until their gazes met, he saw in hers a strength and solemnness which held him captive with its intensity.

Rose turned her face to meet his. She moistened her lips with the tip of her tongue. Her eyes glittered.

The softness of her cheek contrasted against the calluses on his fingertips as he stroked her face. She half-closed her eyes and sighed. The tip of her tongue again moistened her pink, inviting lips.

Could she truly be unaware of her allure? It hardly seemed possible.

Devious?

Or passionate?

Dylan's gaze lingered on her lovely face a moment longer. The insistent throbbing between his legs didn't really care about her motives. He wanted her and she was sending out signals that could not possibly be mistaken for anything but *invitation*.

"I want you, Rose," he said simply.

Her soft intake of breath mingled with his own as he covered her mouth with his. Imitating a more intimate behavior, he probed and withdrew his tongue until she leaned fully against him, moaning in ecstasy which, considering her reaction, surely rivaled his own.

Steam from the hot spring enveloped them, compounded by the cool evening air. Dylan lifted her and carried her to the towels they had placed on a boulder near the lamp. He laid her on the clean linens, his lips never leaving hers as he loosened her dress.

When he dragged his mouth from hers, his gaze searched hers for an answer to his unspoken question. If Rose was merely toying with him, she damned well better confess and end this. Now!

Her nostrils flared delicately as he slipped her dress from her shoulders and removed her modest undergarments, determined no clothing come between them. If she wasn't as eager to feel him inside her as he was to be there, then he hoped she was aware he'd reached and was about to pass the point of no return.

His lips encircled one upthrust nipple. He was eagerly drawing her puckered flesh inward until she moaned and arched against him. Dylan savored the sweet, salty taste of her as he rid himself of his own clothing, completely baring his body to her wandering hands.

Tentatively, he stood, lifted her in his arms and walked into the water until it enveloped them both. He cradled her against him, allowing the water to help support her weight. His lips were free to taste, explore and devour her soft flesh, as the warm water surrounded and cleansed their heated bodies.

"Dylan." Her whisper echoed throughout the cavern, surrounding him with her longing.

His mouth found hers again and possessed it. He was no longer gentle as he pillaged and probed. This woman was his in every sense of the word. All doubts fled—his intentions commanded.

He lowered them both in the water, then emerged

to carry her back to the blanket. This first time, at least, he wanted her on dry ground, where he could meticulously stroke and probe her body in all the right places.

A roaring in her ears made Rose virtually mindless. She knew little sounds came from her lips, but they were uncivilized—even inhuman—as the onslaught of passion claimed and controlled her. His mouth was so wondrous, so delicious . . . so powerful.

How could she have thought, even for a moment, that she possessed enough self-control to use her body in such a devious way? Dylan would not dally long enough for her to demand the location of the gold before he took what he wanted from her.

What she *wanted* to give him.

She ached for answers to these mysteries of her body. Before Dylan Marshall came into her life, she'd been blissfully ignorant of the power of her physical urges.

His mouth tarried, tasted and laved her breasts and abdomen until she thought she'd go mad. A quiver ran the length of her as he kissed his way lower and lower toward that part of her that silently screamed for his touch. She held her breath and bit her lower lip as his mouth made contact.

His seeking tongue descended into her most secret part. He claimed her—branded her flesh.

She was lost.

Rose tried once more to pull back, to recall the reason she'd allowed him to take this beyond the dictates of decency, but he slipped between her thighs and dropped her legs over his shoulders. He buried his face against her insatiable woman's flesh, commanding—unnecessarily—that she yield to his desires. The thought of refusing his possession no longer struggled against this new and wondrous feeling. Her body seemed to leave the cavern floor as waves of ecstasy swept through her.

She was clay—he was a sculptor creating a masterpiece from her madness. Grasping the back of his auburn head with both hands, Rose held him against her. She wantonly arched her hips against him as senselessness consumed her. Higher, higher she climbed until the world as she knew it ceased to exist.

A maelstrom of sensation culminated and she separated from her physical form, floated with the stars in the heavens as oblivion combined with delight to spawn a joy so great she wept from the wonder of it.

Dylan seemed to sense her pleasure, for he finally released her to kiss his way back up to her breasts. Rose winced in stunned joy when he claimed her nipple between his teeth, then drew it into his mouth.

"Please, end this madness," she pleaded in a voice which did not seem to belong to her. The words came from another woman, one who'd forgotten about using her body to coerce this man into relinquishing the treasure.

"Madness, yes," he said, as he climbed farther up to press the evidence of his own desires against the soft flesh of her belly.

Rose's gaze slid downward until she discovered his rigid, male body. Something within her coiled into a tight spring at the sight of his flesh, swollen and throbbing just as she. It seemed right that they join now as one. The hunger within her became all-encompassing, blotting out her determination, her goals, her very purpose.

She reached down to grasp him in her hand, surprised again by how solid he was. She squeezed and slid her hand down, then up to the moist tip. A perverse sense of power swelled within her.

Dylan winced. His eyes glazed over as the veins on his neck became even more prominent. "Don't do that." His voice was harsh yet eager.

Rose released him, relishing her command. This knowledge fueled her desire. She looked at him pleadingly. "Dylan . . . now."

He probed until his maleness separated her protective folds. His rounded tip was barely inside her, throbbing, levying a question of her body—waiting for an answer. She closed around him, drew him inward—answered his silent petition.

His first thrust made Rose feel as if she'd been rendered in two as his powerful stroke severed her maidenhead. Her pained gasp was smothered with a kiss that permitted no protestations. Her body enveloped his, accommodated his insistent maleness.

As he filled her, the burning pain ebbed, replaced by a sensation of completeness Rose had never known before. She shuddered in further anticipation and pressed herself against him.

Dylan's kiss fueled her desire, demanding that she press her hips against his to swallow even more of his large body in the process. Her body seemed to have a mind of its own as it contracted and encased his. She savored the tingling, soaring sensations and consciously—gloriously—followed instinct's guidance.

"Woman, be still." Dylan froze with his body buried

deep within her. She felt his throbbing need match her own. After a moment, his gaze told her he was sorry for his abruptness. "I want this to last."

She had no idea exactly what he meant, nor at the moment did she care. Rose welcomed his thrusts when at last he moved against her again. Her body followed his lead by contracting and possessing him as thoroughly as she possibly could. An exquisite ache replaced her pain and soon gave way to awe.

Each plunge of his body created a soaring glory within her, rivaling even what she'd already experienced. A crescendo was forming, even greater and more devastating than before. Passion overwhelmed her sense of reason as he claimed her as his.

Dylan's movements grew more fervent as she traversed to loftier heights. Rose engulfed his body with a voraciousness which amazed her. Never had she known her primitive instincts could be so powerful, so all-consuming . . . so wondrous.

As her joy erupted in a rush of liquid warmth, Dylan shuddered and tensed against her. The part of him buried within her throbbed—he winced as if in pain. As if in a trance, she reached up to caress his face. But before that movement could be executed, she found another, even more powerful pinnacle.

As Dylan's elixir flowed into her, Rose received it and responded with her own acme. He consumed her like a volcano erupting with hot lava claiming a virgin landscape.

And she saluted his dominion.

He slumped against her as she considered the wonder—and the devastation—of what had just transpired between them. His weight, while moments ago had been quite welcome, now seemed burdensome.

The marriage is binding.

"This wasn't supposed to happen," she whispered without thinking, then covered her face with her hands, awash with shame and regret.

Rose shuddered as the night air enveloped their naked bodies. Her passion cooled as quickly as the mountain air after sunset as the full import of her actions became apparent.

"What have I done?" She shoved at his bare chest until Dylan rolled off and to her side.

"You don't know?" His words were sarcastic, but his gaze was infinitely tender. Those beautiful hazel eyes seemed to caress her as he spoke.

"I'm afraid I do, Dr. Marshall." Rose tried to sit up, but discovered her body felt like lead. Heavy, lethargic and supremely sated. "Don't you see? Now we're . . . stuck with each other."

Dylan flashed her a crooked grin that made her heart flip over in her chest. "I don't think that's necessarily bad, considering what just happened between us." He nuzzled her shoulder with lips that threatened her resolve.

"What happened between us . . ." Rose's voice diminished to nothing as his lips began again to explore her body, taking a swollen nipple between his teeth to rotate, then circle it with his tongue.

Dylan was obsessed with this woman. His blood coursed violently through his veins, making him feel as if he would surely burst if he couldn't feel himself inside her again soon.

Once was not nearly enough.

What was this foolishness taking command of his senses? Rose's ghost had been the lure—a very effective one—to bring him into the trap which had triggered the Keeper's spell. But she wasn't aware of that. She couldn't be.

Every passing moment threatened his resolve. He was inexorably drawn to her. Rose fitted so perfectly in his embrace.

She gazed up at him. "Dylan." Her voice was soft yet daring. "I don't understand this. I try not to feel this way, but I can't help it."

Dylan held her at arm's length to study her face. Dare he reveal to her the emotions raging through him? He shuddered. Cindy'd taken his love and cast it aside with casual efficiency. He held his breath for a moment.

It wasn't fair to expect Rose to give herself to a man from another century—a time traveler. What a bizarre twist of fate this was. Yet he'd already taken her precious virginity, which in this century was a valuable commodity for a woman.

And she was his wife. His responsibility.

"Rose." Dylan swallowed hard and touched her lips with his fingertip. He couldn't say the words . . . not yet. Too many things had happened to simply ignore their implications. He'd been taken captive by the Keeper, cast out of the only life and time he'd ever known. How could he simply forget all that?

But it would be surprisingly easy to drown in her beauty, to permit himself to become enslaved by her. Rose was the woman of his dreams in every sense of the word. A wry smile tugged at the corners of his mouth as he studied her beauty.

Tears trickled down her cheeks. He captured one with his fingertip and brushed it away. "I don't understand what's happening between us, Rose. It's so fast." That seemed such an inadequate explanation, considering how intimate they'd become.

She nodded and lowered her lashes.

He pulled her against him with a fierceness born of desperation. He gloried in her, yet feared her as well. No matter how desperately he wanted her body, he simply couldn't abandon all hope of returning to his own time. The mere notion of remaining in the nineteenth century forever terrified him.

Their lips joined. Dylan knew, in a different time, Rose would be the woman he could love with all his being. Forcing such pressing details from his mind, he probed her soft mouth with his lips and tongue, covering her form on the cavern floor with his body.

The cave was steamy and warm from the spring. His urgent erection signaled his readiness to recreate the bliss he'd found with her only a few moments ago. When she reached between them, down to touch the part of him that literally hurt with the wanting, he released her swollen lips.

"Let's go for that swim." Rose's voice was warm and sultry. There was no trace of her earlier regret. After scrambling to their feet, they waded together into the steaming water. It enveloped them in a gentle caress of ancient origin.

The bottom of the pool was composed of smooth, solid rock. Dylan sighed in anticipation. The hot spring was a haven. He knew it well, because in the future it would be a popular resort. At least the hotel had not yet been built. A smile tugged at the corners of his lips as he considered how the proprietors would react to finding him and Rose in such a clinch.

Dylan savored the feel of the water against his bare flesh. The center of the pool was deep enough to bring the soothing waters to the lobes of Rose's ears. When he released her, she slid along his full length.

The water lifted her legs, supporting her back and shoulders to float on the pool's surface. The liquid lapped against the sides of her golden breasts, liberating a gasp of raw need from deep in his chest.

Mesmerized by the vision of his lovely water nymph, Dylan could only stare for a few moments. Tiny droplets glistened against her bare skin like precious stones. Her breasts stood firm and proud above the water's surface, almost as if they floated apart from the rest of her perfect body.

Her eyes were closed against the outside world, making him ache to join her. This goddess floating before him was his wife.

What more could a man want?

In any time?

Any place?

Forcing serious thoughts from his mind, he turned his attention to his insistent libido. "What have we here?" His light tone masked the gravity of his lechery.

Rose waved her arms in the water and raised her head to peer at him. Sanction blended with raw passion in her expression. "This water feels delicious. I'm glad you thought of it."

"So am I." Other matters occupied Dylan's mind as he took those few steps which separated them. She seemed to recognize his message and returned his gaze with one that took his breath away.

He'd been right—she was a fast learner. In the public schools of the twentieth century, Rose Jameson would have been labeled "gifted and talented," without a doubt.

Dylan reached her just as she permitted the water to float her to its surface once again. A wild thrill pulsed through his veins. He stood beside her, motionless as he studied the intricate details of her body. Her breasts were full despite the apparent poverty she'd lived in with the Sawyer family. Her hips were slightly rounded, and her eyes . . .

Her eyes were those of a passionate and sensual woman, aware of her own needs and those of her partner. But in their sapphire depths, he still saw the sadness of the spirit who'd visited during his sleep a hundred years in the future.

Did he compound her sorrow?

No, he didn't want to hurt her—to make her sad. Dylan wanted only to bring Rose joy and pleasure. There was only one way he knew would banish her sadness—at least, temporarily.

As he reached his hand up to trace the outline of one smooth breast, she sighed in pleasure. Rose continued to float in the warm water, her spirit seeming to meld into her very flesh as Dylan's caresses became more urgent and heated. It was almost as if he could feel her torment, her confusion, the uncertainty that must be ravaging her mind.

Leaning forward, he permitted his lips to rest on the taut peak of her full breast. She doubled up in the water and came back full against him. The impact of their bodies was volatile. He'd known many women, but none in his years of experience had made him burn with such intensity.

Rose was a witch, a goddess, a temptress and a woman of warmth and compassion exquisitely packaged in one irresistible bundle. In this one perfect body he'd found all things. She could be the wife, the lover, the friend, and yes . . . even the whore if she so desired. With a woman such as Rose, a man would never want for anything.

Dylan's lips traversed the distance between her delectable breasts and her mouth. He covered hers in a kiss that was wild, all-consuming and filled with promise. She leaned away from him, permitting his arm to support her back and the water lifted her feet to the surface. She became a toy in his hands. She was his to do with as he pleased.

The azure water was warm against their skin. Rose lifted her head to gaze into his hazel eyes. Blue, sparkling fire radiated from hers and melded into his like pits of violet passion. It was a silent communication between man and woman, an age-old message of mutual consultation and consent.

Rose seemed willing to bow to his every desire, his every wish. For this frozen moment in time, sexual equality and independence paled to insignificance. He felt like a domineering, primitive master—she was slave. When she lay in his arms, her body became his possession—a boost to any male ego.

Rose boldly wrapped her legs around his waist and locked her ankles behind him. The water lightened her weight, making the effort possible. She guided his swollen member deep within her body, smiling when he looked at her, startled.

"You're a fiery little vixen." His whisper was gravelly as he dipped his head to taste her lips again.

They moved together slowly as their obsession mounted. The water swirling about them enhanced the erotic feelings which united them. Dylan felt himself being carried into another dimension of his own existence by this eager and willing woman. His love poured into her with every thrust of his body against hers.

Their passion lapsed into a wondrous world of hidden rapture. Nothing either real or imagined could equal the power of their union, the eclipse, the shattering climax of forbidden love.

As the final spasms subsided, leaving in their wake a mellow but powerful bond, they continued to hold one another in the warm water. Rose showered Dylan's neck and shoulders with tiny kisses. Dylan buried his head against the damp tendrils which clung to her shoulders.

He was frightened by his own staggering feelings. Reluctantly, he released her, permitting her feet to fall to the pool's bottom to support her own weight.

Dylan gazed into her eyes as she stood pressed against him. The throbbing of his climax slowly diminished, replaced by a contentment found only through such intimate contact with a loving woman.

"Airplanes, spaceships, microwave ovens and cable TV, be damned." Dylan didn't care at the moment that she'd overheard. For some reason it no longer mattered. Perhaps, in time, he'd tell her the truth—that he was from the twentieth century, brought back by a visiting ghost. Her ghost. He shuddered, grasping her shoulders and pulling her even harder against him.

"What's wrong?" Rose asked tremulously, seeming to sense his anxiety. "And what was all that about airplanes and spaceships? Micro—something?"

"Jules Verne." Thank goodness someone in the nineteenth century had enough vision to explain some of Dylan's errors.

"You don't believe such nonsense, do you?"

Dylan shrugged and took a deep breath. He held her away from him just enough to permit him to see her face. A pang of guilt swept through him. What would happen to Rose when he returned to his own time? He'd taken advantage of her vulnerability. The circumstances he'd found her in—locked in the cellar to die.

"What's wrong?" She lowered her lashes and bit her lip. Her creamy complexion glowed in the lamplight. "Did I . . . disappoint you?"

"Disappoint?" Dylan shook his head in immediate denial. "Rose, you're . . . incredible. More woman than any man could ever ask for. And far more than I deserve."

She blushed beneath his praise, and when she lifted her gaze to meet his, the expression in her eyes took his breath away.

"You're being silly," she whispered.

Dylan swallowed with difficulty. The Keeper certainly chose the right lure to draw him into his wretched spell. Torn between hatred of himself, anger at his situation, and confusion about his feelings for Rose, Dylan winced. "Oh, I guarantee you there's nothing silly about the way you make me feel, Rose."

She gave him a timid smile. "I must confess—I didn't know."

He cupped her chin in his hand and lifted her face when she tried to lower her gaze. "I . . . had no right."

Rose closed her eyes. "Legally, you had every right."

Dylan gritted his teeth. How could he have a legal right to Rose? He didn't—legitimately—even exist in this time. His credentials, record of his birth, everything proving his validity . . .

"There's more involved here than legality, Rose."

"Is there?" She trembled in his arms and his gut twisted with remorse.

Could he fall in love with a nineteenth-century woman? *This* woman? Enough to forget about treasure? Enough to be content in the Ozarks forever?

Looking down the length of her silken throat to the thrust of her breasts, he sighed. What man couldn't fall for such an enchantress?

But it simply wasn't in the cards.

"Do you like the cabin, Rose?" Why the hell had he asked such a stupid question? "Are you happy there?" *Dylan, what are you doing?*

Rose frowned and looked at him with confusion. "I don't belong here, Dylan. The people don't want me here. I'm an outsider."

Dylan clenched his teeth. Just how the hell was he supposed to respond to that bit of wisdom? If anyone was guilty of not belonging, it was him. "The people will accept you in time." *Time.*

"I've lived here with my mother since I was fifteen, Dylan." Her agitation grew. "I just realized, you don't even know how old I am."

"I guess not." Again, he was reminded of how cruel he was by succumbing to the pleasures of the flesh. He, being the more experienced of them, was responsible for what had happened. What about Rose? What had he done?

"I'm twenty-five, Dylan." Her nostrils flared slightly. "I've lived here in Taney County for ten years. The people have made it perfectly clear—they don't want me here."

"You're different, Rose." Dylan tilted his head to study her. "So am I."

"But you have family here. You belong." Rose trembled and avoided his gaze. "Do you know how much it hurts not to belong . . . *anywhere?*"

How strange. He was from another century, yet he seemed to fit in more than she did. His heart went out to her. Did his feelings of compassion have anything to do with the fact that she'd died? Or was supposed to have died?

How quickly things change.

"I'm sorry." He gathered her close against his chest, torn between a need to run away and to remain in her arms forever. "I didn't mean to make you cry."

She sniffled and laid her head on his shoulder. "Oh, Dylan. I'm being foolish."

"No, you're not foolish." His voice was hoarse with emotion and desire. This lush, naked body pressed so intimately against his was taking its toll on his self-restraint. In his own time, having a short, tempestuous affair with a beautiful woman wouldn't seem so callous and immoral. Generally speaking, twentieth-century women knew the score. But here and now, with *this* woman . . .

She kissed his shoulder. "I don't know. For some reason I feel safe when I'm with you, but—"

"Shh." He felt her hot tears against his shoulder

and kissed the top of her head. "I won't let anyone hurt you. You know that, don't you?"

"Yes." Rose lifted her head to look at him. "I do know that. I don't know why, though—why you would want to bother with me. Since my mother first brought me here, I've been afraid and lonely."

"I understand." He took a deep breath. He had no right—none at all—yet . . .

"You're my wife." Dylan grinned at how odd that sounded. "The people here need a doctor, so they'll be nice to you or they can count me out."

Good God, what am I saying?

"That's blackmail, Dylan." She bit her lower lip, but he couldn't miss the beginnings of the smile she tried to hold back.

He shrugged. "They haven't accepted you because of the Sawyers. Not because of Rose Jameson . . . Marshall." He kissed her quickly on the tip of her nose. "See? Once they get to know you for you, they'll forget about your link to Zeke and his pair of full-backs."

"Fullbacks?"

Dylan threw back his head and laughed. It echoed throughout the cavern. "Someday, I'm going to tell you the whole story of how I came to be in Taney County, Missouri in the year 1894."

Rose frowned and shook her head. "Must be all those Jules Verne novels."

"Could be." His expression grew serious. "What do you think? If I can stand it here—can you?" *I'm totally insane—bonkers—lost it.*

Rose paled. Her gaze wavered and he sensed her withdrawal. "Give up my dreams? Never get out of this place? See my grandmother again? The gold?" She quivered and turned away from his gaze. "I'm . . . I'm not sure."

Dylan couldn't believe he'd actually considered staying in this time just because of an alluring woman. God, what had he been thinking? Cindy'd hurt him that way. Didn't he learn his lesson the first time around? How many times did it take for a man to get it through his thick skull, past the galloping hormones, that women only cared about themselves? "That damned treasure."

"My treasure, Dylan." Her blue eyes glittered as she glared at him. "My father's legacy to me. The reason my mamma died in this horrible place."

Dreams he hadn't even known were growing in his heart, shattered and broke beneath her defiant stare. The pain of losing his wife—his first love—combined with this one and tore at him anew.

Women are all alike.

His heart demanded he wrench himself away from her desirable body, that he reject her for the liar she was, but he didn't. If she wanted to play this kind of game, using her body for monetary gain, so be it.

"Your treasure, Rose? If it's really yours, then— where the hell is it?"

Zeke Sawyer struggled to his feet in the dark cabin. His gut felt as if a badger had torn into his flesh. The hard table hadn't done much for his aging bones either.

He stumbled around the cabin, holding his midsection with one hand, wondering where the damned lamp was. It seemed the doctor and his pretty new bride had left Zeke alone.

A bit of moonlight shone through the window, illuminating the bed in the corner. He swaggered toward it. After all, no one else was using the bed at the moment. Why shouldn't he?

"Zeke Sawyer." An ominous voice infiltrated the cabin from outside. Zeke's mouth went dry.

A memory ripped through him. It had to be . . .

The Taney County Bald Knobbers had officially ceased to exist in 1889, though he knew some of them still operated on the sly when a situation demanded it. But he hadn't done anything to deserve it. Hell, he'd even ridden with the Bald Knobbers for a while.

Looking out the window, he clearly saw a man on horseback on the far side of the spring. A terrifying thought besieged Zeke. Had the man who filled him with buckshot—for reasons he couldn't begin to guess—followed him here? Zeke swallowed, feeling something like he imagined a coon in the sights of Old Bess might feel.

A shot ricocheted off the porch railing, prompting Zeke to slide to the floor beneath the window. He clutched his gut where the doctor had mended it. Religion hadn't played a big role in his life for many years, but Zeke prayed now. Oh, how he prayed.

"Zeke Sawyer. Come out to meet your Maker."

Zeke knew the man would come in after him if he didn't obey. Maybe he could talk his foe out of killing him if he went outside. Sawyer moonshine was considered quite valuable. Bribery sometimes worked wonders.

Zeke crawled to the door, swung it open to pull

himself upright to stand in the doorway. "Hold yer fire," he called, clutching his gut with one hand while he gripped the door frame with the other. "I'm comin' out."

"Zeke Sawyer." The man dismounted and approached him. "You've been tried and convicted by the Taney County Bald Knobbers."

"I never—"

"Silence." The man's voice echoed across the spring as he continued his approach.

Zeke noticed the hideous, horned mask that, to his recollection, only Christian County Bald Knobbers had worn. The white yarn outlining the mouth glowed in the dark against the black mask.

"Taney County Bald Knobbers never wore them masks."

"We do now." The man grasped Zeke by the arm and dragged him around the spring.

Zeke sputtered and staggered. Warm wetness covered the front of his trousers. "Gol-durnit." He tugged at the arm that held him with such iron strength. "Lemme go."

"Your sentence must be carried out."

"Sentence?" Zeke shuddered. He swayed and grasped his throat as an image became visible in the mist. A noose hung from a tall oak, swinging in the slight breeze on the far side of the spring. "Lor' no."

As Zeke was dragged to the tree, he retched and vomited. His gut burned like the fires of hell. But the way things were looking, he wouldn't have to wonder how hot those flames were much longer. He'd have firsthand knowledge.

"Sawyer. Where's the gold?"

"Gold?" Zeke swallowed and held his breath.

"The gold your wife and her kid were lookin' for." The man spat on the ground. "Hell, I oughta just get on with the hangin'."

"I dunno about no gold." Zeke struggled to free himself. "But if you'll spare me, I'll help you find it." Zeke wished he could see the face behind the mask. His heartbeat throbbed in the side of his neck, making the pain in his gut even worse.

"All right. I reckon I can spare you if you do things my way." The man sighed dramatically. "Sawyer, if you double-cross me, you'll die for sure. And hear this, old man—I promise you it'll be one helluva lot more painful than hangin'."

Zeke swallowed. "I dunno who you be."

"When you need to, you'll know." The tall, heavy man released him. Zeke slumped to his knees as the stalker mounted his horse.

"I'll call at your place tomorrow evening. If you know what's good for you, you'll have answers."

Zeke waited until the masked rider vanished from sight. He stood and started walking as fast as his wounded body would permit, not looking back, taking the long way home through the trees.

"Gol-durn Bald Knobbers." He kicked at a tree as he passed, then grabbed his foot and howled in pain. Fearing he might have been overheard, Zeke hopped into the trees until they enveloped him in their protective branches.

Ten

Dylan slipped from the bed, careful not to disturb Rose. Deep in slumber, the angelic expression on her face was the most exquisite thing he'd ever seen.

Angelic but deceitful—what a paradox.

He jerked on his trousers, then opened the cabin door, and stepped outside to watch the morning mist dance among the trees. Stretching, he forced the memory of his argument with Rose from his mind.

The morning was too perfect for such heavy thoughts. He smiled to himself. Who could have thought that after his busy practice in the big city he could find pleasure in the country again?

Uncertainty nagged at him even as he commanded it to leave him be. Could Rose really be capable of treachery at the level he'd accused her of? To give herself to him in order to get the treasure?

Perhaps not directly, but he realized she'd probably do anything necessary to obtain the treasure. But her passion, her innocence, her desire had seemed so genuine. How could such an exquisite experience be pretense?

Stop worrying about it, Dr. Marshall. Just wait this out, then go back to your own time when the Keeper tells you how.

And, in the meantime, continue to live with Rose as husband and wife? He winced. If she was willing to give her body in exchange for the treasure, then she was no better than a prostitute. Why shouldn't he "purchase" her wares?

The idea had its merits.

She certainly was a marketable commodity and he was a very willing investor.

Shaking his head in confusion, Dylan rubbed his hands together and stepped off the porch to attend his personal needs before breakfast. After Rose awakened he would invite her to walk up to the farmhouse with him to check on—

"What the hell?" Dylan froze as he stooped beside the spring to scoop up a handful of cold water. He thought the sun dancing off the trees across the spring must be playing tricks on his vision. He rubbed his eyes with the backs of his hands and looked again.

A hangman's noose hung ominously from a tall oak. It was an obvious threat, but for whom? He walked to the far side of the spring and reached up to jerk the offensive rope down, but it was tied well.

Muttering angrily, he jumped onto a boulder and reached higher to give it another tug. It still wouldn't budge. He burrowed into his pocket to remove his knife and sawed away at the heavy rope. Just as it gave way and slipped to the ground, Rose's scream rent the air in the quiet little valley.

Cursing himself for failing to remove the ominous harbinger prior to her awakening, Dylan threw it down and rushed to her side.

"Rose, it's all right." He gathered her in his arms

to chase away the memory of her deceit. He stroked her hair as she sobbed wretchedly against his shoulder.

"Who . . . ?"

He clenched his teeth. "I don't have any idea, but I intend to find out who and why."

"No." Rose withdrew far enough to meet his gaze. "Promise me you won't."

Dylan had never seen fear as pronounced as what he saw in her gaze at this moment. "What is it, Rose?"

He felt a shudder sweep through her as she leaned against him. She sighed before looking at him again.

"My daddy was hanged." She shook her head as if the memory was too painful to relive. "For murder."

Whoa. "I didn't know." Dylan recalled her mentioning that her father had ridden with William Quantrill in the Civil War. Many of Quantrill's Raiders had turned to hard-core crime after the war. "I'm sorry. You must have been very young."

She laid her head against his chest again. Dylan rubbed her back and shoulders with the flat of his hand. He didn't want to hurt her—so much of her life had already been filled with pain and sorrow. And he was using her, taking advantage of her vulnerability. He silently cursed himself.

"I was fourteen." She trembled again and leaned back to look at his face. "I . . . *saw* my father hang, Dylan."

He flinched. The inhumanity of capital punishment was still alive in his own century. But at least public hangings were a thing of the past—or his present-present—if that made any sense. "How could your mother have let that happen?"

Rose shook her head. "She didn't. She was at home locked in her room that day. My grandfather *wanted* me to see Daddy hang."

Dylan lifted her chin to study her expression. There was no way this terror and grief could be part of any game. Was there? "Why would he do such a thing?"

"Because, he said he wanted me to know what kind of man he thought my father was." Rose turned away and leaned back against him. "That didn't tell me anything—except that society is cruel."

" 'The powerful smash the weaker into oblivion.' " Dylan tried to quote Albert Camus, but knew he fell short. "I'm sorry you had to see that, but this has nothing to do with your father."

"I guess not." She turned to face him again. "It's just that it was . . . so awful. Grandfather died a short time later. Mamma and Grandma never knew what he'd done—that I was there."

Dylan listened to every word, sensing her need to talk. But he didn't believe for a moment that the noose had a thing to do with Rose or her father.

His gut twisted into a knot. A horrendous possibility thrust itself forefront in his mind. Surely not.

Could Rose have an accomplice trying to con me out of the treasure?

"I never knew why she felt this way, but Mamma swore Daddy was framed for the murder because of the . . . stupid treasure." She began to cry again as he turned her to pull her against him.

"That damned treasure. It's more of a curse than anything." Dylan clenched his teeth. He should find a charity somewhere to donate the gold to. Then it would be out of their lives for good. Surely there was some type of organization to benefit survivors of the war. That seemed appropriate.

"Sometimes it does seem like a curse." Rose sniffed, then laughed nervously. "Just think, because of that treasure, I almost—"

"Died?" Dylan arched a brow as she pulled back to look at him. He didn't remind her of the other ways she'd fallen out of character because of the gold. Should he? Now hardly seemed appropriate. He needed to wait—to make certain whether or not she had someone helping her in this little deception.

She nodded very slowly—hesitantly. Turning, she stood on tiptoes and shocked the hell out of him by kissing his cheek. "I almost cheated myself out of knowing what it could be like . . . with you."

Her declaration hung between them. Dylan watched suspiciously as she bit her lower lip and blushed demurely. God, how he wanted to believe her. Was she really glad she'd been spared to be with him?

No, he couldn't fall victim to her charms again. She was a deceitful witch, and it was beginning to look as if she had someone helping her with her dirty work. Yet the fear on her face when she'd first seen the noose couldn't be denied. Not even Rose was such an accomplished actress.

Though she'd certainly been convincing on more than one occasion already.

"Do you really know what you're doing to me, Rose?" Dylan asked as impassively as possible, considering how urgently he still wanted this woman. She was a potent drug with instantaneous addictive properties. Again, his body seemed much more clear on its desires than his mind.

He closed his eyes against the naked truth. He'd lied to Rose about the treasure because he didn't trust her. Yet as much as he wanted to believe her—to feel she trusted him—he just couldn't.

Besides, until he discovered the truth about the rope, he wasn't about to divulge the location of the treasure to Rose. Just in case someone else was after the gold, she'd be considerably safer in ignorance of its whereabouts.

And if this was part of her plan to get the gold, she was going to have a long wait ahead of her.

"I suppose we should get some breakfast." She patted her hair with her hand and slipped from his embrace. "I'm starved, and I know Martha sent some eggs and a slab of bacon."

"Cholesterol heaven." Dylan rolled his eyes as his mouth began to water. It was best to wait and see where Rose's mysterious behavior led. Besides—playing house with Rose, the deceitful wife, was guaranteed fun.

He suspected—hoped—that every opportunity would eventually lead them to bed. The passion he and Rose had shared couldn't be feigned. Maybe her motives were less than honest, but the resulting romp in the cave had been more than mere acting. Of that, he was certain. "Watch out, arteries."

Rose shot him a bewildered look as she turned to go into the cabin. "You talk so strange sometimes, Dylan."

She stopped just inside the door.

"What is it?" Dylan stepped in behind her and grasped her shoulders.

"Do you suppose my stepfather had anything to do with . . ."

Dylan turned her toward him. Her game was becoming more infuriating by the moment. Well, two could play. He'd just pretend to agree with her . . . for now. "Maybe. His wound wouldn't have prevented him from placing the noose in the tree, but his drunkenness might have."

"But why would he do something so cruel?" Rose shook her head. "I'm not so sure."

"Like I said, we're going to find out."

Rose's lower lip trembled. "Promise me you'll be careful, Dylan."

Dylan winked at her, though deep in his gut he felt a fury born of betrayal. She was quite skilled at this flim-flam game—if it was a game. "I promise. I'm not a violent man by any stretch of the imagination, Rose. My mother was a flower child—a hippie when the word was a noun, not an adjective."

"Flower child? Hippie?"

"Uh—er . . ." Dylan laughed at himself, then burst into what he hoped was a tolerable rendition of his mother's favorite song. "The answer my friend, is blowin' in the wind . . ."

Rose clicked her tongue in a fair imitation of maternal tolerance for a wayward youth, then turned her attention to preparing breakfast.

When Dylan picked up a skillet and placed the slices of bacon into it as she carved them off, she gave him a look of shock. "This is woman's work."

Laughter started deep in his diaphragm and grew until he was in the middle of a deep, raucous guffaw. She stared at him in open incredulity.

"What's so funny?"

" 'Woman's work.' " He shook his head in disbelief, then kissed her on the cheek. "Phil Donahue would be proud. I'm a real nineties kind of guy."

"Whatever you say." Rose smiled at him so sweetly his laughter died a quick, clean death.

When he took the knife from her hand and pulled her to him, no humor remained. God, how he wanted her. So much in his life had gone absolutely crazy. He needed to grasp at this one bit of pleasure in the midst of all the uncertainty.

Even though she was the epitome of his uncertainty.

"You're what the natives would call 'tetched.' " Though her words were flippant, her tone was serious.

Dylan took a deep breath and planted another kiss on her forehead. "Shades of Rose . . ." The muse struck him and remained. "You and my dream of the same woman in different . . . dimensions, I guess. Shades is synonymous with . . . ghost, I think. Hmm. Different versions of the same, beautiful woman."

"Beautiful?" Rose blushed profusely. "Really, Dylan, I'm no—"

"Oh, trust me, Rose." Dylan cupped her chin in his hand. "You're that and so much more."

"That sounds kind of nice." She sighed. "You must be a poet."

"Mmm." Dylan kissed her deeply, trying to blot out his feeling of near certainty that she was playing him for a fool. The part of him that prayed it wasn't true reigned supreme at the moment. When they separated, he gazed into her eyes. "Very nice, indeed."

"We're never going to get breakfast if you keep kissing me like that, Dr. Marshall." Rose turned again to the food preparation. "I could use some more firewood, Dylan." She turned to smile at him.

"Men's work, eh?" Chuckling, he stepped outside to inhale the fresh, mountain air. If she was acting, then he could really get into his role. Playing the doting husband alongside her feminine banter would definitely work wonders for his sex life. If that's what she wanted . . .

After Dylan stepped outside, Rose gripped the edge of the table with both hands until her knuckles turned white. There was actually more than enough wood to prepare the meal, but she needed a moment to herself.

The memory of her father falling through the trap door was vivid. His bowels had released as his neck snapped, creating a horrid odor.

The stench of death.

Her grandfather had simply stared in silence as the morbid affair progressed. Rose couldn't recall the old man looking away even once. When the deed was done and his son-in-law's lifeless body dangled from the end of the hangman's noose, the man had sighed in satisfaction.

That's a fine day's work for the sheriff.

Her grandfather's words haunted her.

A fine day's work?

Killing a man was a fine day's work? Rose drew several deep breaths.

Ella Jameson never knew that Rose had witnessed her father's execution. Locked in her room to mourn the loss of her husband, her mother had been oblivious to her daughter's pain. Before anyone began to suspect, her grandfather'd had the decency to die—peacefully—in his sleep.

When Ella Jameson dragged her fifteen-year-old daughter across the country to search for the treasure, Rose's grandmother had said Rose could return whenever she wanted. But Rose's mother was not welcome in her house ever again.

So Ella Jameson had sacrificed herself in a futile attempt to fulfill the legacy of a dead man. Rose rubbed furiously at the tears which threatened to tumble down her face. Her mother was always looking over her shoulder for the man she swore had framed her husband. Whoever he was—he knew about the treasure.

But she'd never revealed the man's name.

"So, the rope was just hangin' there?" Jim asked Dylan after hearing his cousin's story. "You're sure it hadn't been . . . used?"

Dylan shuddered. "Not to my knowledge. If it was, they took the . . . body with them."

"Don't sound like Bald Knobbers to me." Jim rubbed his chin thoughtfully as he packed home-grown tobacco into a corncob pipe. "Smoke, Dylan?"

"That stuff's not good for you." Dylan searched his mind for specific information about the infamous Bald Knobbers. Anyone who'd grown up in southwestern Missouri knew of the vigilante group that terrorized the Ozarks during the late 1880s. "Bald Knobbers."

"Yep." Jim leaned back and sighed. "I never got mixed up with 'em myself, mind you, but I knows plenty fine folks who did." He seemed thoughtful for a moment as he puffed on the pipe. "When they first started up meetin' over to Dewey Bald, we sorta left 'em alone—reckoned they was meanin' to do good."

"Vigilantes." Dylan picked up a stick on the ground near his feet. "Taking the law into your own hands is never a good thing, Jim."

"I tends to agree with you, Dylan." Jim grinned. "They was plumb riled when I wouldn't join up with 'em an' take the oath."

"Oath?"

"Took it under penalty of death, they did." Jim shook his head. "I like livin' too durned much for that."

"I hear that." Dylan chuckled as he used the stick to draw circles in the soil at his feet where one day a cobblestone path would be. "It's even worse than the fundamentalists who are always trying to tell everyone else how to live their lives."

"I don't recollect nothin' about these fundamentalists, but if they's anythin' like them Bald Knobbers turned out, they's no good." Jim drew deeply on the pipe and blew smoke rings in the air. "C'mon. I got somethin' to show you."

Dylan stood when Jim did and followed him behind the house and to the barn. "You remember the litter of pups I showed you the other day?"

Nodding, Dylan wondered if his cousin expected him to be knowledgeable in veterinary medicine. Most country doctors in the nineteenth century probably were.

"I want you to have the pick o' the litter." Jim paused in front of the bitch—she was busily nipping at her eager pups who tried to nurse each time she stood still for more than a moment.

Dylan held up a hand in protest. "That's too generous, Jim."

"No, it ain't." Jim shook his head. "Go on an' pick a pup. Man ought not be without a good dog in these hills."

Dylan considered the events of the night before. "Might be a good idea to have a watchdog." He looked over the puppies, choosing a black and tan male who showed promise.

"Watchdog?" Jim chuckled. "These is prime coonhounds, Dylan. Ain't you never been coon huntin'?"

Dylan laughed. "My grandpa took me once."

"Grandpa?" Jim smiled. "You mean Mary's paw? I thought her folks all died a long time back."

Dylan's face grew warm with embarrassment. His slips of the tongue were becoming more frequent as he relaxed in his new surroundings. He'd let down his guard too much.

"He wasn't exactly my grandpa, Jim." He hated to lie, but the alternative was too bizarre to consider. "He was an old man in our church in St. Louis. Mom and I sort of . . . adopted him as a grandpa."

"Oh, that's a fine thing." Jim seemed satisfied with that explanation. "Old folks can git powerful lonely when there ain't no kin around."

"Young folks, too." Dylan lifted the male puppy he'd chosen, then looked into his amber eyes. "I'll call him Hippocrates."

Jim frowned at Dylan, then chuckled. "You sure enough know lotsa big words. But I reckon that's a good thing for a doctor."

"That it is, Jim. Using big words makes people think we doctors are a whole lot smarter than we really are." Dylan smiled at the pup. He looked down at the bitch. "I think she's ready for him to leave the nest."

"Past ready." Jim chuckled when the bitch stood and walked away, dragging three puppies beneath her as she went. "I'll find homes fer the rest."

"Thanks for the puppy, Jim."

"I'm the one who oughta be doin' the thankin'." Jim smiled and scratched Hippocrates behind the ears. "That's a mighty fine boy you brought into this world."

Dylan blinked hard and fast. If only Jim realized how important that baby boy was to Dylan.

Or was he?

Dylan couldn't exist in two centuries at the same time. Had he simply vanished from the world he'd left behind or had someone slipped in to take his place? Amazing as it seemed, Dylan couldn't see how it was possible for him to live simultaneously in two worlds.

There was only one plausible explanation. What he was living here and now was real.

Did that mean he wasn't the son of George and Eve Marshall? Not the grandson of Sam Marshall? The great-grandson of the Tom Marshall who was now upstairs at his mother's breast? Maybe Dylan had actually become the lost son of the Joe Marshall.

Who the hell am I?

"I been meanin' to ask you . . ." Jim walked alongside Dylan toward the house.

"Uh . . ." Dylan looked at his cousin, or was he his great-great-grandfather? He shook his head in bewilderment. "What is it?"

"Me an' Martha was wonderin' if she'll be able . . ."

Jim hesitated and reddened beneath his brown beard. "You know—have more younguns."

"I don't see why not." Dylan stopped walking toward the house and forced thoughts of his origin or existence from his thoughts. Then he realized how risky it might be for Martha to have a vaginal birth after the cesarean. He swallowed hard. "How old is Martha?"

"Thirty." Jim stopped beside Dylan. "You best not tell her I told you, though."

Some things never change. "If all goes well—and I have no reason to think they won't—she should be able to have more children. She's young yet. Wait at least a year, though." That would give her plenty of time to heal. Maybe he could even teach Maggie Mae how to—

A year? Dylan suddenly remembered the shooting which was to occur in the month of May. Jim Marshall didn't live to father any children beyond May of 1894. That was the reason Dylan had been the last of his line. If he could make sure Zeke didn't kill Jim, then maybe there would be more branches of the Marshall family.

And even if there weren't, he still couldn't let anything happen to Jim.

Jim released a breath he'd obviously been holding. "You had me worried there for a minute, Doc."

"I'm sorry." Dylan smiled. "Your wife and son are doing very well."

"Thank you."

"I guess I need to go into town and pick up a few things for Rose." Dylan glanced at Jim. "You know,

Zeke didn't let her bring anything with her. I'm grateful for the things Martha loaned her."

Nodding, Jim moved toward the front steps. "You plannin' to raise any stock? If you want, I can run what you need with mine. With doctorin', you won't have much time for farmin' or raisin' stock."

Dylan went cold. Raising stock sounded so . . . permanent. But what if he couldn't return to his own time? What if he never found what the Keeper had called the right path? He swallowed and rubbed his forehead with the palm of his right hand where a dull ache began.

He had to give Jim an answer, and since his future was so uncertain . . .

"Being a doctor is busy work. That's true. I guess a steer, a cow, a pig and some . . . chickens." Good thing he wasn't a vegetarian.

"That's a good start." Jim seemed satisfied. "Maggie Mae sure sets a store by your doctorin' skills."

"I take that as a compliment, Jim. Thanks. Maggie Mae's a wise woman—her opinion's important to me."

Jim nodded, resuming his seat on the porch step. "Maggie Mae come here right after the war, when I was just a babe myself."

"She told me she was . . . owned by a doctor before the war."

"I reckon so." Jim shook his head and chuckled. "Maggie Mae's been a blessin' to us folks around here." He turned to face Dylan. "I been thinkin', I reckon it wouldn't hurt nothin' to send for the sheriff about the rope."

Dylan nodded, holding the puppy and scratching it behind the ears. "I do need to find out who hung that rope, Jim." He met Jim's gaze when his cousin looked directly at him. "Rose was frightened." But why should her feelings concern him so much? Her damned treasure was more important to her than he was.

"I reckon as how she would be." Jim flashed a knowing smile. "The two of you sure come to terms in a all-fired hurry."

Dylan's face heated. He squirmed beneath Jim's brotherly gaze. To all observers he and Rose probably did seem like typical newlyweds. But inside he knew nothing could be farther from the truth. He cleared his throat. "She's a . . . special woman, Jim." *God, that's no lie.*

"I know the feelin' well." Jim seemed satisfied with his answer. " 'Course, bein' a doctor an' all, you know they'll be younguns along one of these days."

Dylan swallowed hard. Even though Rose had brought up the same subject, he hadn't seriously considered the possibility yet. What the hell would he do if Rose conceived, then he managed to find his way back to the future?

He looked down at the puppy in his lap, who squirmed and panted happily for the moment.

Children.

If the Dylan Marshall of the twentieth century didn't exist, then he needn't concern himself with genetics. If he did, however . . .

"We'll need to find you a bigger place before then." Jim seemed content to plan Dylan's life without consulting the principal player. "I reckon we could add a couple rooms on the cabin, if you like."

"I'll give it some thought, Jim." Dylan held his breath and clenched his teeth, trying to hide his emotions, though he certainly couldn't have put them into words if his life depended on it at this moment.

Children.

With Rose as their mother.

"The first things I need to take care of are getting my medical supplies and finding out who hung that noose out by the cabin . . . and why." He had to change the subject. His throat was beginning to close with the thoughts scrambling for priority in his mind.

"I'm sorry Rose was sceered." Jim nodded his head. "Womenfolks is like that."

"It was a lot more than that. Rose was shocked because seeing that rope brought back a horrible memory." Dylan wondered if the residents of Taney County knew of Rose's past—of her father. Was it possible they might even know the identity of her accomplice, if there was one? "See, her father was hanged."

Jim took the pipe out of his mouth and sat up straight to stare at Dylan. It was obvious he'd had no prior knowledge of the incident. Why would he? Rose's father had been hanged in Georgia, not Missouri.

"Hanged for—"

"A murder he did not commit." Rose's voice sounded clear and strong from behind them as she stepped onto the porch. "I'm sorry for interrupting, but I want to make certain you understand that my father was an innocent man wrongly accused, tried *and* executed."

Jim rose to his feet. Dylan followed his cousin's example. "I just wondered, Rose. I'm sorry."

"I'm sorry," she whispered, then lowered her gaze, but not before Dylan saw the unshed tears sparkling in her blue eyes. "He was framed. My father rode with William Quantrill."

"Oh." Jim gave a low whistle. "He was in the war, then." The men resumed their seats when Rose sat on the step near Dylan. "That's interestin'."

"Interesting?" Rose's face reddened. "What do you mean . . . *interesting?*"

Dylan took her hand and gave it a reassuring squeeze, though he had no idea why a gesture from him should offer her any comfort. His actions toward her had been anything but consistent. "Rose."

"No, Dylan." Rose jerked her hand free of his grasp and jumped to her feet. "I am so sick of everyone thinking my father was a criminal just because he rode with William Quantrill. Some of the men became criminals after the war. I suppose they were before it, too. But my father was *no criminal.*"

"Rose, we were just trying to figure out who put the rope out by the cabin." Dylan stood and laid a hand on her shoulder. "That's all. No one was calling your father a criminal."

"I . . . I'm sorry, Jim." She bit her lip and lowered her gaze again. "I didn't mean to lose my temper."

"Don't fret none about it." Jim stood and patted her shoulder. "Reckon I'll go see my wife and boy."

"Tell Martha I'll check on her again tomorrow." Dylan held the puppy out for Rose to inspect, wanting very much to take her mind off her father . . . and the rope. "What do you think of Hippocrates, Rose?"

She laughed in delight through her tears. "I'm sorry, Dylan." Her hand trembled when she reached out to pet the happy puppy. "I shouldn't have lost my temper with your cousin."

"He understands." Dylan pushed back a stray strand of hair that had worked itself free from the bun at the back of her neck. The warm spring air made it curl stubbornly away from its confinement. "Don't worry about it, Rose."

He hated himself at this moment. Conflicting emotions fought for supremacy in his mind and heart. This beautiful woman who'd inadvertently lured him into the past . . .

She hadn't been actively involved, merely her spirit had. Rose was as much a victim in all of this as he. At least now she would live. He swallowed the lump in his throat. His breath seemed short and inefficient.

Surely she wasn't deceiving him. It just didn't seem possible. Her grief over her father's execution seemed so real. The terror on her face when she'd first seen the noose this morning . . .

"Jim's a good man." Her smile was shaky but encouraging. "It must run in the family."

He looked at her suddenly, half-expecting to find open deceit in her gaze. Instead, he found her cornflower eyes wide and sincere. Unshed tears filled them to the brims, then one slowly slid down her left cheek. He reached out to capture it on the tip of his finger, to watch the sunlight dance through the tiny droplet.

She's exquisite.

"You think I'm a . . . good man, Rose?" His voice was hoarse and shaky. He should turn around and run, but somehow he just couldn't. The gift of motion momentarily fled. He became a statue, frozen in time, forced to absorb all that transpired around . . . and inside him.

"Oh, it definitely runs in the family."

He kissed her cheek, not trusting himself to do anything more at the moment. "You know, Jim asked me about adding on to the cabin."

Rose seemed surprised. She leaned away from him far enough to see his face. "Why?"

"He thinks we're getting along so well—"

"Dylan Marshall!" Rose gasped in shock. "What have you been telling him?"

He couldn't help himself. Laughter burst forth from deep in his belly. It felt wonderful. "I didn't have to tell him, Rose." He let her take the puppy from his hands. "It's expected."

Before she could protest, he cupped her chin in his hands and kissed her full on the mouth. The puppy, obviously not wishing to be left out, licked the bottom of her chin with his wet tongue.

When Rose pulled back giggling, the happy puppy licked Dylan across the lips.

"Ugh." Dylan wiped his mouth with the back of his hand. "Hippocrates, you're going to learn some manners."

"Why should he?" Rose turned toward the house. "His master hasn't."

"I beg your pardon?" Dylan caught the puppy when she handed it to him. "Miss Manners taught me mine."

"Miss Manners? Who's she?" Rose paused at the doorway to stare at him. "Oh. I suppose you had lots of lady friends back in St. Louis."

"Miss Manners wasn't a lady friend, Rose." The serious moment had passed. Though he knew deep inside they were simply borrowing time until the situation forced them to face the truth, it was a relief all the same not to contend with his confusion for a moment.

A man on horseback approached from the direction of town. They turned to wait for the stranger. He was tall, considerably overweight, at least fifty years of age, with thinning gray hair.

"Howdy." The man reined in his horse and dismounted near the front steps.

"Hello." Dylan held the puppy in one arm as he stepped off the porch. "What can I do for you?"

"You Jim Marshall?" The stranger's ebony gaze went directly to Rose, even though his words were for Dylan.

The way the man looked at Rose made Dylan seethe inwardly. He had no right to be jealous, of course, but he was just the same. It was more than that, though. The man's gaze was insolent, crudely suggestive—even threatening.

"No, I'm his cousin, Dylan Marshall." His words were clipped with intolerance.

The man's eyes widened. "Oh, the doctor." He rubbed his chin as his gaze went to Rose again. "Then this must be Rose."

"*Mrs*. Marshall." Dylan stared at the man. For some reason he felt challenged—intimidated by the stranger. "What business do you have here? I don't believe I caught your name."

"I didn't throw it." The man continued to look directly at Rose. "It's Riordan. Charlie Riordan."

Eleven

Morning fog still hugged the ground as Dylan trudged along the twisting path that led to Maggie Mae's cabin, which was accessible only on foot. Leaning against a gnarled oak, he closed his eyes for a moment and sighed. The scent of honeysuckle permeated the damp morning air, reminding him of another flower.

Rose.

How could he continue to live with her, to make love to her, to want her with such fierceness and still think of returning to his own time? She hadn't mentioned the treasure, or her desire to leave the Ozarks since the night at the hot spring.

Oh, what a night.

But he knew it was on her mind.

He knew she watched him whenever he left the cabin. She still wondered where he'd hidden the gold.

Damn that treasure.

The gold had cost Tom Marshall his life. Rose's father had—allegedly—hanged because of it. Rose had almost died to possess it. Her mother had abandoned her entire way of life to unearth it. And he was stuck in another time—another dimension, because of it.

Rose had haunted him in two centuries. But for the

gold, he might feel almost content in his new life and time. With Rose in his arms, the nagging desire to find the right path almost vanished.

Almost.

What had he lost?

His past?

His identity?

In the nineteenth century he had no past—no identity. If asked to, he couldn't even prove he was a physician. There was no record of his having attended medical school, let alone having graduated at the top of his class.

Hell, there's no record in this time that I've even been born.

Of course, births weren't recorded with any regularity in this time. Many people were born and died in the hills with no record of their existence—unless the revenuers caught up with them, of course.

Then again . . .

Dylan recalled having seen census and tax records at the library when he was in medical school. So there was at least a partial chronicle of the Ozark Region.

But a doctor—even a country doctor—might be asked for his credentials at one time or another. Like if he tried to purchase medical supplies? If he was stuck in this century, then he had to practice medicine. The thought of not being able to work as a physician made Dylan's gut burn.

"Shit."

"That ain't gonna make it no better." Maggie Mac's voice startled him back to the present.

Dylan opened his eyes and smiled at the wiry little woman. The oversized homespun dress enveloped her.

She was just a wisp of a woman, hardly strong enough, it seemed, to endure all she had in life. Born into slavery, then homeless after the war . . .

"What will make it better, Maggie Mae?" Dylan asked cynically, shaking his head in self-disgust. Seeing her reminded him of another error in judgment. "I shouldn't have interfered with Martha's delivery."

Maggie Mae seemed to consider this for several moments. She pursed her lips together until they formed a thin, pale line in her dark face. "That don't matter much now, boy." She clicked her tongue. "You can't change what's already happened."

Dylan laughed. It was a low, frustrated sound. Oh, if only she knew how many things he'd already changed with his mere presence.

An image of the skeleton, then of Rose in the cellar flashed through his mind, making his gut twist. "Maybe not anything else, anyway."

Maggie Mae seemed satisfied with his statement and nodded. "I'm on my way to Bentsen's place. They gots measles."

Dylan jerked to attention. "Measles?" A shudder swept through him. Had vaccines been invented? If only he had his medical books with him, he could . . .

But no. He'd already said he didn't want to change history any more than he already had. "Maybe someday medicine will have a way to prevent measles."

"Lan' sakes." Maggie Mae sighed. "That'd surely be a blessed time to live." She jerked on his sleeve and started walking up the hill. "C'mon. Them Bentsen chillun is waitin'."

Dylan chuckled. What a wonderful old soul. The world would definitely be a better place with more like her. "Will they appreciate having me tag along?" He couldn't help but wonder if he'd be welcome. "I don't recall—" He grasped her arm to bring her to a halt, gently turning her to face him. "Did you say Bentsen?"

"Yep." She looked at him with one eye closed. "You didn't meet 'em at the funeral?"

"No." Dylan shook his head in amazement. Could they be Jeff's ancestors? He could go back to his own time and give Jeff an earful about his heritage. If he could get back.

"Didn't think so," Maggie Mae said, shaking her head.

"Why's that?" They started to walk again toward their destination.

"They don't git 'round folks much." She lifted her bony shoulders in a shrug. "Their maw died with the last youngun." She looked speculatively at Dylan as he helped her step over a fallen log. "I s'pect she coulda used some of the same help you gave Martha."

Dylan winced, but understood her meaning. "I'm sorry to hear that."

"Ten younguns."

"Ten?" Dylan let out a low whistle of awe. "That's a lot for two parents, let alone one."

"That it is." Maggie Mae chuckled. "The Bentsen family lives on up the far side of that knob over yonder there." She pointed toward the west. "T'ain't far."

Dylan walked beside Maggie Mae where the narrow path would permit, until the encroaching vegetation forced him to follow slightly behind. He carried her basket while she used a gnarled walking stick. The little woman amazed him. She climbed the steep, twisting trail with an ease which belied her years.

"Well." She paused and sniffed the air. Wood smoke drifted through the oaks and pines. The dogwood trees had ceased to bloom because it was the end of April, as near as Dylan could determine without a calendar and CNN.

" 'Pears Abel's up to his old tricks." The woman pursed her lips as she looked up the side of the hill.

"Old tricks?" Dylan followed her gaze with his own. Through the thick forest he saw smoke curling upward to the blue sky. Most of it dissipated in the thick vegetation before achieving freedom in the heavens.

"Moonshine. White Lightnin'. White Mule." Maggie Mae arched a wooly white brow as she glanced back at Dylan. "They don't got that in the big city?"

Dylan chuckled. "Oh, yes. But people in town don't make their own as a rule. Nor is it a . . . home business." His face grew hot and his gut twisted as he recalled his first night in the emergency room during his internship. A young girl was brought in by her boyfriend. She died a short time later from a drug overdose. "We have worse things, Maggie Mae."

Maggie shook her head and clicked her tongue. "Well, Abel's liver's been ailin' him some time now. I understand he thinks he needs to make the stuff to sell fer money, but problem is, he samples his wares."

"I see." Dylan grinned despite the seriousness of the subject. "We have that in my ti . . . in the city, too."

She turned back to glance at him and grinned again, almost as if she could read his thoughts.

It was unsettling.

"Menfolks seems to never change."

"Oh, in the city, women are afflicted with alcoholism—are drunks—as well as men." Dylan recalled vividly the mother of a patient of his who came into the pediatric clinic on a regular basis reeking of bourbon. At least her child had managed to avoid fetal alcohol syndrome—nothing less than a miracle.

"Women?" Maggie Mae's mouth dropped open, forming a perfect circle. "Lan' sakes."

Dylan's thoughts turned again to his own problems. He sighed as Maggie Mae paused and continued to peruse him in that knowing way of hers. At the moment, he found her gift more than a little irritating, as thoughts of Rose plagued him no matter how hard he tried to suppress them.

"She's a purty gal. That's fer sure."

"Stop reading my mind, old woman." He sighed when she grinned at him. "Yes, she's beautiful." *I just wish I could trust her.* Maggie Mae's wisdom was etched plainly on her wrinkled visage. "But I had no right to—" He bit his lower lip in consternation.

"To make her yer wife in every way?" The old woman released a wheezing sigh and sat down on a flat boulder at the edge of the trail. "Rest yer bones, boy."

Dylan sat on a fallen log facing Maggie Mae. He stretched his long legs across the trail. The jeans Jim had insisted Dylan borrow, fitted well. He'd have to purchase some in town to replace them. He picked up a stick and twirled it between his fingers, sensing that Maggie Mae was waiting for him to continue the conversation about Rose.

"My wife." Dylan warmed at the thought of her

lovely body pressed against his own in their tiny, mountain cabin. It was the kind of sex dreams were made of . . .

Dreams.

Yet he shouldn't have taken what she'd so freely offered. Even if she was playing a game with him, using her body as ammunition.

A secret weapon the Pentagon would pay dearly for.

He'd taken from her the only thing she was expected to bring into a marriage in this day and age—her virginity.

"Tell me why you don't think you had a right to take yer own wife to bed?" Maggie Mae's frank expression bore no trace of ridicule or disapproval. It was open and patient. "I's lived too many years to start bein' bashful 'bout nature's ways."

Dylan sighed and shrugged. "I don't belong here, Maggie Mae. I had no intention of staying on permanently. Rose Jameson was not mine to take. I knew better, yet I . . . I let myself get carried away."

Maggie Mae was silent for several moments. "It's a tangled web. That's for sure."

"You know Sir Walter Scott?" Dylan smiled at the woman's look of confusion. She'd obviously heard the phrase before, but was unaware of its origins.

"Never heard a him." Maggie Mae tilted her head to the side and closed her eyes, then her wrinkled face split into a wide grin. "But I don't see's how it's wrong." She shook her head. "No, try as I might, there ain't no sign that Rose ain't the woman fer you."

"You . . . you see these things, too?" Dylan swallowed, wondering how he'd transcended the distance from skeptic to believer in such a short time. But then . . . time travel tended to have that effect on one.

"Mostly." Maggie Mae opened her eyes and shrugged. "I sees it as meant to be, boy."

"But—"

"You still wants to go back. Don't you?"

Go back?

Dylan rubbed his forehead with thumb and forefinger, reminding himself she meant the city, of course. He reached down to flip a wood tick, obviously in search of a juicy repast, off his forearm with his other hand. "I do and I don't."

"I see."

"Do you?" Dylan stood and turned his back on Maggie Mae to look back down from where they'd come. Ridges of blue-green mountains stretched as far as he could see. The morning mist had given way to a clear spring day. Honeysuckle and wild violets bloomed profusely along the trail, intermingled with the first signs of the lush ground cover which would soon take its place as spring gave way to summer.

"Yep, I see." Maggie Mae struggled to stand. Hearing her efforts, Dylan turned to offer his hand, which the old woman gripped with both of hers. When he turned away again, she thumped the ground with her walking stick. "Rose is here, but you're in the future."

Dylan gasped and went cold. He was afraid to turn—terrified of facing the old woman. She'd told him she just knew things, but he realized now it was much more than that. Maggie Mae had a phenomenal vision modern science couldn't possibly comprehend.

"I guess maybe you do see." Though her words seemed far too simple to explain something as complex as his situation, they did. Slowly, he turned to face her. The expression in her dark eyes was patience and acceptance. She didn't seem at all shocked by his revelation.

"How long have you . . . ?"

Maggie Mae grinned. "I guessed when you was deliverin' the babe, but I sensed it earlier." She furrowed her wrinkled brow as if pondering the mysteries of the universe. "I know'd another."

"Oh?" Dylan folded his arms across his chest. "You don't expect me to believe people travel through time on a daily basis, do you?"

Shrugging, she turned toward the trail again, talking as they walked slowly up the incline. "I dunno. Could be folks does things like that all the time. I only know of one other, though."

Dylan was properly subdued. How arrogant to believe himself the only person in the history of mankind who'd experienced such an adventure—such a miracle.

Maybe she could lend a clue to the mystery of finding the right path.

"Tell me about the other one, Maggie Mae."

"Well, it was when I was with the doctor down to Washington County, Arkansaw . . . 'afore the war an' all." She chuckled, making the now familiar wheezing sound Dylan recognized as asthma. "This man called hisself Abdul, or somethin' like that."

Dylan assisted Maggie Mae in stepping over a fallen log on the trail. When they were once again slowly moving upward, she continued her story.

"Well, the white folks weren't gonna have none of that. Abdul weren't a proper name fer a nigger."

Dylan shuddered. He hadn't heard that derogatory

term in many years. Again he was forced to reconcile his own feelings toward the crimes of his ancestors against Maggie Mae's people.

"Now, Abdul, he just showed up from nowheres it seemed, on a plantation. The massah there just sorta claimed him since he was on his place an' no one else seemed to own him." She laughed again and shook her head.

"Oh, Abdul was plumb mad. He tried to run away. His massah just put 'im in chains, but still made him work in the fields." Maggie Mae half turned to look at Dylan. "He didn't belong neither."

"No, I'm sure he didn't." How strange it felt to share his secret. Dylan felt his burden lighten as he gazed into Maggie Mae's wizened old eyes. "What time was he from?"

"He said 'twas 1964."

"How did you find out he was from the future?" Dylan paused, waiting for her answer, but then realized how foolish his question was. No one had told her his secret.

"Doc an' I went out to make rounds in the slave cabins. We did that 'bout twice a year to treat fer worms an' such." She closed one eye, then faced forward again to continue their trek.

"That was probably the only medical care the people received," Dylan observed, waiting for her to continue the story.

Maggie Mae nodded slightly as she navigated her way over a large rock in the center of the trail. "When they was a bad accident or sickness we went agin. Massahs took care of their own, mostly."

"Inadequate, at best."

"Anyway, Abdul was called Mose by his massah. He was dragged in to see me an' Doc when we made our reg'lar visit." She laughed and shook her head again. "An' I do mean dragged. That boy was kickin' an' screamin' like somebody was gonna boil 'im in oil."

"So, how did you—"

"He told me. When the doc was outta the room, Abdul looked me right in the eyes an' told me he was from 1964 an' he demanded his civil rights, er somethin' like that."

Dylan smiled knowingly. His own situation was far preferable to this fellow time traveler's. Imagine, being a twentieth-century African American thrust back into the antebellum South. *God.*

"Anyway, Abdul said he needed to git away to find the time door—or whatever—he'd come through. At first, I thought he was plumb crazy, 'til he started tellin' me 'bout the future. He told me 'bout the war and Mr. Lincoln. He told me in his time folks like us had rights. The man was a preacher, he said, an' I believed 'im."

"Why did you believe him, Maggie Mae?" Dylan was beginning to recognize and admire the magnitude of this old woman's gifts.

"I told you before, Dylan. I knows things." She shrugged as if her gift were no different or more spectacular than possessing the ability to see, speak or hear. "Since I was a lil' gal."

"That's quite a gift. What happened to Abdul?"

"I don't reckon you wanna know."

A chill swept through him. He had to know what happened to Abdul. "Maggie Mae. I *need* to know."

The old woman stopped, turned to face him and

leaned heavily on the walking stick. "He runned off lookin' fer his time door, or whatever he called it."

Dylan swallowed hard. "Did he find it?"

She lowered her gaze and mumbled, "I ain't sure."

"Maggie Mae."

With a sigh, she lifted her saddened gaze to meet his. "His massah shot 'im daid before he got away."

The silence of the forest enveloped them as Dylan fought the dizzying thoughts which swept through him. Another man, lost in time just as he.

Was that his destiny? To remain in the nineteenth century for the remainder of his days? Of course, assuming he lived long enough, the turn of the century wasn't far. He almost laughed. Sure, he'd see his own century again—The Spanish American War, World War I . . .

"God."

"It was better that he got kilt than to stay a slave." Maggie Mae's voice was soft and kind, drawing Dylan out of his deep, terrifying thoughts.

"My . . . identity is in the twentieth century. My past. My lineage. My credentials. My ex-wife."

"Yer what?" Maggie Mae's brow furrowed in disapproval. "You got another wife?"

"No, I'm divorced." Dylan forced his thoughts back to the time and place he was forced to live in at the moment. Maggie Mae was an ally. She might be able to help him find his path—his way home. "In my time, many marriages end in divorce."

"Divorce?" She said the word as if it were a vile abomination.

"It means that the married couple don't want—"

"I knows what it means." She cast him a scathing

glance. "You didn't want yer wife anymore so's you got rid of her."

Dylan snorted in disdain. "Not hardly. Cindy didn't want *me*. She got the divorce. Not me."

"Oh. That's why you don't trust folks."

"I suppose," he said with perfect honesty. "Well, we'd better go check on the Bentsen children."

"Yep. I reckon we better." Maggie Mae turned toward the upward trail again, trudging along at her steady pace. "How long you gonna keep your secret from your wife?"

What would it take to get the woman on a different subject? He needed time to think. "Maggie Mae, when I came through my time portal, or whatever you want to call it, I saved Rose from certain death. The Keeper—"

"You knows the Keeper?" Maggie Mae stopped and turned again. Her eyes were wide with wonder. "He comes to me sometimes."

"Can you . . . contact him?" Was that his answer? Could she help him convince the old Indian to return him to his own time? But what about Rose?

"Why?" Maggie Mae's brow furrowed as she frowned at him. "You don't wanna stay here with yer wife?"

"I . . . I—"

"She loves you, Dylan." The old woman snorted in disgust and turned away. "Men is fools."

"She only loves her precious treasure." Dylan touched Maggie Mae's shoulder, prompting her to turn around and look at him again. "She was forced to marry me."

"I don't know 'bout no treasure, Dylan," Maggie

Mae returned in a voice which seemed to combine maternal wisdom with common sense. "All I know is what I sees and what matters. Rose loves you—you loves her. You're just too big a fool to see it."

"I don't belong here. I—"

" 'I don't belong here,' " she mimicked, making him realize how sickening he sounded.

"I'm whining. Huh?" Dylan grinned at himself. Hearing Maggie Mae repeat his words reminded him that Rose used the identical phrase even more often than he did. "Rose says she doesn't belong here either."

The old woman stopped and turned on him again. Her expression wasn't fierce, but it was accusing. She obviously thought Dylan a fool. She shook her head and turned toward the front again, mumbling under her breath. Her words were barely discernible.

"Maybe that's why you belong together."

Dylan was struck dumb.

Her words made sense, yet he wasn't ready to accept them. Was that his answer? His right path? Had the Keeper chosen him to lure into his spell because he was the right man for Rose?

C'mon, Dylan. Get a grip. Cindy always said you thought you were God's gift to women.

He swallowed hard, staring at the narrow, stooped back that continued up the trail. Hurrying his pace, he caught up with her. "It isn't that simple."

"Maybe, but I reckon it's a whole lot simpler than you thinks it is." Maggie Mae shrugged, but didn't halt her steady pace.

Dylan followed with the basket of herbs. He patted his fanny pack to make certain it was there just in case he needed something from his dwindling supplies. But there was little to do for measles, one of those ailments that ran its course despite modern medicine.

Maggie Mae was obviously ready to drop the subject of his relationship with Rose for a while, and he was more than willing to oblige. His mind was in enough turmoil without throwing destiny into the ball game.

Meant to be.

He shook his head to rid himself of such foolishness and took a few hurried steps to catch up with Maggie Mae, who had quickened her pace as the terrain leveled off. She glanced over her bony shoulder once and smiled. It was that infuriating way she had of letting him know she sensed his every thought.

Damn you, old woman.

Well, he'd just change the subject enough to interfere with her reception a bit. "My best friend's name was—is—will be—Bentsen. Jeff Bentsen. If he's related to this family we're going to see, I can just imagine Jeff's reaction to learning his ancestor was a moonshiner."

"Probably is the same family." She stopped, lifting her gnarled hand to point through the trees at a dilapidated shack. "Here we be."

Dylan wrinkled his nose in disgust at the sight of the shack, which could hardly be called a cabin. Empty jugs, fruit jars, burlap bags and a few cans were neatly stacked near the porch. A stench came from behind the little structure, indicating an outhouse which hadn't been properly maintained or constructed.

"Whew."

"Yep. It's a mess." Maggie Mae shook her head. "When the missus was alive, it was different."

"Abel Bentsen." Maggie Mae shouted with her hand cupped to the side of her mouth. "Abel Bentsen."

Within a few moments a man appeared from the far side of the cabin carrying a double-barreled shotgun. He was tall and thin; his skin and the whites of his eyes bore the pale yellow tinge of early jaundice. Maggie Mae had certainly been right about his liver.

"Maggie Mae." The man stepped forward, removing his floppy hat to offer the old woman his arm for support as she stepped across the mud to the stoop. "I thank you fer comin'."

"You know'd I would, Abel." Maggie Mae's tone was almost maternal with Abel Bentsen. "Fer Mary Jane an' the chillun."

"Yep. Fer Mary Jane." The man nodded in Dylan's direction as they stepped into the cabin. "Who's the stranger?"

"Dylan Marshall." Maggie Mae paused to grin at her companion. "He's a school-learnt doctor."

"Gol-durn." Abel glanced at Dylan with an expression suggesting a mixture of awe and uncertainty. "I dunno if I want—"

"He gots the gift fer healin'." Maggie Mae's words seemed to settle things for the man. He nodded, which was apparently the closest thing to a greeting Dylan could expect.

In silence, Dylan followed the pair into the squalid enclosure, as clean as could be expected for a dirt floor. There was almost no furniture, save a bench and table where the large family must have eaten in shifts.

His eyes adjusted to the dim interior as he looked

at the surroundings for any sign of the children. A ladder in the center of the room caught his attention. Following the rungs to the top with his gaze, he saw three faces in the square opening at the top. When the children realized they'd been seen, they vanished.

"Can you get up that ladder, Maggie Mae?" Dylan knew the moment the words left his mouth he'd made a mistake.

Maggie Mae snorted in obvious contempt. "Fetch a pail of water, Abel." She looked him up and down. "The good stuff you use at the still."

Abel blushed, but didn't utter a word in his own defense. Maggie Mae was respected in the hills. Despite her race and gender, she was regarded with more admiration and respect than a college-trained physician could command. Dylan knew that all too well from the reactions from some of the few patients he'd seen since his arrival.

"Maggie Mae?" he asked, realizing his services weren't needed or desired.

She turned from a point halfway up the ladder to peer down at Dylan. "Yep?"

"I'll help Abel get the water and be up in a few minutes."

"Oh, it'll be hard, but I reckon I can handle things by myself fer a while." Maggie Mae grinned. "Been doin' fine before you showed up."

"Indeed." Dylan saluted the woman and turned toward Abel. "Let's get that water."

"Yep. Reckon we best hurry." Abel hitched up his breeches and stepped out into the fresh air. He took a deep, appreciative sniff. "Love springtime."

"Me, too." Dylan looked at Abel in profile. The

shape of his head and the narrow, aristocratic nose were nearly identical to Jeff's. He hadn't realized until this moment how much he missed Jeff. At least now, if he ever returned to the twentieth century, Dylan would be able to tell his friend that male pattern baldness definitely ran in his family.

"So, you're a real doctor, eh?" Abel's voice penetrated Dylan's thoughts.

"Yes." Dylan stepped off the porch. "Which way to the water?"

"If you know where my still is . . ." Abel shook his head. "Don't rightly know I likes that idea at all."

Dylan smiled. "I like a good shot of whiskey myself every once and a while, Abel. Your secret's safe with me."

"Well." Abel put the hat back on his head. He was the image of one of the hillbilly actors who paraded around Branson in the twentieth century. "All right."

Following his host up the hill, Dylan smelled the sour aroma of corn liquor which hadn't yet mellowed with age. Smoke curled up toward the sky, indicating the exact location of Abel's still.

Dylan followed his host's example and retrieved two pails from pegs nailed to a tree near the still. Abel then turned downhill, went approximately one hundred feet and dipped the pails into a clear spring-fed stream.

"This here water's the secret." He cupped some of the water in his dirty hands. "See? Water's as clear as a newborn's skin."

"That it is."

Abel grinned. His jaundiced complexion didn't seem quite as pronounced now. He straightened and walked back to the still, where he placed the pails on the ground and picked up a jug. Looping a finger through the handle, he let the jug fall against the back of his hand and took a long pull of the contents.

"Ah. That hits the spot." Abel wiped his mouth with the back of his hand and held the jug out to Dylan.

Dylan shook his head at first. "Ah, hell, why not?" He wiped the mouth of the earthenware jug with his sleeve and imitated his host's actions.

The liquid burned like the inferno of perdition as it slid down his throat. "Lord." Passing the jug back to its owner, Dylan formed a circle with his lips. "That's good stuff."

Abel smiled and nodded his head, seeming satisfied with Dylan's reaction. "Reckon my secret is safe with you." He placed the jug on the ground near a tree and lifted the two pails. "We better git back before Maggie Mae starts a hollerin'."

Dylan felt a warm glow down to the tips of his toes. "Damn good stuff," he said under his breath, following Abel back to the cabin with the pails in tow. "How do you make moonshine, Abel?"

Abel looked back over his shoulder and arched a brow. "Thinkin' a makin' it yerself?"

Dylan stepped over a fallen log and paused near the front porch. "Just curious."

"Well, it's a secret recipe." He shrugged and chuckled. "Really, just the water's the secret."

For a few moments Dylan had almost forgotten about the children. Making moonshine in the woods had become more important than tending patients.

No, that wasn't exactly true. He smiled. This was

simply the first time he'd truly relaxed since his journey through time.

Except for those blissful moments in his wife's arms.

But even those precious minutes were fraught with guilt and misgivings. He had no right to Rose. She wasn't his for the taking, yet he had taken.

And—Lord help him—he knew he'd take again.

It was unlikely as hell he'd be able to deny himself the prohibited fruit once he'd sampled its pleasant flavor.

Dylan stepped into the cabin with his two pails of water. Maggie Mae peered down from the opening at the top of the ladder. " 'Bout time."

"Yes'm." Abel grinned as he started up the ladder with both pails. "I told you it weren't hard measles. This be the easy kind, I reckon."

"Yep. You was right." Maggie Mae reached down to drag one pail up through the opening. "Where's Henry off to?"

Abel released a long sigh and reached down the ladder to pass Dylan's pails up through the opening as well. "I wish I knew, Maggie Mae."

"He runned off agin?" Maggie Mae clicked her tongue. "It's hard fer a boy to be a man too soon, I reckon."

"Yep."

Dylan followed Abel through the opening. The stench of a sickroom permeated the air in the closed loft.

He squinted as his eyes adjusted to the dimness. Two bunks lined one wall, while a pallet on the floor provided space for four children of assorted sizes and genders, ranging from about four to eleven years, he guessed.

All together, there were eight children in the small beds. An older girl moved around helping Maggie Mae. Dylan's gaze discovered a small window at the end of the room. He immediately went to it and threw open the shutters. Sunlight and fresh air suffused the stale environment.

Abel scratched his head as he looked from child to child. "I thought it best to keep 'em warm, Doc."

"That used to be considered the right way to do it, but trust me—the fresh air will do them a lot more good." Dylan approached the first of the two smaller beds, where two girls peered at him from beneath a worn, patchwork quilt. Their hair was matted and their faces soiled. "Cleanliness would do all of you some benefit as well."

"I tries, Doc, but—"

Dylan shook his head. "The garbage and stench are places for germs to grow. Germs spread disease. I want you to clean it up, inside and out." He glanced out the window, wrinkling his nose when he realized the air wasn't quite as fresh as he'd thought. "And do something about that outhouse."

"All right." Abel looked at his worn boots and shifted his weight. "I reckon Mary Jane wouldn't like it neither. Eh, Maggie Mae?"

"That's fer sure."

Dylan's trained gaze immediately recognized the rash which covered the children's faces and arms. "Rubella," he muttered aloud as he glanced around the room. "Make sure you keep the children away from preg . . . expectant mothers for a while."

"Beg pardon?" Abel screwed up his face in obvious confusion. His oldest daughter blushed.

"Uh, this type of measles isn't serious for the kids, but can be very dangerous to an unborn child." Dylan looked at Maggie Mae, who smiled in obvious approval. "If the mother catches this, it can hurt the baby."

"Oh, I didn't know that." Abel nodded.

"I learn somethin' new ever'day." Maggie Mae bathed the children in cool water and offered Abel some words of advice, which made perfect sense to Dylan. His daughter nodded and resumed assisting Maggie Mae.

"All right. I'll keep 'em in bed fer a few days, give 'em plenty to drink an' soft foods when they's ready." Abel seemed quite capable of seeing to the children's needs. "I's shore glad this ain't the hard measles. Susan Jane here had those when she was a youngun and we purt near lost her. She's had this kind, too. Reckon that's why she didn't git 'em agin."

"I'm glad this ain't the hard measles, too." Maggie Mae's lips formed a thin line. "That's always bad."

"It still is."

Abel shot Dylan another look of confusion, but Maggie Mae nodded in comprehension. "Reckon you can handle this now. I gots to git over Miz Wilkes' way," she said, winking at Dylan from behind Abel's back.

"Oh, is her rheumatiz' actin' up agin?"

Maggie Mae started down the ladder, seeming satisfied that Susan Jane was capable enough to handle the children's illness. Dylan and Abel followed her example.

"Do you want me to come with you, Maggie Mae?" Dylan hesitated, knowing some of the woman's patients wouldn't appreciate his presence.

"Nope. Don't reckon you better." Maggie Mae chuckled. "Miz Wilkes'd just soon shoot you as look at you."

"I'll just skip that visit, then." Dylan grinned and Abel chuckled in agreement.

"I'll check on the younguns in a few days, Abel." Maggie Mae shot him a measuring glance. "Stay away from that liquor, boy."

"Yes'm." Abel looked at his feet again. "I'll try."

Dylan wasn't sure why, but for some reason he remained behind with Abel. Maggie Mae had made it perfectly clear his services weren't wanted at her next patient's home, and Rose was visiting Martha and the baby, where he was to meet her later in the day.

"So, Doc." Abel grinned sheepishly as they stood outside in front of the shack. "You wanna learn more 'bout makin' white lightnin'?"

"Abel." Dylan placed his solemn physician's expression on his face and used a firm voice. "Maggie Mae's right. Your liver's failing and you should stay away from alcohol—liquor."

"I know." Abel reddened beneath his jaundiced complexion. "I just can't all the time. It's like a . . . a sickness."

Dylan sighed. "Abel, it *is* a sickness. It's called alcoholism."

"Well, just cuz I can't drink it, don't mean I can't make and sell it."

Dylan shook his head and weighed his options. He was intrigued by Jeff's ancestor and could use a little male companionship, not that he could make true confessions or anything of the sort. Abel Bentsen would probably have him locked up if he were to hear Dylan's entire story.

As they ambled through the woods toward the still, Abel shot Dylan a measuring glance. "Understand you hitched up with Zeke Sawyer's stepdaughter."

"Yeah, I did."

Abel chuckled. "At the end of his shotgun, I reckon."

Dylan nodded, then regretted the action. He hadn't let Jesse Whorton assume the worst. It wasn't fair to Rose to permit people to think . . .

What?

The truth?

He hadn't agreed to the marriage, nor had she. It had been forced on them by her fanatical stepfather, whose intelligence rivaled that of a fetal pig, no doubt.

"That's how it happened, yes. But—"

"Ah, don't fret, Doc." Abel grinned again, displaying two missing front teeth. "These things always works out fer the best."

Dylan looked at Abel Bentsen in a new light. "You're pretty smart for a hillbilly, Abel."

"Hillbilly." Abel chuckled and shook his head. "I come from back East with my folks when I wuz just a boy. My paw had a hankerin' to go West. This was as fer as we got. Buried both my folks when I wuz eleven year old. Was alone till I got hitched." He stopped and stared off toward the high ridge to their left where three crude crosses marked the family graveyard. "Now that she's gone . . . the younguns is all I got."

Dylan swallowed the lump in his throat. He placed a reassuring hand on Abel's shoulder. One of those "younguns" would be Jeff's direct ancestor. "That's all the more reason to take care of your health, Abel. *They* need *you.*"

Abel removed his hat and scratched his head. "Damned if you ain't right, Doc. I'm sellin' out. That's it. I'll sell you my still an' the white lightnin' that's done made and stored up."

"Hold on a minute there, Abel, I—"

Abel turned toward him with a wide, pleading expression. "Don't you see? I can't just quit with it here."

Dylan sighed. Hell yes, he understood. How could anyone expect Abel to give up drinking when he manufactured it on a continual basis? Surely Dylan could find some medicinal purpose for the jugs of corn liquor.

"All right, Abel." Dylan reached into his pocket and pulled out five twenty-dollar gold pieces. He wrapped his hand around them for a moment, wondering how much they'd be worth in his own time.

A helluva lot more than a lousy hundred bucks.

Abel stared in awe at the coins Dylan placed in his open palm. "This is too much, Doc." He shook his head and held his hand out for Dylan to take back part of the money. "I can't."

"For prime stuff like you make and the secret recipe to go with it?" Dylan chuckled and shook his head.

He felt wonderful.

Fabulous.

The wretched treasure was finally beginning to do someone some good instead of harm. "And this is only the down payment. There will be nine more payments equal to this amount—*if*—"

"I know'd it." Abel sighed. "What?"

"You have to promise me you'll stay sober for the children—and for yourself." Dylan didn't take his gaze off Abel while the moonshiner pondered his options. He sensed that when the man gave his word it would be for keeps. "For every week you stay sober, I'll give you one hundred dollars until you've collected an entire thousand."

Abel swallowed hard. His Adam's apple bobbed up and down in his long neck. A film of sweat coated his brow. "Done."

Twelve

Rose stepped out the back door of the farmhouse to replace the pail at the well. She paused for a moment to gaze up at the sky. Clouds were gathering. Springtime in the Ozarks often brought violent weather.

Martha and the baby were napping and Rose had spent the day baking bread and doing the churning. There'd be enough bread and butter, along with the remaining items Martha had put up last fall from the garden to last them at least a week.

By then Martha would be up and about, at least enough to handle the light chores. Jim could help her with the rest.

Dylan had mentioned something about needing to purchase medical supplies. Would he take her to the city with him?

To Springfield? Civilization?

How long had it been since she'd seen a community any larger than Dogwood, Branson or Forsythe? She recalled Atlanta with its bustling citizens and excitement. She and her mother had traveled to Springfield once on the train the year before Ella's death.

What a wonderful experience that had been. Rose hugged herself in recollection of her awakening. The women carrying signs down the main street had stunned her at first. But while her mother saw the special doctor there who'd given them the bad news about Ella's illness, Rose had received an education.

Those women with the signs were suffragettes. The New Women. Their lives were dedicated to freedom from men, liberation from oppression.

Rose bit her lower lip as she recalled her own weakness for men. At least, her weakness where one man was concerned. Some strong, independent New Woman she'd turned out to be. She'd fallen into bed with the first man who came along.

But Dylan was her husband. Even though they'd been forced to marry at the end of Pappy Zeke's shotgun, they were still husband and wife. Morally, that made her surrender to his seduction quite acceptable—expected.

But as one of the New Women, it made her a failure.

"Warm today."

Rose whirled around to ascertain the owner of the voice intruding on her thoughts. Charlie Riordan, the new farmhand Jim had hired, smiled at her as he removed his hat. His silver hair glistened in the sunlight; his dark eyes crinkled at the corners when he smiled.

"Didn't mean to frighten you, miss." He grinned sheepishly and looked at the ground.

"Not at all, Mr. Riordan." Rose returned his smile, then turned toward the house.

"Mrs. Marshall?"

Rose stopped and turned to look at him again. He shifted his weight to his other foot, then looked up at her. "I heard Jim Marshall talkin' to a man at the mill down in Dogwood earlier."

"Yes?" Rose felt uncomfortable, wondering what gossip this man had overheard.

"Well, not to be eavesdropping or anything, but I heard the man say your maiden name was Jameson." He turned the straw hat in both hands.

Rose reddened. He must have been talking to Zeke or one of the boys. "Yes, it was."

"I knew a man name of Jameson back in the war, and—"

Rose took a startled step toward him and reached for his hand which still clutched the hat. "You knew my father—Hank Jameson?"

"Hank. Yes, ma'am. I sure did." Charlie looked at her and grinned. "He was my partner. We rode with . . ." He looked from side to side. "William Quantrill."

"I know." She waved her hand to dismiss his obvious anxiety about his wartime activities. "Quantrill's a legend around here, Mr. Riordan." Her heart beat wildly in her throat. Her father. How she'd ached for stories about him—to know him as she'd never been allowed.

"I'd sure like to look him up." Charlie's expression seemed eager. "Does he live nearby?"

Rose lowered her gaze. "My father died eleven years ago, Mr. Riordan." Surely, if he'd spoken to her stepfather, Charlie must have realized her mother couldn't have remarried otherwise.

"I was afraid of that when I heard Zeke Sawyer claim he was your stepdaddy." Charlie shook his head. "I never knew your mother, but I can't imagine why she'd marry up with someone like that old hillbilly. No disrespect intended, ma'am."

"None taken, Mr. Riordan." Rose released his hand and sighed. "I'd like to hear about my father, if you don't mind talking about the war and all. I never really knew him. He traveled a great deal even after the war."

"Why, I'd be proud to tell you about Hank, Mrs. Marshall." His expression was solemn and he seemed sincere. "He was quite a character. I never knew a soldier as brave as Hank."

Rose brightened and smiled. "Really? Truly?" Her grandfather *had* been mistaken. "My grandparents thought he was—"

"Oh, he spoke of his wife's family during the war." Charlie winked. "There was no love lost there."

"No." Her face grew warm with embarrassment. "Come inside for some coffee and fresh bread."

"Oh, I couldn't—"

"Yes, you could." Rose took his hand and gave it an encouraging tug. "It's just out of the oven."

"Well, how can a man resist fresh bread? Thanks, Mrs. Marshall."

Rose flinched at hearing him address her as Mrs. Marshall again. Each time she heard her married name was a painful reminder of what a sham the liaison truly was, and what a failure she was as a suffragette dedicated to a noble cause.

This man had known her father—that made him practically family. "Please, call me Rose, Mr. Riordan." She released his hand and stepped into the kitchen while he held the door for her.

"Well, thank you, Miss Rose." Charlie stepped in, permitting the door to shut behind him. "Your daddy was fond of roses, as I recollect. I think he said it was your mamma's favorite flower."

"It was." Rose took a deep breath and trembled slightly. Her voice dropped in volume as she fought against her demanding tears. "It was."

"Forgive me." Charlie stepped up behind her at the table and placed his hand on her shoulder. She turned to face him and he pulled her into his arms for a fatherly hug. "I didn't mean to make you cry, Miss Rose. Your daddy'd shoot me for sure if he was alive to know I made his little girl cry."

A sob tore at her throat and she laid her face against his chest. He felt warm and safe, like the father she'd lost so long ago. Tears streamed down her face as she wept in silence for several moments.

"Forgive me, Mr. Riordan, I—"

"Charlie." His voice was soft and comforting. "You call me Charlie, now. Hank's girl calling me 'Mr. Riordan' don't set right somehow."

"Charlie." His arms were still around her when the back door swung open. Expecting Jim, Rose was stunned to look up and meet the smoldering hazel gaze of her husband.

"Rose. Riordan." Dylan's voice was tight and gruff as he crossed the room to the back stairs and left the room without another word.

Rose pulled against Charlie's embrace to follow her husband, but the large man gently restrained her.

"Let him be." Charlie's voice was slightly scolding. "If he's good enough for you, he's good enough to understand this. Your father wouldn't have wanted his daughter to crawl after a man who didn't really want her."

Rose froze.

A man who didn't really want her.

No, Dylan didn't want her. Her face flooded with heat and her stomach twisted. She forced herself to meet Charlie's gaze, shocked to discover that he seemed to know everything.

"You know?" Her voice quivered.

Releasing a long sigh, he permitted her to move away as his hands dropped to his sides. "It's the talk of the town. I didn't wanna tell you, but figgered you'd find out for yourself soon enough."

Rose's eyes widened and she bit her lower lip. "The talk of the town?" A nervous, tittering laugh bubbled forth from her distress. "Rose Jameson—the girl who doesn't belong anywhere—married to a man who was forced at gunpoint."

"Stop this right now." Charlie's voice was firm and level. "Your daddy wouldn't like this one bit. Even though you weren't born when I knew him, he often spoke of the day when he'd have children. He loved your mamma very much, and I know he'd be right proud of you."

"Thank you, Charlie." Rose turned toward the loaf of bread covered with a cloth on the sideboard. "Just let me slice some of this bread for you."

"No need." Charlie reached for her shoulder and turned her toward him. "What I want is to make sure you're happy. See, your father saved my life during the war and I owe him. Since he's not around to repay in person, well—"

"Charlie, that isn't necessary." Rose smiled at his tender words. "It's very thoughtful, though."

"More than thoughtful. It's duty. I want to. I could be sort of an . . . uncle, maybe."

Rose stared at Charlie in amazement. "Uncle?" The thought appealed to her. Having family again . . .

"Why not?" Charlie chuckled and patted her cheek with a beefy hand. "I'll protect you like your daddy would if he was around." He glanced meaningfully up the stairs. "I know he wouldn't put up with any man mistreating you."

"Dylan hasn't mistreated me." Rose shook her head, awash with guilt for speaking ill of her husband. Not that he'd displayed any intention of making their marriage permanent.

Except in bed.

"Maybe not . . . physically." Charlie's face reddened with anger. "If he ever so much as looks at you the wrong way, though—"

"But it won't be necessary." She pulled away from him and sliced the bread, knitting her brow in consternation.

The passion in their marriage bed had been so intense she almost forgot sometimes that Dylan had been forced to marry her.

At the end of a double-barreled shotgun.

Held by a maniac.

She didn't stand a chance. Dylan might have wanted her physically . . . at first. But passion waned in time, or so she'd been told. Some stronger bond held married couples together.

Love.

Not just mere physical lust, though it could prove quite pleasant indeed. She felt hot all over just thinking about the way Dylan had touched her, branded her—made her his woman.

His wife.

"I'd best be getting back out to the barn." Charlie gave her hand a squeeze, then released her. "Can I call on you sometime, Miss Rose?"

Rose shook her head. "Oh, of course, Charlie." She forced a smile, even though her body burned with longing and her heart constricted with doubt. "We live down by the spring."

Nodding, he donned his hat and left the house, whistling a tune her father had liked.

"It's almost like having Daddy back."

"What?" Dylan held his breath, hoping he hadn't heard what he thought.

"I reckon you heard me good enough." Martha held her healthy son to an engorged breast. The baby rooted and settled in for serious nursing right away. "I weren't dreamin'."

Dylan's face grew warm. "Martha, you were heavily sedated. I don't think—"

"I know what I heard." Martha lifted her chin. Her flaming red hair hung around her shoulders in a riot of curls and her blue eyes flashed angrily. It was clear she meant business and wouldn't accept any excuses or flimsy explanations.

"Tell me again what you think you heard, Martha." Dylan pulled a chair near the bed and sat down. How the hell was he going to get out of this mess?

"I heard you sayin' you'd just delivered your own great-grandfather." Martha's eyes glistened as if they were filled with tears. "Now, don't set there an' tell me I was dreamin' it. I know t'ain't so."

Dylan lowered his gaze and cleared his throat. Folding his hands in front of him, he rested his chin on them for a few moments while he considered his rather limited options.

She knew the truth. That's all there was to it. At least, she knew a part of the truth. What must be running through her mind right now?

He had to tell her . . . everything.

"Yes." Dylan lifted his gaze to meet the shocked expression in his great-great-grandmother's blue eyes. "I'm Dylan Marshall, M.D., born in the year of our Lord . . . 1961." She gasped, but he rushed on. "And your great-great-grandson."

"How can it be?" Martha leaned forward with the baby still pressed to her breast. "How—"

"I don't know how exactly." Dylan sighed and stood to walk over to the window. "I was asleep in this room. March the twenty-ninth, 1994."

"Go on," she urged in a hushed tone.

Dylan could tell by the sounds Tom made that she was changing breasts as he stared out the window. He didn't have to look to identify the mewling of a hungry newborn.

"The view from this window is much the same a hundred years from now." He turned toward her. "Grandma."

"Grandma." Martha said the word as if trying it out for size. Her lower lip trembled. "The Lord do work in mysterious ways, boy. See this baby? He sent you here to save him."

"Martha, if this baby hadn't survived, *I* wouldn't

exist." He held his hands up helplessly and approached the bed. "I meddled in history."

Martha frowned, then smiled. "No, He wouldn't a brought you here if it weren't for a good reason. Every woman dreams of seein' her grandchildren. Now, just think—I'm here with my own great-great-grandson."

Dylan had to smile. It was indeed a miracle to be here in the room, sharing himself with Martha Marshall—a woman who'd only existed as a name in the family Bible in his time. He reached out to touch her cheek.

"You must be right, Martha." He released a sigh. "You and Maggie Mae are the only people who know the truth."

"Well, I'd like to hear the rest of this story, Dylan." Martha was using her "no nonsense" voice Dylan had heard before. "Set yourself right down here and tell me how you got to go back in time."

Dylan did as he was told. It was plain Martha wouldn't tolerate any reluctance on his part. Where to begin? Well, he could hardly tell her he was lured here by an insatiable ghost.

Despite his best efforts, he started to laugh. He laughed until he couldn't bear it, yet it was healing, soothing to his frazzled mind.

"Dylan." Martha chuckling and grabbing her incision with her free hand. "It hurts me to laugh."

"I'm sorry." Dylan dried his eyes with the back of his sleeve. "To me, it feels good to laugh."

"Fine, now tell me."

Dylan leaned back in the chair and crossed his legs. "Well, the cabin down by the spring was . . . haunted."

"I don't believe in hants."

"Neither did I, but it was a fact. The ghost in the cabin was . . . Rose."

"*Rose?*" Martha gasped and leaned toward him. "Are you sure?"

"Positive." He cleared his throat as the memory of his powerful dreams returned. "Very sure."

"How?"

His expression grew somber. "Tom Marshall—the first one, that is—sealed her in the cellar with—"

"Gold." Martha frowned and her face reddened. She lowered her gaze for an instant, then looked at him again. A tear trickled down her cheek. "I done a terrible thing, Dylan. I kept the gold a secret from Jim."

Dylan stared at her in horror. Even his own great-great-grandmother was in on this? "How did you know about the gold?" His insides twisted. This torture had to end soon. He couldn't take much more.

She sniffled. "I'm the one who found Tom that mornin' real early." Her lower lip trembled and another tear escaped. "A pouch of gold coins was in his hands when I found 'im. I was gonna show it to Jim the mornin' you showed up. I didn't wanna lie to him, but I just knew he'd go tell the law."

"You wanted it for yourself."

"Not really." She leaned closer and whispered. "I just figgered if word got out there was gold around these parts, folks'd be crawlin' on every inch a ground we got lookin' for more."

Relieved, Dylan returned to sit down in the chair he'd vacated earlier. He was cognizant of another memory niggling at the edges of his mind, but it seemed reluctant to make itself clear yet.

"I understand, Martha." It seemed strange to address her by her first name now that they were out of the closet about their true relationship.

"Do you?"

Dylan straddled the chair and laid his chin on the backs of both hands. "Yes, I do."

"Then, you'll help me tell Jim?"

Zeke Sawyer shot and killed Jim Marshall over a pouch of gold . . .

Relief mingled with uncertainty glutted him. Had history already been altered enough to ensure Jim's safety on May eleventh? Dylan couldn't take any chances, but this was good news. At least Jim didn't know about the pouch of gold that could get him killed.

Dylan lifted his brows and grinned, wondering how she'd react to the rest of his story. "I think it's best to keep it a secret a while longer. Please, Martha? Besides, don't you want to know how much gold there really is? And where it is?"

She stuck out her chin. "No."

"A fortune."

She gasped. "Really?"

Dylan nodded. "Rose supposedly came across Tom down at the cabin by accident while he must've been hiding the treasure in the cellar. From her story, it sounds like he went a little crazy before he put that old tree stump table over the opening. He . . . he sealed her in the cellar with a lantern."

Martha paled. "Dear Lord. Poor Rose." The woman wiped a tear away and stared at Dylan. "I just don't hardly see how Tom could move that table by hisself. Guess that's what killed 'im."

"I'm sure it was the catalyst. I had to have help moving it myself." Dylan shuddered. His lovely Rose locked in that cellar to die a slow, terrifying death . . . His voice diminished to little more than a tortured whisper. "It's no wonder she haunted the place. What a terrible way for her to . . . die."

"Why and *how* did you git here?"

"My grandfather—Sam Marshall—"

"Sam? And to think we thought you was Joe's boy."

"It was convenient." Dylan arched a brow and smiled. "Anyway, my grandfather left me this farm in his will, but there was a condition to my inheritance of the land where the cabin and spring are."

"Oh?"

"I had to move in and live there for at least thirty days." Dylan shook his head. "I can't begin to tell you how terrified I was to do that. When I was a kid, Jeff Bentsen and I—"

"Bentsen?"

Dylan nodded. "Abel's descendant. Jeff and I saw . . . her."

"Rose?"

"Yes . . . her ghost." Dylan felt cold. The thought of Rose . . . "We never went back to the cabin. So, when I learned I had to live in it . . ."

Martha chuckled, then frowned. "I see. But near as I can figger, you musta saved Rose, since old Tom's dead an' she ain't."

Dylan sighed. "The Keeper—you've heard of him, I trust . . . ?" She rolled her eyes and nodded. "He apparently cast some sort of spell on the cabin after Tom entombed Rose. When I moved the table blocking the trap door and opened the cellar I saw—"

"Oh!" Martha covered her mouth with her hand. "Lord. You seen Rose."

"Her . . . remains." Dylan's voice grew weak. The true impact of what would have happened to Rose had he not traveled back in time seemed even more horrifying when spoken aloud.

"So, you did save her." Martha seemed relieved. She leaned her head against the pillow and sighed. "I'm glad. Zeke's trash, but Rose an' Ella always seemed like nice folk. A bit queer, mind you, but nice." She chuckled and shook her head, placing the baby on her shoulder and patting his back. He grunted in apparent satisfaction.

"Rose was always purty outspoken as I recollect," she continued after the baby dozed off on her shoulder. "When they first showed up here, Rose raised all kinds of trouble about there bein' no school in Dogwood. She was hankerin' to finish her schoolin'. Her mamma got the town to open the church durin' the week for school. Ella taught for a few years, before she took sick."

Again Dylan felt that prick of penitence for his deceit. In hiding the treasure from Rose he had forced her to continue her exile. He had firsthand knowledge of how intelligent and determined she was. All she wanted was to return to her family in Georgia. Who was he to deny her that opportunity?

Against his will, Dylan recalled the sight of his wife in Charlie Riordan's arms downstairs. His blood boiled at the mere thought of another man touching her. The fact that Riordan was an old man did little to appease Dylan's jealousy.

"What about the gold, Dylan?" Martha tilted her head. "Did it travel back in time with you?"

Dylan nodded and swallowed hard. "I've hidden it."

"I see. What of your wife?"

"She was searching for the gold." He frowned and his stomach churned. "Her mother came here looking for it and ran out of funds. That's why she married Zeke Sawyer."

Martha nodded as if that made sense. "Go on."

"Rose's father rode with Quantrill in the war." He paused to wait for any reaction from Martha. Seeing none, he continued, "Apparently, he hid the gold in a cave. Before he died, he told Ella Jameson how to find it. Obviously, his instructions weren't specific enough, because she never did."

Martha pursed her lips. "But Tom did. An' so did Rose, it seems."

Dylan's guilt resurfaced. "So did Rose." It wasn't his gold to hide. Didn't Rose have a right to it? But did he have a right to Rose? His insides wrested.

"Will you . . . stay?" Martha looked at him anxiously.

Dylan's heart raced. "I seem to have no choice in the matter—one way or another."

Reaching for the doorknob, Rose hesitated, listening to Martha's question. *Will you stay?* Dylan's answer . . .

She restrained the sigh which threatened to betray her presence. Leaning her forehead against the cool doorjamb, she strained to hear their conversation. Did Dylan mean to take the treasure and abandon her? Leave her stranded for eternity in this godforsaken place?

She wouldn't tolerate it. Taking a deep breath, she lifted her gaze, watching Dylan in profile as he conversed with his cousin. If only she'd arrived a few moments earlier, perhaps she could have overheard more of what had led up to his declaration.

No choice in the matter.

Was he speaking of their marriage? But they'd been talking about the gold when she first discovered the door open just enough to permit her eavesdropping.

My gold.

Dylan bobbed his head. His auburn hair fell across his forehead in disarray. His obvious state of anxiety accentuated his strong cheekbones and aquiline nose. His hazel eyes were hooded and unfathomable.

Was he truly considering leaving her?

But why should he remain? He was a physician, capable of making a successful future anywhere of his choosing.

And he was a dashingly handsome man. Women would fall at his feet, no doubt.

Most women.

But not me.

Yet isn't that precisely what she'd done? As she considered her behavior in Dylan's presence, Rose felt her face grow hot and her legs weak.

Her passion-starved body had responded to his touch like a timberland to flames after being denied precious rain. To think her entire life had been spent in contented ignorance of the pleasures of the flesh, only to have her carnal nature burst to fruition with the barest impetus.

And, oh how she'd gloried in it—those stolen moments in Dylan's arms. Try as she might, Rose could not deny the truth. She did not regret her surrender.

She reveled in it.

Yet it was temporary at best. Dylan would leave her and she would once again be stranded in the Ozark Mountains, far away from what remained of her family in Georgia.

No. I won't let it happen.

Somehow she had to prevent the inevitable. Dylan was free to leave, of course. She had no way of preventing him from doing so. But not with her treasure—at least not all of it. No matter what it took, Rose would not be stranded again.

But the thought of him leaving—though she told herself it didn't matter—tore at her. Rose felt unshed tears stinging her eyes, threatening to trickle down her face at any moment.

Dylan's going to leave me. He doesn't love me.

"So, you don't wanna stay?"

Martha's voice invaded her thoughts. Rose returned her attention to the pair inside the room. There was always the possibility that Dylan would betray the location of the treasure.

Her treasure.

Her parents' legacy. What right did anyone have to deny her the very thing her parents had both died for?

Dylan shrugged. "I'm not sure what I want, Martha." His voice sounded sad—almost desperate.

"Is it . . . Rose?"

The hairs on the back of her neck pricked to life at the mention of her own name. Rose held her breath in anticipation of Dylan's next words. Would he deny the feelings which were growing between them?

"I had no right to . . . to touch her." Dylan looked away from Martha, turning completely away from the doorway to face the window. "She's young. Someone else will come along."

There will never be anyone else.

"She's married to you, Dylan. Whatever you wants to say or think, she can't wed another when she's already married to you." Martha shook her head as she looked anxiously at Dylan.

"But is it a legal marriage, Martha?" His voice rose as he turned to face his cousin. His nostrils flared in obvious anger. There was something like desperation in his voice. "How can it be legal when I do not even exist?"

Totally baffled, Rose bit her lower lip. What nonsense was this? Of course he existed. There he was, talking to his cousin.

"That's just foolish talk, Dylan." Martha sighed, shifting her infant son to her other shoulder. " 'Course you exist."

"Do I?" Dylan stood and paced the room with his hands shoved deep in the pockets of his dungarees. She could see them balled into fists, those hands that had touched her with such tenderness.

"Dylan—"

"Tell me, Martha. How can I exist in both places at once? How can I lead a double life? Does the Dr. Dylan Marshall who practiced pediatrics in St. Louis really exist?" He returned to his seat and slumped into it. "Think about it."

"I . . . I dunno." Martha furrowed her brow as she obviously struggled with the question he'd dealt her. "I don't see how you could be two people, but—"

"I've been robbed of my identity." His chin touched his chest in obvious despondency. "And I've taken something precious from Rose—something she can never give again."

Rose lifted her fingertips to still her trembling lips as the full meaning of his words became clear. He regretted taking her virginity. At first the realization that he was ashamed of having ravished an innocent brought her pleasure and a perverse sense of satisfaction. But upon further reflection, she discovered hurt and rejection.

He regrets the difficulty he will have leaving Dogwood with a wife and possibly a child in the way.

Heavy footfalls resounded from the stairs, prompting Rose to pull the door quickly to, and tiptoe down the hall. Glancing around in momentary terror at being discovered eavesdropping, she quickly threw open the doors to the tall cupboard at the end of the hall where Martha stored clean linens.

"Hello, Rose." Jim's voice rattled her nerves. After quickly removing a pair of linen towels, she turned to face the master of the house, coercing a reluctant smile to her lips.

"Jim." She moved toward the master bedroom. "I believe Dylan is in with Martha and the baby. I was just heading that way with these towels." Did her trembling voice betray her?

"Good. Reckon I'll just peek in an' see how they're doin'." Jim smiled at her in his gentlemanly way and moved down the hall. He knocked, then opened the door in one smooth motion.

Rose exhaled the breath she didn't even realize she'd been holding until now. Weakly, she leaned against the wall for support, the towels still clutched in her hands. The knuckles on both hands had turned white from the ferocity of her grip.

Dylan's going to leave me.

She had to accept it. Even though she'd told herself repeatedly he didn't matter to her, that her carnal urges were simply physical responses she was too weak to control, it suddenly seemed quite shocking that he truly wasn't going to stay with her.

Her right hand released its death grip on the linen and trembled as it traveled up her bosom where her husband had caressed and kissed her. Her fingers touched her lips, and despite her self-directed lies, she discovered a truth which rendered her numb with dread.

God help me—I love him.

A tear trickled down her cheek and was soon followed by several more. Rose wiped furiously at the liquid traitors and pushed herself away from the wall. Her mother's face flashed before her eyes, reminding her of their mission.

"Heavens, for a moment I became misdirected," she murmured to herself and turned toward the stairway to make her way back down to the kitchen. She placed the clean towels on the table and stepped outside.

"Evenin', Miss Rose." Charlie Riordan walked toward her from the well just as she felt the cool evening air envelop her. Lightning flashed in the distance, promising a dousing later in the evening.

"Good evening, Charlie." Rose hoped her discomfiture wasn't obvious, but upon meeting his gaze she realized how futile it would be to keep her secrets from this kind man. Her lower lip trembled.

Charlie stepped toward her and reached for her hand. "What happened?" Concern filled his eyes as he waited for her answer.

"N—nothing." Rose shook her head. This wasn't the time or the place for secrets. "It seems I've made a serious error in judgment."

"Did your husband say something to hurt you, Miss Rose?" Charlie's nostrils flared in obvious fury. " 'Cuz if he did . . ."

Rose averted his gaze. Dylan hadn't hurt her physically by any means, yet hurt her he had. But wasn't she the one who'd hurt herself by allowing such fantasies to interfere with what was truly important?

"He means nothing to me," she lied, sighing and meeting Charlie's gaze again. Allowing her anger to steady her nerves, Rose knew what she must do. "If I don't permit myself to care about him, then how can he hurt me?"

Charlie seemed unconvinced. "I see." He removed his hat and released her hand. "Then, if he don't mean nothin' to you, why do you live in that cabin with him?"

Dylan remained in the shadows of the kitchen as he waited for Rose's answer. Her words stripped him bare to the soul, forced him to reconcile some of his own confusion. If how Rose felt about him mattered so much, then that must mean . . .

No!

Why do you live in the cabin with me, Rose? Her answer—he had to hear it.

"Why, Charlie." Rose laughed, but it wasn't a pleasant sound by any means. Her voice became harsh and filled with anger as the laughter subsided. "I only remain with Dylan Marshall because he has hidden something important which belongs to me."

Thirteen

Dylan bit his lower lip and forced himself to watch the exchange. He'd been right. Rose had sacrificed herself—given him her body—to lower his defenses, to coerce him into giving her the gold.

Heartless bitch.

Charlie fidgeted with the hat in his hands and licked his flabby lips. "Uh, what is it he took that belongs to you, Miss Rose? I can sure try and help you get it back—whatever it is."

Rose seemed to study Charlie for several moments, then shook her head. Dylan released his breath, relieved she hadn't told the man about the treasure. The reason he felt such relief didn't matter at the moment. He'd analyze that later—hopefully about a hundred years later. There was something disturbing as hell about Charlie Riordan . . .

"No thank you, Charlie." Rose looked toward the brewing storm. "I'll bide my time just a while longer."

"But . . . if you wait, you have to keep livin' with a man you don't love." Charlie reddened. His eyes became glassy as Dylan continued to watch from the kitchen door. "You're shamin' yourself, Miss Rose. It ain't right. Somehow I don't think your daddy'd like knowin' his little girl was havin' to . . . be with a man she didn't love."

"Charlie." Rose covered her mouth with her hand and blushed profusely as her husband clenched and unclenched his fists in increasing rage. "That is quite unseemly."

"Well, I'm sorry, Miss Rose, but I can't help the way I feel." Charlie lifted his gaze to hers and sighed in a manner which Dylan felt was a bit over-dramatic. "I don't want you to be hurt—or used."

Dylan almost laughed out loud. If anyone in this situation was being used, it was him. Used by Rose . . . and the Keeper. His fury mounted as he considered all he'd been robbed of simply to save Rose Jameson's life.

And how ungrateful could a human being be?

He trembled in silent rage. Rose was his willing partner in bed. Fine—if she wanted to continue living with him as his "wife," simply to obtain the information about the treasure, then who was he to deny her an opportunity to at least try?

Rose seemed to struggle with her composure after the man's frank words. Good. Dylan was glad she was finding it hard to live with her lie. How could he have been so stupid? But he saw her clearly in a new light, now. The memory of her surrender had been so sweet.

A delectable lie, if ever there'd been one.

Rose had said outright that Dylan meant nothing to her. He rubbed his forehead with his thumb and forefinger, recalling against his will the day Cindy'd told him she wanted a divorce. His gut twisted into a knot.

Dylan kicked the door and let it swing wide as he swaggered outside. He felt like a nineteenth-century version of "The Terminator."

"Ready to go *home,* Rose?" His words were clipped as he stopped beside his wife and gripped her elbow with more force than necessary.

"Yes, I'm ready whenever you are." She glanced at him, then lowered her guilty gaze and bit her lower lip. "Good evening, Charlie."

Charlie stepped aside and watched as they walked away. Dylan felt the man's gaze on his back and knew it was murderous. For some inane reason, the man had appointed himself Rose's guardian.

How much of their conversation had he missed? Were Rose and Charlie lovers? It seemed impossible, yet the suspicion wouldn't leave his boggled mind.

Glancing sideways at his wife, Dylan clenched his teeth, working the muscle in his temple to the rhythm of his hurried steps. The storm continued to brew, seeming to hold itself back to build. Empathy with the building tempest surged through him. That's precisely how he felt at the moment. He was a storm waiting—holding himself in check until he exploded.

But why the hell should he hold himself back? Rose didn't mind sharing her body with him. He wasn't foolish enough to think she was feigning pleasure when they made love. No, she couldn't deny that. Even if she claimed to be with him simply to get something which "belonged" to her, he knew the truth.

And by God he'd make her admit it—one way or another.

As they neared the cabin, a lump formed in Dylan's throat. The memory of the evening he'd carried Rose from this very spot assailed him. Despite his heart's disappointment, his body still wanted her.

And she was willing.

Deceptive.

Treacherous.

Why should he deny himself when she was so willing and eager to spread it around?

He hadn't touched her during their walk—until now. He reached for her arm just as she put her foot on the porch step. Pulling with very little force, he twisted her body until she lost her balance and pitched toward him. His mouth covered hers in a kiss that would abide no protests.

He felt Rose tremble as his grip tightened. His tongue plummeted and possessed her. He would permit no denials of what truly existed between them. This was an affair, whether they be married or not. They were . . . servicing one another. Nothing more. He wouldn't—couldn't—let it be anything more.

Never again.

She gasped and twisted her face away from his kiss. "What do you think you're doing?"

Dylan's breath scorched his own hand where it was wrapped around her neck to hold her against him. Their faces were mere inches apart.

"Why, I'm giving you what you want, Rose." His voice was mocking, filled with the betrayal he felt to his very core. "Sex—gratuitous sex. This *is* the nineties. You're one of the . . . New Women. Liberated. A suffragette." He threw his head back and laughed. He knew it was an insane sort of laugh, but at this moment that was precisely how he felt.

Ignoring her shocked expression, Dylan picked her up and went inside, kicking the door closed behind them. He crossed the small room and dropped his bride on the quilt, scorning the flashbacks of earlier sessions of lovemaking he'd shared with this gorgeous creature.

Falling down on top of her, his mouth possessed hers with savage passion. He knew his kiss was punishment and anger as he staked his claim. It was his intent, he realized without surprise, to make Rose regret the words she'd spoken to Charlie. She would want him this day.

She would beg for him.

But would she *care?*

Determined to cleanse her mind of any further thoughts of the damned treasure, he vowed that all she would feel was him. He jerked at the front of her mockingly demure dress until the buttons yielded to his superior strength and scattered across the room.

Rose trembled beneath his near-violence, but Dylan's anger and lust culminated into a ruling passion. He never had—and never would—force himself on any woman, but he knew that wouldn't be necessary. Rose's passion would rule in the end. He was certain of it. Her past performances were too unrestrained to have been total pretense—regardless of what she'd told Riordan.

Raw, naked need permeated him, burning deep within Dylan. He would damned well give her something to remember after he was gone. No other man would ever possess her as completely as he would this evening. She would learn the full extent of his possession.

He wanted her to think of this night—the moment when he'd fully claimed and possessed her—each and every time she tried to tell her sweet lies to Riordan, or any other stupid male who might fall victim to her charms.

The muslin shift tore easily in his hands, revealing the beauty he sought. This body he'd touched with such gentleness in the past belonged to a woman who'd lied in the worst possible way. She'd rejected the feelings growing between them.

Tonight there would be no repudiation.

Rose professed to dislike his rough treatment when his mouth left hers for a moment to slip her clothing from between them. But her blue eyes glittered with a reckless light in the brief, intermittent lightning flashes. She was like a wild animal, with her hair tousled in ebony curls across her bare shoulders. Her breasts rose and fell with her rapid breathing.

Dylan reclaimed her mouth, shutting off her protestations—her lies. Parting her lips with his tongue, he searched for the eagerness he'd felt in the past. Her lips trembled slightly.

Then he felt her response.

Rose's tongue probed his in return, transforming his blood into a raging furnace. Such desperation coursed through him that he feared he might succumb to his own feelings before he brought hers into focus. This was something he'd never felt before, but he knew the spirit of his flesh would rule until it was sated.

Their passion was all they had—there was no love. There couldn't be. He'd never surrender to such foolishness again. Women were too deceitful—they couldn't be trusted.

When he tore his mouth from hers, gasping for air, Rose didn't even flinch as his gaze possessed her.

Without preamble, he ravenously sought and claimed one passion-swollen nipple.

He devoured her. He took her breasts repeatedly, punished them with lips and hands bent on possession of unparalleled dimensions. He was aware of the shift in her role, the moment when her passion soared to a point that no longer permitted her to deny him anything.

Rose moaned and writhed with need as his onslaught continued. Her breasts swelled and filled his mouth. His stubbled chin scraped her tender flesh, making her crave more of his coarse treatment.

And hate herself for wanting it so.

Dylan searched and found the soft concentration of senses between her thighs, stroking her until she was a quivering mass. He released her nipple long enough to scorch her flesh with his hot breath.

"You like it. Don't you, baby?"

His mouth covered hers with such force that Rose felt as if she were being smothered. The feeling of suffocation soon vanished, replaced by the flames which claimed her woman's flesh. He mercilessly brought her body to the limits of passion as she whimpered and contorted beneath his skilled touch.

Why is he doing this? It's so cruel—so wonderful.

Rose shattered. Each fragment became nothing more than his toy, his possession. Nothing else mattered or even existed in her conscious mind for an interminable twinkling. She wanted nothing more than always to feel as she did at this moment.

Dylan's mouth left hers and returned to her tender nipples, torturing beyond any reasonable level of endurance. This must end. "I can't . . . take this," she pleaded. "Please, Dylan."

"Not yet." He chuckled as he ruthlessly possessed her breasts, first one then the other with his tongue and teeth.

"Dylan."

Recognizing only one defense against his sadistic yet inspiring intent, Rose traced a delicate line across his swollen manhood with her fingertip, wondering when he'd removed his clothing. She couldn't recall, but he was as naked and hot as she.

Swollen, starving flesh pressed against flesh. Her insides coiled into a tense spring, on the verge of unwinding with explosive force. She was like the breaking storm outside. The wind howled as rain beat against the solid walls of the rustic cabin.

Like her, the tempest seemed intent on releasing all its fury—its passion. Dylan was like that tonight, too. What had happened to make him so . . . desperate?

The cruel world ceased to exist. Every curve, every hollow, every nerve of Rose's body came to life in a new, raw version of its former existence. She begged, pleaded for him to release her from his spell. He was the only one who could give her what he alone had made her crave.

Dylan further staked his claim with his mouth and hands in ways and places she couldn't have imagined before. His mouth found the softness between her thighs which was already exploding with desire. Tantalizingly—determinedly—he coaxed and forced his way into her soul, into her very essence.

The world grew darker and hotter with every passing second. How could she think anything at all? He wasn't giving her the opportunity to feel anything but him, his tongue, his body pressing against her own.

In the past, every time they'd come together had been so beautiful. But this was different; it was maddening. There was nothing beautiful about what was happening between them. It was primal, basic hunger. They were yielding to their most carnal wants, their most animalistic desires.

Rose felt as if she left the bed's surface as her senses created an eruption within her. Incoherent sounds of anguish, pleasure and longing escaped her parted lips, but she didn't care. She was unable to heed them.

She groaned, growled, cried, but still he didn't do what she knew he must want with as much desperation as she. Only he could alleviate her suffering. Why didn't he give her what they both wanted so desperately? It was so cruel to delay the inevitable. She must feel him inside her soon or die.

Decisively, she lifted herself and shifted so her head was opposite his. Rose hesitated only a moment, then took his smooth, hot erection into her mouth, flicking her tongue against its silken tip. Dylan flinched and groaned in what she knew was disbelief mingled with pleasure. She fought back with the only ammunition she had—making him suffer just as she.

They inflicted upon one another such mounting pleasure that Rose thought death was imminent. She'd never known something that felt so good could actually become torture. But this was indeed torture. Someone had to give. She sensed his mounting frustration, his inner battle to maintain control.

Violently, he jerked her away and pinned her beneath him. He plunged into her as if probing for something new that had never been present before. The depth of his possession unhinged her. Their bodies brutalized the other in their quest, striving to give and to take from the other.

It was fury, their love-lust aflame, the crashing of waves against the rocks on the seashore. It was everything—it was the only thing. Carried into another dimension, the shuddering of their bodies reached something Rose felt certain neither of them had ever felt before.

A unique completeness filled Rose as her body finally gave way to its augmentation. She grew hotter, her muscles constricted, her body craved more yet could take no more. She heaved a sigh of contentment as she felt Dylan unleash his own completion within her.

His seed spilled into her, staking total possession, claiming something more from her—something Rose could not quite comprehend. Yet she sensed something different.

Something powerful.

Sweat formed between them, but they didn't venture from the comfort of their embrace. As rationality began to return, tears pooled in her eyes and slid down her cheeks. Rose shuddered, and when lightning flashed, she turned her face away from his haggard expression. Something in that gaze tore at her—threatened everything she'd sworn not to feel.

Dylan's expression was haunted. "God forgive me. I don't know what came over me," he whispered in a ragged voice. His fury was gone. "I've never—" He clenched his teeth as if biting back his own words. "It's late. You need rest."

He started to move away, but she reached for him and pulled him back. For some reason she couldn't let him go—not yet.

"Not rest, Dylan."

A flash of lightning clarified the expression of shock evident on his handsome face. Rhythmic flashes of nature's fury bathed the cabin with periodic light from the small window above the bed.

Dylan's breath came out in a rush as his gaze swept her. He seemed stunned by her words. There was something like remorse in his eyes . . . and an unfathomable emotion which stole her breath.

All thoughts fled her save one—he was hers, at least for now. Nothing could change that fact. When Dylan eased his weight from her and lay on his side, the pain in his eyes made her tremble. There would be no remorse, no denials, no holding back, for she wanted this man with such force it was frightening.

"I want you, Dylan." Rose's invitation was clear. She would deal with the why later. Right now she only knew that she needed and wanted this man. Not treasure, not independence, nothing else.

He sighed. A muscle twitched in the side of his jaw as the storm passed and moonlight streamed through the small window. "I wish you really meant that, Rose."

A sense of purpose filled her. She didn't know or care why. Though she couldn't say the words, she had to let Dylan know how much she needed and wanted him—that she didn't hate him for making her see this. "I do."

Dylan looked at her as Rose reached out to touch him. Her heart seemed to skip a few beats. She wrapped her legs around him, drawing him against her body. Not a fraction of space remained between them as they lay transfixed.

He began slowly to kiss her all over, seeming intent to explore every inch. With searing lips he tasted each toe, finger, the lobes of her ears, her eyelids and he playfully tickled her navel with his tongue. Greedily, his mouth claimed one eager nipple.

Each caress, every kiss was gentle but intense. Mind and heart were silenced. Rose permitted her body to rule. She was amazed that the innocent brush of his lips against her toe could cause such violent tremors of exhilaration to dash through her.

The slow progress his loving made brought her to new and unexpected heights of yearning. This was right and it was wrong—it was heaven and it was hell. She writhed as perspiration coated them both. His dallying was some new form of torture he'd conjured up for her.

But if it was torture, it was a divine agony.

As his lips slowly made their way up her legs, traveling to the tender flesh of her inner thighs, Rose felt a brief void until he crept back up her body. Swells of longing shot through her loins as he moved higher.

She gasped when Dylan rolled away and onto his back, gently coaxing her until she sat astride him.

Driven by mutual need, Rose slid her body down onto his throbbing hardness. He pervaded her with an efficiency that rendered her breathless. She could not move for one glorious moment as the splendor of it swept through her. She was filled only with him, with her need of him, with her own desire to please him as much as herself.

An even trade.

Dylan pulled her upper body forward. She was on her knees, permitting him to position her, still stunned by the depth of their union. When he laved first one, then the other of her swollen nipples with his tongue, Rose began to move gently, rhythmically against him. It was as if nature had provided her body with instincts about such things. But she did not take the time to sort through these jumbled thoughts as the flames of passion burned brighter between them.

The power of their coupling was unique. Rose felt as if she truly belonged to someone, that she'd discovered something she'd never even realized was missing from her life.

Her breasts tingled deliciously from his ravenous assault, intensifying the heated pulsing of her female flesh. Her insides felt like warm honey, all soft and heated as the explosive rapture grew. His teasing lips never left her as the new experiences drove her to higher plateaus.

They clung together. Their bodies were blending into infinity as the flux of gratification lapped over her. When they rocked together in the final paroxysms of surrender, neither of them moved or even breathed, for countless moments.

As Rose slumped against him, Dylan stroked her back while their breathing returned to normal. She treasured the stolen intimacy, sensing somehow that things might never again be the same between them. Sadness gripped her with an overwhelming intensity.

What had prompted him to be so harsh earlier? Why

had he told Martha he was going to leave her? Wasn't that what he'd said—what he'd meant?

Dylan tensed beneath her and she rolled away from him, sensing the moment of unity had passed. The rain-washed evening air was chilly against her bare flesh. The sense of loss that permeated her soul was torture. He didn't love or want her. Charlie'd said as much. She was shaming herself by succumbing to the weakness of her flesh. How could she be so weak?

Run—get away—hurry!

Suddenly, she had to distance herself from him—from herself. She couldn't face the emotions swirling through her. She couldn't look into those hazel eyes right now.

He might see . . .

Rose moved from the bed in one smooth motion and pulled her dress over her head. Most of the buttons were gone from Dylan's earlier impatience, but she managed to partially cover herself. Without a word, she turned to the door and walked outside, desperate and alone.

Tears slipped down her cheeks in increasing numbers. She stood on the porch for several moments, heard Dylan's angry muttering and what sounded like a shoe hitting the wall. She wiped at her tears and stepped off the porch.

I can't love him. God help me, I just can't.

Fourteen

Dylan opened his eyes and stared at the beamed ceiling. Without looking, he patted the empty space beside him in the bed.

She was gone.

That was no big surprise. Why would she want to stay with a man who'd practically forced himself on her? The memory of his actions made his gut twist in deserved punishment.

Still, his guilt didn't lessen hers.

Damn the woman, anyway. She was driving him crazy with wanting her, with not being able to trust her, with loving her . . . He shuddered in denial.

Dylan was haunted. Possessed. Bewitched.

Definitely.

Rose was like a bad penny. No matter where he was, where he went, what *century* he lived in, she was there. She was on this earth to torment him, to confuse and tempt him. She'd haunted him in the future . . . and she was haunting him now.

"Damn."

He rolled out of bed and pulled on his clothes, not bothering with breakfast. The way his gut felt right now, any food he managed to force down his throat would probably beat a hasty retreat anyway.

After stepping outside, he paused to pat Hippocrates on the head, then walked toward town, trying to suppress his memory of the angelic face he'd grown accustomed to seeing each morning.

When did she leave? He vaguely remembered seeing and hearing her return to the cabin very late. Neither of them had spoken a word when she lay down on the bed at his side, distancing herself so as not to touch him. During the night, he'd heard her sobbing, but he'd resolutely kept his back turned, vowing not to offer aid and comfort to the enemy. She—not he—had declared this war with her words to Charlie Riordan.

Let her live with her deceit.

Wherever she was.

He hadn't visited Dogwood since the day of Tom's funeral. Dylan had left word that if his services were needed, he could be sent for. Since that first day, his only patients had been Sarah Jane Whorton, Martha and Zeke. He knew Maggie Mae would send for him if it became necessary.

But today he needed to keep busy. Hanging around the cabin would give him too much time to worry, and he certainly wasn't prepared to face Martha this morning.

An old hound, tail wagging and tongue lolling out the side of its mouth, greeted Dylan at the edge of town. But before Dylan passed the first building on the outskirts of Dogwood, he froze.

There was Rose.

Alone and carrying a painted sheet draped across her front.

Vote for Women!

A barrage of emotions surged through him as he

watched her stern expression and heard her shout the words painted on the sheet.

"Vote for Women!" she repeated over and over . . . until she saw him. Rose faltered as their gazes met.

Dylan's gut twisted again. *Damn.* She was gorgeous. Remorse filled him. He shouldn't have treated her so harshly, but her words to Charlie Riordan plagued him. She didn't love him—didn't care. The knowledge that his own feelings for her were building to a dangerous level tore at him.

Rose only stayed with him because of the treasure.

She lifted her chin a notch while he stared. Rose was a lone soldier in her cause. Only the hound and Dylan were aware of her vigilant march for women's rights.

His feelings evolved, surprising him as he stood watching his wife march back and forth down Dogwood, Missouri's only street. Pride in her efforts filled him, even if they were wasted on the small community. She'd fit right in if . . .

No.

What a ludicrous thought. Imagine, considering taking the deceitful Rose, back with him to the twentieth century.

I must be a glutton for punishment.

Turning resolutely away from the marching figure, Dylan paused when he noticed a building he hadn't paid attention to on the occasion of his first visit to Dogwood. A sign painted in large white letters read: The Branchwater.

When he walked past the saloon, the mongrel deserted him and went through the swinging doors.

"You drunken beast." Chuckling, Dylan hesitated,

then took a backward step, his gaze riveted to those swinging doors.

I need a drink.

Remembering Rose, he swallowed hard.

Hell, I need several drinks.

A nineteenth-century saloon was just the bit of Americana he could deal with at the moment. Sighing, he checked to make certain there were no messages on his office door, patted his pocket to ensure he'd brought along a few coins, then noticed with an infuriating pang of disappointment that the lone suffragette was gone. Disgusted with himself for caring, Dylan went inside the dank environment.

Only one customer occupied the establishment—Zeke Sawyer. Turning to beat a hasty retreat before his stepfather-in-law saw him, Dylan lost his thirst in a big hurry.

"Hey, Doc." Zeke's words were slurred, indicating his state of intoxication.

Busted. Slowly, Dylan turned to face the old man. He sighed and took a few reluctant steps toward the bar and stood next to Zeke. It was a losing battle. First Rose—now her stepfather. He was obviously doomed to spend some time with one of them. Though Rose would have been far more pleasant company, Zeke was safer.

As he waited for the bartender to take his order, Dylan recalled with a start that the date was quickly approaching when the newspaper clipping had indicated Zeke shot and killed Jim. A feeling of momentary terror gripped him. Jim Marshall was far more than merely a name from history to Dylan now. Jim was a flesh and blood human—someone he cared for and respected very much.

"What's the date today?" Dylan asked the bartender after ordering a shot of whiskey. He continued to ignore Zeke's ramblings while the heavy man flipped over the calendar hanging on the rough wall.

"May tenth."

Dylan went cold. The shooting had occurred on May eleventh. What could he do to prevent it from taking place? He didn't care that he was meddling in history again. History be damned! When it came to saving Jim Marshall's life, he'd meddle as much as necessary.

"Damn."

"What's matter, boy?" Zeke leaned toward him as he spoke. His breath smelled like he hadn't been sober for several weeks—maybe years. "That high-spirited filly wearin' you out?"

Dylan clenched his teeth. A muscle twitched in his jaw as he pondered his options. He could either lay Zeke out like he really wanted, or he could use his brain to find a means of preventing the shooting—if he hadn't already done so by appearing in the nineteenth century. He exhaled and gripped the glass the bartender placed before him.

Choosing to ignore the man's crude question, Dylan took a sip of the burning liquor. It warmed him instantly, but he shook his head when the bartender offered a refill. Suddenly, it seemed critical that he remain sober. Besides, drinking before eight in the morning and on an empty stomach wasn't his usual style.

In his friendliest voice, Dylan turned to the ugly old man. "How's that wound in your side, Zeke?"

Obviously surprised by the amiability in Dylan's tone, Zeke grinned, revealing several missing teeth—most of them, in fact, were missing.

"Fine. Fine. Thank you for askin'." Zeke drained his glass and waited until the bartender had refilled it before speaking again. "I hear you an' Rose is gittin' on well."

"Oh?" Dylan arched a brow and folded his hands on the bar in front of him. It was going to be difficult to maintain his composure if Zeke insisted on talking about Rose. The ability to think clearly fled Dylan when the topic of conversation turned to his deceitful wife.

"Folks talk."

Determined to change the subject, Dylan released a ragged sigh and mentally counted to ten. "Tell me, Zeke—how well did you know my, er, grandfather?"

"Tom?"

"Yeah, Tom."

"Well, yer grandpaw an' me was partners long time back." He shook his head and ran his dirty fingers through his long, greasy hair.

"Partners?" Dylan frowned, wondering what his family and Zeke could possibly have been partners at.

"We sure was. Me an' Tom went to Californy together back in '49."

"The gold rush. And?" *Seems like it always comes back to gold.*

Zeke chuckled and drained his glass. "Tom an' me staked us a claim and went to diggin' for gold, see."

He seemed to forget what he was talking about while he watched the bartender refill his glass.

"This is the last one, Zeke." The heavy proprietor's voice was stern. "Them jugs you brought me ain't worth more than this."

"Hell. All right, you swindler."

"I ain't the swindler here."

Once Zeke finished grumbling about the deal he'd gotten for his moonshine, Dylan prodded him for more information. "What happened in California, Zeke?"

"Tom lost the claim while I wuz in town doin' . . . bizness."

The bartender passed by and Dylan nodded toward Zeke's empty glass, indicating with his expression that he would pay for the old man's drinks. Zeke took another sip of the amber liquid and wavered as if he might fall.

Dylan steadied the hillbilly and grinned. "Best take it easy there, Zeke," he said in a friendly tone which belied his true feelings for the old man. "Can't have my father-in-law falling down and getting hurt."

"Thanks, Doc." Zeke seemed truly pleased with this turn of events. "I reckon it helps to have a doc in the family."

"Now, what was it you were saying about Tom and California?"

"Oh. Well, see Tom let some claim-jumpers take over the mine whilst I was in town, doin' bizness, like I said."

"Go on."

"Them boys was slippery'n a water moccasin. They had papers they said proved the claim belonged to them."

"How'd they get the papers, Zeke?"

"Made 'em. They wasn't real."

"I see." Dylan rubbed his jaw thoughtfully while the bartender refilled Zeke's glass. If he could determine a means to detain Zeke until the day after the shooting was supposed to occur . . .

"I s'pect old Tom hid some a the gold."

A nagging suspicion originated in the pit of Dylan's stomach. The single sip of whiskey he'd consumed didn't help much either. "You mean there was some gold with you when you came home?"

"He hid it from me." Zeke belched.

Waving his hand before his nose to clear the air after the old man's gaseous exhalation, Dylan was beginning to understand. At least . . . he hoped he was. The pouch of gold that had been on Tom's body when he died could easily be mistaken by an illiterate like Zeke as something other than what it was. Perhaps the old hillbilly would believe it was part of a cache supposedly brought back from California.

"How could Tom have brought back something as heavy as gold without you knowing it, Zeke?"

Zeke seemed confused for a few moments. "Oh, that's easy. We didn't come back together, see."

"Oh."

"Tom sorta runned off after we lost our claim."

Dylan pondered this bit of information. "But what makes you think he brought back some gold?"

"Hell, ye've seen that fine house, Doc. How the hell do you think he was able to build it?"

Dylan frowned. This wasn't heading in the direction he'd intended. Zeke had backed him into a corner by asking a question he couldn't answer.

Then an idea crossed Dylan's mind. Could Zeke be bought off? With enough gold in his hand, could the old man be convinced to leave the Ozarks forever? The idea had some merit, though the possibility that Sawyer would simply drink away any payment he received was very real.

In fact, it was a near certainty. Dylan would have to simply detain the old coot until he slept off the effects of so much whiskey. And it would certainly be at least beyond May eleventh before such an exorbitant amount of alcohol could be metabolized.

"Zeke." Dylan rubbed his palms together. "C'mon up to my office. I want to talk to you about something. We'll check that wound and make sure it's healed up properly, first."

"I dunno . . ."

The bartender paused in front of them, gesturing toward Dylan. "He leaves, you get no more drinks, Zeke." The big man received an obscene gesture from the target of his declaration.

"C'mon, Zeke." Dylan used a patronizing tone with the old man, knowing that when someone was as drunk as Zeke, they were usually extremely gullible.

Dylan tossed a gold coin onto the counter and winked at the bartender's shocked expression. "Keep the change."

Zeke swayed and staggered against his son-in-law as they made their way to the mill and up the narrow stairs to the doctor's office. Dylan released a sigh of relief when they were safely inside, grateful they hadn't tumbled over the side because of Zeke's staggering and stumbling.

"What you . . ." Zeke's eyes rolled into the back of his head and he hit the floor with a loud thud.

Dylan contemplated the situation. The old man was obviously in no condition to discuss business and wouldn't be until tomorrow.

But tomorrow might be too late.

He had to make absolutely certain Zeke couldn't carry out his destiny. The gold pouch Martha had told him about could be the key. With it out of circulation, maybe—just maybe—history'd already been changed for the better. Jim had to live, to father more children, to grow old with Martha.

Searching through the cupboard against the wall, Dylan found several leather restraints, probably used for surgery in lieu of anesthesia. *Perish the thought.* Glancing at Zeke, he wondered if they'd really be necessary, but decided against taking any chances.

"Well, Zeke," he said, grinning mischievously. "You're in need of a medical procedure which requires you to be totally still. Now . . . don't you move an inch."

Charlie Riordan waited across the street until he saw Dylan leave the saloon with Zeke in tow. After the pair had staggered up the stairs and disappeared into the doctor's office, Charlie ambled across the street and into the saloon.

"What can I do for you?" The bartender asked distractedly when the large man sat down at the bar. He was still staring at the twenty-dollar gold piece in his hand.

"What you got there?" Charlie couldn't help but

notice the gold coin. It wasn't every day one of those appeared in a town like Dogwood.

The bartender scratched his head and chuckled. "Durn fool doctor give it to me to pay for Zeke's drinks." He shook his head in amazement. "Never got such a big tip before."

"Lemme see that." Charlie's hand snaked out and grabbed the heavy coin from the bartender.

"Hey!"

"I'll give it back. I just wanna look at it." Charlie's expression warned the bartender not to challenge him.

He turned the coin over in his palm. It looked familiar. *Very* familiar. His chest tightened in expectation. It wasn't a current United States Government issue, but it looked new. Squinting, he read the date that curved around the coin's base.

1860.

He nearly whooped in delight. His treasure—at last, he'd found it.

Part of it, at least.

Reluctantly, he passed the coveted coin back to the bartender, who seemed much relieved to have it in his possession once again. "You said the doc give this to you?"

"Yeah. Who figgered he had this kinda money to throw around?"

"Yeah. Go figger."

Charlie forgot about the drink he was going to order. There was a lot more where that coin came from.

And he was going to have it.

No matter who got in his way.

* * *

Panting in exhaustion when she reached the cabin, Rose grimaced and threw down the banner she'd so carefully made before the sun even rose. What a joke. Marching down the streets of Dogwood, where half the residents were illiterate, with a banner demanding women's vote.

But she'd needed to do it for herself—to validate her strong feelings for women's rights and independence, despite her behavior with her husband.

Shaking her head, she commanded her traitorous tears to cease and went about her morning chores. Recalling the expression on Dylan's face when she'd seen him in town, she winced. Her eyes stung again and she angrily swiped at them.

When she'd returned last night from her short walk, Dylan hadn't even looked at her. It was clear he hated and resented her. It didn't really matter. She'd heard him say with his own voice that he intended to leave her.

With a sinking feeling, she groaned in recollection of his words to Martha . . . and his actions toward her last night. Her muscles ached, reminding her of their fiery, animalistic lovemaking.

Love?

How could she call it lovemaking when it was more like "hatemaking"? The expression on Dylan's face . . . the brutal way he'd possessed her . . .

Her face flashed hot as she went out and splashed it with cool spring water. She saw her reflection in the water as the ripples subsided. It annoyed her.

"Miss Rose." Charlie Riordan's voice penetrated the still valley, calling from the meadow just beyond the spring.

Rose winced. Though Charlie was a pleasant sort, she wasn't in the mood for any company this morning. Especially not someone who might see through her facade, which he seemed very adept at doing.

Resolving herself to entertain Charlie whether she wished to or not, Rose straightened as he approached. She would just be very careful to avoid the subject of her husband.

Just the thought of Dylan made her insides twist and burn in agony. Why had he brutalized her, then shown such tenderness?

"Good mornin'. I seen you leavin' town this mornin' in an all-fired hurry. I wanted to make sure you was all right." Charlie stopped in front of her. His smile vanished as he looked at her with a knowing expression. "He hurt you."

Rose gasped and stared at Charlie in amazement. "How did you—"

"I'll kill him for hurtin' you."

"No, he didn't hurt me, Charlie." Rose shuddered, sensing the fury emanating from the man. "We . . . we simply had a disagreement."

"Don't you lie to old Charlie. I can tell he hurt you." Charlie's voice was ominous. "I can't let him get away with that, Miss Rose. Hank wouldn't want me to let it pass."

Rose winced at the mention of her father's name. Her father had wanted his family to have the treasure. Her eyes burned.

"No, Charlie." She shook her head and pursed her lips. "He didn't hurt me. I . . . I hurt myself."

"Ah, Miss Rose . . ."

Rose wept openly as he pulled her against his broad

chest and stroked her hair in a fatherly manner. All the pain and anguish bottled up inside her spilled forth. She sobbed like a small child against her mother's bosom.

Oh, how she needed her mother right now. A woman's guidance was just what she lacked. But that could never be. Ella Jameson Sawyer was dead and gone. Rose pushed herself away from Charlie. When he released her, she dabbed at her tears with her sleeve and tried to smile.

"I'm sorry, Charlie." She covered her face with her hands. "I'm being foolish."

"You ain't foolish." Charlie patted her arm. "I seen him in town."

Rose's tears ceased as she glanced up at her visitor. "Oh?"

"He was with that worthless Zeke Sawyer."

"What would Dylan want to talk to Pappy Zeke about?" Rose furrowed her brow in concern. Then she recalled the conversation she'd overheard between Dylan and Martha the day before. "Oh, no."

"What is it?"

Rose swallowed hard and turned toward the cabin. She walked over and sat on the step. Charlie knelt at her feet. His gaze was patient and expectant, though something much less benign burned in his eyes.

"Dylan's planning to leave me."

"Why would he wanna do a fool thing like that?" Charlie chuckled, but his eyes glittered strangely.

Rose shook her head—stunned that Dylan might, at this very moment, be making arrangements to return her to the Sawyer cabin. "Because he wants it all for himself."

Charlie straightened—his dark eyes were glazed, sinister. "Wants what?"

Rose shook her head and swallowed hard. "I'm just being silly again."

"No you ain't. What does he want?"

"Something of mine . . ." Rose grew pensive and turned away. "Charlie, I'm really not in the mood for callers this morning."

Ignoring her plea for privacy, Charlie's breathing became very loud. "I think I know a way to make him give . . . it to you."

Rose froze, then slowly turned to face him. "What . . . are you talking about?"

His evil—maniacal—grin gave no warning of his intentions. She gasped when he reached for her, pulled her hard against his chest, pinning her arm behind her back.

"Let me go."

His wicked laughter sliced right through her. Rose cringed as he glowered down at her.

"It ain't yours, pretty lady. It's mine."

Rose closed her eyes. How could he treat her this way? He'd ridden with her father.

Ridden with her father? "Oh, my God." *Mamma, is he the one?* Rose swallowed hard as the memories formed a lump in her throat. *Someone who rode with your father in the war framed him for murder,* her mother'd insisted. Rose opened her eyes and looked at him accusingly.

"You're the one," she said quietly, suddenly realizing how mistaken she'd been about Charlie Riordan. The minute he'd admitted to having known her father, she should have suspected him. But instead she'd imprudently welcomed him with open arms. "You killed my father."

"Hank was a fool, but I ain't." Charlie shoved her inside. "C'mon, Miss Rose, we're gonna find us some treasure."

Dylan leaned back in the chair, tilting it until the front legs came off the floor. The office had a spacious closet in the back, where he'd dragged Zeke and the chair he was tied to. The old man would be stiff and sore when he woke up, but all in all, except for an unavoidable hangover, he wouldn't be any the worse for wear.

All he had to do was keep Zeke under wraps for about thirty-six hours. Then the date of the shooting would have passed and Jim would be safe.

Hopefully.

Dylan closed the closet door twice during the course of the day when patients showed up at his door. He kept it open when he and Zeke were alone to make certain the old man had plenty of air. So far, except for an occasional snore, he hadn't made a single sound.

As evening approached, Dylan replaced the medical book he'd been perusing all day, and checked on his prisoner. Zeke was still out cold. Shaking his head, Dylan tied a gag over the man's mouth. He felt certain that old Zeke could holler to wake the dead if he wanted to.

And when Zeke Sawyer awakened tied and gagged in a closet, Dylan knew the entire town of Dogwood would know it right away.

As Dylan walked toward the farm, his steps quickened. The thought of seeing Rose, of smelling her sweet aroma, of touching her velvet skin spurred him on. The expression of pain in her blue eyes last night tormented him. He shouldn't have taken her in anger. She didn't deserve that. No one did. Even though he'd made tender love to her afterward, it didn't make up for his rough treatment.

Darkness blanketed Serenity Spring by the time he reached the cabin. Pausing on the porch, Dylan wondered why Rose hadn't lit the lamp. But he knew the answer to his silent question before he even opened the door.

"She's gone."

He slowly opened the door and stepped inside, striking a sulphur match to light the lamp. His suspicions confirmed, Dylan walked around the room in dismal confusion. He really shouldn't be surprised. She'd been quite outspoken about her feelings toward remaining with him in the Ozarks.

"The gold."

If she discovered the gold he knew he'd never find her. She'd be gone from Missouri as fast as possible and never look back.

Never give him a passing thought.

Coldness built from inside his gut, then gripped him hard. Walking out onto the porch, Dylan put the lamp down and gazed across the spring. Part of him wanted to march right to the cave and check on the treasure, but he stood frozen.

Another part of him didn't want to know.

Rose had betrayed him—abandoned him after he'd given up his entire life to save hers.

But of course she didn't know that. She had no idea of the price Dylan had paid to rescue her from certain death.

Chuckling at the irony of their situation, he shook his head. As his gaze swept the little valley, the deep, penetrating cold seeped into his heart. Loneliness. Rose had become far more important to him than he cared to admit. Her absence left an incredible void.

He walked back inside the cabin, his gaze riveted to the narrow bed in the corner. Its brightly colored quilt contradicted the true spirit of the cabin's most recent occupants.

Rose.

His memory conjured up the image of her smile, the tempting way she moistened her lips with the tip of her tongue. His heart seemed to swell within his chest as he recalled the sound of her laughter.

It was just like when Cindy'd left him.

The emptiness.

The rejection.

The pain.

How could she?

Her ghost had lured him into a trap. Dylan placed the lantern on the table, the very object which had been used to imprison Rose in the cellar. Cursing, he threw open the trap door and went down into the dark cellar to retrieve one of Abel Bentsen's jugs.

Returning to the room, saturated with the silence of Rose's absence, Dylan ran his fingers through his tousled hair in desolation. A fury gripped him as he reached for the brush Martha had given to Rose.

Hoisting his arm back to throw, he paused. His grip on the brush handle was like death as he slowly lowered the object until it was in front of his face. Long, wavy strands of ebony hair clung to the bristles.

It smelled of rosewater.

Dylan swallowed hard. His eyes burned as he gingerly placed the brush on the mantel and blew out the lamp. Darkness surrounded him, bathed him with a soothing, mocking ambience.

Simon and Garfunkel would've found it inspiring, no doubt.

Dylan found it tormenting.

Something wasn't right.

Almost mechanically, he moved outside and took a deep breath. The moon, which had been full last night after the storm when he and Rose . . .

Clenching and unclenching his fists, he stepped off the porch and went behind the cabin. The nearly full moon bathed the countryside in surreal light as he walked up the slight incline toward the cave in the side of a limestone cliff.

If Rose had truly left him, then the gold would be gone as well. If not . . .

Dylan's pulse raced as he quickened his pace. Soon he would know the truth.

And he hated himself for needing so desperately to know. He'd vowed not to care after overhearing her conversation with Charlie Riordan, but he couldn't help himself. He needed her. Something inside him—a deep, primitive male instinct—cried out for her. For her only.

Rose.

Panting and perspiring by the time he reached the limestone cliff, Dylan squeezed past the boulder. It was dark inside the small cave; the moonlight couldn't reach beyond the boulder he'd so carefully placed.

Dropping to his knees, he felt around the floor of the small cavern until his groping hands discovered what he sought. The heavy cloth bags were still neatly stacked in the corner where he'd placed them with his own hands, along with his cellular phone, wallet . . .

And marriage certificate.

Confused, he returned to the cabin and relit the lamp. He searched the cabin for some evidence of what had happened to Rose. If she hadn't found the gold, it didn't make sense that she'd leave. That treasure had been his ace-in-the-hole, his means of holding her even before he realized how much he wanted to keep her.

But Rose was gone—the gold was still safely hidden away.

"Dylan."

Jim's voice echoed through the still night. Dylan jerked open the cabin door and stepped outside with the lamp in hand.

"Letter come to the house for you." Jim held out the sealed envelope. "It was left on the porch. Don't know who brung it."

Dylan swallowed the lump in his throat and sat on the step, placing the lamp at his side. Jim sat nearby, silently waiting.

Dylan tore open the envelope and read the words quickly, then scratched his head in confusion. "Damn."

"Bad news?" Jim's voice was calm and soothing. He didn't press for information, simply sat stroking his long beard.

"Uh . . ." Dylan struggled with his words. The horror of reality descended upon him to blot out the images which had plagued him earlier. Uncertainty surged through him. Was this true? Could it be true?

He glanced at Jim, his cousin—his great-great-grandfather—who was supposed to die tomorrow at the hands of Zeke Sawyer. It was too dangerous—he couldn't involve Jim in this mess.

Rereading the letter, Dylan cleared his throat. "It's from Rose," he said finally in a voice he felt certain couldn't belong to him. He wasn't really lying, because the letter was in her handwriting.

"Oh." Jim looked away, glancing out across the spring. "She's gone, then."

"It . . . it would seem so." Dylan nodded as a thousand possibilities raced through his mind. "She didn't want to marry me, Jim. You know that."

"Well . . ."

"Thanks for bringing it." Dylan stood beside him and shook his hand. "I'll be all right. You go on back to your wife and baby." *And please—just stay there—hide for at least thirty-six hours.*

"If you're sure, then I'll head back." Jim took a few steps, then paused. "I got me a powerful hunch Rose might be back."

Dylan tried to smile and failed miserably, electing to nod instead. "Thanks, Jim."

"Sure." Darkness swallowed the tall man after only a few moments.

"Damn." Dylan sat beside the lamp to read the letter a third time. Hippocrates nuzzled his way into Dylan's lap, pushing his head beneath one of his master's hands. Absently stroking the hound's head, Dylan felt his blood pressure rising as he read Rose's words.

Dear Dylan, I've been kidnapped and he means to kill me if you don't give him the gold. He will send word about where and when to deliver it. I'm frightened. Love, Rose.

He closed his eyes and looked again at her neat signature.

Love?

The image of Rose in Charlie Riordan's arms assailed him, making Dylan leap to his feet, sending the surprised puppy tumbling to the ground in his usual clumsy manner. This was nothing but a ploy to get her hands on the treasure.

Rose was using this as a means to force him to relinquish the gold. It made perfect sense. Blackmail.

Lord knew she was capable of it. Hadn't she been sleeping with him all along simply to get her hands on the damned treasure? She'd admitted as much to Charlie Riordan.

Riordan.

Charlie Riordan was her accomplice.

Dylan raked his fingers through his hair, longer now than he'd worn it in the twentieth century. What a mess he'd be when he . . .

Returned to his own time.

"Damn."

He leapt to his feet and rushed into the cabin, put out the lamp and stuffed the offensive note in his pocket. Enough was enough. Once he was certain Jim was safe from Zeke Sawyer, he was going to find the Keeper and demand that he return him to his own time.

Slamming the cabin door behind him, Dylan walked toward the town of Dogwood for what he hoped would be the last time.

Fifteen

Rose stared in horror at the man who dragged her into the shack she'd hoped never to see again. The rank stench of Sawyer moonshine assailed her nostrils from the back of the ramshackle cabin as Riordan shoved her through the door and slammed it shut behind them.

She knew the shack well—intimately—from her years of exile within its walls. Covertly, her gaze darted about the room, ascertaining that her stepfamily was not in residence at present. For once, she actually longed for their presence. Despite her distaste for the Sawyer family's way of life, none of them had ever mistreated her.

The moment Charlie's back was turned, Rose bolted for the back door and tore at the latch pull to no avail. Her captor moved far more quickly than she'd suspected his bulk would allow him to—foiling her escape.

She clawed at the beefy hands that wrapped around her middle to drag her unceremoniously across the dirt floor. "Let me go."

"We're gonna have us a fine time waitin' for your doctor to come up with the gold." He smacked his lips as he threw her onto the bed she had once occupied in the Sawyer cabin. "Yessiree, a fine time."

Rose threw one leg off the straw tick the moment her body made contact with it, straining against his huge bulk to free herself. She had no inclination to remain beneath him long enough to find out what his intentions were. The lecherous expression on his puffy face left little room for doubt.

Charlie pressed her back onto the bedding and placed one knee against her abdomen. The pressure of his massive weight against her midsection forced the breath from her lungs. Rose immediately ceased her struggle while he bound her hands to the bedposts with thin strips of leather.

He stood back as if to admire his handiwork. "You are a looker. We're gonna have us a high old time. Hank'd roll over in his grave if he knew what I was thinkin' about his little girl right now."

Rose glowered in silent rage at the monster whom she had foolishly befriended and trusted. She should have realized when he showed up here in this backwater place, and just happened to have known her father . . .

That wretched treasure.

"Why are you doing this?" Her instincts told her the answer, but she needed to hear him admit it. After everything she and her family had gone through because of that contemptible gold, it would all end here—like this.

His chilling laughter penetrated her flesh and crawled inside her as he knelt beside the bed and ran a rough finger across her cheekbone, down her neck and across the narrow plane between her breasts. Rose shuddered in revulsion, squeezing her eyes shut to pray for escape—or even a sudden and merciful death.

Anything but this.

He leaned forward—his hot breath scorched her cheek. "Oh, you know what I want, Rose."

"N—no." She shook her head, trying to shrink back as deep into the straw tick as possible to avoid contact with her captor's lips. Consciously, she ignored the fingertip which continued to toy with her throat and bosom, threatening to become more intimate at any moment. "I don't know what you want."

"The gold." He arched a brow and grinned with no trace of humor. *"My* gold."

Rose bit her lower lip and turned her face toward the wall, but his hand snaked out to capture her chin in an iron grip, forcing her to return his gaze. His face was dark with rage as he glowered down at her.

"You *do* know where it is." He tilted his head to one side as if considering the entire situation in a new light. "At least your . . . husband does."

"Dylan?"

Charlie's thumb brushed against her nipple, making Rose shudder in revulsion. Such intimate contact with Dylan had been so wonderful. With Charlie Riordan it was living hell.

He released her suddenly and strode across the room to the cold hearth. His back was to her and Rose breathed a sigh of temporary relief. At least, for the moment, he wasn't touching her. How could she have trusted him?

Rose didn't speak—he seemed deep in thought. She tugged at the leather bindings, but to no avail. Where were Pappy Zeke and the twins? Surely they weren't involved in this.

Or were they?

It didn't make sense that Charlie would bring her

to this cabin unless the Sawyers were already involved. Dylan would have no way of knowing where she was being held until her captor was ready to inform him. And if her relatives were involved with Riordan . . .

There was no hope.

As if in answer to her unspoken question, a pounding at the back door distracted her abductor from his musings. As he moved cautiously toward the portal, he withdrew an ominous-looking revolver from the saddlebags slung over the back of a chair in the corner.

Dylan?

"No, Dylan!" she shouted, jerking against her restraints, praying he heard her warning.

"Hush!" Charlie's words were hissed from between clenched teeth as he peered through a crack near the door. "Well, it's about time you showed up."

Rose's eyes widened as he swung open the door to reveal her very drunk stepfather and his sons. By their lack of surprise, she realized they were most definitely in cahoots with her captor.

"T'ain't your husband, Rose." Zeke staggered toward her with his jug clutched in his hand. "That scoundrel tied me up an' locked me in a closet. I gots half a mind ter sic the sheriff on him."

"Please, do." Rose wondered where her courage came from. "Can't you see that this . . . scalawag is holding me prisoner?"

"Now, Rose . . ."

"Shut up, Sawyer." Riordan's voice was ominous as he placed the revolver back in his saddlebags and walked over to stand beside the bed and Rose. "You boys don't try nothin' foolish."

"I done told 'em." Zeke appeared uncomfortable.

He glanced from Rose to his sons, then down at the jug. "Need myself a refill."

Rose closed her eyes in dismay. There was no hope. Dylan would choose the treasure over her. And why shouldn't he? She'd made it abundantly clear she had no intention of remaining with him once she found the gold.

Now he had no one to share it with. He could keep it all to himself.

What have I done?

Dylan paced the small office in agitation, looking again in the closet where he'd left Zeke. The only thing the hillbilly'd left behind was his stench.

"Where the hell is he?"

Running his fingers through his hair in turmoil, Dylan looked at the untouched jug of moonshine he'd brought along. The last thing in the world he needed at this moment was a drink. Jim was in danger and it was imperative Dylan have his wits about him.

The sun was beginning to rise as Dylan stepped onto the landing at the top of the stairs. He'd been up all night. Between the shock of Rose's abandonment, and finding Jim's prospective murderer missing, sleep hadn't been uppermost on his list of priorities.

Two days' of beard growth covered his chin. Rubbing it with his thumb and forefinger, Dylan leaned against the door frame to contemplate his strategy.

He had to find Zeke.

Closing the office door behind him, he started down the stairs just as Ida Whorton started up.

"Doctor Marshall." She seemed frantic as she carried her bundle up the steps toward him. "Sarah Jane's sick."

Sighing, Dylan pushed his other concerns from his mind and reached for the child. She was burning with fever. Even through layers and layers of blankets, her fever was indisputable.

Without a word, he turned and rushed back up the steps, unwinding the stifling blankets as he did. Once inside he laid the infant down on the small examining table and disrobed her until the frail child wore nothing but a diaper.

"I thought it best to keep her warm." Ida wrung her hands and bit her lower lip.

"No—cool's better." Not taking time to worry about Ida's feelings, Dylan retrieved his stethoscope from the fanny pack and listened to the baby's chest. Her heart thudded along steady and regular, though at a more rapid rate due to the fever, typical for such an elevation in temperature.

But the rubbing sound in her lungs set off every alarm Dylan had developed since his first year of medical school. Closing his eyes for a moment, he cursed the lack of modern antibiotics.

After starting a fire in the small pot-bellied stove in the end of the office, Dylan left Sarah Jane to rest on the table with her mother's protective presence. He placed three kettles of water on the stove at once to boil. It was the closest thing he could get to a humidifier.

"My kingdom for penicillin."

Ignoring his whispered plea, Ida didn't look up when he came back to stand beside her. "My husband don't want her, Doc." Her lower lip trembled as she looked at him with wide, frightened eyes. "When she took sick, he carried her out an' left her in the woods."

"What?" Dylan clenched his fists to prevent fury from overtaking his ability to reason. Sarah Jane was critically ill. Pneumonia had taken the lives of many children during the nineteenth century, and he knew from personal experience how much more vulnerable a child with Down Syndrome was.

"He said the Injuns had the right idea 'bout . . . deformed babies." Huge tears trickled down Ida's puffy face. "He said they took 'em out an' let the w-wolves have 'em."

"Oh, God." Dylan reached for Ida as her grief overwhelmed her. Keeping one steadying hand on Sarah Jane, he rubbed Ida's shoulder in reassurance. "I'm sorry, Mrs. Whorton. You should have told me. Maybe I could have spoken with him."

"He done told her brother and sissie that Sarah Jane died." Her voice was pleading. "He don't know I followed 'im an—"

"I see." Dylan sighed and let his hand drop to his side. "Sarah Jane is very ill, Mrs. Whorton. She has pneumonia."

He turned his attention back to the most immediate concern—saving the child's life. But he couldn't prevent the thought from crossing his mind that Sarah Jane's life would be something considerably less than ideal even if he managed to save her. She was susceptible to diseases in a medically impoverished society . . . and her own father didn't want her.

Another thought suddenly struck him. Children with Down Syndrome were considered highly adoptable in his time. Maybe there was hope.

"Mrs. Whorton." He looked at her as he turned Sarah Jane across his palm and pounded on her back in an attempt to alleviate some of her respiratory distress. He'd need to construct a tent of some sort to concentrate the steam from the boiling water to a more confined area. "Is there a chance that maybe another family might want to adopt Sarah Jane? Are there any orphanages—adoption agencies—maybe in Springfield?"

If only Rose was here. She's more worldly about such things.

"Lan' sakes, Doc." Ida's horrified expression told Dylan he'd made a grievous error in judgment. "I couldn't give 'er away. 'Sides . . . they'd just send her to some horrible place. Most folks don't want babies like Sarah Jane."

Dylan knew she was right. If only there was some way to transport Sarah Jane to his time, where prospective parents tended to have more liberal viewpoints about what made a child adoptable.

Maybe there is.

The Keeper had said Dylan needed to find the right path. Wasn't helping Sarah Jane a path? He could take her back with him, see to her health and find a permanent home for her in the twentieth century.

It was certainly worth a try.

It was obvious Ida wasn't going to give the child up, though the position she was in more than forced the issue. Though it was against every principle he'd ever valued, Dylan knew he would have to simply keep Sarah Jane, rather than send her back to a home where she wasn't loved and wanted.

If he could save her at all.

Steam began to fill the office space as Dylan continued pounding on the baby's back. She wasn't in serious respiratory distress yet. Her color was pale, but not blue. He glanced up at Ida.

"I need to tend her around the clock for a while, Mrs. Whorton." He avoided the woman's gaze as he searched his mind for ideas. "Maggie Mae can help me if I take her out to the farmhouse. She can have constant care until she's out of danger."

Ida seemed relieved and Dylan suddenly realized this woman had little say in the future of her child. What an injustice for a mother to be so vulnerable to the cruelties of her spouse. Nodding, Ida gave her consent.

As Dylan wrapped one thin blanket around Sarah Jane to prevent a chill, Ida banked the fire and removed the kettles from the stove. "You go on, then." She kept her face averted as she tended the fire. "I'll take care of the fire."

Dylan stared at her straight back as she lifted the heavy pails from the stove and placed them on the floor. The woman was very brave. He regretted what he planned to do until he looked into the tiny face of the child cradled in his arms. A surge of protective, fatherly love burst through him as he recognized something within himself.

If he managed to save Sarah Jane and found a way to take her with him into the future, he wouldn't place her for adoption. She was a link to his adventure—his journey through time. They were connected by that bond and something far deeper. Sarah Jane represented his coming of age.

Suddenly, without preamble, fanfare or drum rolls, Dylan knew his path. He would return to his own time and continue to practice pediatrics. But his patients wouldn't be the spoiled children of St. Louis yuppies. They'd be children like Sarah Jane. Children without medical insurance, babies whose parents were unemployed.

And his clinic would be in Taney County.

He was going home . . . to stay.

Jim rubbed his beard as he glanced at Dylan's burden. "I dunno, Dylan."

"I'm sure she isn't contagious, Jim." Dylan arranged the small room off the kitchen that doubled as a pantry for Sarah Jane with one hand as he clutched the child in his other. "Once she's out of danger, I'll take her to the cabin with me."

"Can't understand folks who don't want their own babies." Jim shook his head and Dylan knew he was recalling his own children who hadn't survived.

Dylan placed Sarah Jane on her side and propped her with a rolled up towel placed behind her back. The water he'd placed on the stove was boiling, so he stepped out of the pantry and retrieved two steaming kettles. After placing them on the floor beneath the drawer he'd transformed into a bassinet, Dylan draped a sheet from one of the high shelves to the door frame, allowing it to cascade around the makeshift bed until Sarah Jane was enclosed in a tent of soothing steam.

"There."

Jim stepped out of the room. "You say that'll help her breathe?"

Dylan pulled the door shut behind him, but remained nearby where he would be able to hear the baby if she woke. "I hope so."

"You ain't heard from Rose?"

Dylan shook his head. "I was wondering if you'd fetch Maggie Mae for me." He wasn't ready to talk about his wife's betrayal, yet. The wound was too raw—too deep.

"Sure. Just lemme tell Martha where I'm goin'." Jim turned and went up the stairs.

Dylan stepped outside and filled two more kettles with water from the well, then hurried back to place them on the stove. He opened the pantry door a crack and listened. Sarah Jane's steady snoring told him she was still breathing and asleep. That was best. She'd breathe more deeply asleep than awake.

If his treatment was successful, she'd soon be hungry. How was he supposed to feed her? It wasn't as if he could rush to the supermarket for disposable diapers, bottles and formula. He'd have to ask Martha where he could obtain the necessary equipment and try to concoct his own formula.

"Jim told me you got a sick youngun here." Martha came into the room garbed in a shirtwaist dress which was gaping where her swollen breasts strained against the buttons. She was the picture of new motherhood, blooming with health and . . .

Milk.

"Yes." Dylan cleared his throat. How did one politely ask a woman to breastfeed another child? Of course, Martha knew his secret. Perhaps she could overlook his bluntness if he just came right out and asked.

"She ain't carryin' sickness Tom can catch. Is she?"

"No." Dylan shook his head. He felt certain what Sarah Jane suffered from was bacterial, not viral.

"We'll keep her down here away from Tom, though—just in case."

"If there ain't no danger of me catchin' it an' passin' it to Tom, I'd like to help tend her."

Dylan smiled. "Thank you." He cleared his throat and stepped over to check the water on the stove. Tiny bubbles were beginning to gather around the edges of the kettles, but he needed to wait until the water had reached a full boil. "I was wondering . . ."

"Wonderin' what?" Martha folded her arms across her bosom where a damp spot had formed from the copious amount of milk she was producing.

Far more than young Tom required.

"How do people feed babies when the mother can't—or isn't available?" Dylan's face grew warm as he looked again at the kettles of water.

"Well, some folks uses a bottle, but most often another mother can wet-nurse . . ." A frown creased her brow when Dylan looked directly at her again. "Whortons ain't gonna take her back. Is they?"

"No."

She sighed. "Dylan, I gots more milk than Tom knows what to do with. But you already know'd that."

Dylan met her gaze and felt a huge burden lift from his shoulders. "I confess. I was hoping you'd offer."

"Just lemme know when." She glanced down at her breast where dampness had spread halfway down her shirtwaist. "Tom done ate an' went to sleep. So anytime'd be right fine with me."

"Thanks, Martha . . . Grandma." It was good to share his secret with her, to be able to come out in the open on occasion in her presence. "The more we can get her to nurse, the better. She's nearly dehydrated as it is from the fever."

Nodding, Martha followed him into the small room, which was now filled with steam. Brightly colored jars of preserves, pickles, fruits and vegetables lined the top shelves in the pantry.

Dylan set the two cooling kettles outside the door and replaced them with the new ones while Martha cooed and spoke to the little girl. She sat down on the bench beside the makeshift bassinet and stroked Sarah Jane's cheek with her fingertip.

Instinctively, the child turned toward the finger and made a sucking motion with her mouth. Dylan's heart swelled with love and concern. She was so tiny—so weak. Her oral motor strength would be poor from the extra chromosome she carried and even more pronounced due to her illness.

"She may need some coaxing at first," he said quietly as the baby opened her eyes and screwed up her tiny face. When she woke, her wheezing seemed more pronounced, but he suspected that was because she was preparing to emit a scream.

"We'll be fine." Martha picked up the baby and unbuttoned the front of her dress. Her engorged breast seemed as eager to offer sustenance as the child was to receive it. It was a good sign that Sarah Jane seemed hungry.

A very good sign.

"There, there . . ." Sarah Jane turned her head away from the friendly nipple. Martha continued to stroke the side of the baby's cheek with her reddish brown nipple until Sarah finally rooted and settled into the task at hand. "She ain't like Tom."

Dylan recognized the expression on his great-great-grandmother's face as one he'd seen on many new mothers. It was maternal love—unconditional and complete. His heart went out to this woman, his ancestor. She had room in her heart for Sarah Jane, too. He'd been wrong to consider taking the baby with him into the future.

Even if he'd found a way.

"Do you . . . understand about Sarah Jane?" Dylan stood in the small steam-filled space while his tiny charge took sustenance from his great-great-grandmother's breast. He knew when the milk let down because of Sarah's sudden burst of rapid swallowing. She pulled away to cough once and milk continued to spray across her cheek.

Dylan couldn't prevent the chuckle which bubbled from his chest. Martha simply urged the infant back to her breast as soon as the coughing had ceased. Several times she had to tickle Sarah Jane's feet and face to wake her. The more milk they could get into her, the better.

Martha shrugged. "I see she's weaker'n most babies—different, I reckon. But she needs love, warmth, milk . . . like all babies needs."

"Good." Dylan nodded. He couldn't have said it better himself. Sarah Jane was different, but the same. She was in good hands. The best.

"Jim told me about Rose."

"Oh?" Dylan leaned against the door, where the sheet partially hid his face from Martha's knowing gaze.

"You can't lie to me, Dylan Marshall." Martha's

voice took on the maternal tone Dylan had grown accustomed to. "I knows you love her."

Closing his eyes, Dylan knew she was right. From the first night Rose's ghost had visited his bed he was destined—or doomed—to love her. She was everything he'd ever wanted in a woman. She was beautiful, passionate, intelligent, outgoing.

Deceitful.

The anger he'd held so carefully under control combined with his fatigue to compound the pain. Yes, he'd loved her, even considered abandoning his desire to return to his own time for her.

For what?

To feel the pain of rejection and betrayal slash through him again, even more devastating than when Cindy'd left him?

Never again.

"Yes." Dylan shifted his weight to his other foot and forced the image of Rose's face from his mind. "But it doesn't matter."

"Humph." Martha burped the baby and placed her back in the makeshift bassinet, then buttoned her dress. "I reckon the Lord know'd what He was doin' when He give me enough milk for two."

"Thank you."

The woman gave him a motherly hug and stepped past him and into the kitchen. "I'll just put these kettles back on to boil again."

Dylan examined Sarah Jane, noting the contentment on her face. He suspected that Ida had been under so much stress from her husband's rejection of the child that her milk production had been affected. Though the baby was still wheezing, her color already showed improvement. With any luck, lots of Martha's milk, and plenty of moisture in the air, Sarah Jane just might make it.

Covering her with a thin blanket, Dylan stepped from the pantry to speak to Martha when a memory assaulted him.

"Zeke."

"What?" Martha turned toward Dylan as he moved rapidly toward the door. "Dylan, what's wrong?"

Dylan looked at his great-great-grandmother, feeling the urge to reveal to her the secret burden he carried from the future. But he halted himself, realizing that the last thing in the world this woman needed to know was that her husband was about to be murdered by Zeke Sawyer.

Today.

Sixteen

Rose refused all food and water offered by her captors. At least her stepfamily's presence had halted Charlie's obscene overtures. He now kept his distance, refraining from speaking to her at all. But those dark eyes burned her with lechery that made her flesh crawl and her stomach churn.

She sensed that the moment she was alone with Charlie, he'd take liberties. More than once she'd noted the hard bulge in his trousers when he stood and stretched after watching her for an extended period. Each time, her stomach rebelled at the mere thought of him touching her.

"When you plannin' to send fer Doc?" Zeke asked the morning after her abduction, when he seemed more sober than he'd ever been. "If you're so all-fired sure he's got the gold—"

"I'm running this, Sawyer. Butt out." Charlie walked over to his saddlebags and withdrew a pencil and tablet. Leaning against the wall, he wrote for several moments, then chuckled.

"Miss Rose?" He said in a sickening tone, obviously mocking her as he approached the bed where she'd been tied for many hours. "You're gonna write a little note to your dear husband."

Rose shook her head, then she immediately regretted the action. Charlie reached out to grab a handful of her hair, then jerked her head back until she felt as if her neck would snap. Glancing at Zeke, he nodded his head toward Rose. "Untie her."

He freed her hair after Zeke had released her bindings. Tentatively, she pushed herself up to a sitting position, feeling her head swim with the effort. Lack of sleep and food, combined with the misery of having been in one position for so long, had sapped her strength. Her hands trembled as she rubbed her sore wrists.

"Now, Miss Rose . . ." Charlie's voice was ominous. "You will write exactly what I have here on this sheet of paper. Won't you?"

Rose glanced at the page where he'd scrawled out a message, demanding the gold in exchange for her safe return. What a joke. "There's just one problem that I see." She tilted her face until her gaze locked with his. "Dylan doesn't care about me."

"We'll see." Charlie folded his arms across his huge belly and waited. When she made no move to retrieve the pencil he'd dropped in her lap, he reached down and grabbed her hand and forced her fingers to close around the instrument. *"Write."*

"You told me you wasn't gonna hurt 'er." Zeke moved toward them, but halted when Charlie's fierce gaze pinned him. Something resembling regret crossed the old man's features as he turned away like a wounded hound.

Rose copied the message precisely. Tears burned her eyes, but she refused to permit them to expose the heartache which threatened to betray her at any moment. Writing Dylan's name on the paper tore at her, jeopardized her resolve. But she did it and thrust the offensive document at her captor. The pencil rolled onto the dirt floor.

"Good girl." Charlie read the words with obvious satisfaction. "Loverboy'll come for sure."

"No . . . no, he doesn't care about me." Rose lifted her chin in defiance, though her heart seemed to swell in her throat at the truth in her statement. "Dylan doesn't want me, so he won't give up the gold for me."

Obviously choosing to ignore her, Charlie moved toward her stepfather. "Sawyer, you deliver the note." He glanced over his shoulder at Rose. "And take both the boys with you."

Zeke seemed taller somehow as he straightened to face the larger man. He glanced at Rose—compassion flickered in his eyes. "No. I ain't gonna leave 'er alone with you. I owes her maw that much."

Rose heaved a sigh of relief. Never in her entire life would she have expected to feel grateful to Zeke Sawyer, but at this moment he was her hero.

Charlie stared long and hard at Zeke. The tension in the tiny cabin was thick, palpable, reminding her of the heavy atmosphere just before a violent storm broke. Rose bit her lower lip while the nonverbal battle played out between the pair. Though Zeke was far smaller in stature, Charlie was outsized twofold by her stepbrothers, who moved to flank their father.

Remembering the gun hidden in the big man's saddlebags, Rose watched him closely, prepared to warn her stepfamily if Charlie so much as looked at the leather pouch which contained the weapon. It felt very strange to actually feel grateful and protective toward the Sawyers.

Grumbling, Charlie thrust the folded note toward him. "You win . . . *this* time, Sawyer." He glanced at the boys. "They can stay."

"Where you want me to take it?" Zeke looked at Rose, then back to the big man. "The cabin?"

Charlie shook his head slowly. "Nope. Take it to the farmhouse again. I wanna make sure somebody's around to take the note in person."

"That'll put the blame on me."

"That's right." Charlie glowered at Zeke. "And lead the doc right to this cabin."

Maggie Mae took over Sarah Jane's care, praising Dylan's use of steam and Martha's milk to treat the child. After adding some herbs to the pails of boiling water, the old woman pulled a rocking chair into the tiny pantry and looked pointedly at Dylan.

"Jim sent me on ahead." Maggie Mae's expression was filled with concern as she looked directly at Dylan. "Said he was goin' to Zeke's place, lookin' for Rose."

"On May eleventh? Good God—not today." Dylan knew Sarah Jane was in good hands as he turned and ran from the house. Slamming the back door behind him, he almost ran right into the man who was in the process of attaching a note to a board near the door.

Dylan reached for the piece of paper, grabbing Zeke's bony wrist with his other hand. As his gaze scanned the words in his wife's handwriting, his gut twisted. But as long as the old man was here delivering ransom notes, he couldn't be shooting Jim Marshall.

"Where's Rose?" His voice was low and ominous. A fury built in the depths of his soul and spread gradually outward. *"Where—the—hell—is—she?"*

"Charlie just told me to bring this." Zeke's eyes grew round and frightened as Dylan's anger gained more and more control of his typical manner.

"Riordan?" The image of Rose in Riordan's arms flashed through his frazzled mind. Her words haunted him.

"Yep. He's got 'er." Zeke trembled in Dylan's grasp. "Why'd you tie me up?"

"How'd you get loose?"

"The boys." Zeke attempted to free his wrist from Dylan's brutal grasp, but to no avail. "C'mon, cut me loose, Doc."

"Not until you tell me what Rose is trying to pull." Dylan dragged Zeke down the steps toward the well. He raised the bucket with one hand while continuing to hold Zeke with the other. Lowering the filled pail to the ground, he placed one hand on the back of Zeke's neck and forced his face into the water. Though he was a pacifist at heart, sworn to saving lives, at this moment Dylan believed murder was not beyond his capability.

Zeke kicked and bubbled beneath the cold water until Dylan pulled his head back with a handful of the man's silver hair. "Where is she?"

"My . . . cabin."

Zeke gasped for air as Dylan continued to hold him by the scruff of the neck. "You'd better not be lying to me, Sawyer. Do you know what Rose is up to?"

"Rose ain't up to nothin'." Zeke spat on the ground and shook his head. Droplets of water showered them both. "Riordan's holdin' her."

"Sure he is. And Ross Perot's a liberal Democrat." Dylan started to force Zeke's face back toward the bucket of water.

"No!"

"Talk."

"I'm tellin' you the truth, Doc." Zeke's tone was pleading. "Rose ain't got nothin' to do with nothin'."

Dylan wanted to believe him. He ached to learn that Rose hadn't deceived him after all. But the overwhelming evidence refused to allow his easy acceptance of Zeke's claims. With his own ears, in this very spot, he'd overheard Rose telling Riordan that her husband meant absolutely nothing to her.

"Why should I believe you?" Dylan's blood boiled. He couldn't recall having ever been this angry before. The fury that possessed him threatened to rule until appeased. He would have revenge—one way or another.

"I owe Rose's maw." Zeke lowered his head as he spoke. His voice was low and seemed sincere. "Ella was a good woman. Better'n I deserved."

"I'm sure that's an understatement, but still doesn't convince me you're telling the truth."

"Lookee here, Doc . . . las' time I seen Rose she was tied to a bed in my cabin." Zeke's nostrils flared. He was obviously angry now. "Read the note. I can't read nor write, so's I ain't sure what it says."

Dylan pulled the paper from his shirt pocket with his free hand, never releasing his grip on Zeke with the other. His eyes scanned Rose's words again. Could this be true? Was Rose being held against her will by Charlie Riordan?

Sighing, Dylan realized he must make absolutely certain. If there was even the slightest possibility Zeke was telling the truth, then Rose was in danger. He couldn't return to his own time without ensuring her safety.

After all—she was the only reason he was here in the first place. What a shame to have given up so much only to have Rose Jameson die before her time by other means.

To have Rose die at all, whether he'd made a sacrifice or not, cut Dylan to his core. He couldn't bear it—not Rose.

"Dylan." Jim Marshall's voice carried from the far side of the spring house as he rushed toward the pair beside the well. "I seen Zeke from up on the bluff headin' this way, so I never got to his place. What's goin' on?"

Dylan looked from his great-great-grandfather, a man who was supposed to die on this very day at the hands of Zeke Sawyer. As long as Zeke was preoccupied with Rose's predicament, and Martha remained silent about the pouch of gold . . .

Maybe saving Rose's life had already altered history enough to prevent Jim's murder. Rose was responsible for keeping Zeke occupied long enough to prevent it. But for Dylan, Rose wouldn't be alive to have been kidnapped in the first place.

"Read this, Jim." Dylan handed the note to his great-great-grandfather. His heart thundered wildly in his chest. "You seen Riordan lately?"

"Nope." After reading the note, he shook his head in disgust. "What's this about gold?"

Arching a brow as he contemplated these developments, Dylan instantly realized what he had to do with the treasure. But not yet. He had to keep it until he was certain of Rose's safety.

Shrugging, he released his hold on Zeke. "He claims Rose is being held at his cabin."

"Is that a fact?" Jim frowned, pointing an accusing finger at Zeke Sawyer. "You ain't never been no good, Sawyer. But this here is lower than I thought even you was. Ella was a good woman an—"

"Tarnation, Jim." Zeke released a loud sigh, looking from one Marshall to the other. "I know that. That's why I wouldn't let Charlie make the boys come with me. I didn't wanna leave Rose alone with 'im."

Dylan's gut twisted into a painful knot as he considered the possible implications of his wife alone in the cabin with Charlie Riordan. Scanning his memory, he recalled Rose's claim that her father'd been framed by someone who wanted the treasure. Riordan obviously knew about the treasure, and unless Rose had told him about it, the only way he could be aware of its existence was if he knew Hank Jameson during the Civil War.

"Oh, God." The facts were falling into place now—why hadn't he seen this coming? He should've been able to protect Rose.

From everything Zeke had told Dylan, he had to face the truth. Rose was in real danger, being held against her will by a man who was more than capable of rape and murder. Dylan squeezed his eyes shut.

"Jim, can you send for the sheriff?" His voice carried a raspy quality he knew reflected his emotions.

"He's over to Forsythe, but I can do it."

"Good." Dylan faced his stepfather-in-law with purpose. "All right, Zeke, listen. This is what you're gonna do . . ."

"It's about time." Charlie's words sounded more like a growl than a human voice when the cabin door swung open and Zeke entered. "What took you so long?"

"I had to wait 'til no one was lookin'." Zeke blatantly avoided Rose's gaze as he spoke. He went directly to his jug of moonshine and removed the cork. After taking a long pull of its contents, he sighed in apparent satisfaction.

Rose watched the men move about the room. The aroma of baking cornbread drifted to her nostrils. Her stomach protested loudly. A pot of beans bubbled over the open fire as well. But she wouldn't eat. Riordan would have to play his sinister game alone—she had no intention of helping. Cooperation was the one thing she could continue to deny her captor.

The entire time Zeke had been gone, Charlie'd tried every ploy imaginable to get the twins to leave him alone in the cabin with Rose. But Tem and Abner had refused. They obviously realized why their father didn't want Rose left alone with her captor. Impossible as it seemed, she had cause to feel very grateful to her stepfamily.

"The doc was hangin' around outside." Zeke walked over to the hearth and removed the lid from the pot to sniff appreciatively. "The only thing better'n beans'n cornbread is fried taters with beans'n cornbread."

"Did he see you?" Charlie seemed impatient as he walked over to Zeke, then struck a threatening affectation.

"Nope."

Rose couldn't help but notice Zeke's agitation as he moved around the small cabin. He glanced once in her direction, but quickly looked away when her gaze met his. There was something different about him. She furrowed her brow in confusion. What had happened during his short absence to change his mood so drastically?

"Well, did you hang around to make sure the doc picked up the note?" Charlie leaned against the hearth, obviously waiting for Zeke to explain.

"Yep. I seen 'im pick it up with my own eyes." Zeke took another pull from the jug.

"Then it's his move." Charlie dished himself up a plate of beans and took a slice of cornbread from the pan placed near the hearth on a rough table. Leaning against the stone fireplace, he ate in silence, but his gaze seemed riveted to Rose.

Swallowing was difficult—nearly impossible—as she tried to avoid that menacing gaze. Somehow, she knew Charlie Riordan had no intention of releasing her even if he succeeded in procuring the gold.

There was something else he wanted—her.

It didn't take much experience in the ways of men to recognize the primal male hunger in those dark eyes. The man was determined to have her. But she wouldn't let that happen. She'd rather die than succumb to his lust. Bile rose in her throat at the mere thought of his beefy hands touching her.

"Rose, you hungry?" Zeke paused beside the bed until she turned toward him and shook her head. Sighing, he pivoted away, his expression haunted—sad.

Charlie finished his plate of beans and sopped the broth from his plate with the cornbread. Rose looked away to count the cracks between the logs on the wall beside her. Again.

Would Dylan come for her?

Surely he wouldn't give up his treasure for her. Why should he? She'd given him no reason to believe she would be willing to make such a sacrifice on his behalf.

Tears stung the backs of her eyes, but she blinked rapidly to prevent their escape. What did it matter? She was better off dead than held prisoner by Charlie Riordan.

Dylan wrote until his fingers cramped from the effort. His words could have a significant impact on history, and on the future of Taney County. He must choose them with care.

Even though his heart wanted him to drop everything and run as fast as he could to Rose, caution mandated patience to ensure her safety.

Her safety and his return to the future.

He knew the time was near. The Keeper had said when he found his path, he could return. Sarah Jane had shown him his path.

But what about Rose?

He swallowed hard and rubbed his tired, burning eyes.

When he opened his eyes, he looked around the room. The farmhouse would still be part of his life in the twentieth century. But Jim and Martha, little Tom and Sarah Jane would be *here*—where they belonged. He knew without being told that Jim and Martha would keep and raise Sarah Jane. Once he saw Martha lay her loving hands on the child, he knew she belonged here with them.

Not in the future with him.

But Rose . . .

Logic insisted that Zeke had spoken the truth, but a part of Dylan still doubted her. Hating himself for needing absolute proof, Dylan knew he had to learn for himself whether or not she was being held against her will, or perpetrating a complicated scheme to force him to relinquish the gold.

That damned gold.

Glancing down at his words scrawled on the paper, Dylan knew he was playing a dangerous game. But the cursed treasure had to go. The little bit of good it had done Abel Bentsen wasn't enough to compensate for all the harm. Maybe if he could ensure that it would do a great number of people good, the curse might finally end.

Folding the pages and sealing them in an envelope, Dylan addressed it to: the Citizens of Taney County. He sighed and said a silent prayer—*Martha's influence, no doubt*—that his instincts were accurate.

And that they'd heed his suggestion about future building on high ground.

The quiet house called out to him—saying goodbye?—as he made his way down the stairs to the small room where Maggie Mae dozed in the rocking chair beside a very content Sarah Jane. With his stethoscope, he listened to the baby's breathing and smiled. Definite improvement—no doubt about it. Thank God.

Glancing at her small hands curled up on either side of her little head, Dylan felt a lump form in his throat. For a very brief time he'd thought of her as his. He'd never realized how much he wanted children of his own until now. He owed Sarah Jane a debt of gratitude for making him realize this. After he returned to his own time and recovered from . . .

Rose.

His heart constricted as he thought of her. She was his wife. Maybe it was legal—maybe it wasn't. It wasn't as if a precedent had been established regarding time travelers and matrimony. What did it matter anyway? In his time it certainly wouldn't. But he thought of her as his wife.

His soul mate.

His . . . love.

"It's time. Ain't it?" Maggie Mae stirred, her voice a soft whisper in the small room.

Dylan understood somehow what she was asking and merely nodded in response. Yes, it was time. The lantern's low flame cast just enough light for him to see her wrinkled face when he looked at her.

"I'm going to miss you, Maggie Mae." He reached down to pat her shoulder. "I've learned so much from you—from all of you here. More than I ever learned in medical school."

"And we you, boy." She covered his hand with hers

and gave it a squeeze. "Ye've found your path. I can feel it."

"Yes." Dylan was strangely calm. Even though he was about to face an enemy who threatened someone he cared very much for—loved—he felt tranquil. Maybe because he knew the end of his adventure was near. Soon, his exile to the nineteenth century would end.

One way or another.

"I need a few supplies," he whispered, moving away from her to place his stethoscope back in the fanny pack. He paused before closing the pouch and removed the instrument again. Turning, he handed it to Maggie Mae. "You keep this."

The old woman took it in her hand and stared in awe. "Thank you, Dylan. I'll 'member you always."

"And I you, old woman." He grinned despite the certain danger about to confront him. "Take care of everyone here for me. And will you please give this letter to Jim when he comes home?"

"River's up. It'll take 'em all night to git here." She knitted her brow in concern. "Usually only takes half a day. Will that be soon enough?"

Dylan sighed. "It'll have to be."

"What kinda supplies you need?"

A mischievous grin tugged at the corners of his mouth. He narrowed his eyes meaningfully as he met her curious gaze. She obviously thought he'd gone mad—"tetched."

"Castor oil—as much as you've got." A malicious thought coursed through him. "I know a bunch of hillbillies who need a spring purge."

Maggie Mae chuckled. "Ye're a wicked boy." She

shook her head, then nodded. "It's in my cabin. Take all you need."

"Thanks, Maggie Mae." Dylan kissed her wrinkled cheek. "I'm just the doctor whose gonna give Charlie Riordan a prescription he'll never forget."

Seventeen

"You have found the right path."

The Keeper's voice filled the tiny valley at Serenity Spring. Dylan had known when he left the farmhouse—for what he felt certain would be the last time in this century—that he'd find the old Indian of legend.

It was time.

Past time.

He felt no fear of the spirit now. A strange peace had settled within him. It seemed almost to surround him as he waited for the Native American's words.

"In this journey you have learned many things."

"I have."

"You have grown as a man . . . in here." The figure touched his breast with his right hand. His face was wise and serene. "It is time for you to return from whence you came."

Dylan's heart raced.

Go home?

Leave Rose in the clutches of Charlie Riordan?

"No, not yet." Dylan shook his head, scarcely believing the words had left his lips. "I've prayed for this moment, but I can't leave Rose in danger. I'm the one who saved her life the first time and I'll be damned if I'll leave her in danger like this."

The spirit seemed to look at him, through him and beyond. It was evident his old dark eyes saw much more than what and who stood before him. Dylan knew without a doubt that the Keeper was living up to his reputation.

"You must return the woman known as Rose to this valley—where the living water comes from the ground—in there." He lifted his arm and pointed to the cabin.

"And then?" Dylan's pulse leapt again, racing out of control. Would it be possible to save Rose and return to his own time?

"All will be as it should."

"What the hell does that mean?" But Dylan's desperate query merely echoed through the empty valley. He was alone, standing in the darkness beside the spring.

The Keeper was gone.

All will be as it should.

Dylan searched his mind and heart. That could mean anything, nothing . . . or everything. Part of him knew the only way all could be as it should, was if he and Rose were together.

Yet this was her time—not his.

First things first. The castor oil he'd retrieved from Maggie Mae's cabin was in a jug that had formerly contained moonshine. The thick, potent liquid should serve his purpose quite well.

Charlie Riordan would rue the day he'd tangled with Dylan Marshall.

Taking a deep breath, Dylan headed in the direction

of Zeke Sawyer's cabin on the far side of the mountain. Though he'd never been there, he felt confident he'd be able to find it from the directions Maggie Mae had provided.

Quite soon Rose's captors would taste the potency of his fury.

Damn straight.

"Dammit, Sawyer." Charlie paced the room, repeatedly slamming his fist into his open palm. "Can't you make her eat? She's *your* stepdaughter."

"Rose's always been hardheaded. Right, boys?"

The twins guffawed and elbowed one another in obvious agreement. Zeke took another long drink from his jug and passed it to his sons. "If she don't wanna eat, she ain't gonna."

"But she'll be too damn weak to travel if she keeps this up."

"Travel where?" The front legs of Zeke's chair came down to the earthen floor with a soft thud as Rose tried to concentrate on the words being exchanged between the men.

"You heard me." Charlie stopped his pacing to grin in a superior fashion. "I'm plannin' to take Rose with me when I ride outta here . . . with *my* gold."

"I dunno about that." Zeke shook his head. "You said you'd let her go."

"Changed my mind." Charlie moved toward the door and peered through the crack. "He oughta be here soon. Note told him to come by sunrise."

"They's hours before sunrise."

"Damn. I'm going to the outhouse." Riordan slammed the door on his way out of the cabin.

"Rose." Zeke's whispered words were very near her face. She grimaced at the foul stench of his breath. "You gots to eat, girl. Keep up your strength. Doc'll be comin' for you soon."

"No." Rose looked away. "Dylan doesn't want me. He won't come."

"He will." Zeke shook her gently by the shoulders. "Dammit all, Rose. Your maw was a good woman, but she was a scrapper. You gonna quit? Or you gonna fight?"

Rose turned to face her stepfather. She had to trust him. What choice did she have? The worst thing Zeke had ever really done to her had turned into the most wonderful experience of her life. "How can you be so certain Dylan will come?"

"Shh." Zeke swallowed hard—his Adam's apple bobbed up and down in his long, skinny neck. "I know 'cuz I talked to 'im."

"And?" Rose's heart dashed as if running a horse race at the Taney County Fair. Could it be true? Would Dylan come for her? Did he really care?

"Shh." He leaned closer. "I dunno what he's got cooked up, but he ain't plannin' to let Riordan have you—I can tell you that for sure."

Rose shook her head again. "I can't hope for . . ." She bit her lower lip as tears burned her eyes, then slid down her cheeks.

From behind one of a thousand trees, Dylan watched as Riordan moved away from the outhouse and went back into the cabin. Dylan's fury knew no bounds, but he forcibly quelled it. Rose's life was in danger and he had to keep his wits about him in order to save her.

"Chill out," he whispered to himself and the squirrels.

Stealthily, he moved toward the pail used to bring water from the well and poured a generous portion of castor oil into it. He knew a large portion of the liquid would settle to the bottom of the water, but at least some of it should get inside his intended victims. With any luck, by morning the four men would be fighting over the one-hole outhouse, and in no condition to prevent him from taking Rose away to safety.

Two jugs sat near the back door. After making certain they weren't empty, Dylan poured in the castor oil—flavor enhancer. He carefully recorked the jugs, then darted behind the well just as he heard someone opening the door from inside.

"I'll fetch it, Paw."

One of Zeke's linebackers stepped out and retrieved both the jugs of tainted moonshine. Dylan smiled to himself, satisfied his plan would work.

He retrieved the burlap bag full of tools he'd stashed behind the outhouse, then removed a sharp saw. Dylan stepped into the obligatory facility, holding his breath against the nearly overwhelming stench. His stomach roiled in protest.

God, how he missed modern plumbing.

Slowly and methodically, he sawed around the hole in the rough bench seat until it was much larger than the original opening. He carefully replaced the pieces of wood he'd cut away, giving the fraudulent impression the bench was untouched. Until someone sat on it . . .

With any luck, his wife would not be escorted out to utilize the facilities, such as they were. But that was a risk he'd simply have to take.

Dylan returned to the edge of the dense woods surrounding the Sawyer cabin, then slid to the ground and leaned against a tree. As long as Rose's stepfamily was present, he didn't have to worry about Riordan abusing his captive. He might just as well settle down for the night, to wait for sunrise.

Or for the first scream from the outhouse.

A smile tugged at the corners of his mouth as fatigue overtook him. He'd been awake for two days and nights. During his residency such marathons had been a necessity. He was too damned old for all this nonsense.

Just a little sleep was all he needed to renew his energy before the castor oil took effect. There was nothing to do now but wait.

Dylan's path involved much more than he realized before. He saw it clearly now. His future must include Rose.

There was no other way.

Eighteen

A blood-curdling scream rent the still air.

At least an hour of darkness remained when Dylan jerked awake, blinking in confusion and wondering for a moment where in the hell he was.

Then he remembered.

Rose.

His wife.

The scream shattered the silence again with a string of profanities Patton would have envied. Dylan stood, hiding behind a tall oak to watch the dark outline of the outhouse. A devilish grin tugged at his lips.

Zeke's voice came from inside the outhouse again. "Gol-durn shit everywhere! Git me outta this stink-hole!"

Dylan couldn't prevent the chuckle that flowed from deep in his chest. His "gift" had obviously taken effect and his stepfather-in-law was the lucky individual to test the renovations in the outhouse first.

Not his first choice of victims, but still appropriate.

Just be patient, man.

But knowing Rose was inside with Charlie Riordan did little to promote tolerance. Just as his anger began to build again, the back door swung open and Zeke's offensive line came racing toward the outhouse together, their red flannel underwear glowing in the darkness.

"Paw!" One of the boys threw open the outhouse door and reached inside. "He plumb fell clear through."

"Tarnation, Paw. I gotta shit somethin' powerful an' ye broke the gol-durned outhouse."

"Shet up an' pull me outta this shee—it!"

Dylan held his breath in an attempt to stifle the loud laughter that threatened to burst forth at any moment. When the threesome emerged from the outhouse together, running into the woods in the opposite direction from his hiding place, he knew they'd be occupied for some time.

"Hey, that's my tree."

"Was mine first."

Their arguing eventually faded as pressing business obviously took precedence. Dylan straightened and let out a sigh of relief. He hoped Riordan would be suffering similar effects quite soon. The longer he was alone with Rose the less Dylan liked it.

"Damn."

But Riordan really *was* alone with Rose—a complication in his plans he hadn't anticipated. But it stood to reason, since Charlie was so heavy, that the castor oil would take longer to kick in for him.

Dropping to the ground, Dylan crept toward the cabin on all fours. He stopped at the side, listening for any sound from within the rough walls. Surely, if Riordan had consumed even a portion of the castor oil the Sawyers had, he'd be feeling some consequences soon.

Before he touched Rose.

Rose stared in horror at her captor as he approached.

She knew what was on his mind. There was no mistaking the lust glowing in the ebony gaze which scathed her with obvious intent.

"Now . . . we're gonna have us some fun." Charlie took a knife from his boot and cut open the front of her frock. He held the point near her throat. "Tell you what I'm gonna do to you. Girlie, you ain't never felt a man like me before. That puny doctor can't measure up to this here old bull. I know you're gonna cooperate with old Charlie. Ain't you, girl?"

Nausea churned within her. Rose didn't even blink— she didn't dare. With her hands still tied to the bed frame she was completely vulnerable—at the mercy of this madman.

It was the most horrible feeling she'd ever known.

The point of the blade pressed against her throat. The simple act of breathing could cause the blade's tip to prick her flesh. Where were the Sawyers? Why had they all left at the same time?

Leaving her at the mercy of this monster?

Charlie continued to hold the blade against her while he stripped her naked with his free hand. He bared her body to his roving gaze within seconds. Her clothing lay in tattered shreds on the earthen floor beside the bed.

Rose wanted to die.

A tear rolled from the corner of her eye as his gaze violated every inch of her. His eyes glowed menacingly as he released his belt and stood long enough to drop his trousers beside the remnants of her clothing. His swollen manhood stood out beneath his rotund abdomen, obviously eager to invade her body.

Opaque fluid dripped from the tip in apparent anticipation of complete release, oblivious to her wishes.

And she most assuredly did not share his desires.

Before she could scream in protest, he covered her
with his heavy frame. His wet lips pressed against
hers until she tasted her own blood. Using her teeth
as a barrier to his probing tongue, she vowed silently
to deny him entrance to every possible portal of her
body.

He assaulted her with rough hands as he continued
his efforts to deepen his invasive kiss. Surely the Sawyers would come back soon. They had to.

As Charlie dragged his mouth from hers, he lowered his head to encircle her nipple, nipping at it with
his teeth. Rose groaned in shame and agony. It was
repulsive to be touched in such a vile manner. Only
Dylan should ever touch her so intimately.

"No." She couldn't bear it. The thought of anyone
but Dylan touching her body made her stomach lurch.
She wanted to die—right here and now.

The back door swung open as her death wish filled
her mind. Rose stared in shock as the figure of her
husband came toward her captor like a charging bull.

"What the hell?" Charlie leapt from the bed, staring
in shock and still naked from the waist down.

Without a moment's hesitation, Dylan charged
Charlie Riordan's huge bulk. With his head down, he
rammed into the obese man's gut, sending the heavier
figure to the dirt floor with a loud thud and a string
of expletives.

"You damn son of a bitch." Charlie immediately
lurched to his feet and came toward Dylan with surprising speed for such a large man.

Rose struggled against the leather bindings with all her might. She had to help Dylan. Riordan was so much larger.

"Jeez . . . he's a damned sumo wrestler, with the speed of a New York Knicks guard." The older man had Dylan's head in a vise within a few moments. Dylan's face turned reddish purple as Charlie's grip tightened.

"Have it your way, old man," Dylan whispered. It was obvious he was having trouble breathing. "I can . . . fight dirty, too. You leave me . . . no alternative."

With the obvious skill and knowledge of a physician, Dylan grabbed a handful of the man's genitals and gave a decided twist. Riordan let out a howl of pain that undoubtedly woke the neighbors for ten miles in either direction.

Rose continued to tug on her bindings while the men struggled. If she could only free herself . . .

Charlie's saddlebags.

The gun.

Rose watched her husband struggle with the tenacity of a bulldog. He hung on to Riordan's offensive flesh, twisting and pinching until the man released Dylan's head.

Overcome with relief, Rose watched as Dylan gasped for air. Riordan grabbed his huge belly with one hand, while continuing the struggle to free himself from the straits of a physician's death vise.

Twisting and turning, Riordan continued to moan in agony. Dylan didn't budge. He ignored the blows Charlie inflicted to his face and head as the man fought to free himself.

Rose felt the bindings slip. Her left hand tore free and she used it to release her right arm. Without hesitation, she swung her legs to the floor and leapt to her feet.

The room spun. Grabbing her head, she braced herself against the wall for support. Two days without food had taken its toll. Zeke had been right in telling her to keep up her strength.

But there was no time for that now. Taking a deep breath, she steadied herself and girded her resolve. The saddlebags were only a few feet away.

Blood spurted from Dylan's split lip where Charlie's merciless pummeling continued. She had to help him. But his grip on Riordan's male organs seemed quite effective.

Rose reached the saddlebags and found the gun. The smooth metal felt foreign in her hand. It was extremely heavy as she lifted it from its hiding place.

"Riordan," she said in a voice filled with far more courage than she felt at the moment.

Dylan and Charlie both looked in her direction at the same time. Rose noticed her husband's eyes widen in amazement as she steadily aimed the weapon toward the man who had ceased his merciless beating.

Hesitantly, Dylan released the man's vitals, which Rose noted with a sense of satisfaction, were no longer standing at attention. Dylan moved away from the larger man as she kept the gun raised in a threatening manner.

"Now, Rose . . ."

"Don't you dare speak my name again." Her nostrils flared as anger filled her, clouding her judgment.

"You . . . you framed my daddy. Made him hang. Didn't you?"

Silence.

"Didn't you?" Her voice raised in hysteria when he simply stared at her. His gaze swept the length of her; he seemed unruffled by the weapon.

Dylan moved to her side and reached for the gun very slowly. "I'll hold this, Rose." His voice was calming, soothing, drawing her back from the world of insanity which had temporarily gained control. "It's all right now."

Shaking, she let Dylan take the gun from her grasp, then turned toward him, engulfed with tears. His free hand pulled her into a protective circle.

"Now." Dylan's steady tone gave the impression he remained unaffected by the events which had just transpired. "You're going to the sheriff."

"Oh . . . my gut." Riordan doubled over, grabbing his abdomen with both hands. "Got . . . gotta git to the outhouse."

Dylan arched a speculative brow and nodded. Rose stared in confusion at the smile which spread across his handsome face.

"Oh, by all means, allow me to escort you."

Dylan released her and shrugged out of his shirt by switching the gun from hand to hand, then passed the garment to her. "Here, Rose." His warm gaze gave her badly needed reassurance.

With shaking fingers, she buttoned the large shirt, which hung to her knees. Her nudity was shielded from Charlie Riordan's roving gaze at last, though he seemed occupied with other problems now.

Breathing a sigh of relief, she watched in confusion

as Dylan—eagerly—led her captor at gunpoint to the facilities behind the cabin.

When Riordan entered the outhouse in pre-dawn light, Dylan waited outside and leaned against the door grinning. It was the most purely devilish grin she'd ever seen in her life. Stepping completely outside, Rose wondered why in the world her husband should take such pleasure in leading a criminal to the necessary house.

A scream, followed by a stream of profanity that made her blush, provided a partial answer to her mental question. Dylan doubled over in riotous laughter. Tears of mirth streamed down his face.

Rose shook her head in bewilderment, wondering what sort of prank her husband had played on her captors.

"Dylan!" Jim's voice echoed through the trees.

"Up—here—Jim." Dylan's laughter subsided, but the cursing and yelling from inside the outhouse seemed endless.

"What in tarnation is goin' on up here?" Jim glanced at Rose and reddened beneath his beard.

The sun bathed the forest with light by the time Jim's companion reached the clearing where the Sawyer cabin stood. He had all three Sawyer men lined up at the end of his shotgun.

"Was they involved in this, Miss Rose?" the sheriff asked, looking quickly away when he obviously noticed the state of her attire.

Rose looked at Dylan, then at her stepfather who also clutched his abdomen. Zeke's face was a peculiar shade of green. Curiously, Abner and Tem seemed afflicted with the same malady.

"No, Sheriff," she said in a voice that was now calm and serene. She exchanged knowing glances with her husband—the man she loved with all her heart. "My stepfamily tried to help me. The man who abducted me and tried to . . ." She looked down at her clothing for emphasis, taking a deep breath for courage. "He's in there."

She pointed toward the outhouse. The string of oaths had ceased. The only sounds emitting from the primitive structure were groans.

"He's all yours, Sheriff." Dylan handed the gun to the lawman, who had released the Sawyer family with a perfunctory nod.

"I gotta find me a tree." Zeke, followed by his sons, vanished into the woods.

Jim, Rose and the sheriff glanced after the threesome in bewilderment. But Dylan burst into renewed gales of laughter which Rose found herself drawn into. By the time her husband had joined her near the door, she was laughing as hard as he.

But she had no idea why.

"What in tarnation happened in here?"

Rose chanced a furtive glance when the sheriff opened the door to the outhouse. All she saw of Charlie Riordan were his legs, arms and the top of his head. The remainder of his huge bulk was submerged.

"Oh!" Rose reddened at the spectacle and cast her husband a look of suspicion. "I trust you had something to do with this?"

"Oh, yeah. And I enjoyed every damned minute of it." Dylan swept her into his arms and kissed her soundly on the lips. When he lifted his gaze, his hazel eyes had darkened to a deep greenish-gray. "I love you, Rose."

"Oh, Dylan." She laid her head against his chest and sighed. "I love you, too—always have, but was too stupid to see it."

"Enough to forget about that wretched treasure?"

She nodded. There was no doubt in her mind. "I never want to see or hear of it again."

"And you're willing to live with me . . . *anywhere?*" He cupped her chin in his hand and lifted her gaze to meet his. An unmistakable challenge tinted his voice.

"Anywhere."

"Even if it's something like a Jules Verne novel?"

Frowning and grinning almost simultaneously, she nodded. "Even there."

"Let's go home."

He held her hand as they stepped off the porch and paused beside Jim. Dylan extended a hand to his cousin. There was something distressing—final—in Dylan's voice.

"I'm going to miss you, Jim."

Rose glanced at her husband in surprise. Were they leaving the Ozarks? For some reason she wasn't as pleased with that prospect as she once would have been. She'd miss Jim and Martha very much.

"Ye're leavin' us then?" Jim didn't seem surprised at all by this revelation. "Don't you worry none about Sarah Jane. She's got a home with us." His expression seemed wistful. "I gotta tell ye, Dylan . . . Martha told me . . . everythin'."

A huge smile split her husband's face. "Great-Great-Grandpa. I'll miss you."

"It's been a heck of a treat . . . meetin' my own . . ." A catch in Jim's voice prevented him from finishing his sentence. He cleared his throat and embraced Dylan. "Take care, Son."

Great-great-grandpa?

Rose looked from man to man. They were nearly the same age. This was ridiculous. Was her husband losing his mind? But steady, reliable Jim seemed in complete agreement with this insanity.

"Let's go home, Rose."

Without explanation, Dylan led her through the forest and down the hill toward the cabin. He glanced at her from time to time and just smiled with a curious tranquility in his eyes.

When they reached the cabin, he pushed open the door, then swung her into his arms. He spun her in a circle, clutching her against him, reminding her that beneath his heavy shirt she had no clothing whatsoever.

He held her for a few moments, then sat her on the edge of the bed. "Riordan didn't . . . ?"

She knew what he meant and swallowed the lump in her throat. "No, but he tried." Rose noticed Dylan's face relax even more.

"Good. I'm going to get you something to eat."

She started to protest, but remembered how weak she'd felt this morning. Nodding, she merely smiled and watched him prepare a plate of bread and cheese. When he brought it to her with a cup of spring water, she ate every bite and drained the cup.

"Thank you." Her gaze swept him. He was magnificent, bare chested with rippling muscles beneath smooth skin. Setting her plate on the floor, she reached out to lay the flat of her palm against his smooth chest.

"I love you," she whispered, downright giddy with the knowledge that he returned her feelings.

Dylan's mouth covered hers in a kiss made all the more spectacular by the fact that they had openly declared their feelings. They were married and in love— what better combination could there be?

She melded herself against his hard body, felt her insides grow warm and jellylike as he caressed her. When he laid her back against the bed, she released the buttons on the front of the shirt, baring herself to the hands that roamed over her shoulders, down her arms, over her breasts and belly.

He dipped his head to kiss her neck while his hands tested the weight of her breast. A feral hunger pounded a steady rhythm in her body as his mouth encircled her upthrust nipple, drawing it into his mouth as his tongue urged it to almost painful sensitivity.

His beard stubble rasped against her flesh as his hot, wet mouth continued to drive her into a frenzy of raw need. He suckled as she writhed beneath him.

She arched, pressing her tender flesh against his possessive mouth, eager to please and be pleased. His hands cupped the sides of her breasts, massaging and bringing them into even more prominence.

The world spun ever onward as desire controlled her every thought. The need to be consumed drove her. Dylan enticed her on a journey through a vortex of brightness. Though her eyes were closed, she sensed their voyage.

When he released his trousers and slid between her thighs, Rose encompassed his waist with her legs to draw him close, but he evaded her attempts to possess him. He seemed intent to tarry, to torture her with the ache he'd created deep within her.

Dylan kissed his way downward, burying his auburn head in the dark, crisp hair which shielded her female flesh. She was his, lost to reality and glad of it.

A fire, as sure and hot as any deliberately set, raged within her—an inferno, determined to possess and ravage until it burned itself out. She was powerless to extinguish the flames herself. The one who had started the blaze must douse it as well.

Lost in a swirling eddy of pleasure, Rose wrapped her legs around the back of his neck. His hands busied themselves with her aching female body, filling her and coaxing her into a whimpering mass.

God, how she wanted him to fill her, to end this misery. At last their lovemaking was really that—*love*-making. That knowledge fueled her passion, sent her soaring up toward an elusive brightness, a glow that promised solace from the agony.

Then a cry left her lips as blackness appeared before her eyes. Slowly, as her body seemed to leave this world and enter another, bright lights exploded behind her eyelids, blotting out the darkness, offering relief and ecstasy like she'd never known before.

Growling with a need which surely matched hers, Dylan left her throbbing flesh, which strangely wanted more, and slid upward until his rigid maleness pressed against her. She opened to him—his penetration unhinged her. Her second explosion came almost instantaneously as he entered and withdrew, pressing himself deeper with each thrust.

Spiraling, she felt as if they were floating through air, no longer anchored to the bed—or even to the earth itself. They were spinning, being swallowed, sucked deep into another world—one where she knew love would rule.

Through closed eyes, Rose saw the bright, swirling lights. They seemed intent on possessing her mind. At this moment she didn't care what happened as long as Dylan didn't stop his marvelous loving.

The lights grew brighter and moved faster in the maelstrom as she reached the pinnacle. Her body bucked against his as she swallowed his seed with a ravenous hunger that made her bite her lip until she tasted blood.

Then blackness . . .

Nineteen

Dylan sighed in contentment. He felt like maple syrup during August dog days. The supple form dozing against his chest moaned slightly, but didn't awaken as he yawned and stretched.

It was late afternoon, by his calculations. Hippocrates nudged his hand with a cold, wet dog nose. Chuckling, Dylan's gaze swept the room—then stopped short.

It couldn't be. Could it? A miracle—an apparition—leaned against the wall near the door. He rubbed his eyes and looked again.

"Oh, my God."

There sat the backpack he'd carried down to this very cabin the day he first moved in.

Hooting in delight and amazement, he looked down at Rose, who had awakened to his raucous behavior and stared at him in indisputable bewilderment. Dylan swung his legs out from under hers and padded barefoot to the pack, throwing it open to peer inside.

A couple of moldy sandwiches, tools . . .

He looked at Rose and smiled. The cellar door was propped open—the way he'd left it when he first climbed down the ladder.

His heart did a little flip-flop in his chest as he glanced from Rose—alive and well—to the trap door.

A cold sweat beaded his brow as the memory of the sight he'd first seen when he opened the cellar door assailed him. He had to look, though deep inside he knew. Rose was alive . . . here with him in the twentieth century.

Nothing less than a miracle.

Too good to be true?

Slowly, while his wife stared at him in total confusion, Dylan walked over to the trap door and looked down. He saw nothing but darkness.

Then he remembered having brought two flashlights with him when he moved into the cabin and returned to his backpack to find the spare. When he flipped it on and shined it down into the dark cellar, he released a breath he hadn't known he was holding.

"Hot damn. Nothing but old Abel Bentsen's moonshine and still." He clenched his fist in victory. "And my missing flashlight."

Dylan sat back on his haunches and laughed until he cried. Rose simply stared at him, concern etching her fine complexion while he struggled to his feet.

"Dylan." Her voice was firm. "Dylan Marshall."

"Rose, it's gone. There's no treasure down there. No . . . no skeleton."

"Skeleton? What are you talking about?" Obviously concerned, Rose walked over to stand beside her husband and gaze into the dark hole.

When Dylan again turned on the flashlight, she gasped and jumped back. "What's that?"

Dylan frowned, then laughed again. He wrapped her in a bear hug, rejoicing that Rose was in his time . . . and that her skeleton wasn't in the cellar.

He kissed her soundly on the lips. Here she was—

his one hundred and twenty-five-year-old bride. His eyes widened. "When's your birthday, Rose?"

"My birthday?" She frowned at him. "Dylan Marshall, you're acting like a fool."

"When is your birthday?"

Sighing, she placed a hand on her hip and stepped away to stare at him in open disdain. "June third."

Dylan cleared his throat and assumed a very serious tone. "My dear, this will come as a shock to you, but . . . on June third you'll be a hundred and twenty-six years old."

"Nonsense." Rose reached for the flashlight. "Now . . . tell me what this thing is."

He let her take it from his hand. She turned it over in her palm and examined it carefully. When she flipped the switch and the beam came on, she dropped it on his foot.

"Ouch!" Laughing, he stooped to retrieve the object. As he straightened, he couldn't resist pausing to kiss his way back up the front of her abdomen.

"Dylan."

She was really pissed now. He couldn't postpone telling her the truth any longer. He swallowed hard and straightened. "I'm sorry, Rose." He released a pent-up sigh—one he'd been holding for a century. "It's time you heard the entire story."

"I should say so."

As he was leading her back to the bed, she looked around the room in confusion. "What happened in here? Everything's so . . . so old and dusty."

Dylan wisely resisted the impulse to say "especially you" and sat down beside her on the edge of the bed.

Holding her hand in his, he maintained his serious tone. "It doesn't matter."

"This is really strange, Dylan." She reached up to press her cool hand on his forehead. "I think you have a fever."

"Strange—yes. But you caused my fever, Rose." He shook his head and sighed. "This is going to be the hardest thing in the world for you to believe, but you have to listen to all of it."

She nodded, her gaze wide and frightened.

"I was born in the year . . . 1961."

"That's ridiculous."

"You're supposed to listen, remember?" When she nodded, he smiled and squeezed her hand. "I inherited this farm from my grandfather in the year 1994. His will required me to live in this cabin for thirty days, for some eccentric reason only he understood."

She frowned and tried to pull away. "This is scary."

"I know, love. And . . . it gets scarier."

"All right. Go on."

"This cabin is—was—haunted."

"I told you before I don't believe in ghosts, Dylan."

Dylan smiled at the irony of the situation. *"You were the ghost of Serenity Spring, Rose."* He reached up to caress her stunned face with the back of his hand. His voice became hoarse with emotion as he tried to help her understand the truth. "You . . . originally died in that cellar and haunted this cabin for a hundred years."

He knew she was reliving the nightmare of being sealed alive in the cellar when her face paled and her pupils dilated. "Rose, it's all right. You're alive."

"I'm . . . I'm listening." An unmistakable tremor

altered her voice. "Tell me the rest—not that I believe any of this."

"Your ghost . . . visited me when I first moved into the big house—the farmhouse."

"Ah, so that's why . . ."

"Why I accused you of coming to my bed." He grinned and stroked her bare shoulder. "You had."

"Humph."

"Your ghost had." He shuddered. "When I moved in here and opened the cellar door, I looked down and saw—"

"Oh!" She covered her mouth with her hand. Her eyes grew even wider. "You saw me!"

"I saw . . . your . . . remains." Dylan pulled her against him. Stroking her hair, he closed his eyes, then opened them again to ensure she was still in his arms—that she was real.

And alive.

"And?" Her voice was barely audible. The pupils of her blue eyes dilated as she stared at him.

"The gold." He gritted his teeth, recalling his avarice. "I was willing to go down there for the gold. Little did I know that when I did, I'd travel back in time a hundred years."

"To the night Tom Marshall sealed me in that cellar?"

"Yes." Dylan squeezed her. "God, it feels so good to hold you, to know you're here with me—*alive.*"

"As good as it feels to be held, I hope." Rose trembled and pressed herself against him even harder. "So, you're telling me that we're back in . . . your time?"

"I think so." Dylan shook his head in wonder. "That

backpack over by the door was left in this century before I went down in the cellar."

"I'm so confused." Rose leaned away to stare up at his face. "I want to believe you."

"It must be as hard for you to accept this as it was for me to believe I was really in the nineteenth century."

She laughed. It was a nervous, hesitant sound—not her usual happy giggle. "And you were escorted to the preacher by a drunk hillbilly."

"Yeah, and I owe him a debt of gratitude."

She frowned and tilted her head to the side. "How do we . . . make sure which century we're in? Assuming, of course, that this isn't a figment of your overactive imagination."

As if in answer to her question, a sound drifted into the cabin. It was a dull roar, faint as if it came from a great distance.

Straight up.

Excitement filled him as Dylan released her and rushed to the backpack. He withdrew two pairs of jeans and T-shirts he'd packed for his thirty-day vigil in the cabin. Tossing one of each to Rose, he pulled on the others.

"Hurry. You aren't going to believe this." He rushed out onto the porch to look up at the sky.

"I already don't believe this, Dylan," Rose murmured while pulling on the jeans. Following Dylan's example, she joined him on the porch, then shaded her eyes and looked up at the bright, afternoon sky.

The dull roar grew louder as Dylan held her hand and glanced down once to grin at her. He looked like a little boy at the carnival.

Rose returned his smile despite her trepidation. What nonsense was this? Time travel? Did he actually expect her to accept his bizarre tale?

"Look."

Obeying his excited command, Rose shaded her eyes again to gaze up at the blue sky. Her breath caught in her throat as a giant silver . . . bird passed overhead. Sunlight glistened from its wings and twin tails of white smoke followed behind for some distance.

"What . . . what is it?"

"A jet. An airplane." Dylan pointed up as the object vanished from their line of sight. "They're as common in this time as trains were in yours."

Rose swayed and clutched his arm for support. "It's true. We've . . ."

"Traveled forward in time a hundred years."

Dylan seemed ecstatic—a total mystery to her. His happiness was somewhat irritating at the moment. Rose covered her face, shook her head and pulled away from him, turning to go back into the cabin. Perhaps this was a dream. She was still asleep and none of this had really happened.

That's it.

"Dylan!"

"Jeff!"

Rose paused in the doorway to stare at the stranger running toward them from the far side of the spring. He was tall and slender and seemed very pleased to see Dylan.

"Where the hell have you been?"

Dylan laughed as he embraced his friend. "How long have I been gone? I lost count."

"Weeks."

"You aren't gonna believe where I've been, Jeff." Dylan threw his head back to laugh again. "Actually, come to think of it, I never really left here. I did spend more than thirty days in the cabin."

"Uh-huh." Jeff shook his head. "I came out here, had the sheriff out and your cousin—"

"Cousin?" Dylan frowned and rubbed his chin in that familiar fashion as Rose continued to watch from the cabin door. He ran his other hand through the unruly mass of auburn hair she'd grown to love. "I have a cousin?"

"Stop joshin' me, Dylan. You know damned well you do. Jim Marshall. Your cousin? Remember? Earth to Dylan?"

Dylan sighed and smiled. "That's the most wonderful news I've ever heard. It means . . ." He sobered and turned toward Rose. "Jeff, this is . . ."

"Yes?" Jeff looked at Dylan expectantly. "Aren't you going to introduce the lady, Dylan?"

"You've never seen her before, then?" Dylan sideglanced at Rose. "You're sure?"

"Never." Jeff looked at Rose again and extended his hand. "Well, if he's not going to introduce us, I'll do it myself. Jeff Bentsen."

Rose nodded. "I'm . . ."

Laughing, Dylan reached for Rose's hand and drew her off the porch. He sighed and kissed her softly. "You're not a ghost," he whispered in her ear.

"Ghost?" Jeff frowned, then chuckled. "C'mon, Dylan. You know I have superhuman hearing. You never could keep anything from me anyway. And I sure as hell don't believe in ghosts."

"Good." Dylan nodded and squeezed her hand. "That makes two—three of us."

"Now tell me who this lovely lady is, where you've been and what's going on?"

"It's a long story, Jeff." Dylan slapped his friend on the back. "Come on in and we'll give you the full report. By the way, this is my wife, Rose."

"Wife?"

"Yep." He gave her hand a possessive squeeze and looked at her in a manner that made her blood warm and her knees weaken. "My wife, in every sense of the word."

"Well, I'll be. Congratulations! This is great news. Guess you finally took my advice." Shaking his head in obvious amazement, Jeff followed Dylan and Rose into the cabin. Stopping short, he stared at the furniture and let out a low whistle of admiration. "Valuable antiques."

"They were part of the package." Dylan grinned, then sighed. "Have a seat, Jeff. I think you're going to need a drink, too." His face brightened. "Hey, how long does moonshine keep?"

"Moonshine? You really have lost it, Dylan."

Jeff frowned and rubbed his chin, leaning against the oak tree stump which had once been used to entomb Rose in the cellar. She shuddered, beginning to actually feel the age Dylan claimed she was. This was all too much to absorb in one day.

Or a hundred years.

But this helped her understand some of the inconsistencies in her husband's behavior. As she sat down beside him on the bed, which was the only real place to sit in the cabin, other than on the edge of the table, Rose began—little by little—to accept the miracle.

She'd never belonged in the Ozarks of the nineteenth century, but perhaps the twentieth would be different. Gazing at her husband's profile as he explained the miracle they'd experienced to his friend, she relaxed. This was fated—inevitable. She and Dylan belonged together . . . in any place . . . anytime.

For all time.

"So you really expect me to believe you've traveled through time?"

"Yes, I do." Dylan's tone had roughened. He released a frustrated sigh. "Maybe it was a mistake telling you. If you don't believe me, nobody will."

Jeff rubbed his thigh and shook his head again. His expensive-looking clothes seemed out of place in the old, dusty cabin. "You got that right, Dylan. I don't think it would help your reputation any to go blabbing this all over the county."

"I know—if it's still there." Dylan went outside. "C'mon."

Rose merely offered a shrug to Jeff's questioning glance. "Let's go see what he's up to," she suggested.

Dylan ran up the hill at the back of the cabin. Holding up the too large jeans with one hand, Rose tried not to notice when Jeff's hair caught on a branch and slipped right off his head.

Blushing, he righted his hair and offered her a sheepish grin. "Male ego."

Frowning uncertainly, Rose noticed Dylan standing in front of a large boulder with his hands on his hips. He was scratching his head in obvious confusion.

"I should've known," he whispered when they reached him.

"What is it, Dylan?" Rose touched his forearm.

"This is where I hid the . . . the gold." He reddened and offered her a shrug and a grin.

"It's gone." Rose's heart thumped in her breast. Part of her prayed the gold was really gone—it had caused enough trouble already.

"I left a letter telling where it was hidden and what it was to be used for." Dylan shook his head again. "But I wasn't really looking for the gold. I left some other things in the cave. Let me have another look."

Slipping behind the boulder, Dylan vanished inside the small cave, whooping in delight a moment later. "It's still here. Come see. Jeff. Rose."

Sighing, Jeff poked his head around the boulder just as Dylan started out with something in both hands. "My cellular phone." He held up a badly corroded object which Rose vaguely recalled having seen at their wedding. "I tried to use it, Rose. Remember?"

She nodded. "I didn't know what it was, though. I still don't."

Jeff reached for the phone. It was in two pieces. "Color me strange, but I was hoping for the gold."

"My wallet." Dylan laughed, holding his hand out to display a very old leather pouch. As he opened it, several cards fell out. "American Express, Visa, Master-Card." He grinned at Rose. "I think you'll like these when you learn how to use them. Then again, maybe I shouldn't explain them to you."

"All right." Jeff looked stunned. His voice diminished to a faint whisper. "Don't ask me how or why . . . but I believe you."

Dylan patted Jeff on the shoulder. "I knew I could count on you." He nodded and glanced at Rose. "I'm definitely going to need some rather . . . unusual assistance from you, old buddy. Old pal."

Jeff stared long and hard at Dylan. Rose sensed that he was trying to decide whether or not his friend was crazy. She was still wondering about her own sanity, for that matter.

"I know you're up to something when you call me old buddy. But old pal, too?" He shook his head and sighed.

Dylan held a badly decayed parchment in his hands. His gaze locked with hers. "Rose, do you remember this?"

"Our marriage certificate." She touched the fragile document.

"The date is still legible." He held it up for Jeff's inspection.

Jeff sighed and nodded. "All right. Dylan, believe it or not, I think you're telling the truth." He laughed, obviously at himself. "It explains a lot, actually."

"Such as?"

Jeff glanced from Rose to Dylan. "Walk up to the house with me and we'll go for a drive. I'll show you what I'm talking about."

Dylan brightened as he grasped her hand and gave it a tug. "I want to put these treasures in the cabin first." He looked at her. "Are you ready to witness the miracles of the twentieth century, Rose? They're not all good, but they're sure as hell impressive."

"Are we talking about that Jules Verne nonsense

again?" She couldn't prevent skepticism from entering her tone.

"Not exactly."

They bypassed the farmhouse and went directly to Jeff's Volvo. Rose hesitated when Dylan opened the door for her. She gazed up at him; uncertainty flickered across her face. Her blue eyes asked a question.

Dylan nodded and gave her hand a reassuring squeeze. "It's all right, love. This is a car. An automobile, which I believe were already developed in your time. It's the most common form of travel in America, now."

She swallowed hard. "Yes, I read about Mr. Ford's invention."

After they climbed into the car, Dylan related some of the more recent history of Taney County to Rose. He pointed to the dam across the reservoir. His gut twisted with the pain of remembrance. Dogwood was submerged beneath the vast, rippling water. The mill . . . his medical office . . . the saloon . . .

All gone.

"You don't remember the hospital or the statue, then?" Jeff asked as they drove slowly along the curvy highway.

"No." Dylan reached down and checked to make certain he'd fastened Rose's seat belt. He'd have to teach her so many things. But there was no doubt in his mind that she possessed the intelligence and fortitude to accomplish anything. After all, she'd managed to teach him how to love again. "Do you remember ever hearing about a town called Dogwood, Jeff?"

"Of course." Jeff frowned as he gazed at Dylan and shook his head. "This is weird. You grew up here but really don't remember."

Dylan swallowed hard and looked out across the lake. "It's under the lake." Hearing Rose's tiny gasp, he covered her hand with his and patted it. "The dam held back the river and covered the town."

"How barbaric!"

Jeff frowned again and pointed to a large building high on a hill overlooking the massive lake. "Up there's the hospital. You really don't remember it?"

"The treasure." Dylan sighed, remembering his letter to the citizens of Taney County. "I gave the county the gold to build a hospital with. I guess they paid attention when I insisted it be built on high ground. That's it?"

"You'll see for yourself in a few minutes."

A winding road led up the hill behind the hospital. *Dogwood Memorial Hospital.* Dylan nodded in satisfaction. The memory of the little town lived on. "Perfect."

"There's more." Jeff drove through a parklike setting behind the hospital where carefully manicured grounds led up to a huge statue, surrounded by a pond full of ducks.

Jeff parked the car and Dylan showed Rose how to unfasten her seat belt and open the door. They all climbed out in the warm air and walked around the pond.

Rose's gasp caught Dylan's attention. He turned

slowly. A premonition gripped him. She was looking up at the statue, her expression filled with awe.

Following the direction of her gaze, Dylan lifted his head and stared in wonder.

"It's you, Dylan." Rose's voice was filled with surprise and obvious appreciation for the likeness the statue bore to her husband.

"Well, I'll be." Dylan walked around the statue until he faced it again. A plaque at the base near the water caught his attention. He squinted to read the raised letters.

"Dedicated to the memory of Dr. Dylan Marshall, whose generous contribution to the citizens of Taney County and the town of Dogwood made this hospital more than just a dream."

"And the date, Dylan . . ." Jeff's expression had changed to one of reluctant acceptance. "See what I mean about this explaining a lot?"

"1894."

"Folks around here have always wondered about the resemblance between you and this statue." Jeff shook his head. "I can't believe you don't remember any of this. There's even a picture in our high school yearbook of you standing beside that statue." He chuckled and gave them a sheepish grin. "We were loaded, of course."

"Loaded?" Rose echoed, frowning.

"Uh, I'll explain it later, Rose." Dylan shrugged and smiled at his wife. "I guess they probably thought I was a throwback, eh?" He laughed out loud. "God, was I ever a throwback."

"Something like that, except there was never any record of a Dylan Marshall living in the nineteenth century . . . except for this statue." Jeff chewed his lower lip, obviously deep in thought. "Your family always claimed Dylan was the long lost son of Joe Marshall."

Recalling Martha and Jim's kindness and generosity, Dylan smiled. "He was."

"If you say so." Jeff rubbed his jaw and sighed. "This is so strange."

"I guess I must have appeared from nowhere, then vanished. I can't wait to tell you everything I did. I met Abel Bentsen, your great-great something or other."

"Abel? Really?" Jeff chuckled. "I heard he was a rascally moonshiner."

"He was, but I convinced him to give it up for his health." Dylan winked at Rose, who simply stood in silence absorbing it all. "His still, supplies and jugs full of one-hundred-year-old moonshine are in the cellar at the cabin. A museum might want the still."

"I want the moonshine."

The men laughed as the sun lowered behind a mountain in a fiery ball of crimson, then they climbed back into the car. A short time later, they were at the Marshall Farm again. Dylan sat in silence for several moments, contemplating his situation.

"So, I have a cousin?"

"Yep. He's your only relative, but he's married and his wife's expecting their first baby. They live here at the farm."

"Then . . . then it's not mine." The joy of discovering he had a family mingled with his disappointment at not owning the farm he'd originally planned to sell. "What about—"

"You inherited Serenity Spring, Dylan."

Sighing, Dylan gave Rose's hand a squeeze. The cabin at the spring would be their home in this century as well as the last. He could practice medicine at Dogwood Memorial Hospital . . . and maybe Rose could go to college in Springfield, if she wanted.

His gaze swept over her in the twilight. She seemed so vulnerable in his oversized clothing in a time and place as foreign to her as her time had been to him. He gave her hand another squeeze.

"Look," Jeff said, pointing toward the front of the farmhouse.

Dylan turned and saw a tall thin man near his age leaning against the porch railing. Except for the clean-shaven face, he was the image of their mutual great-great-grandfather. Dylan's heart swelled in his throat and his eyes burned.

"My cousin?"

Jeff nodded.

"I'll be damned." He turned to his wife, judging from her expression that she saw the resemblance as well. "Think you can handle this, Rose?"

Rose smiled. Tears sparkled in her cornflower blue eyes and she nodded almost imperceptibly. "I can do anything as long as I have you, Dylan."

"There's a forger over in Branson I defended once," Jeff began pensively, then sighed. "I can't believe I'm doing this. I'll arrange for some . . . documentation for Rose. It'll be illegal, of course, but she'll need a birth certificate and Social Security card. When's your birthday, Rose?"

Dylan melted into her smile. He nodded, knowing

what she was thinking. They'd shared quite an adventure, a past, a mystery . . . and now a future.

"June third . . . 1868."

Epilogue

Rose trembled as Dylan brought the car to a stop in front of the Taney County Courthouse. "Can this be real, Dylan?" she asked, searching his face for answers.

"Yep." He turned to face her. "You, Rose Jameson Marshall, college student, are about to vote for the first time in your life."

The anticipation was killing her. "For president." She bit her lower lip, then smiled, remembering all the times she'd tried to tell other women in Dogwood—even her own mother—that they deserved the right to vote. "I'm really going to vote for the President of the United States of America?"

Dylan nodded and squeezed her hand. "Thanks to Jeff's master-forger. This time, and every four years for the rest of your life, love."

She reached for the door handle. "Let's go."

Dylan held her hand as they ascended the steps of the impressive structure. Joy filled her as she glanced at the man at her side—a man who loved her. He was all she'd ever hoped for . . . and so much more. Sometimes she had to pinch herself to make sure she wasn't dreaming.

And what a dream.

Inside the dim building, they waited in line for their

turn to enter the voting booths. "Do you need some help, Rose?"

"Only one at a time in the booth," an elderly woman said in a dreary voice. "Sorry."

Dylan shrugged and gave Rose a thumbs-up gesture, then went inside the booth next to hers. A dark curtain closed around him.

Filled with exhilaration, Rose imitated her husband's behavior. The voting booth was dark and private. She was charged with the enormity of her decision as she scanned the list of candidates.

She'd studied the various candidates and made her decision weeks ago. But the desire to prolong the exquisite moment was simply irresistible.

A slow smile tugged at her lips as she made her choice and left the booth. Dylan was waiting, smiling when she paused and sighed in satisfaction.

"Well, are you going to tell me who you voted for?" he asked with a smug expression. "I hope you took my advice this first time."

Rose lifted her chin and leveled her gaze on him, then shook her head. "My vote is confidential, Dylan. Surely you know that."

He chuckled. "All right. Don't tell me, then. It doesn't matter. I'm sure you took my advice."

"No, I made an informed decision and voted for the best . . . person for the job."

"What?" He knitted his brows together in confusion. "Well, tell me who you voted for, then, Miss Know-it-All."

She leaned over and whispered a name in his ear, feeling him tense at her side.

"Oh, God—not her!"

Dear Readers:

When I reached adulthood and made the shocking discovery that everyone didn't have stories playing through their minds, I was worried. Then a miracle occurred—I found a socially acceptable means of breathing life into my imaginary friends. Writing!

My family claims writing is an obsessive-compulsive disorder, because when I'm working on a new book my characters take over every moment of my life—awake and asleep. They say I'm possessed, but I think they're beginning to relent. At least they've stopped threatening me with exorcism.

This book is really my parents' fault—my mother's for giving birth to me and my father's for sharing his stories about growing up in the Ozarks. The legend of "Serenity Spring" evolved from his mysterious tales. I placed some of my fictional companions in this mystical place, and *Shades of Rose* was born.

As Dylan and Rose embark on their individual quests for self-identity, they learn that love transcends time and plays a role in shaping their destinies. *Shades of Rose* is a story of romance, time travel, and fantasy, but it's also about self-discovery. I hope you enjoy sharing this adventure with all of us: Dylan, Rose and me.

I'd love to hear from you. Write to me at P.O. Box 25602, Colorado Springs, Colorado 80936-5602.

Deb Stover

If you liked this book, be sure to look for the July releases in the **Denise Little Presents** line:

Leopard's Lady by Mary Gillgannon   (0153-4, $4.99)
  Leopard's Lady begins outside a nunnery in 13th-century England. Astra de Mortain is unaware of the presence of an unseen watcher. Nor is Astra aware that the watcher will change the course of her life. Later, when that same knight rescues her from deadly danger, she can only wonder who the man is. Richard Reivers, a stalwart knight in the service of King Henry III, is both her savior, and the man who will lead her into the most difficult test of life and limb, heart and spirit that she will ever face. He is her destiny. As these two courageous people unite against an uncertain future, they discover that only love can give them the strength to prevail.

Race Against Time by Lynn Turner   (0154-2, $4.99)
  Fast-paced, suspenseful, with the fate of the world hanging in the balance, and with two strong romances in two completely different times—that's *Race Against Time!* When Samantha Cook wakes up in Washington, D.C., in a strange bed, in a strange time, with Special Agent Joseph Mercer of the F.B.I. breathing down her neck, she hasn't a clue what's going on. Little does she know that back in her own time and place, Valerie Herrick is in the same predicament. And newsman Lucas Davenport isn't going to stop asking questions until he finds the woman he loves. But it won't be easy. Samantha and Valerie are caught in a vortex of time and destiny. They've switched places—and unless they can solve each other's problems, they're stuck. Can Valerie and Samantha save the world? Can Lucas and Joe come to terms with what has happened to the women they love? And will love or the laws of physics triumph?

AVAILABLE IN JULY

**If you liked this book, be sure to look for others
in the *Denise Little Presents* line:**

MOONSHINE AND GLORY by Jacqueline Marten (0079-1, $4.99)

COMING HOME by Ginna Gray (0058-9, $4.99)

THE SILENT ROSE by Kasey Mars (0081-3, $4.99)

DRAGON OF THE ISLAND by Mary Gillgannon (0067-8, $4.99)

BOUNDLESS by Alexandra Thorne (0059-7, $4.99)

MASQUERADE by Alexa Smart (0080-5, $4.99)

THE PROMISE by Mandalyn Kaye (0087-2, $4.99)

FIELDS OF FIRE by Carol Caldwell (0088-0, $4.99)

HIGHLAND FLING by Amanda Scott (0098-8, $4.99)

TRADEWINDS by Annee Cartier (0099-6, $4.99)

A MARGIN IN TIME by Laura Hayden (0109-7, $4.99)

REBEL WIND by Stobie Piel (0110-0, $4.99)

SOMEDAY by Anna Hudson (0119-4, $4.99)

THE IRISHMAN by Wynema McGowan (0120-8, $4.99)

DREAM OF ME by Jan Hudson (0130-5, $4.99)

ROAD TO THE ISLE by Megan Davidson (0131-3, $4.99)

*Available wherever paperbacks are sold, or order direct from the
Publisher. Send cover price plus 50¢ per copy for mailing and
handling to Penguin USA, P.O. Box 999, c/o Dept. 17109,
Bergenfield, NJ 07621. Residents of New York and Tennessee
must include sales tax. DO NOT SEND CASH.*

IF ROMANCE BE THE FRUIT OF LIFE—
READ ON—
BREATH-QUICKENING HISTORICALS FROM PINNACLE

WILDCAT (772, $4.99)
by Rochelle Wayne

No man alive could break Diana Preston's fiery spirit . . . until seductive Vince Gannon galloped onto Diana's sprawling family ranch. Vince, a man with dark secrets, would sweep her into his world of danger and desire. And Diana couldn't deny the powerful yearnings that branded her as his own, for all time!

THE HIGHWAY MAN (765, $4.50)
by Nadine Crenshaw

When a trumped-up murder charge forced beautiful Jane Fitzpatrick to flee her home, she was found and sheltered by the highwayman—a man as dark and dangerous as the secrets that haunted him. As their hiding place became a place of shared dreams—and soaring desires—Jane knew she'd found the love she'd been yearning for!

SILKEN SPURS (756, $4.99)
by Jane Archer

Beautiful Harmony Harper, leader of a notorious outlaw gang, rode the desert plains of New Mexico in search of justice and vengeance. Now she has captured powerful and privileged Thor Clarke-Jargon, who is everything Harmony has ever hated—and all she will ever want. And after Harmony has taken the handsome adventurer hostage, she herself has become a captive—of her own desires!

WYOMING ECSTASY (740, $4.50)
by Gina Robins

Feisty criminal investigator, July MacKenzie, solicits the partnership of the legendary half-breed gunslinger-detective Nacona Blue. After being turned down, July—never one to accept the meaning of the word no—finds a way to convince Nacona to be her partner . . . first in business—then in passion. Across the wilds of Wyoming, and always one step ahead of trouble, July surrenders to passion's searing demands!